To Stan West

May the ancestors

Echoes of Mercy

Whispers of Love

Enfold your heart
with joy & fill each
day with great peace.
And may God bless
your family with
love, faith & hope.

Elaine Ferguson

Echoes of Mercy
Whispers of Love

ELAINE R. FERGUSON

LAVONNE PRESS • CHICAGO, IL

Echoes of Mercy, Whispers of Love
Copyright © 1995 Elaine Reginia Ferguson

Lavonne Press
5oo North Michigan, Suite 1920
Chicago, Illinois 60611

ISBN: 1-878743-53-8

Cover illustrations: Donna Blake Fizer

Cover concept: Elaine Ferguson

Cover design: Angelo Williams

Manufactured in the United States of America
99 98 97 96 95   10 9 8 7 6 5 4 3 2 1

Perfect submission, perfect delight,
Visions of rapture now burst on my sight,
Angels descending bring from above,
Echoes of mercy, whispers of love.

- Blessed Assurance, Second Verse

❧ Dedication ❧

For my ancestors:

Grand Parents -   Sarah Mae Garrett Collins
                            Roy Dolphus Collins
                            Eula Tecora Mansell Ferguson
                            Homer Ferguson

Great Grand Parents -   Mary Ferguson
                            Daniel Ferguson
                            Matilda Shoemaker Garrett
                            Jesse Garrett
                            Mary Mansell
                            Frank Mansell
                            Hannah Robinson Collins
                            Spencer Frank Collins

To my great-uncle Reverend Raymond Wellington Collins
1892-1995
whose life was an inspiration to all.

And for all of those who dared to survive,
not only to give us life, but that we might be free.

Table of Contents

Amazing Grace!

How sweet the sound,
that saved a wretch like me

one

The leaves of a thick, damp forest surrounded me. An inescapable chill pierced my shivering body. Overhead, through a clump of thick leaves, an incandescent gray light filled the air with a shroud of luminous danger.

Where am I? How did I get here? I want to go home.

The presence of evil descended upon me. Its eyes bore down on me like two laser beams, penetrating my flesh to the core of my being. From a remote hiding place its raging thirst for blood assaulted me. My heart pounded with a paralyzing fear. A loud clap of thunder shattered the silence and shook the earth beneath my feet. Suddenly, heavy footsteps, crushing leaves and underbrush began rushing toward me. My body trembled with terror.

Without thought I burst into a run. I ran as fast as I could through this unknown forest, with the darkness surrounding me. Hundreds of wet leaves and small branches launched an attack upon me, slicing my face and exposed hands. My cold, wet clothes buffered most of my body from the direct assault. From my forehead, drops of blood mixed with sweat quickly flooded my eyes, burning them and clouding my view. My hands rose instinctively to shield my face, and as I ran faster, wet hair plastered over my eyes, briefly blinding me.

The faster I ran, the closer it got. Its powerful footsteps grew louder. Fear flooded my body and coursed through my veins. Who was it? What was it? And why was it trying to destroy me? I needed an answer.

My nostrils were on fire; the cold, burning air forced desperate gasps and collapsed against my exhausted lungs. Death seemed inevitable. Images of my flesh being ripped from my bones raced before me. I saw my body being devoured, eaten alive.

Midway down a steep gully, I lost my footing and fell face first. My body tumbled over and over, where my fall ended in a small creek. I didn't have time to be repulsed by the mud filling my mouth and covering me. I stood up quickly, and started running again. I didn't want to die. Waves of sweat burst from my pores. My body was drenched with sweat, soaking my clothing, and the cold wind pierced through to the marrow of my bone. It seemed as if I had been running for miles. I was losing this battle as the footsteps drew closer and closer.

Exhaustion circled over me like a family of ravenous vultures and finally descended, pecking away at my flesh. I was hollow; an empty shell of fading life. Yet, my will to live refused to let me stop. I couldn't surrender my freedom. I was too stubborn to give into defeat, although my body was totally depleted of any hint of reserve. Every muscle ached, begging for rest.

Desperately, I tried to scream out or cry for help but nothing happened. Nothing but silence. Even if I could, I knew that my cries would only fall on the ears of the one seeking to trap me.

I felt the movement of a huge muscular hand stretching out to capture me, reaching, getting closer and closer, brushing against my back. My fate was finally sealed. I was within its grasp. Now I could turn around and face my captor. I didn't care anymore. I didn't want to know anymore. I didn't need to see his face.

In that final moment of freedom, its claw clamped down and locked on my shoulder, ripping into ripping into my flesh. I screamed, as the pain tore me apart.

It was over.

Just as suddenly as my ordeal began, it was over. My body was shocked, suddenly transported to another place.

For a brief moment, everything stood still. I was in another place, another time, a different world. I turned my head as I felt my husband John vigorously shaking my left shoulder. It was the same one that only a split second ago was being ripped apart. Thank God he had rescued me from that horrifying world and returned me to ours. I was at home, safe and sound in our bed.

In the twilight space that lies between being here and there, I remained in the claws of a paralyzing fear. Even though I knew it was all over, my heart continued to pound with terror, while my body trembled with terror. I was grateful, so very, very grateful to be back in my world.

John, half-awake himself mumbled a few words, then clearly asked, "Baby, what's wrong?"

"Nothing," I quickly replied, still short of breath, panting and terrified.

"No, baby, I don't think so," he replied, moving closer to me. "I've been shaking you, trying to wake you up for at least a three or four minutes, or longer. So I'm gonna ask you one more time and I want you to tell me the truth. What's wrong? Were you having a nightmare or something?"

Realizing that my husband was far more alert than I had suspected, I whispered softly, "Yeah, you could say that."

"Say what?' He said, reaching out and pulling me into his arms. "Baby, tell me what's wrong with you."

My voice trembled, and cracked with fear. "It was the worse thing that's ever happened to me. It was real. I don't know where I was, but it really happened."

John's broad, rich brown forehead contracted like an accordion and shrunk into a frown. He looked deeply into my eyes, probing to see what was severely troubling me. Confusion filled his face. "You were where? I want you to tell me everything that happened to upset you so much.

"What was real? Angie, I've never seen you like this before. Look at you, you're terrified! Your nightgown is drenched, and your heart is pounding like it's about to leap out of your chest." He placed his hand over my heart and said, "See, it must be beating over a hundred times a minute!" John reached over and picked up my quivering left hand, cupped it between his and gently kissed it. I could tell he noticed it was trembling, because he looked at me gently and kissed it again. As his soothing lips brushed against my hand, my heart felt no need for words, his kindness said it all. He knew I was in deep pain.

"Okay honey, you're right." I sighed, while I snuggled closer into the hollow of his chest.

I was still scared to death, and I couldn't explain why. All I knew was that it wasn't a nightmare.

"Whatever happened to me, really happened in another place. Something, some kind of creature was after me. I must've run for miles, and the faster I ran, the closer it got. I tried my best to get away, and just when my body was about to collapse, it caught me, and was ripping into my flesh when you woke me up."

He pulled me closer, held me tightly in his arms and whispered softly, "Ang, it's over now. It's gonna be alright."

As I rested in his arms, he gently stroked my hair. Quickly, a wave of soothing comfort filled me. I drifted into a place of peace. Like sunshine dispersing clouds, his soothing touch brought light into my dark pain and chased away my seemingly unreasonable fears. Laying there in his arms, feeling safe and sound and so far away from that place of distant terror, I began to feel a little silly— after all it was just a dream, or so I tried to tell myself.

In his own way, John is the sweetest and most protective man I've ever known. His tenderness has always been the source of deep healing for me, like an ancient balm that over the years has comforted my wounds and fears. Sometimes, it seems a bit old fashioned, but I always find his protectiveness quite endearing. For most of my life, he has been my beacon, my strength and my light.

He reassured me again, "Baby, its gonna be alright. It was just a bad dream." His deep, rich, melodic voice, with a whiff of his mother's Georgian accent, was soothing music to my ears.

I was home. Looking around the room, I smiled when the first rays of a new day began to slowly enter our room, bathing it in a soft, but unusual glowing peach light, casting a warm glow over our bedroom's white and gold trimmed French provincial furniture and light pumpkin-colored walls. I looked around, just to make sure I was really in my room, and found everything was still in place. The wall of photographs and paintings of African children that I had collected over many years decorated the wall above the chaise lounge. Their bright smiles sparkled brightly. But my favorite was of two small boys, taken in Senegal, West Africa. The boys were squatting, exploring something on the ground. Their skin glowed with a rich, black velvet sheen.

On my side of the bed was our ivory French provincial dresser filled with almost a dozen neatly arranged portraits of our family: a color photograph of our wedding in an ivory frame, others of our children, different sizes and frames, captured stages of their childhood. My favorites were the old baby pictures of our two teenagers James and Ashley in silver frames, my parent's silver anniversary in a larger fluted silver frame, and John's favorite, a slightly faded and battered black and white photo of him, his brother and two sisters when they were all less than seven years old in a brown wooden frame. Betty, his baby sister, always stood out. Sitting on John's lap, she was a plump round baby, about six-months-old, with the prettiest, most enchanting smile imaginable that captured everyone who looked at the picture. Her entire cherubic face glowed, beaming her light in every direction. It was the prettiest smile I'd ever seen. Betty's eyes were barely open, two little beaming half moons, her cheeks round and full, and her entire face radiated the innocence and happiness that only a child can possess. Looking at those pictures, feeling my family's spirit helped to lift the last residue of fear that had followed me back home. Finally my ordeal was over.

Lying in my husband's arms, I peered through our balcony's white vertical blinds facing our bed, as a slice of an orange sun cautiously rose over the scant sections of the rugged brown, barren San Gabriel mountains that cradled our city. Strips of the half dozen cypress trees that border one side of our pool stood at attention, reaching toward the sky, gently swaying in the bosom of a soft early morning breeze. Our home is perched on a mountain in the Baldwin Hills section of Los Angeles facing due east, and blessed with a magnificent, breathtaking view of the city. It gave us the gift of majestic sunrises, especially on those rare clear smog-free days that happen every other blue moon.

John had gracefully wrapped the rest of his body around mine, while I continued to rest my head in the hollow of his chest. I felt the warmth of his body, his heart beating against my cheek—the pounding of his heart was so strong, so certain, so assured. I felt the hidden strength of the muscles sculpting his arms. They were firm, powerful and sturdy against the softness of my own.

Yet, there seemed to be something different about being in his arms this morning. Maybe it was me, I don't know. Perhaps my fear and vulnerability caused me to look upon my husband with fresh, new eyes. After twenty-five years of marriage, in some ways we'd both come to take each other for granted. But this morning, I saw my husband with new eyes.

Slowly, almost with caution, I explored the depth and breadth of his magnificent body. A portion of his torso and legs were silhouetted, outlined by our peach satin sheets. There was something fresh and surprisingly new about his body. John was in excellent shape for a 47-year-old man. He worked out regularly by lifting weights, playing tennis and basketball on the weekends and golfing every now and then with friends whose bodies were attacked by the signs of old age. My husband could easily pass for a man ten to fifteen years younger than his actual age. Looking at him now, more than two and a half decades later, remarkably, he looks essentially the same as when we first met.

I smiled, still admiring him and my mind flashed back, returning to the first time I saw his face. That was almost thirty years ago in nineteen sixty-five, when I was a freshman at Howard University in Washington, D.C. Sports was the last thing on my mind, and track was at the bottom of the list. I had absolutely no interest whatsoever in wasting my time at a track meet, but my roommate Rhonda talked me into going.

"Come on, Angie, you need to spread your wings, get your head out of those books."

"I can't. I have to study."

"Midterms are over. One afternoon off isn't going to kill your G.P.A."

She'd asked me several times before, and I always found an excuse. But this time she wouldn't take no for an answer.

Rhonda Gilchrist and I came from two very different worlds. I could never figure out why she took such a liking to me. I was unsophisticated, awkward and plain—an uncomfortable cross between a frightened sparrow and a clucking goose. And in terms of Howard's rigid social pecking system, I was half way from the wrong side of the tracks. My father worked at a beer factory in Milwaukee, while many of my classmates, including Rhonda, came from the sophisticated Black-upper class, a world I'd never known.

Rhonda was a graceful swan, pretty, sophisticated, urbane and very bright. A genteel, almost intoxicating Southern charm wafted around her. She was a cotillion debutante, popular, yet a part of her spirit seemingly remained untouched by all that life had given her and the constraints of her privileged world. I realized she was a free spirit, wishing desperately to chart the course of her life, instead of the one her family had chosen. She was expected to get her degree in liberal arts and to find a husband of equal stature to marry and settle down with, preferably in Atlanta.

Her boyfriend, Ray Townsend, fit the bill. He was a big track star, a talented athlete who was handsome, a big man on campus and most importantly from an almost equally prominent Philadelphia family. Yet, I think in spite of expectations, she genuinely liked Ray.

After I stalled as long as I could, Rhonda looked at me with plaintive disgust and said, "You know I know what you're doing."

"What are you talking about?" I replied with great naiveté, while putting on the fourth or fifth outfit from my limited wardrobe.

"You think making us late will force me to leave you here, don't you?"

"Rhonda, I don't know what you're talking about. I just can't find the right thing to wear."

"Okay, if you insist. But I just want you to know, that you are going, no matter how late we are."

Sitting on the second row from the top of the bleachers on a crisp, unseasonably cool afternoon in the spring of sixty-three, just a few days before cherry blossom time in Washington, I looked to the bright, clear blue sky for comfort. In less than ten minutes after our arrival, I was completely bored.

"Isn't this fun?" she asked, with a perky smile.

I couldn't pretend. "No," I whispered dispiritedly. I didn't want to offend her. She was one of the few true friends that I had.

After stewing in my boredom for some time—I couldn't take it anymore, so I decided to just get up and leave, without excuse or pretense. Rhonda, sitting next to me, was so caught up in the event that she didn't notice me standing.

As I rose from my seat, I looked down on the field and was thunderstruck, jolted by the presence of the most handsome man I had ever laid eyes on. John was preparing to throw the javelin. His concentration had stolen him away, into a world that was composed of only him and his javelin, consuming him and overwhelming me. He slowly and methodically studied it inch by inch, watching it move while still holding it in his hands. Aside from his unbelievable level of concentration, he was strikingly handsome. John looked like a bronzed god that had stepped through the pages of time from an ancient myth and onto Howard's track field.

I couldn't believe my eyes. His presence swept me away. I slowly and carefully sat down, absorbing every detail I could of this spectacular specimen of a man. I didn't want to blink, out of fear that I might miss an important detail. His closely cropped hair was a perfect crown for his broad and prominent forehead. His deep-set, piercing almond-shaped brown eyes were possessed, locked into a steely determination. His perfectly chiseled cheekbones, a determined square jaw and a broad, round nose were all the more striking before the sun's bright light. His skin was a rich, dark bronze, and had a sheen like satin as it glowed, covering a finely sculpted mass of muscles that enveloped his entire frame. The muscles in his arms were so dense that they looked like they were about to rip through his skin. His body, like the wind, was a primal force of nature, possessing thick legs like tree trunks, an even thicker torso like an impenetrable tank. He moved with the strength of a lion and the grace of a gazelle.

Rhonda leaned over and whispered in my ear, "Somebody caught your eye?"

Since I couldn't say a word, I nodded in reply.

"That's John Stewart. He's co-captain of the team with Ray. And he's headed for the Olympics.

"You've got good taste. If you want to meet him, I can arrange that. He and Ray are very good friends."

I still couldn't speak. I just sat there, dazed, completely captivated by this man. For me, it was love at first sight. I knew then that this man was going to be my husband.

John continued to go through a finely tuned routine during his warm-up, trotting around, jogging in place, rotating his arms throwing an imaginary Javelin, then going through the motions once more with the real one. He was filled with a deep grace and a determined poise, oblivious to the fact that he had mesmerized the vast majority of women in the bleachers and pissed off most of the men. On that day, his first javelin throw broke a school and conference record.

After the track meet, I seemed to see him everywhere on campus. Suddenly our paths crossed on a daily basis, at the cafeteria, on the quad, in the library and even in the city at the hangouts frequented by Howard students, like Billy Simpson's.

As I lay there, wrapped in the warmth of my husband's arms, I began to feel quite awkward and uncomfortable, almost queasy, as my stomach began to churn. I wondered if the fear from my nightmare was returning. But this was different, seeming to be of this world and not the other. Why am I feeling this way? I wondered, as the discomfort within me grew. I closed my eyes, trying to shove away the gnawing presence in the pit of my stomach.

Suddenly, my mind was filled with shadows, distorted visions, images lacking pure form. I was startled when I saw a man's face, bruised, swollen and bloodied emerge. His eyes were as big as ping pong balls, about to burst out of their sockets. At first I didn't recognize the face, it was too horrible. Gradually, it took a recognizable form, and as the distortions resolved, I realized I was looking at the face of Rodney King. My body trembled with anger, now filled with a fresh rage. I wondered again how he'd survived such a savage attack from that vicious circle of men.

Over the years, I've witnessed many times, more than I care to remember, the results of the unbridled brutality that has been heaped upon a people lacking the resources to fight back and demand justice. I've seen the impact it's had on the lives of my clients—broken limbs, maimed minds and residual pride extracted. When I think about it, I feel nothing but a helpless rage, knowing that one day, my own, son or husband, for no good reason, could suffer the same atrocities.

Throughout the city, after the change in venue, most of the black folk I know fiercely believed that moving the trial of the policemen to Simi Valley in Ventura County was done to ensure an acquittal. I disagreed. I reasoned that anyone with eyes who saw the videotape would have to be convinced of their guilt. Yet, as the trial progressed, doubt crept into my mind. Now since the jury's been deliberating for several days, I'm beginning to feel that maybe there will be an acquittal.

What's taking them so long? I wondered. Isn't this an open and shut case? What more do they need? A corpse?

I was so caught up in my thoughts that when John tapped me on my shoulder, I almost jumped out of the bed. I thought he'd gone back to sleep.

"What's wrong now?" he asked.

I knew he was reading my mind again. It's the weirdest thing that happens between us. Sometimes, especially when one of us is upset, the other, no matter where we are, instinctively knows to call and find out what's wrong.

"I don't know," I replied sheepishly, while shrugging my shoulders. "It's nothing serious."

"And, come on, baby. Don't put me through this again. I want you to tell me what's wrong. Is that dream still worrying you?"

"No, it's not that."

"Well, then, what is it?"

"I don't know for sure. I just have this terrible feeling that something bad is about to happen."

"Now, Ang, you know I'm never going to let anyone or anything hurt you or the kids. You shouldn't be worrying like this. You need to get some more sleep before we have to get up."

"Honey, I know that. But this feeling I have is about something that is beyond your control."

"Woman, what are you talking about?"

"I don't know for sure. But I think it has something to do with the Rodney King trial. I have an is awful feeling that the jury is going to find those animals not guilty. They've been deliberating for days. Those bastards need to be in jail!"

"Listen to you! I haven't heard that tone in your voice in a long time. Not since the movement. You sound like the man was a friend or relative of yours."

"Well, excuse me," I said sarcastically sitting up in the bed, and releasing my body from his embracing arms. "I suppose you think they ought to go free."

"Hold on a minute! Baby, calm down. I'm on your side. They ought to be in jail for a long, long time."

I felt an invisible knife rip through my heart, as tears welled up in my eyes. "Every time I see those policemen, I think of the cop who killed my cousin Jesse in Detroit. That was almost twenty-five years ago, but I haven't forgotten. No, not one bit. I still remember how those defense attorneys got the trial moved over three hundred miles away to that little bitty all-white Alpena. Remember how they acquitted him, in spite of the fact that he had confessed? They did it without blinking an eye."

Looking away from me, staring across the room, he nodded in solemn agreement.

"And what about Anthony?" I asked. "How could we ever forget what happened to him? Do you remember the way your best friend was murdered when we were in Mississippi? And what about the men that killed him? They never spent one day in jail, even though there was sufficient evidence to arrest and convict them. He was murdered in cold blood, just like the hundreds, if not thousands, of other black people who've been killed in this country, while their killers have gotten off, scott free.

"I'll never forget the look on his mother's face when she saw what they did to her child."

"But, Angie," pleaded John. "You might be right, but, baby, that was over 20 years ago. Am I supposed to think that things have changed very little since then, and that justice will not prevail?" His flickering eyes winced in anguish, desperately seeking an escape from a part of the past that had caused him unbearable pain.

After a few moments, he sighed, and said, "I think not."

I nestled close to him again, looked into his eyes and I squeezed his hand and said, "Honey, what do you really think is gong to happen?"

"I don't know for sure," he sighed. "A lot has changed since the sixties. Yes, we've made plenty of gains. Look at us. We have a good life. We've done well in spite of all the obstacles we've faced—what we have now is beyond my wildest dreams.

"But there's a flip side to our prosperity. Look at what's going on with a lot of our people throughout this country. There are fewer opportunities now, more isolation, so much more hopelessness. The sixties were a mixed blessing. We all wanted to believe that things were going to get better for the vast majority of our people, and that didn't happen. The pain and the misery I see my brothers and sisters carrying around today is much heavier load than the burden we carried twenty or thirty years ago. At least back then, people believed they had a chance. Now, they don't. Yet, most of us, to one degree or another, pretend that nothing is deeply wrong. All over this country there's something wrong. Not just in our community, but throughout this entire society. How do we fix it? How do we restore our communities?

"I wish I had the answer but right now I don't see a way out of this. This society thrives denying its problems, until they explode. Then it's too late.

"Each and every day I see what the unyielding hand of racism is doing to our people. Back in the eighties, I was in Chicago on a business trip, when I ran into Larry Johnson, one of my partners from Howard. Larry runs an agency in a housing project. I can't remember the name of the place. It's somewhere on the north side of town, within walking distance of the Gold Coast—the richest neighborhood in town. Larry told me about an incident that happened in the early eighties. When a policeman was hit by a sniper's bullet, the entire complex was locked down and the cops went from apartment to apartment illegally searching and terrorizing thousands of innocent people. Not only the adults. They put guns to the heads of children and babies, threatening to kill them. Some of the older children were so traumatized that they had to call in volunteer doctors and psychologists to evaluate them and provide counseling. The agency wanted to sue the city on behalf of the victims, but it didn't have the money to pay the lawyer's fees. So they had to drop the case. The saddest part about it is that that was only one incident. That kind of police brutality goes on all the time, just to a lesser degree.

"So baby, to answer your question, I don't know. Simi Valley might not be that far away from L. A., but, as far as I'm concerned, a change in venue is a change in view, and that jury just might just set those bastards free." John placed his hand on top of mine and stroked it. He sat up, kissed me on the cheek and said, "You know I love you madly, but sometimes you can get so lost in your thoughts and fears that you spend too much of your time worrying about things before they happen.

"I know why you feel the way you do, probably much better than you could ever imagine. You don't know how hard it is, being a black man in America. I realize each and every day that it could've been me, or our son James, or my brother, or one of my friends, instead of Rodney King. We've just been lucky. I know I'm not safe on the streets. When I see a police car, I'm on guard until it passes me by. But this time, I really want to believe there is too much evidence, and that finally for once, justice will prevail. Come on honey, they caught 'em on video. What more do you need to convict?"

"What about a little less prejudice and racism, and a lot more humanity in their hearts?" I replied.

"You're right," he said.

I looked over at the clock. It was five thirty. I kissed John on his cheek, hopped out of the bed and threw on my sweats. I raced out of the room to leave all of the morning's trauma behind. Part of my daily routine includes doing yoga postures early in the morning by our pool. I usually got in at least a half hour, then I'd shower before making breakfast for John and the kids. It was the only time of the day I really could call my own.

By the time I finished doing my yoga and showering, it was almost six-fifteen. I threw on my robe, and continuing my daily routine, I walked down the hallway to my children's rooms. Every morning between six-fifteen and six-thirty, I wake them up. But this morning before getting them up, I stood in the doorway of each bedroom for a few moments and watched my son and daughter, sleeping so peacefully, and thanked God for their presence in my life. The safety of our home, the strength of my husband and his unyielding love, the presence of my children, are the filaments of light that give my life radiance, and this morning I remembered how grateful I should be.

When we got married, we decided to start a family immediately. We tried for several stressful years, more than I care to remember, to maintain a pregnancy. We both desperately wanted to have a large family, lots of kids. I'd get pregnant and during the fourth or fifth month I'd miscarry. After my seventh miscarriage, visits to more fertility specialists than I care to remember, tons of painful invasive tests, and years of severe emotional turmoil, John convinced me it was time for us to look into adoption.

"I don't want to keep putting you through this. It's too hard on your body and your emotions. Baby, we can adopt. After all there are plenty of black children out there who need a home and two loving parents like us."

Less than two months after our first visit to an adoption agency, I was pregnant again with James. I was so afraid that I was going to lose him. John still teases me to this day. He swears that I held my breath during the first four months of the pregnancy. My mom even came and stayed with me. I have a weak cervix, the mouth of my womb opens up too early. So I restricted myself to bed rest as soon as I found out I was pregnant. That time in bed was the longest, most anguishing period of my life. And I did the same thing when I was carrying Ash. Only it was harder then, because James was just beginning to learn how to walk. But thank God, we have our two beautiful children, and if I had to do it all over again, I would.

James, our first born, is sixteen. He's a junior in high school. He's tall for his age, almost six feet, and lanky with very long arms and even longer legs. I tease him a lot and tell him that because he's all bones and no meat, that he's just a tad heavier than a bag of wet toothpicks. Of our two children, James is the introverted one and a loner at heart. He is such a sweet, gentle spirit, and he carries the aura of an ancient soul, who for some reason or another decided it was time to visit this earth again.

Lately I've seen signs that indicate my son is beginning to slowly emerge from his childhood cocoon, and thrusting himself into the world. He has a few friends, and has taken a few girls out. James is very bright, and a good, conscientious student—a far cry from my daughter.

Physically, he's a blend of his father and me. He has his dad's forehead and chin, my small, round brown eyes, John's radiant sunburst smile and my copper brown complexion. But when it comes to sports and athletic abilities, he is the complete opposite of his father, and much more like me, lacking coordination and even the most rudimentary skills. Since he was in daycare, James has been far more interested in music and art than basketball or track. He's never liked football or basketball or any other sport for that matter. When he was in elementary school, he tried out for the Little League team, I think more to make my husband happy than anything else, and fortunately he didn't make the team.

However, as soon as James learned how to pull his body up, he would crawl over to the piano we had in our living room at our first home in Englewood, and bang away on the keys for hours. Now he plays three instruments: piano, trumpet and guitar. Although his interest in music is currently focused on rap and hip-hop, for the sake of our hearing and sanity, I hope this is a brief phase of interest that won't last much longer.

Ashley, our fourteen-year-old baby, is a little whirlwind, a vibrant spark of life. She rushed into this world at birth, and has yet to stop to let the rest of us catch up with her. Our daughter is a mixture of little girl daintiness, teenage perkiness and athletic prowess. She doesn't look like either one of us. John swears she is the spitting image of his Aunt Bessie, one of mother's sisters who died when he was a teenager. I've only seen one picture of her, and I've yet to see the resemblance in Ash. The only resemblance between the two that I saw was perhaps their similar zest for life.

When Ash was a baby, I used to think she looked like my mother, but not any more. Her beautiful oval face with her sparkling and delicate doe eyes, huge eyelashes, sloped nose, beautiful white teeth are surrounded by a wide mouth with thick, rich lips. She inherited her father's athletic prowess and muscular build. And in spite of a mild case of childhood asthma, Ash has been a track star in her own right since the sixth grade. In the span of just a few short years, our daughter has broken many state records, and her one hundred yard dash continues to improve, of course, under the watchful eye and guidance of her proud father. I love to watch Ash run. She possesses the grace of a gazelle and speed of a young colt. A typical teenager, she's not very interested in books. Clothes, fashion and movies have been her adolescent focus. And now boys are beginning to call, which is a development that her father certainly doesn't like at all. Most of the time, she's usually pretty easy to get along with. But that girl has a stubborn streak wider than the Grand Canyon. She's been that way since she was a little baby. James ate whenever I fed him, but not Miss Ashley. She ate according to her schedule, and, of course, I had to accommodate her.

She's feisty, independent and manipulative. And she has her father wrapped around her baby toe. She might think about trying to get away with murder, but Ash is shrewd enough to know where to draw the line, before I draw it for her.

In contrast to the handful of friends that my son has, Ashley has more friends than I can count. She spends more time on the phone in a week than I do in six months.

Ashley and James are two good kids, and we are both very proud of them. They never give us any problems, and we haven't gone through that stage of adolescent rebellion that most parents speak of like the plague. However, sometimes I do become concerned about their preoccupation with material things. Often, I think we give them too much. They have rooms filled with toys, games, TVs, stereos, compact discs, cable, video games, musical instruments and closets full of clothes. To help them see how blessed they are since they were toddlers, I frequently take them down to the center where I work on the weekends. Now that they're much older, they take it upon themselves to tutor some of the younger children. It's a great opportunity for them to see a harsher, more difficult side of life, and to appreciate how fortunate they are. They view their work as being fun and rewarding, and look forward to it.

Although we're Baptist, and have been all of our lives, James and Ash attend a private Catholic academy in Los Angeles. We decided to send them to St. Ignatius School because it has an excellent educational achievement record. Graduates have attended Howard, Morehouse, Spelman, Harvard, Yale, Stanford and Princeton. James and Ash doing well at 'St. Ig.'

Making breakfast for John and the kids, getting them off to school and preparing for work diverted my focus away from my fears. By the time I arrived at the agency, the old Angela had returned. I'd finally put that nightmare behind me. All of my earlier emotional darkness had quietly retreated into a distant corner of my mind.

I'm a social worker at the Mary McCloud Bethune Social Service Agency, located in South Central Los Angeles, one of the toughest neighborhoods in the city. I've worked here for over fifteen years, ever since we moved to Los Angeles. Over the years, the community has changed dramatically, and most of the changes have been for the worse. The ravages of high unemployment, a rotting, ineffective education system, teenage pregnancy, single-parent homes, crime, inadequate health care, police brutality, isolation and municipal insensitivity have all taken their toll on the clients our agency serves. Also, our client population has changed. During the last fifteen years, there's been a huge influx of Central Americans; Mexicans, Guatemalans and Costa Ricans.

All of my life, I've wanted to help people. When I was a little girl growing up in my neighborhood in Milwaukee, whenever one of my playmates got hurt, or if they had a problem, I was the first one to volunteer to help. I also used to nurse everybody's pet that was injured.

My mother used to tell my father, "That girl's gonna to work herself to death trying to help these children." Momma was right. Helping came very naturally to me. So when I entered Howard University, I initially planned to major in psychology and become a child psychologist until I quickly discovered that my sociology class was the most exciting and stimulating one for me. I couldn't wait to get to class to hear Professor Arthur Dillingsworth lecture. He was a noted scholar and a highly respected academician who discussed the dynamics of the family. During my summer breaks, my experiences in the civil rights movement further cemented my desire to help others.

Shortly after my graduation from Howard, we moved to Cleveland, John's hometown. I taught elementary school for a couple of years, but after my third or fourth miscarriage, I desperately needed something to look forward to. I decided to go back to school, and earned a master's degree in social work at Case Western University.

I love my work. Second only to my family, my work has been the most rewarding portion of my life. Through all of my subsequent miscarriages and other trials and tribulations, my work has been the glue that has held me together. When James and Ash were born, I only took off a few months from work. A few years ago, when John's business took off, he wanted me to quit, to stay at home and take care of the kids. For several months, the thought of quitting my job flickered across my mind, but when I finally had to put my cards on the table, I couldn't. In my heart I know I'm a much better mother, because I feel whole and fulfilled in my life, and my work has a lot to do with that.

We've developed and launched several innovative programs at the agency that have had a tremendous impact on the lives of our clients. Almost three years ago, I became the director of family assistance programs. My department coordinates services for smaller agencies and satellite offices within our organization. Bethune is the largest social service agency in metropolitan Los Angeles, providing comprehensive services to over twenty thousand residents in our community. Our headquarters has the traditional social service components, plus on-site job training for high-tech jobs, a family oriented educational center and a fully staffed drug rehabilitation program. We have a half dozen senior citizens day care centers located throughout South Central L. A. and Englewood, four homeless shelters, numerous outreach programs for substance abuse, domestic violence, teenage pregnancy, a nutrition center, a dozen day care centers and a few innovative programs to help people get off welfare. Over the years, services were expanded to meet the needs of the tidal wave of unemployment caused by the departure of several major employers from the area.

In spite of the fact that the agency has received numerous awards and citations, we still struggle every month to pay all of the bills on time. John has been a big supporter of Bethune. He put together a group of entrepreneurs who have become regular contributors to our organization. They've provided us not only with money but with skills and technical advice that we otherwise could not afford.

Although my position is an administrative one, I still make an effort to find the time to do a little bit of hands-on counseling for a few of my long-term clients. I've seen lives changed with our assistance. One of my favorite success stories is the Collins family. Mr. and Mrs. Zachariah Collins were one of the first families that I worked with shortly after coming to Bethune. They have seven children, four boys and three girls. We've provided services to the family for about fifteen years. They first came to us after Mr. Collins lost his job as a semi-skilled laborer at a local factory that moved to Mexico. In spite of sporadic employment, financial instability and major illnesses, they not only managed to survive, but thrive. All of their children are college graduates, and they are all doing well in their chosen professions. A couple are teachers, one is a chemist, another a psychologist and three own their own businesses. I am most proud of their baby girl Latesha who was six or seven when I first met them. She is currently a medical student at Stanford. When she graduates in the spring, she plans to return to L.A. to do her residency at Martin Luther King Hospital and eventually practice medicine in this community. A few years ago, the children pooled their resources and bought their parents a beautiful split-level home.

On the way to my office, I noticed throughout the corridors many of the staff seemed to be preoccupied. I'm sure that the pending verdict was hanging heavy on their minds. Even our clients in the reception area, who were usually a rambunctious group, were unusually quiet and subdued.

Later that morning, during a routine staff meeting with my department, I had to repeatedly ask the same questions about a client. After I tried several times to capture their roaming attention, I got downright tired of talking to myself. I picked up a heavy directory and dropped it on the floor. When it slammed onto the floor's linoleum surface, my twelve staff members all jumped in unison.

"Now that I finally have your attention, I want you to know that this meeting is adjourned. I know you're probably very preoccupied and anxious about the verdict. I am too, but we still have an agency to run and clients to serve. In spite of your appropriate concern, I must remind you we can't afford ourselves the luxury of becoming distracted to the point of rendering ourselves ineffective. Too many people are depending on us."

"Mrs. Stewart, how are we supposed to act like this is just another normal day?" asked Anita, my youngest and least experienced social worker.

"Yeah, people in the community are mad, very mad about the way that brother was beaten. How can we pretend that nothing is going on?" harped in David, one of my project leaders, who lives in the community, only a couple of blocks away from the center.

"David, I'm not asking that you pretend anything. All I'm requesting is that today in spite of the situation at hand, that each and every one of you do the most you can to carry out your duties to the best of your abilities."

"Mrs. Stewart, that might be easier said than done," he replied.

"I hope it's not."

After the end of that unproductive meeting, I returned a few phone calls and escaped to lunch at Chez Georgette's a popular Creole restaurant located about five miles away from the office. The restaurant's quiet, relaxing and homey atmosphere is a great diversion from my characteristically hectic day. It possessed a quaint and tranquil ambience, dark oak paneled walls, and small vases filled with bright red and white carnations which enhanced the checkered red and white table cloths.

The paneled walls were lined with an interesting and eclectic collection of African American, Caribbean and African art. Paintings of happy, small sunkissed children picking cotton beneath the rays of a bright sun; ballet dancers caught in graceful movements; an old, mournful musician playing the saxophone, another on the drums; beach scenes with palm trees and beautiful sunsets. Photographs of our heroes Dr. King, Malcolm X, Fannie Lou Hamer, other black leaders and a few movie stars were intermingled with paintings of old slave men and women of the eighteenth century, with hoes in their hands, dull, tattered clothing covering their bodies, peering down at us—their descendants. Sometimes the aching silence of their long, drawn faces speaking thousands of words through their eyes, haunting me in a way that I cannot find the words to explain.

My all-time favorite painting held court on the paneled wall facing the restaurant's entrance. It had greeted me there for months, and I desperately wanted to take it home with me. It was a huge, almost life-size oil painting of an African moor, swathed in layers of a flowing robe of handwoven cloth, the color of glistening elephant tusks. He stood in regal splendor, before the steps of a rugged arched brown doorway laced with streaks of gold. Ready for battle, he held an elaborate sword at his side. Its ornate gold handle sparkled with encrusted jewels, rubies and sapphire.

The African possessed a compelling, inescapable presence. He was striking, regal, handsome and rugged. His rich ebony skin shimmered. While he possessed the essence of unbridled masculinity, a gentle countenance could be noted by a careful observer. His luminous presence radiated throughout the entire building. I knew this African lived before, and somehow his spirit transcended the portals of time. I don't know what it is that makes me cleave to him. Perhaps he reminds me of one of my African ancestors.

I've told John on several occasions while eating there that I am going to buy the painting. The price $45,000 is a bit steep, but it's a priceless treasure. I can see it now holding court in our living room, and filling our home with its regal aura. John usually rolls his eyes at me and then jokingly tells me, "First you need to find two more husbands who can jointly afford to buy it."

The restaurant is frequented by a healthy blend of L.A. It is a regular tourist stop for those bold enough to venture past Crenshaw Boulevard and into the heart of South Central. Chez Georgette has become a phenomenal success in the heart of the city's most economically blighted area. The food is absolutely divine, but a significant measure of its success can be attributed to the way the owners lavish their attention and genuine affection on their customers.

Bill and Georgette Dumas, the owners, are from New Orleans, and like us settled in Los Angeles during the early seventies. They are a very attractive, stylish couple, both in their late fifties. They're charming, genteel Southerners, lacking any hint of pretense, in spite of their success.

Over the years of eating there John and I have become good friends with Bill and Georgette. Bill and John have been playing golf together for over ten years.

Normally, I have lunch at Chez G's at least three or four times a week. Most often, I eat with Geneva Green. When I arrived at the agency, she'd been there for over ten years, and next to our founder and executive director, Doc Whitney, she's been there longer than anyone else. Geneva, the administrator in charge of the day-to-day operations, was second in command, but after her husband had a stroke, she stepped down from that position, and now directs the senior citizens programs. She's a handsome Southern woman, and like Georgia, she's also in her late fifties. Her caramel colored face possessed a few scant wrinkles and continues to possess a tawny, youthful glow. I didn't know if it was her genes or the way she takes care of her self, but she looked at least fifteen years younger and is frequently mistaken for a forty-year-old woman. Geneva is a lady with an engaging, sparkling smile, an exaggerated Southern charm and appropriate grace that is abridged by the merest whiff of playful flirtation. Geneva is the epitome of a Southern belle in a modern world. She usually wears a smart, well-tailored designer suit and matching accessories. On this particular day, she wore a striking tailored black linen suit with a vibrant fuschia satin blouse with a matching handkerchief carefully tucked into her lapel. The colors went well with her shock of gray hair, a cascade of loose silver curls that flowed over her head, perfectly draping her square face and huge brown eyes. She was delicate and fragile on the surface, yet strong and determined, possessing the grit of a steel magnolia.

At lunch, she erupted into her usual, incessant flow of chatter about office gossip. Her long, red lacquered fingernails moved with a irritating intensity, making dramatically exaggerated gestures, as though she was conducting a wildly dissonant symphony. Normally, I found her theatrics funny and entertaining, but today I just wasn't up for it. As usual, she was so wrapped up into her performance, she failed to notice that I wasn't even there. I picked over my favorite Creole meal of chicken etouffee, red beans and rice and cole slaw on the side, aimlessly searching for something, trying to entice the return of my absent appetite.

"Sugah, what's wrong? You're not paying attention to me. You haven't heard a single word that I've said since we walked into this place, and that's not like you."

"Yes, I am Gen. I've heard everything that you've said so far," I replied, quite sheepishly feeling like a little girl caught and scolded by her mother for not listening.

"Well, if that's true, what did I just say?"

"You said...that...Mrs. Wellington is...going to..."

"Uh-huh, go on."

"You said," I paused for a moment, took a deep breath, cleared my throat and looked directly into her eyes and said, "Gen, I'm sorry. I really don't know. You're right, I really wasn't paying attention, and I hope you'll forgive me. Don't take it personally, I've been distracted all day."

"Sugah, what ever in the world is wrong? What's got you so preoccupied that you're acting like a toad sitting on a lily pad, looking for shade on a hot summer day?"

"Oh, I don't know Gen," I sighed, shrugging my shoulders, "I guess it's a lot of things."

"No, come on now, I know you better than that. What is it?"

"Well, to be perfectly honest with you, even though I've tried not to think about it, the verdict is weighing heavily on my mind."

"Relax," she whispered softly, gently touching my hand. "Sugah, I don't know what you all are so worried about. It seems like everyone at the agency is walking around holding their breath, waiting for something terrible to happen. Like—"

"Like they're going to be found not guilty?"

"Now, Sugah, I don't know why you are even giving that one thought. Those beasts are going to be convicted. Come on Angela! This is America! Where is your head? They have all the evidence they need to convict, on videotape."

"Gen, I don't agree. If that's the case, what's taking them so long? They've stayed out too long for a guilty verdict. And you know how frightened a lot of white folk are."

"Darlin, I don't know why they're staying out so long. Like I told that precious husband of mine this morning, before I left home, 'Abe darlin, mark my word, justice shall prevail.' You two worry warts can rest assured of that. And like it or not, there's nothing we can do, but wait. So stop worrying your pretty little head. Worrying causes wrinkles, and where I come from, worrying is considered to be very unladylike for women to do such a thing. That's a man's job!"

She smiled, coyly batting her charming Southern eyes. "Things have certainly changed during my thirty years on this earth! And not all of that change has been for the better."

I howled, doubling over with laughter. "Gen, you know you're a mess. If you're thirty, them I'm fifteen, and my children have yet to be born!"

After lunch, when I returned to the office, I finally plunged once more into my normal working state of mind, and plowed through several stacks of paper that seemed to have been sitting on my desk for years.

At 3:30, I had an interview with an applicant for the assistant program coordinator's position. My previous coordinator resigned last fall to move to Denver with her new husband. Since Peggy's departure, I'd had a very difficult time finding a suitable replacement.

The latest applicant, a young woman in her late twenties, was quite impressive. She had a strong academic background, received her master's degree in social work from Tulane University, and had worked for a large private social service agency in Dallas. The interview was progressing quite well.

In the middle of the interview, my secretary, Dora, bolted into my office unannounced with distress and anger bursting from her eyes. I'd never, not in the ten years that she's been my secretary, seen her like this. In my heart, I knew that whatever prompted Dora to interrupt me was a significant emergency. She stood in the middle of the room for a moment, shaking and stomping her feet. Finally, she opened her mouth and said on the verge of tears, "Ms. Stewart, please forgive me. I'm very sorry for the interruption, but I thought you might want to hear the news as soon as possible."

I turned to the applicant and said, "Please excuse me, just for a moment, Ms. Jordan."

She nodded her head, smiled nervously and replied, "No problem, Mrs. Stewart, no problem at all."

I stood up to leave my office, to speak to Dora in her adjoining office. The tears that had welled up in her eyes rapidly streamed down her anguished face. "Ms. Stewart, you don't have to leave the room. I just wanted you to know—" she suddenly stopped speaking, tears exploding forth from her eyes. I stood up to walk over and comfort her, but before I could take my first step, Dora screamed out, "The jury...can you believe that they found them not guilty?!"

I was stunned.

I was crushed by the shocking news. I couldn't breathe. For a few moments, I was completely numb by the news. Finally, when

I recovered and slumped back into my chair, disbelief washed over me. It was followed in close pursuit by a searing, intense flash of white hot anger that burned through my entire being. Even though I had anticipated this verdict, I couldn't believe my ears. "Not guilty? That can't be true, it's not possible!"

"I'm sorry Ms. Stewart," she said crying, "but it's true,"

I placed my hand on my forehead, stunned with disbelief and anguish. I felt like I was in another world, where down was up and up was down; where right was wrong and wrong was right. Faces, hundreds of faces, rushed through my mind. Some were shadows, silhouetted against the backdrop of their assassination, bowed heads, wrenched necks dangling lifelessly from trees; some shot point blank in the head; others were drowned attached to huge rocks that held them at the bottom of a thousand nameless rivers and creeks. I tried to recognize who it was that was being lynched shot, killed, beaten and maimed for no reason other than the fact that God gifted their birth with rich, dark skin. Then I saw faces I recognized: Emmett Till, the little teenager killed in Mississippi nearly forty years ago for looking at a white woman; my cousin Jesse; John's best friend, Anthony, all rushed through. I saw the faces of our slain leaders, Dr. King, Malcolm X, Medgar Evers, those four little girls killed in Alabama in a church bombing while attending Sunday school, and many more I couldn't recognize.

In my heart of hearts, I knew they would be acquitted. Yet when it finally did, I couldn't accept the verdict, even though it was the one I'd expected. I don't know why I wanted to believe it might be different this time. So many thoughts flashed through my mind, I was in a daze. My eyes gazed around my office, searching, trying to get oriented to this painful new reality. The strong surge of disbelief had left me sick to my stomach.

I thought about Rodney King, and wondered what he was feeling now. Although I could never completely know what he was experiencing, in my heart I was certain that I was feeling at least a part of his pain. All that he had gone through for a not guilty verdict. I remembered the first time I saw him being interviewed during the press conference that was held a few days after his beating. He looked so pitiful. He looked more like a corpse than a living man. I remembered how I felt when I saw his beating. Each time his body received a blow, mine jumped, seeming to absorb the same forceful, abusive trauma. Then I thought about his mother. I wondered what she was experiencing right now. Somehow, if my own son had been beaten, I know I would be angrier than I am now, although I don't know how that's possible. How did she feel after watching that videotape of her son, her own flesh and blood, being so savagely beaten, almost to death by the men our judicial system proclaimed now to be innocent—not guilty of any crime.

"Even worse than that, Ms. Stewart, people all over the city are very angry," whimpered Dora. "You know, for weeks there's been talk about what would happen if the police weren't convicted, and I just got the word on the street that the trouble is about to begin. Dr. Whitney has scheduled an emergency executive staff meeting to discuss the situation in ten minutes."

I made the appropriate apologies for the obvious inconvenience to the applicant, and asked Dora to reschedule the interview. As I rushed down the corridor to the agency's conference room, I noticed that the gray halls were filled with several groups of three to five employees huddled together, whispering, venting, voicing expressions of anger, shaking their heads in utter disbelief.

People were already taking to the streets. From the windows facing the street, sounds invaded the building. Cars were honking incessantly, up and down the street. I began to hear angry, pained voices shouting and screaming, "No justice, no peace!"

"No justice, no peace! No justice, no peace!" vibrated through my body. The anger from the people on the streets blended with mine. I felt like I was about to explode, filled with a rage I had never known.

When I entered the conference room, Doc Whitney was pacing back and forth at the head of the large oak table that filled the room. Most of the department heads were already seated at the table, anxiously observing his movements, as the remaining staff trickled in one by one.

"Doc," as we affectionately called him, has been a part of the South Central community for over thirty-five years. He was deeply respected and loved by those who worked with him and especially the members of the community he served. Not only did he work here, but unlike the majority of our staff, he lived in South Central. He raised his family here, and for over forty years has been a shining light and a beacon of hope for this devastated community. Over the years, Doc gained the respect of so many different sections of the community, from the preachers to the gang bangers. He's tall, a robust giant of a man, almost six feet and five inches tall. Yet, the strength of his character looms over his frame. Every inch of his vibrant presence emitted an unavoidable, magnetic charm. Any room he enters is immediately overwhelmed by his commanding presence. His charm had a magical way of quickly disarming the intimidated, especially men. A silver white arc of hair from ear to ear encircled his huge shiny bald spot, that we jokingly called his crown. It added to his aura of dignity and grace.

We tease him a lot, asking if the spot glowed in the dark. He always responded in equal measure, saying, "Oh I don't know for sure, you gotta ask the Missus about that. And if she can't tell you, maybe one of those sweet young actresses that I know might be able to tell you. They've got much better eyesight than older women like you."

From the other end of the long room, through the sealed windows, we could still hear muffled voices shouting, "No justice, no peace! No justice, no peace!" growing louder and louder. The tension in my body grew tighter, settling like a noose around my neck.

Doc Whitney stopped pacing and stood at the head of the conference table, gripping the edge with both hands, his deep rich baritone voice rose over the cacophony from the street. He announced, "I know all of you are very familiar with how verbose and long-winded I can be. This is going to be the briefest meeting I've ever conducted in my tenure as director.

"As you know, many of our community leaders have been preparing for an acquittal. Let us pray that our efforts will be successful in averting a disaster, like the one that happened in Watts almost thirty years ago. Already, there are early reports of scattered violence in the area. I think it's going to get worse.

"Therefore, we're closing the office indefinitely. We'll notify you by phone as to when we'll reopen. Go home immediately! It's too dangerous for anyone to be here. And please be careful. It looks like all hell is breaking loose. " He paused for a moment, pulled a white handkerchief out of his gray jacket and wiped the sweat from his brow. He slowly looked around the table, making direct eye contact with each of us, and whispered in a choked voice, that was full of emotion, "God be with you, until we meet again."

We quickly filed out of the room in silence and fear. Many of the staff had lived through the Watts rebellion. During the meeting, I saw even more severe fear and concern moving through them. I rushed down the hallway into my department. Staff members were racing toward the main entrance, on their way home, hopefully to safety.

I quickly filled my briefcase with papers and reports. The faces of my children, James and Ashley, flashed across my mind. I looked at the clock, It was a little after four o'clock. They should be home by now. I called and they were there. I instructed them to stay put, and not to leave the house under any circumstances. Then I called John on his cellular phone. When I reached him, he was already on the freeway, somewhere in the valley heading home.

"Angie, I'm fine. You don't have to worry about me. But baby, I'm very concerned about you. Looks like you're down there smack in the middle of it. I want you to get home as fast as you can. I guess you were right. It seems like this is the beginning of another Watts. I know our people were looking for a sign from the system that their lives are of equal importance. Today we received yet another rude awakening."

"You're absolutely right. Honey. I'll see you shortly. I love you, and please be careful."

"I love you too, Baby, and you be very careful, too. Call me when you get home."

"Okay, I will." I threw the rest of my papers into my briefcase, fastened it quickly, locked up my office and made sure that the rest of my staff had left or was about to leave.

When I walked outside, the anger filling the air took my breath away. I stood in front of the agency for a moment. The first thing I noticed was that the noise on the street was much louder than I had imagined. I could feel a new wave of rage erupting like a volcano into the air, rising from old, unhealed wounds festered by abuses and decades of neglect. People poured into the street, yelling, screaming, shouting, crying out, begging and pleading for answers. Why did this happen again? I saw groups of teenagers and adults, anguished men and women and teenage girls too young to be mothers carrying their babies. Young men pounded their rage into on cars, smashing windshields, breaking windows. A few stood on the hoods, shouting over and over, "No justice, no peace! No justice, no peace!" Grown men paced back and forth in agonized pain. They were angry, dazed and disheartened with hurt and hopelessness boring deep holes in their hearts. Deep down inside, I knew they wanted to believe that justice would prevail, but today they received another great slap in the face that proved otherwise. The verdict rendered a stunning blow, and told them in no uncertain terms that their lives were not of equal merit in the eyes of this system of justice.

The angry cries of "No justice, no peace! No justice, no peace!" assailed my body.

"No justice, no peace! No justice, no peace!"

two

Most of the staff had rushed out ahead of me, and except for three other cars, the lot was empty. My royal blue BMW was parked on the far side of the lot, facing a couple of weary unattended bushes on the small strip of undeveloped land that separated the cars from an adjacent vacant lot. Just as I put the key into the door, from the passenger's side a loud moaning noise—like the sound of a dying, wounded animal—assailed me. It unnerved my tense body even more. I knew someone was in deep pain. In all of my life, I've never heard such pained and burdened sobs. The moaning turned to shrill cries and sobs, and the deep, guttural noise continued, forming a piercing and unrelenting ache which raced through me and settled in my heart. As fast as I could, I opened my door, threw my purse and briefcase onto the floor of my backseat, and walked over to the passenger side. I wondered if someone had been shot or injured. To my surprise, I discovered an old woman, sitting on the adjacent space's cement parking barrier, with her head bent over, weeping loudly. Her hands cupping her face in her swaying lap as her knees moved rhythmically back and forth, almost in synchronicity with her wailing as her back leaned into Mrs. Townsend's dark blue Cadillac.

Her clothes were soiled with portions of caked, thick pieces of dirt; the colors were faded, barely noticeable and tattered, with huge, gaping holes; which looked as though an animal had chewed them. A raggedy, dirty brown button-up sweater covered her torso, with holes exposing both of her elbows. A dangling wisp of gray hair was suspended in mid air, peeking from beneath an old dingy scarf of dull blue. She wore a skirt made of a heavy black burlap-like material, with patches of red and yellow gingham covering some of the holes, while a tattered, unraveling hem brushed against the parking lot's asphalt. I'd never seen anything like this before. My heart gasped at her horrid appearance. How could anyone let a pitiful woman like this roam the streets without helping her, I wondered.

The anger laden shout of, "No justice, no peace!" snapped my attention back to the impending danger we both faced.

"Ma'am is something wrong?" I asked, bending over to touch her back. She continued to wail, seemingly oblivious to my presence—I wasn't sure if she heard me or not. Maybe she was deaf.

"Can I help you?" I asked, raising my voice as I squatted and leaned closer. I placed my hand on her back, stroking it with the kind of soothing circular motions my Mama and grandmother used to make to calm me down whenever nothing else could console me. Her wailing continued, unrelenting for what seemed like an eternity. Finally, she became aware of my presence. Slowly, very slowly, this little old lady turned her head in my direction and peered up at me, out of the corner of her right eye. She looked at me for no longer than a second or two and quickly covered her face again, and returned to sobbing.

The brief glimpse of her eye hinted a fragile, glassy disorientation. I wondered if she had Alzheimer's disease. I tried to reach out to her again, but her mind slipped quickly through my fingers. Maybe she had been recently released from a mental institution or abandoned by her children. I gently shook her body while she continued to wail.

"Ma'am, Ma'am," I pleaded, "Is there anything I can do to help you?" Her frail body continued to shake back and forth, to and fro rattling with anguish. Leaning even closer on her left side, I looked at the hands shielding her face that were apparently caging her in, and separating us. Thin, almost translucent, shiny brown skin covered her long, slender fingers, grossly disfigured at the joints into a stiff, frozen claws. Her short, stubby nails contained deep ridges and grooves, some stained with a brown pigment. Darker brown spots of varying sizes speckled across her hands, clumping together in the middle. Coarse scars, too numerous to count, filled the spaces between the spots, while tortured, dark blue veins threatened to burst from beneath the loose, dangling skin. Her hands were rough, brittle and ashen.

Her body continued to wail and convulse in unspeakable and seemingly confused anguish. She was totally unaware of the imminent danger we were facing, "Ma'am," I pleaded again, "Please let me help you!"

Several people raced through the parking lot shouting, "No justice, no peace!" intermittently banging on the few remaining cars. I knew we had to get out of there.

Finally, she uncovered her face, lifted her head and looked up at me without moving her frail torso and said, "I is lost. I is lookin foh my husban and my chilrens. I been lookin fo such a lon, lon time an I cain't fine dem," she whispered and sobbed in a soft husky voice, choking, seemingly gasping for air, as tears streamed down her face.

"Ma'am, do you know where your family lives? If you do, I'll take you there."

Her face was blank, frozen, exempt of expression, while her eyes suddenly became very glassy. She looked through me, without responding. I studied her face closely, while she continued to gaze through me. Her deep owl-shaped brown eyes were haloed by bluish gray circles. They were two cloudy, tortured pools filled with ancient anguish and confusion.

Her warm brown face, the color of fresh almonds, was sculpted by deep seams of wrinkles. Hallmarks of old age and a hard life filled her face, cascading around her eyes, ripping across her forehead, tracing her passage from one era to another. Heavy, burrowed, crevices intermingled with dangling flesh, tracked across her face melding into her sagging brown skin, with a sallow, yellow tint blanketing her complexion. Her long and very angular chin jutted forth to greet me. Her reddish brown lips contained hundreds of fine, broken lines; a pattern that escaped into the surrounding areas above and below the lips. Her neck's prominent veins were surrounded by loose ripples of flesh that settled at the junction where the neck ends and the chest begins. More loose flesh appeared to droop from her arms, replacing the muscles that once fortified and strengthened her stature. After several moments passed, again she began to slowly notice my presence. Her glassy disorientation began to give way to her returning awareness. Her knees began to sway again, seemingly shaking off and releasing her pain through movement. A full view of her hands revealed them to be more like claws than I had initially imagined. They were curled over, deformed into a frozen, claw-like position, attached to her large, distorted, bony wrists.

Silence enveloped us. Her eyes drifted away from me again, into the distant world that was hers and hers alone. In my heart, I sensed what this fragile carriage, this tenuous blush of life, once was. My mind saw an image of her forty, fifty years earlier—a young, strong, powerful and determined woman, full of life, presence and stature, sturdy, strong like an oak tree. Now she was a mere shadow of that woman.

I touched her hand, purposefully, and whispered in her ear, "Ma'am, please let me help you. Where do you live?"

"I doesn't lives no wheahs. I ain't got nothin, I ain't nevah had nothin," she cried through her hands.

What could I do with this woman? How could I leave her here in the midst of all this madness so helpless and alone? I knew this neighborhood was about to explode, about to burst into flames in any minute. I couldn't take her back into the agency—everyone was probably gone by now. Hundreds of thoughts ran through my mind. My conscience asked, "What if this was your mother? What would you want a stranger to do?" With that question, suddenly, my heart decided to put her in my car and take her home. If I didn't take her with me, God only knows what would happen to this poor old woman who couldn't fend for herself.

In that split second, I knew I had no other choice. It was the only thing I could do. "Ma'am, I want you to come with me." I bent over, placed my hand under her right armpit and lifted her up. I had to grab her tightly because she had very little muscle on her arm to hold on to. She resisted initially, but eventually yielded to my strength. Once I got her upright, her body remained slightly bent over. I turned her in the direction of my car, only a couple of steps away, and lead her to the door. She staggered and hobbled about like a little sparrow with a broken wing, trying to fly, dragging her right foot a bit, struggling with a heavy, awkward limp.

When I opened the door on the passenger's side and tried to help her in, she stopped moving and asked, "Whot is dis?" She seemed very confused about getting in.

"A car."

"What's a cah?" She asked, trying to pull away from me.

"Ma'am, please get in," I pleaded. "I don't have time to answer."

She tried to yank her arm away from me again.

"Listen," I said firmly. "I want you to come with me. I've gotta get both of us out of here. It's too dangerous for you to be out her by yourself."

She pulled away from me once more and said, "No, I don wonts go wid yah. I wonts tah fine mah familee."

"Ma'am," I pleaded. "If you come with me, I promise you. I promise I will help you find your family."

"How does yah knows where dey is?" she demanded.

Across the street at the stripmall, a large storefront window crashed, and the harsh sound of glass crashing startled both of us. The noise was so severe, she literally leaped into the car. Her cooperation surprised me. I hopped quickly into my side and sped down the street, as fast as I could to the freeway.

Through the windows, I could still hear the loud, angry chants, "No justice, no peace! No justice, no peace!" richoceting through the air. I thanked God when we made it safely to the Harbor Freeway.

My passenger sat motionless, in a state of suspended animation, barely breathing, staring straight ahead, totally unaware of me or the danger we were leaving behind.

Looking out of the window as my car sped along, I could see plumes of thick black smoke rising from the city's floor.

The fires had begun.

My body turned ice cold as the memory of this morning's nightmare flooded my senses.

Now the meaning of that experience was clear.

I turned on the radio to a news station to find out what it had to say about what was happening.

"Whot's dat?" she asked, as shock passed through her body. "Who dat talkin? Wheah is dat man? Dere ain't no man in heah?" she said looking in the back seat. From the corner of my eye, I saw her looking at me, her face filled with a disbelieving confusion.

I replied softly, seeking to calm her with a reassuring tone, "Ma'am, that's the radio."

"What's dat?"

Pointing at the dashboard, I replied, "As I said—it's the radio."

"Whot is ah ray-dee-oh?" she snapped.

"Ma'am, don't you know what a radio is? I'm sure you just forgot."

"No, I doesn't. I ain't nevah heard ah no ray-dee-oh. Wheah is dat man who be talkin? Is dis heah thang haunted wid speakin haints?"

"No, Ma'am, I assure you it's not." I turned the radio to several stations, so she could hear the different sounds. "Ma'am, a radio is an electrical instrument that picks up sound waves from different stations."

I looked over at her and she was gone again. She slumped back into her seat and returned to that strange catatonic state. "Do you hear me? Do you understand what I'm telling you? "

No response. She was lost once again to another world.

As I drove along the expressway, I saw a couple of white people being pulled from their cars and beaten. What I saw pained me. I wanted to stop and rescue them, but I felt so defenseless, as a woman I knew there was very little I could do. My mind replayed Rodney King's beating. I wanted to know, why do we do this to one another? Yet, no answer came.

I exited from the freeway and made my way through our neighborhood, quickly climbing up Baldwin Hills. When I turned the last corner onto my street, I was ecstatic to see the street sign, "Vallejo Drive" beckoning me home. I took a deep breath and sighed, while I whispered a silent prayer, thanking God for getting us home, safe and sound. I wondered, now that we were finally out of harm's way, who this woman was and where she came from. I drove my car into the circular drive that formed an arc around our dry, minimally green lawn. A white gray fountain of a cherub holding a bucket on his shoulder sprinkled water into the basin.

Waves of relief washed over me. I had never been so grateful, in the eight or nine years that we've been here, to get home. But it actually had taken us forty-five minutes to make a fifteen minute trip. Not knowing who this woman was or what she was going to do next unnerved me.

Gazing at the front of our home, I smiled at the white stucco, Spanish structure that I'd proudly called home for almost a decade. Seven arcs surrounded the house, glowing before the sun. The four larger ones located directly in front of the house are two stories high, while the three smaller ones lined the walkway linking the garage to the house.

John discovered our home, one day many years ago, while driving through Baldwin Hills to visit a friend. He made a wrong turn and ended up in front of this house, which had a for sale sign in front of it. He fell in love with the house immediately and so did I. It is a beautiful home.

In my wildest dreams, I never thought I'd ever find myself living in such luxury. The main floor is actually the second level. It has a huge white foyer, peach marble floors and a gorgeous one-of-a-kind large, art-deco chandelier that I picked out myself, shortly before we moved in. This hallway runs the entire length of our home, linking our two story living room, kitchen, breakfast nook and library. My favorite room on that level is the living room. I've never seen anything like it before. It's two levels, with the front side covered by a wall of windows. My favorite part of the house is our rock wall fountain. Instead of a fireplace, we have an entire wall covered with a rich, brown granite rock. Streams of water flow down the rock into a pond filled with exotic and rare goldfish, while tropical plants rest at the base of the wall.

The first or ground level contains our huge family room. In the center of the room is a large 'U' shaped black leather sofa, that

rests behind a plush, white shag rug, accentuating the rich black
marble floor, facing the wide screen television John bought a few
years ago to watch the Lakers and Forty-niners games. We spend
most of our time down there. The wet bar on the side faces the
wall of glass overlooking our patio and pool. The room is chock full
of entertainment, including a billiard table, a wide-screen television, a pingpong table and video game machines. The adjacent
soundproof music room lets me listen to my music while my son
plays rap. We also have a smaller game room, an office and a large
guest suite. I occasionally use the office on that level, although I
really prefer working in the breakfast nook area, because of the
view it offers of the city and the bright sunlight that streams into
that space. Our third level has the four other bedrooms. James
and Ashley's bedrooms are there, another smaller guest room, as
well as the master suite, our bedroom which is the piece-de-resis-
tance. Our huge bedroom has his and her bathrooms, connected
by a space containing the jacuzzi, sauna and a small exercise room,
walk-in closets and a dressing room, plus an office for John that
he rarely uses. He prefers our statelier, more formal library downstairs, adjacent to our dining room.

I parked the car in front of the house, turned to our guest,
smiled and said as cheerfully as I could: "We're home!" She continued to stare straight ahead, as if in a deep hypnotic trance. When
I helped her out of the car, she offered no resistance. I took her
hand and led her into the house. She stumbled along, a half step
behind me dragging her right foot, barely lifting it off the ground.

Once inside the foyer, I called the kids on the intercom system, "James, Ash, hi sweeties. I'm home."

"Hi, Mommie!" squealed Ashley. "We're down in the family
room watching TV."

"Okay kids, I'll be down in just a minute."

My little companion held on tightly as I led her down the
hallway to the kitchen, continuing to stagger very closely behind
me, like a broken shadow. I wondered why she didn't have any
possessions other than the tattered, dirty clothing on her back.
She had no bags, no purse, no identification or money. Once in the

kitchen, I led her over to the glass table in the breakfast nook, and helped her take a seat.

I stroked her right hand while she sat there, looking straight ahead, out the window overlooking the pool in our backyard. I whispered, "Ma'am, I am going to go downstairs to see my children. I'll be back in just a few minutes. When I do, I'm going to get you out of those dirty clothes and fix you a nice hot meal. Okay?" She grasped my hand with her long, deformed fingers, looked up and squinted at me. She appeared to be a little less disoriented, although she didn't respond to what I said. "It's going to be okay," I reassured her. "I'll be right back."

I ran downstairs to greet Ashley and James, and to prepare them to meet our unexpected houseguest. My children were glued to our wide screen television, watching the live reports about what seemed to be the beginning of a massive rebellion.

James was sitting in the middle of our sofa, his legs were crossed on the coffee table, while Ashley was lying on the plush white long-haired shag rug. Without looking in my direction, still focused intently on the television, James asked, "Mom, do you know what's going on?"

"First of all, I know you need to take your feet off my coffee table. You know better than that." His feet snapped to a hurried attention on the floor as he sat up straight in his seat. "Well, son, a lot of people are very angry about the verdict. And they are venting their anger and frustrations in the only way they know how."

James had a stymied expression on his face as he said, "Dad called just a few minutes ago to see if you'd gotten home yet. He was worried about you and when I asked him the same question, all he did was mumble something about how disgusted he was.

"Mom—" he continued anxiously.

"Yes, dear."

"What does all this mean?" he asked, folding his arms across his chest, the way he did when he was a frightened little boy.

Seeing my children so perplexed made me wonder how could I ever possibly find the words to adequately explain to them what was in my heart. And more importantly, how can I protect them from the hatred and anger I know they will one day have to face alone? "James, you have to understand that your father has good reason to be upset. It's very tough and frustrating for him, as it is for most of us to see those policemen get off, knowing what they did. Your dad's lived through a lot of bad experiences, being a black man in this world."

Ashley rolled around, turning away from the television to look at me and said, "Mommie, if it was wrong for those policemen to beat up Mr. King, why aren't they going to Jail? And why are those people fighting and burning down everything? It looks kinda scary down there."

"Ash, you know that it was wrong for the policemen to beat Mr. King like that, or anybody for that matter. Your father and I have told you time and time again that there is a lot of injustice in this country, especially when it comes to our people, and that's what happened today. But it doesn't make any sense to destroy your own neighborhood. Now does that seem right to you?"

"No, Mommie, it doesn't," she sighed, still perturbed.

"Are you mad?" interjected James.

"Yes, I most certainly am," I replied forcefully as my anger resurfaced.

"Well, I'm mad too," replied my son in a surprisingly forceful manner, reminding me that he was growing up. "I want to know what kind of justice this is if those cops could get off like that?"

"Baby, it's racism, pure and simple. But before we go any further, I want to tell the two of you about our houseguest."

"Houseguest?" they replied in unison.

"Yes. On my home, I found her crying next to my car in the parking lot. She doesn't remember very much, if anything about her life. So I want you to be very nice to her and to be on your best behavior."

"What's her name?" asked James.

"I'm not sure," I answered.

"But Mom, what are we supposed to call her if we don't know her name?" demanded James.

"Calling her 'Ma'am' will be sufficient," I replied sternly.

"What's wrong with her? Why doesn't she remember her name?" chirped Ashley.

"Ashley, I don't know for sure. She's very confused right now."

"How long will she be here with us? Is she going to stay for a long time?"

"Young lady, I don't know that either. Maybe she'll be here for a few days, maybe a little longer. It just depends on how long it takes us to locate her family, and how long this violence lasts."

"Mom, how long do you think that's gonna take?"

"James, I don't know. I hope it's over as soon as possible."

"I'm going to go upstairs and bring her down here to meet you. Remember, I want the two of you to mind your manners, and be on your best behavior."

At the top of the stairs, I looked across the stretch of the room, and found her still in the same frozen position she was in when I left her about five minutes ago. Sitting there, she looked very frightened and so desperately alone in the world. My heart felt the pain of her loneliness and confusion. I wondered where her family was, certain they must be worried sick about her. In that moment, I suddenly realized that for the time being we were going to be her family because we were all that she had. Leaning across the table, I gently touched her shoulder so as not to startle her. "Ma'am, I want you to come with me," I said, reaching my hand out to her.

"Oh, Lawd," she cried out, rolling her head around. "Wheah is we goin now? Is we goin back in dat fast movin carriage?"

"Shh, Shh, Ma'am it's okay," I whispered. "No we're not. We're at home now, and I want you to meet my children. And we're going to get you out of those dirty clothes and into some clean ones."

"Oh yeah?" she grinned a semi-toothless grin. The few teeth she had left were very yellow and appeared to be rotting. A couple on the lower gums possessed very dark brown stains. Talking about my children seemed to relieve her of some of her pain and calmed her down a bit. "You gots chilrens, too? How many does yah haf?"

"Two, a boy and a girl."

"Dat all?" she asked.

"Yes, Ma'am that is."

I took her by the hand and lead her through the kitchen to the stairway leading down to the first level. Her right hand held onto the bannister for dear life, while her left hand clamped down like a wrench onto my arm. Her fingers dug deep into my flesh. The appearance of her hands were quite deceiving. Although they were fragile and obviously crippled they yielded an unexpected current of strength. I carefully guided her into the middle of our family room.

"James and Ashley, I want you to meet our houseguest. Say 'hello.'"

"Hello" they replied dryly looking in our direction.

Standing there, next to the couch, she had drifted back into a deeper state of absence, failing to recognize the children were speaking to her. When she didn't respond, James reacted, his words rattling with irritation, "Mom, what's wrong with her?"

"Watch your manners, boy! As I told you, about a minute ago, she's a little disoriented right now, still trying to figure out where she is. But she's going to be alright because we're going to help her."

"Why didn't you take her to a shelter or some other place instead of bringing her here?" demanded James once more, sounding too much like his father to suit my liking.

"Wait one minute!" I exploded with firm anger. "Boy, where's your home training? Let me make myself perfectly clear. You have no right whatsoever, and I repeat no right, to ask such a rude and unnecessary question. I will discuss this matter with you later. In the meantime, I expect you and your sister to be on your best behavior, and to help make our guest's stay as pleasant as possible.

"Do I make myself perfectly clear?" I asked.

"Yes, Mom," they replied, barely above a whisper. They knew I was serious. Serious enough to corral them back into their appropriate adolescent place.

I led the little lady into our guest room, and sat her down on the yellow flowered chaise lounge. The room's bright canary yellow wallpaper and matching bedspread temporarily lifted my spirits. I bent my body to her level, looked directly into her eyes and said, "Ma'am, I'm going to give you some clothes to put on and run you some bath water so you can take a nice, hot bath. Okay?"

Once more, she appeared to be very confused, and asked, "Whot does yah wants me to do?"

"I want you to go into the bathroom, through that door over there," I said, pointing at the bathroom door, "and take a nice, hot bath."

"Yes, Ma'am. How does I gits outside? Does I goes through dat dooh?"

"No, Ma'am. You don't have to go outside to take a bath. There's one in the bathroom. We have running water in our house." I felt so sorry for her. The thought of inside running water had confused her. I wondered what part of the deep South she was from. I know there are still places in remote impoverished areas that lack running water. She must be from one of those places. But that was virtually unheard of in 1992.

I left her alone for a moment, walked into the family room and asked my daughter, "Ash, would you please run upstairs and get one of Mommie's clean terrycloth robes, that green pair of sweats, a pair of white socks, and those blue houseshoes?"

"Okay."

I walked through the guest room into its attached bathroom. I turned on the bathtub's faucet, and heard her soft, occasional whimpering seep in from the bedroom. I poured a handful of a mineral bath solution in to the warm water, and walked back into the bedroom. "Ma'am, I'm running your bath water. It will be ready for you in just a few more minutes."

The sound of my voice agitated her. She moved away from me.

"I doesn't need no hot baf. I ain't had one in a lon, lon time." My pity for her surged as I wondered how long she had been homeless, and denied the most basic of human needs.

Ashley cautiously entered the room with all of the clothing I'd asked her to bring. She placed them on the chaise lounge and literally ran out of the room.

Suddenly, the woman returned to her catatonic state. I touched her right shoulder and shook it gently. Once again, she failed to look at me.

"Ma'am, do you need me to help you get undressed?" Once again, she failed to respond.

Her clothes were filthy, caked with layers of dirt. Because I was so preoccupied with getting us out of harm's way when I discovered her, I didn't realize just how dirty she was. Over the years, I've seen literally thousands of homeless people in my line of work, more than I care to remember or can count, but I'd never seen anything like this. She sat there, oblivious to her surroundings. After I turned off the water in the tub, I walked over to the chaise lounge, got down on my knees and pulled up the tattered hem of her long, dirty skirt to take off her shoes. As I moved it, I noticed beneath the top layer of burlap-like cloth, she had on another skirt, a dirty, orange calico with several tears and holes. She wore a pair of old, decrepit brown brogan shoes. The worn, old tongues hung lifelessly from the middle of the shoe. The right lacked a shoe string, while the left possessed only a short stub, lacing only the first two of a dozen or so rows. Several gaping spaces between both shoes at the soles were filled with foul smelling dirt. I lifted her leg and pulled the shoes off one by one. As the first shoe came off, a putrid odor, worse than rotten sardines, filled the air, burning my nostrils and choking my throat. I gagged uncontrollably. Most of her black socks were missing, eaten away, through the large holes in the soles of both shoes. I was horrified when I saw her right foot covered with a horrible, strange looking rash, like a black cauliflower, covering most of the bottom of her foot and the side. Portions of the rash oozed a clear, white fluid. Some sections of it exposed tiny slivers of raw, pink flesh. The growth extended into the spaces between most of her toes, and to the surface of her right foot. I've never seen anything like it before. I realized it must have caused her severe pain to bear weight on her feet. No wonder why the poor thing could barely walk. I assumed she had arthritis. It was apparent to me now that this rash was the cause of her awkward gait.

"Ma'am, would you please stand up? I'm going to help you take off your clothes." I stood up, placed my hands under her armpits and lifted her. She continued to stare straight ahead into space. When I began to unbutton her sweater, she slapped my hand, and screamed, "Don't touch me! Stop dat! Stop dat right nawh! I can takes mah own clothes off!"

"Okay, I'm sorry, I did not mean to offend you. You don't need me to help you get in the tub?"

"No, I doesn't needs yah tah do nothin, I knows how tah clean mah own body."

Without speaking another word, I quietly retreated from the room. A knee jerk response from childhood had returned without invitation. My mother taught me never to challenge adults, even when I was right.

About a half hour later, she and Ashley emerged at the top of the stairs holding hands. I caught a glimpse of them out of a corner of my eye as I searched through the refrigerator adjacent to the stairwell. "My, don't you look pretty!" I said cheerfully. She looked much better and refreshed. Ashley had plaited her thin gray hair into three braids, one at the top of her head, and two in the back.

"Thank yah, Ma'am," she replied with a faint smile. "I does feels much betta now." She seemed a bit more alert and aware of her surroundings. I suppose the hot bath had done her some good.

"Come on over here and have a seat," I said, pointing to the table in the breakfast nook. "You can keep me company while I finish up dinner. It's almost ready. And I know you must be hungry."

"Yes, I is a bit. Some vittles would hep dese ole bones. It bin a mighty lon time since I et hot food."

"Ash, sweetie, thanks for bringing our guest upstairs. You can go back downstairs and watch television with your brother until dinner is ready."

"That's okay, Mommie. I'll stay up here and help you."

As I set the table, I looked at the little old lady and asked, "Ma'am, what's your name?"

"Mah name?" she replied.

"Yes, Ma'am. Do you know your name?"

She paused for a few moments, looked a bit perplexed, as if she were searching the ancient recesses of her memory. "I doesn't quite remembas. It bin such a lon, lon time since I heards it."

"Think hard," encouraged Ashley. "You can remember. I know you can."

"Let's me see heah," she said, looking down into the palm of her hands. "Yah know, I jist doesn't remembas mah name. It ain't wid me rite nah. Dat makes me so sad. I jist doesn't knows whot to do." She bent her head, her hand covered her heavily wrinkled brow and shook it in despair. I walked over to her and wrapped my arm around her shoulders. She began to sob again. But her sobs were much softer, less pained this time.

"Don't worry, honey. Maybe after you have a nice, hot meal, you will remember. It's not that important right now anyway," I said trying to console her once more.

Because we were hungry, I decided not to wait for John, and we started dinner without him. I didn't call him on his cellular phone because I didn't want to have to tell him about our houseguest guest over the phone. My heart told me he was safe. Knowing him, I thought this surprise would go over much better face to face.

We ate dinner quietly against the presence of the day's events. The children were on their best behavior. We ate baked chicken, corn on the cob, left over collard greens from Sunday's dinner, corn bread and peach cobbler. Our guest ate as if she hadn't eaten in years, gobbling the food on her plate with a ravishing, reckless abandon. The poor thing ate so fast, I thought she might choke. A couple of times I caught her eating with her hands.

John walked into the kitchen during dessert. He appeared exhausted and shaken. It was around seven thirty, and he was actually getting home an hour earlier than usual. Tonight his haggard expression carried the stresses of a long and very difficult day.

"Daddy!" screamed Ashley. "I'm so glad you're finally home!" She jumped up from the table, ran across the room and leaped into his arms.

"Baby, I'm very glad to be home, too. It's been quite a day for your dad," he replied, kissing her on the cheek.

"Dad, what took you so long to get home?" asked James.

"Son, it's crazy out there. I was stuck on the freeway for over three and a half hours. I'm just glad I finally made it home."

As he walked towards the table, he stopped in his tracks, looked at me, pointed to our guest, who was slurping down her second helping of peach cobbler, and asked, "Who's that?"

"She's our houseguest," I replied.

"Our what?" he snapped sarcastically, still pointing in her direction.

She looked up and dropped her fork, suddenly becoming very self-conscious, as she wiggled nervously in her seat.

"Ma'am, I want you to meet my husband John Stewart. John this is our houseguest.

She managed to create a brief, delicate, tentative smile that extended across her face. My husband responded to her gesture by asking harshly, "What's your name?"

"John, let's talk about that a little later," I replied, trying to divert his attention. "Honey, why don't you sit down and let me fix your plate. I'm sure you're hungry."

"No, I want to know who this woman is right now!" he demanded.

"John, I said this isn't the right time or place."

"Yeah, right..... later." He turned and stomped out of the kitchen.

"Where are you going?"

"Upstairs to get out of these sweaty clothes."

While Ashley and James cleaned the kitchen, I took our mystery guest downstairs to her room and put her to bed. After I pulled the covers back, handed her one of my old yellow and white flannel nightgowns that Ashley had collected for her, I said softly, "Ma'am, this has been a very long day for all of us, but especially for you. Why don't you go on in the bathroom, and change into this gown, so you can get yourself a good night's sleep?"

She nodded in agreement, "Yes, Ma'am. I needs tah do dat."

I sat down on the chaise lounge as she staggered into the bathroom. The weight of this most difficult day fell upon me like a ton of bricks. Every fiber in my body ached. And with the conversation with my husband looming before me, and I knew it was not going to be a pleasant one. I had to explain to him, in a way that he would understand, why I brought her home.

In the midst of my thoughts, she emerged from the bathroom. The nightgown literally swallowed her up. In spite of her age, her braids and the gown made her look like a little girl wearing her mother's clothes.

"Now don't you look ready for bed?" I asked wearily. She staggered once more over to the bed and climbed in slowly. I walked over to the bed and leaned over to tuck her in.

Her eyes were refreshed, crisp and clear, glowing with new clarity. Something made me kiss her goodnight.

She grabbed my hand. Squeezing it tightly she said, "Ma'am, I remembas. I do remembas mah name."

"You do?" I replied, startled by her abrupt discovery.

"Yes, Ma'am. I knows mah name. It Zoli. Dey used tah call me 'Momma, Momma Zoli.'"

three

I doesn't knows how I gots heah an I cain't remembas wheah I bin. De las thin I remembas is dat I was jist outsidah Vidaylia, an I lay down dat evenin aftah dark. De stars in de sky was v'ry brite dat nite, an I remembas wonderin if any of mah youngins was ah lookin up at dem stars like I was. Befoh I wents to sleep I gots down on mah knees like I al'ays do an say mah prayahs axin de Lawd tah gif me jist one moh day to fine mah chilrens. Den I lay down 'neath dis heah big weepin willah tree dat was bout firty feet from de road dat I bin journeyin on. I stretch out dese ole weary bones on dat raggedy blankut of mine, an foh some reason I say mah prayahs agin. When I woke up de next mawnin I was in dis heah strange place. I doesn't knows wheah I is or who broughts me tah dis heah place. But dere is one thin dat I knows foh sho—dis heah worle is a shock to mah system.

When I wokes up dat next mawnin I was in dis heah place. It ain't nothin like I has evah seen befoh. Dere was dese big old trees wid a funny brown bark, dat had dese long ole leaves dat looked like ah heap ah fans at de top. De trees was purdy, but I ain't nevah seen nothin like dem befoh. An de grass was yellah an green, not like dat ole thick green grass in 'Sippi. I looked aroune me an mah blankut an mah ole bag was gone. De firs thing dat I reckoned when I woke up an foune mysef in dis heah strange an diff'rent worle, is dat Momma Zoli had done died an gone on tah heaven, to be wid mah Lawd. I was happy tah knows dat I done made it ovah, but sad 'cause I ain't found mah chilrens yet. Dats de God hones truf. I dropped tah mah knees an thanks de Lawd foh bringin me ovah. I ain't reckon dat heaven would be a lookin like dis. But I ain't knows wheah else I could be. Dere was a few peoples walkin aroune mindin dey own affairs. An de streets was filled with dese big ole buggies an carriages dat was movin aroune on dey own. Dey ain't haf no horses or mules pullin dem. I didn't knows whot tah thinks bout dem machines. Dey was somethin else, dey way de be movin movin real fast. An dere was mostly darkies ridin arounee in dem. I guess dey was on dey way tah de pearly gates, too. So I went a lookin foh Saint Petah. Alon de way I was seein all dese thangs dat dese eyes ain't nevah seen befoh. De sun was jist a shinin, it was so brite an purdy. Dis is ah brite an wondahful place, but I ain't knows dat heaven was gonna be lookin like dis. I kept on walkin aroune justah lookin foh Saint Petah or ah angel to help me on mah way. De air was funny. It had a bad smell to it, an it was burnin in mah troat an made me coff. An dere was peoples ev'rywheah. Most of 'em was colored folk. I doesn't knows why dey was lookin de way dey was lookin. I woulda thought dat peoples in heaven was gonna be happy an smilin once dey got dere. 'Specially us darkies. But dey faces was drawn up wid pain, an some of 'em looked downrite mean. I ain't see no smiles on dey face, dey jist looked like dey was in a worle of dey own. Mos of dem ain't even look at ole Momma Zoli. Dey acted like dey was 'fraid, like somethin was wrong wid of Momma Zoli. Ev'rythang is v'ry diff'rent 'bout dis heah worle from whot I is used tah.

I mustah walks aroune dis heah place an nobody ain't say nothin to me. I was gittin hungry an vary tired. Mah stomach was justa growlin, cause I had mah last good food bout two weeks ago, days foh I made it to Vidaylia. Some croppahs took me in an fed me in a farm two days outsidah dat town. All I had tah do was look aftah dey youngins while dey was in de fields. Dey wanted me tah stay wid em, but I said "No," I had tah keeps movin on til I fine mah own chilrens an mah husban.

I ain't knows if yah can gets hungry in heaven. An mah empty stomach brought tah mind a bit of ah worry dat maybe dis heah ain't heaven. I ain't nevah thought too much 'bout whot happens when yah dies. But Momma Zoli sho nuff did den. An den I starts gettin riled up. If I wadn't in heaven den Lawd have mercy on me, wheah was I? Wheah was de angels? I went into dis heah place dat looked like it was ah store wid some food in it. I seen pictas of food hangin in dah windahs of de store. Dey looked so real til I thought I could eat 'em up. So I went in tryin tah gits some hep. An de people dat was inside was some kinda people I ain't nevah seen befoh. Dey was short an dey skin was real yellah, an dey eyes was li'l bitty slits. Dey looked jist a little bits like dem Injins I seen in Jackson when I was a li'l gul, but I didn't knows wheah dese folks came from. I was axin dem tah heps me, an dey was jist yellin at me, sayin words dat I couldn't undahstands. I ain't undastan nothin whot dey be sayin, an I was gettin moh an moh scared. Den de next thang I knows a whole heap of colored folk ran up in dere an startin beatin on dem. I gots vary scared, den I started wonderin if dis was heaven den why was dese people fightin like dis? I jist don't knows why dey took tah beatin dem folk foh nothin. Den I thoughts to mysef, wid all dis fightin, maybe dis is really hell. I ain't knows whot de Lawd had in store for me next. I axed de Lawd whot did I do tah gits sent tah hell.

Mah heart got so heavy, I jist started cryin, an I kep on cryin til I was los in mah own teahs. I tried tah know foh mysef whot I be doin wrong foh de Lawd tah send me tah dis heah place. I mustah done somethin awful bad tah git heah. Ev'rybody was yellin an screamin, shoutin an fightin, runnin up an down de streets like de worle was comin to ah end. I thought dey was gonna hurt Momma Zoli. Mah heart starts hurtin seein dem folks get beat like dat. I can remembas how it feels tah gits beat foh no good reason. I gots so scared dat dem folks was gonna each othah. An if I knows somethin I knows dat heaven ain't 'pose tah be like dis.

I reckon I cain't remembas much ah happened next. Seem like mah head got a big ole hole in it. Cause de next thin I knows, jist ah li'l bit latah I is gittin outta dis heah carriage without no hoss, an dis heah purdy li'l colored lady takin me inside dis big ole house dat looked like a king or queen lif in it. I ain't nevah seen nothin like dis, not wid mah own two eyes.

I is scared, so v'ry, v'ry scared. I doesn't knows how I is gonna gits back tah 'Sippi. I gots tah fine mah chilrens and mah husban. I love dem moh dan any thang else is dis heah worle, an I always will. I gots tah leaf dis place soon as I can.

I bin ah lookin foh mah family, mah husban an mah seben chilrens, Nehemiah, Homer, Eula, Tecora, Raymond, Roy an mah youngese Jeremiah foh moh dan two yeahs, an I ain't foune a trace ah dem yet. Since de day dey took mah first chile away moh dan fifty yeahs ago I bin waitin an prayin foh de Lawd tah set me free so dat I could fine dem. It hurted me so much tah lose mah chilrens. Ain't a day passed by when I wadn't feelin dat pain. I nevah thought dat mah heart could carrys so much pain. But Momma Zoli ain't de only one tah lose a chile. So I made do wid whot I had, an each an ev'ry nite foh all ah de days dat I can remembas, I said mah prayahs axin de Lawd tah keeps mah chilrens safe, an dat somebody mite be lookin out foh dem since I cain't be dere wid dem. I axed Him tah one day send all ah dem back tah me.

De sweet chilrens in dis house makes me thinks ah mah own. Maybe I gots granchilrens somewheah. An dey is de only ones heah dat believes me. Dey knows I is tellin de truf. But bein aroune dem makes me miss mah own even moh. Yes, Lawd have mercy on me, I gots tah fine mah youngins. I is ah ole woman, an I knows dat I ain't gots much time left on dis heah earf. I doesn't knows who brought me heah or why. I jist needs tah gets back tah 'Sippi.

Mah firs chile was only ten yeahs ole when dat ole Massa Steadwell took 'em from me. I mustah cried each an ev'ry day foh six monfs. But it didn't make it no bettah. He took mah boy from me, an I ain't nevah bin rite since. An mah heart ain't gonna be rite til I fines each an ev'ry las one of mah chilrens. An dat is somethin dat I is gonna do, foh I lays down mah head one las time on dis heah side ah Jordan. Walkin all ovah 'Sippi an some parts of 'bama, a bit of Tennahsse, an a li'l part of Floreedah. An if I had tah, Momma Zoli will walk 'cross de face of de earf til I fines 'em.

I doesn't knows wheah dey is. Dere is no tellin. Dey coulda been sole anywheah in de south from Texas tah Virginny. Each time one of dem was taken away from me, I would stop an pray, pleadin wid de Lawd tah keeps de rest of dem close tah me, evens if I couldn't bees wid dem, it was bettah dat dey be close by.

An I kept ah hopin an a prayin one day I would fine at least one of dem. But mah luck wadn't goin de way I axed de Lawd tah let it be. I ain't bin able tah fine not even one of mah chilrens an I been lookin foh dem for almos two years. I been walkin, justah walkin from one farm to de next, one town to anothah, and ask questions. But nobody seemed tah knows anythang abouts mah family an wheah dey mite be. But who could knows wheah dey mite be? I doesn't knows 'zactly whot dey name is and since dey bin grown whot dey looks like rite now. I ain't knows if dey is dead or if dey is alive, but I knows I haf tah fine some kine ah trace of dem foh mah sake, so mah mine won't go downrite crazy.

Alone de way dere was al'ays some colored folks on de road ah lookin foh dey family too. Sometimes othah womins travels wid me. Most of de time I was on mah own. Sometimes some kinely soul would take me in an feed me, give me a warm place tah stay. I gots by by doin a li'l bits an pieces of work ev'ry now an den. Cleanin house, workin in de fields, mostly pickin cotton, sometimes indigo. It seems like each an ev'ry day I done de same thang day in an day out. Ev'ry nite I would fine a quiet safe place tah sleep.

But I cain't give up on findin dem. Dats whot keeps me goin. I knew de Lawd had kept me alive foh dis one reason. An dat reason was tah git us back togetah agin under one roof. De way a familee is 'pose tah be. I knows mah time is runnin out, cause I is gettin ole. I know de Lawd is gettin ready tah bring me on home.

I gots tah git back tah 'Sippi so dat I can fine mah own.

four

I couldn't believe it. I couldn't believe my ears. After all these years, I never thought my wife would do something like this. But she did. Why did she have to disrespect me like this? I'm the head of this house, the man in charge. Why did my wife of twenty-five years bring a stranger into our home without consulting with me? We had an understanding, an agreement that we weren't going to make a major decision without first discussing it together. It's been that way with us for years. But today, she willfully and boldly disrespected me by going off and doing exactly what she wanted to do. I was fuming.

As I changed and put on my favorite Howard U sweatsuit, Ashley walked in the room, asking, "Daddy, what's wrong?"

"Nothing." I replied.

"Daddy, are you mad at Mommie because she brought that lady home?"

She's very keen for her age, doesn't let anything slip by her and is much sharper than her brother. Not wanting to put her in the middle of our argument, I cut the conversation short and said, "Look Ash, it's been a long, long day for your dad. There's nothing for you to be worrying you pretty little head over. Everything's going to be alright."

"But Daddy—"

"No buts, you just scoot on downstairs and help your mother. Seems like she's got her hands full."

"Daddy, did something bad happen to you coming home? I saw a lot of people getting beat up on the freeway when I was watching TV. Did you see it happen?"

"No," I replied gruffly. "I'm exhausted. It's been a very long day so I want you to go downstairs and give your daddy a chance to catch his breath."

"Aren't you going to eat dinner?" she pleaded, continuing her intense one-on-one evaluation of me.

"No, I'm not hungry. I don't have much of an appetite right now. I'll be okay."

"Okay," she sighed as she shrugged her little shoulders and backed out of the room. On her way out, she continued to carefully examine my face, watching me, like a lioness observing her cubs for any signs of distress.

I picked up the remote control that was sitting on my nightstand and turned on the television. As I flipped through the channels, I noticed that every local station had a flock of reporters on the street covering the outbreak of rage. It was a madhouse, absolute chaos in South Central and the violence was rapidly spreading to other parts of the city. One station showed a crowd of several hundred people marching on police headquarters downtown in Parker Center, where they overturned and set fire to a couple of police cars. The protesters then fanned out into the Civic Center area, torching other cars including more police cars, breaking the windows of office and government buildings, attacking passersby and torching several businesses. Another report showed protesters over at Lakeview Terrace, the very site where Rodney King was beaten over fourteen months ago. They were about the only ones who had peacefully assembled to express their outrage toward the verdict. Other areas throughout the city also reported violent incidents, and attacks on motorists getting pulled from their cars, poor souls who happened to be in the wrong place at the wrong time. It looked like this situation was going to get worse tonight. To add insult to injury, the police were nowhere to be found. I haven't seen anything like this since the sixties.

On my way home, on the radio I heard the mayor say, "I'm just stunned, shocked ... Today this jury told the world what we saw way with our own eyes wasn't a crime ... The jury's verdict will never outlive the images of the savage beating ... Today the system failed us." People from across the country, including several legal experts, were interviewed, and each one said he believed the verdict had more to do with the preconceived notions of the jurors than the actual facts of the case.

More people from all walks of life expressed their disdain with the verdict. Most of those interviewed felt it was a travesty of justice of the highest order. One elderly Black woman said, "I has seen a lot of things in my life. If a picture is worth a thousand words, then justice must be deaf, dumb and blind." A young white woman, said, "Today I am more than embarrassed to be an American. I am ashamed, very ashamed that my country, claiming to possess a thousand points of light could set those brutal officers free. I just don't believe it."

A middle-aged white woman interviewed on the streets said that American was on trial, and the verdict proved that the jurors believed what they heard and not what they saw. I wanted to ask her when it comes to Black people isn't that normally the case?

It's unbelievable to think that those jurors saw what we saw and then failed to convict. Even the lawyer for the guy who filmed the beating said his client is having a difficult time reconciling how his tape could've been so important when the four officers were found not guilty.

As I sat there watching clippings from earlier in the day when the defendants left the courthouse, an angry crowd assembled outside and shouted "Racist" and "Guilty" as the officers and their entourage rushed by. I thought that they were going to get attacked. The television graphically depicted the raw emotions that characterized the racial tension in the streets of our city. They aired a clipping of two Black women arguing with a white woman on a downtown street earlier in the day. One of the sisters said, "There is no justice in America." The white woman responded, in a taunting manner, "LAPD keep doing your job, protect our rights."

The other black woman responded, "Who gave white people the right to beat a man, a Black man, nearly to death?"

A leader of a national civil rights organization said, "I am shocked, outraged and frightened for our nation. We all cried and prayed for our nation. Even in Johannesburg, South Africa, they have begun to punish white officers who assault Black people."

An interview with Rev. Edwards, a local minister, summed it up when he said, "The tragedy of the verdict was not that it was unbelievable, but that it was believable to those who have lived the Black experience."

After a few more minutes of watching, I'd had more than enough. I was sick to my stomach so I turned the set off. My heart pounded and my anger was flaming, even more than after I first heard the verdict. I think it's going to get a lot worse on the streets before it gets better.

I escaped downstairs to the library to be alone. Because I'm the only one who normally uses the library, I consider it my own private domain. The only piece of furniture I picked out for the house is there, my cavernous mahogany desk.

I sat there fuming, mad at the police, mad at my wife, mad at the world. Overhead, the unsettling roar of police helicopters scurrying about disturbed my attempt to block out everything. I moved my chair closer to the glass wall, adjacent to the right side of my desk so I could look outside easier. From the window, I could see thick, heavy black smoke billowing up, blanketing the city. I guess there was no escaping the turmoil. I tried to figure out how many buildings were burning, and if one of them was mine.

A few minutes later, I heard Angle's soft, but certain footsteps in the hallway approaching the room. When she reached the door, she stopped and just stood there watching me. Although she was facing my back, I could feel her watching me. Still looking out the window, I asked, "What do you want?"

"I want to talk to you. Honey, what are you so upset about?" She asked softly.

"What am I upset about? Who ever suggested that I was upset?"

"John, I don't have to be a Rhodes scholar to figure out this one. There's obviously something bothering you. So why don't you just tell me what I've done that's got you all bent out of shape?"

"Tell you? The question is why didn't you tell me?"

"Tell you what?" she replied innocently.

"I don't believe you!" I yelled, finally turning around to face her. "Don't play dumb with me. You and I have a long standing agreement, one I might add that you initiated yourself, to bring more 'mutual respect into our marriage' as you put it. And now without my knowledge or approval, you bring a complete stranger into my house. To add insult to injury you're acting like I've committed the sin. Woman, you are too much!" I felt triumphant, briefly. I'd finally said what was on my mind.

"Honey, what's the big deal?" she asked. Her strained voice was half an octave higher than normal rattled with the irritation and stress. "You're acting like I've disrespected you intentionally and insulted your manhood on purpose. All I did was to bring a helpless little old lady home, getting her out of harm's way. Lord only knows what might've happened to her by now if I hadn't found her."

"That's not the point," I replied.

"Well then, would you mind telling me what is the point?"

"The point is that you should have respected me as man of the house as you are supposed to. Why didn't you call me on your way home if you were so concerned about your safety or even once you got here?"

"John, think about it. You yourself told me to get home as soon as I could. Look at what's going on down there. We were in the middle of a race riot. Let's suppose I stopped in the middle of helping this lady and called you. We could've been hit by a sniper's bullet, or Lord knows what else could've happened. I didn't have a lot of time to decide what to do with her. There were hundreds of people in the streets, throwing rocks, pulling folk from cars and beating them half to death."

"Angela don't play that with me. All I know is that you could have called me if you wanted to. But no, this is just like you to wait 'til I got home to spring one on me."

"I thought about calling you, but I thought you would understand that it would be easier and much safer for both of us to discuss this matter once you got home ..."

"Ah-ha," I broke in sarcastically. "So you admit you should've called!"

"I'm not admitting anything, I'm just trying to explain what happened. When I got home, I figured it would be easier to wait until you arrived. This is a very unusual circumstance. My God, man, I did what my heart told me to do. Tell me this. How would you feel if your mother was lost down in South Central and needed help? Wouldn't you be grateful that a good samaritan helped her get to safety?"

"Don't bring my mother into this. You and I both know that she is safe and sound in her own home in Cleveland. She is not homeless nor will she ever be as long as I am alive. My mother has nothing to do with what you did."

"Honey, you just don't get it. Do you?" she asked pacing back and forth in front of my desk, her voice was getting higher and higher, taut with emotion. "In this day and age, you never know what's going to happen, or who your mother, the kids or I might need to help us. Life is just too unpredictable."

She stopped in her tracks in the middle of the room and said, "I am very sorry that you're upset. I really am. But I am not upset that I did what my conscience told me to do. I can go to sleep tonight with a clear one, and I don't regret my decision. And for the last time, I didn't disrespect you!"

"Look Angela, it's just this simple. You've gotta stop disrespecting me and I mean that! I am the man of this house. You want me to be your protector when you're afraid, but when you wanna get bold because you're feeling your oats, you go off and do whatever you want to do. I'm a reasonable man, but you're going to stop treating me this way.

"I've got too many things on my mind. Now I have to worry about protecting my family from this stranger in my house."

"John, what are you worried about? She wouldn't hurt a fly."

"You don't know that. As a matter of fact, exactly what do you know about this woman? Nothing, not one thing. I took a good look at her, and she looks a little off to me. She might be crazy. For all we know she could've been one of those early releases from a state mental institution. I'll bet good money that she hasn't told you one thing about her life. Tell the truth—has she?"

"As a matter of fact, you're wrong. She did tell me her name when I put her in bed. I'll bet good money, that poor little woman is perfectly harmless, she wouldn't hurt a fly, much less one of us!"

"What's her name?" I insisted.

"Zoli."

"Zoli what?"

"I don't know, she didn't tell me her last name," she mumbled.

"She didn't tell you because she doesn't know. Where's she from?"

"I don't know."

"Angela, how could you bring a complete stranger into my house?"

"Your house? That's the third or fourth time you've said that. I thought this is our house."

"I'm the man of this house and you know that."

"I never said you weren't."

"You didn't have to say it. You treated me like I'm not, which is even worse."

"Okay, so what do you want me to do? Put this helpless woman out in the streets, tonight of all nights? This is probably going to be one of the most violent nights this city has ever known. And what am I, what are we, supposed to tell our children? We've always talked to them about helping others. We've told them our movement stories ad infinitum, about my work, how I help people for a living, and how you've helped so many others. Yet, the truth of the matter is that they've only seen us do it from a distance. This is the first time they see a living example inside of our home, of us practicing what we preach, being good samaritans, and you want me to abort it. Tell me John, what does that really tell them about helping others?"

She stood silently in the door for several moments looking around the room, at everything but me. I could see her mind working, trying to come up with something new, searching for a new strategy, one that would work this time to change my mind.

Then she took a good long look at me, and said with her "Miss Know It All" voice of authority, "I know you. And this is not like you to get this upset about helping someone in need. I'm willing to bet good money that it's not about this little old lady's presence in our home. It's something else. Remember, I've known you for over twenty-five years. Yes, something else is going on here and I'm pretty sure I know what it is."

"Oh yeah? Like what?"

"Um-hmm. Yes sir, I most certainly do. You're not really upset about me bringing her home. I know you because you would've done exactly the same thing if it had been you. As big and generous as your heart is, you know I know you. I know what's wrong— you're worried about Stewart Computers, and you're using this other situation to ignore what's really bothering you."

"There you go. That's the most ridiculous piece of psychological garbage I've ever heard! Any additional thoughts from our local analyst?"

"You know I'm right!" she replied laughing and giggling like Ashley. "Look at you, all of a sudden you've become real quiet on me. You've sunk down into your seat, it looks like that chair is going to swallow you up. You're pouting like a little boy. Honey, you are too much!

"Darlin, why don't you come on down to the kitchen and let me fix you something to eat. I know you're hungry and tired. A little bit of food will make you feel better."

"I don't want to eat anything. I'm not hungry."

"Okay, suit yourself, Mr. Stewart. You and I both know that you are, but if you want to sit up here and mope around, be my guest if that's what it takes to make you feel better. I'll be in the kitchen heating up your dinner."

"Don't waste your time. I'm not eating."

It wasn't going to work. Not this time. She thought she could sweet talk me, and make me forget what she did. This time my wife had failed miserably.

I just sat there, really pissed off. So many thoughts ran through my mind, I couldn't keep up with all of them. When I heard that those cops had been acquitted, I couldn't believe it. For a split second this afternoon, I felt enough rage, enough to want to kill one of those cops.

On my way home, I thought about going down to the community rally at FAME Church, but then decided against it. What good would it do?

Across the country tonight, my people were once again trying to overcome yet another deep wound. How much more must we bear? This society tries to convince us that racism doesn't exist anymore, and that it's only a part of our distant past. Yet, each and every morning that I wake up usually before I leave my home, if I have any contact with the outside world, through the phone, television or radio, in some way, shape or form, I am reminded that I am a Black man living in a hostile world. A world that deems me the "Enemy" because of the dark color of my skin. In spite of everything that I have accomplished in my life I am still a suspect, the most feared and dangerous figure in the eyes of most of white America.

When I'm out conducting my business, it doesn't matter if I am in downtown L.A., Santa Monica, Bel Air, or Beverly Hills, I am still a Black man, hated, denigrated and feared. It doesn't matter what I'm wearing or how I'm behaving, all that matters is that I'm a Black man. I can be walking down the streets or step into an elevator wearing one of my impeccable Italian suits and carrying a briefcase, but women still clutch their purses and shudder with fear, thinking I'm going to attack them. They don't know that I have more money than most of them.

My wife, like most women, just doesn't understand what I go through each and every day of my life. I don't blame her for that. She can't possibly know because she's not a Black man and hasn't had to live through the horrors and abuses I've known. And I'm glad that she's been spared.

I can't count the number of times I've been stopped and harassed by the police. Sometimes it was insignificant, no big deal. But there have been times when I almost lost my life. I've had guns pointed at me, some placed on my temples and the triggers pulled, been forced to down on the asphalt spread eagle, searched and threatened. I wonder how I escaped Rodney King's fate. I never told my wife about these run-ins with the police. Why should I? What could she possibly do? Nothing but get upset and worry every time I leave our house. Plus, I was too humiliated to tell her. After all, I am the man of the house. What would she think of me if she knew how helpless I've been? She would've thought less of me, as a man, that I was a punk or something less than what she deserved. And it got worse after I bought my red convertible Jaguar. I was stopped each and every day the first month I had it.

The last time I got stopped, a couple of months ago, I was in Brentwood. I was driving through a residential neighborhood minding my own business, when I saw the police car's flashing lights in my rearview mirror. I pulled over and the cop on the driver's side got out of the car with his gun drawn. I was calm, and thought I was taking it in stride. After all, it had happened so many times.

"Nigga, put your hands up and get out of the car!" The officer shouted through the window. He was a big, fat greasy policeman with a snout for a nose, and loose, floppy ears and about fifty pounds of fat hanging out over his belt. He pointed his gun at my head as he approached my car.

"Officer, is there a problem?" I asked calmly.

"Shut up, boy! Give me your registration and get out of the car."

"I don't care if you have a gun, I am not your 'boy.'"

"Nigga, I said shut up!" he said cocking the gun.

I reached my left hand slowly into my pocket, pulled my wallet out and handed him my driver's license and registration.

"Boy, where did you git this car from? Where did ya steal it?"

"This is my car, officer. I bought it. As you can clearly see on the registration, I am John Stewart, the owner." I stood there, leaning over my car, arms rigidly attached to the hood, feeling totally defenseless, with this deranged authority figure who could blow me away if he felt like it. Then they'd call it justifiable homicide or something like that. My murder would have been a total whitewash.

"See this here gun?" He asked, placing the gun next to my temple. "How would you like it if I put it between your legs and blew off your smart ass balls?"

I heard the patrol car's door open and footsteps raced in our direction. His partner rushed over to my car and said, "Harry, come on and leave this guy alone. Put the gun down."

My body betrayed me, as sweat poured down both sides of my face and my heart pounded. I didn't want to show my fear, but I couldn't help myself.

His partner pulled him away from me. I wanted to give that slimy excuse of a human being the beating of his lifetime. I wanted to drag him down the streets and humiliate him, the same way he tortured me.

"Come on, leave the guy alone. He hasn't done anything."

He stood there for a second, probably deciding whether or not he was going to shoot me. "Yah know what, boy? You is one lucky nigga tonight. I don't think I'm gonna shoot off your balls tonight. But you betta not let me catch you out here again driving around in this fancy car, or I will have to shoot off your balls. And I'll send 'em to your wife on a silver tray. I bet she's a real hot Black bitch, now isn't she, boy? So when I shoot your balls off, she'll need a real man like me to take care of her. Now won't she nigga?"

He walked away laughing. I thought about rushing over to the pig's car, catching him off guard before he loaded himself inside and giving him the ass kicking of his lifetime. I wanted to stomp him into his grave.

As I got my off the hood readying for attack, suddenly a soft, faint voice resembling my mother's began pleading with me. "John, slow down," whispered the urgent, small voice. "It's alright. Everything's alright. Just get back in the car." Suddenly my rage disappeared. I got back in my car, knowing there wasn't anything I could do. What good would filing a police report do? It would only be my word against his. I felt like I had been castrated and my balls were dangling from a rope on a tree. To this day, I still have flashbacks and nightmares. I see his face and him shooting me in slow motion. I'm trying to dodge the bullet, and when I think I have, it changes its course and hits me right in the middle of my forehead. I wake up drenched in a cold sweat. I'm grateful that Angie sleeps like a log, so she never hears me.

My son wants me to buy him a car. I keep putting it off because I don't want him to be out driving a car alone, or with his friends. It's just too dangerous.

Later, I calmed down long enough to try to look at the situation from my wife's perspective. When I thought about it, calmly I realized that my wife probably did do the right thing. After all, she really had no choice, and I had to adjust to the fact that our guest is going to be with us for at least a few days, until this uprising is over.

I had decided to go downstairs and apologize to Angie when she appeared again at the library's doorway. Lost in my thoughts, I didn't hear her footsteps this time.

When she walked over to my desk, I was still sitting there looking outside. She whispered in my ear, "Honey, I'm very sorry about arguing with you. I apologize for not talking this situation over with you first. Please understand that it was not my intent to disrespect you when I decided to bring her home." She leaned over and kissed me on my cheek, then gave me a long, deep kiss on my lips. I stood up and held her in my arms. But this time, unlike early this morning, it felt like she was holding me, I felt her tiny, narrow arms that looked more like two twigs than arms because she's so petite, wrap around my neck.

When we were at Howard, I used to call her "Sparrow" because that's what she reminds me of, a little brown bird, flying around in a big world. Angie is about four feet eleven, although she swears on a stack of Bibles that she's five feet two inches tall. She might reach that height wearing spike heels. My wife is beautiful, but for a very long time she hid and denied her beauty, because she didn't see it with her own two eyes. When I first met Angie she was shy and extremely bashful. She always wore these baggy clothes, never put on any makeup and hid her face behind a huge pair of glasses that looked more like goggles than anything else. But beneath all of those layers, I discovered my beautiful brown angel's warm honey colored skin, small brown eyes, little lips and big round nose. I often teased her about hiding such a pretty face, but she didn't believe me, she thought it was just a line. Now, nearly thirty years later, she still doesn't know what to do with her hair. Sometimes she braids it, occasionally she wears it straight. Then a few years ago she went through this, I-need-my-life-to-be-simple phase, so she cut it off and wore it naturally. I liked that style best. Her face is so pretty that she really doesn't need to wear makeup, and I really like her au naturel. But when we go out to a fancy affair and she gets dressed up, she is so stunning people often mistake her for a movie star, and I am the proudest man in the room.

But aside from her physical beauty, I have always been overwhelmed by her sweet, beautiful spirit. Her vibrant eyes sparkled with sunlight, and she possessed such a powerful spirit; a vibrant, magical essence that radiated her passionate zest for life. I was surprised she wasn't involved with anyone else, but I'm glad that was the case. From the first time I saw her, I wanted her to be mine. I was completely disarmed by her. Her innocence charmed me, she could've gotten anything that she wanted out of me, but she never knew.

For a long time, she absolutely refused to accept the fact that I was interested in her. "Why me? What's so special about me?" she'd ask. "If you don't know, how could I ever tell you?" Her innocence disarmed me. She just didn't know how special she was. Angie was a serious student, didn't have time for the superfluous parties and social gatherings on campus. She wanted to make a contribution and was very committed to what she believed in. I found her to be the exact opposite of many women on campus who were far more concerned about money and social status than principles. Because I was a track star and a big man on campus, most, if not all of the women I dated wanted to go out with me and were more interested in being seen with me than being with in me. While this sort of attention was certainly flattering and stroked my ego well, I ended up not wanting to be bothered. By the time junior year rolled around, I'd grown completely bored with being a campus celebrity and the women that notoriety had provided.

I never forgot what my mother told me when I was a young, poor boy growing up on the streets of Cleveland. Momma said when looking for a wife, I'd better look beyond the physical. "Son, you better look past what your eyes can see. What's pretty on the outside can be pretty empty on the inside. You can pick out something pretty if you want, but what's going to happen when the pretty is gone?"

"Baby, I'm sorry, too. I shouldn't have been so hard on you. But I'm just very wound up. I didn't realize how much faith I had put into justice being done. And it's made me very mad to have the truth slapped in my face again. When it comes to the police, why should we expect better?"

"Honey, we all wanted to believe it would be different this time."

"I had no right to speak to you the way I did. Will you ever forgive me?"

"Of course I do," she smiled. "But only if you forgive me first. Come on, let's go downstairs and I'll heat up your dinner."

"Baby, I'm not really hungry. After this long and trying day, I don't have much of an appetite."

She paused, studying me, decoding my statement with her razor sharp mind. Her eyes and mind were working together, like mental laser beams slicing through my camouflaged words to find the truth. "John, did something happen to you on your way home?" she asked softly.

"No."

"Yes, it did. You saw something, didn't you?"

"Put it like this, as you would say, you didn't have to be a rocket scientist to figure that one out. Anybody out on the street today probably saw something."

"That maybe true, but you saw something that really upset you. So tell me, what happened?"

"Driving down the Hollywood freeway, I just missed getting hit by a huge chunk of concrete that two stupid kids dropped from the overpass. Then to add insult to injury, I saw the man in the car next to mine get shot at the next overpass. It happened so fast, the best I could tell was that the bullet hit his shoulder. That bullet could've taken me out."

"Honey, why didn't you tell me when you first got in?"

"You're supposed to lean on me. I'm the man, remember?"

"Honey, you are too much. I don't know what I'm going to do with you. We're supposed to share our burdens with one another. I'm just grateful to God that you made it home in one piece."

"Angela, it's my responsibility as the head of this house to protect you and my children. I guess I was a little on edge when I got home, but I'm alright now. I am very sorry for going off on you about bringing that old lady home. I understand what you're saying about doing the right thing. But there's something about her, I don't know what it is that gives me the creeps but she makes me very uncomfortable."

"Honey, you only saw her for a quick second. Give her a chance. You'll see, she couldn't hurt a fly."

Maybe my wife was right. I had so much on my mind and probably wasn't thinking clearly. Since I first heard what was going on in South Central, I had been a little concerned about my building's safety. Maybe it's bothering more than I'm aware of. I just didn't want to let on to Angie how I feel. My body was pretty tense, and I couldn't relax. So I decided to stay up and watch television. Maybe I'd be lucky enough to catch a glimpse of it. We walked downstairs to watch television in the family room. By the time I got down there, the kids and our mystery guest were already in bed.

By nightfall, all hell had broken loose. Although South Central seemed to bearing the brunt, there were reports of violence across the entire metropolitan region. I saw people from all over the city—Black, white, Hispanic—taking part in the mayhem. I must've watched the beating of the truck driver that happened on Florence and Normandy at least five or six times. It was unbelievable. This poor guy was snatched from his cab and beat unmercifully; ferocious blows to the head, chunks of concrete smashed into his body and kicked in the head. They had even stolen his wallet. I'd never seen anything like that in my life; it was sickening. Somehow the poor guy made it back into his cab, and four black folk rescued him and took him to the hospital just in time. The doctor said one more minute and he would've died. According to the reporter, two of the good samaritans were at home watching the beating on live television and left the safety of their home, ventured out into that madness to help him. It was really a weird scene watching that beating. It was the mirror image, the exact opposite of Rodney King's only a lot more graphic because of the quality of the pictures.

We watched clippings from the community rally held at FAME Church. The vast majority of the speakers were visibly shaken by the verdict. Everyone begged for calm, pleading with people to keep a lid on the hostility and anger generated by the verdict. But it just didn't seem to make a difference. The people had already taken to the streets.

The Harbor Freeway from the Santa Monica junction to Century Boulevard was closed. So much smoke had plumed up in the air that the air traffic controllers were so worried about it interfering with the visibility of planes landing and taking off that LAX Airport had to shift its landing pattern. I couldn't believe it, but according to the television reports, the fire department was receiving three to four calls per minute for fires. A television helicopter hovering over Washington Boulevard almost crashed because the smoke was so thick. Around nine o'clock the mayor had declared a local state of emergency. By ten thirty Bradley issued a message pleading for peace.

I wanted to ask the mayor, "Do you really think anyone is going to listen?" I don't think so. By midnight, Governor Wilson had declared a state of emergency and called out the National Guard.

Sitting there in my family room with my wife at my side, I felt fear in a way I've never known before. It was like watching an uncontrollable force of nature gathering up speed and force and not being able to do a damn thing about it.

For weeks there had been talk about what would happen if the police were set free, but I don't think anyone was prepared for what was happening. One young man, who might be characterized by the media as a 'gangbanger' asked, "How can you look at that video and say that those four white officers were innocent? Screw it—we ought to burn this city down!" I understood his rage, but I couldn't justify all of the destruction that was flashing before me. Looking at his young, anguished face, faces of other young men came to my mind. For example, all of my friends who'd been in the movement with me during the sixties. I wondered about them and all of the sacrifices we'd made. Thirty years after the movement, was it worth it? In light of the way racism seems to be entrenched in this society, even more so now than it was before. I thought about all of those people who willingly made great sacrifices, a few paying the ultimate price by losing their lives to make this world a better place.

For several hours, Angie and I just sat there silently, frozen in front of our television. We didn't talk a lot, there really wasn't much to say. I think we were both in shock. Sometimes when I looked at her I'd see tears collecting in the corner of her eye.

Finally, I'd had more than enough. I turned the set off around eleven and turned on KGBF, the black talk radio station. People were calling in expressing their outrage and anguish. Some cried, others pleaded for calm, while a few suggested the city needed to be torn down. After an hour or so of listening to that rhetoric, I decided to turn the television on again. Maybe by midnight the madness would begin to quell. All I saw on television convinced me that was wishful thinking on my part. Between worrying about my business and my rage about the verdict, I was caught between a rock and a hard place. My feelings about the situation fluctuated dramatically.

When will this country learn? When will it finally live up to its creed? The verdict brought to mind the Supreme Court decision, Plessy vs. Ferguson, in which the court ruled nearly a hundred years ago that a Black man had no rights a white man was obliged to respect. If this verdict didn't prove that truth, I don't know what did.

My fear of losing everything was eating me up. Maybe I won't be able to support my family. I saw myself penniless, homeless, losing everything, being forced to live on the streets.

Angie tried to stayed awake as long as she could. She knew I was all wound up, but after all she'd been through, she was exhausted too and fell asleep shortly after midnight. I'm sure her day had been worse than mine. First thing this morning, she had that horrible nightmare, then she was down in South Central during the beginning of the madness, and finding the homeless woman. That's a lot for anyone to have to deal with on a given day. She finally fell asleep snuggled against my shoulder. I didn't have the heart to wake her up so I just picked her up and carried her upstairs to our bedroom, took off her clothes and put on her white laced nightgown and tucked her in the bed. She was dead to the world and never woke up once. I laid down on top of the covers. But I couldn't relax, my mind wouldn't slow down. Thoughts were racing around in my head like I was in the Indianapolis 500. Every time I closed my eyes, I saw my building going up in smoke, as huge flames consumed it.

Around one o'clock, I went to bed. Lying in my bed, my body felt like it was resting on top of a bed of nails. My muscles were so tense, they felt like they were going to tear away from the bones that held them together and rip through the surface of my skin. I laid there for a long time in darkness, trying to fall asleep, but couldn't.

My thoughts then drifted to our houseguest, the stranger in our midst. Angie was right, she does appear to be harmless, but who knows for sure? There's something about that Miss Zoli that just doesn't sit right with me. I may have only seen her for a few seconds. But there was something very strange and unsettling about this woman that just didn't click. She doesn't look like a typical homeless person.

I think that she was in a mental institution. We know nothing about her. My wife admits the poor old woman doesn't even remember her own last name. She doesn't know where she's from, her age, address or the name of her closest of kin.

I went downstairs to check on her. She was dead to the world. She probably hadn't had a good night's sleep in a bed in years. On my way back to the bedroom, I checked the kids' rooms, and they were both fast asleep, dead to the word. I got back in the bed and still couldn't fall asleep. Angie rolled over and asked, half-awake in a groggy voice, "What's wrong, honey? You can't fall asleep?"

"Don't worry, I'm okay."

Finally, I saw the sky begin to lighten up a bit and I finally began to relax. I dozed off and fell into a deep, dark dream. My building was on fire, and each time the fire department extinguished the fire, as soon as they left, the ashes would reignite. I pulled myself out of that dream and woke up. I know I wasn't asleep for more than a few minutes. I tossed and turned for what seemed like an eternity.

I knew I had to get down there to my office to find out whether or not it had survived the night. By early morning, more than a thousand fires had been set. From South Central to Westwood, Long Beach to Compton, the whole city had descended into chaos. There was looting, arson, assault on properties, sporadic gun fire, firemen trying to put out the fires were fired upon, and one reporter suggested the Police Chief Darryl Gates was behaving like Nero, who fiddled while Rome burned. Gates was reported to have attended a fund-raiser last night while L.A. burned. Throughout the night, the violence flared like a ferocious, uncontrollable firestorm.

The Harbor Freeway was still closed in South Central and the National Guard was being deployed. Beverly Hills and Bel Air had been cordoned off. Last night, three people were killed in Beverly Hills when their car struck a fire hydrant and flipped over, while trying to elude the police during a chase. And more than a dozen people had been killed since the verdict was rendered. Hospitals throughout the city had been deluged with injuries. Victims of gunshot wounds, stabbings, beatings, and God knows whatever else had clogged up the emergency and operating rooms. Our mayor had announced shortly after midnight that the violence was diminishing. That must have been wishful thinking on his part. He had apparently failed to watch television last night. Otherwise, he would've known better.

It was almost daybreak. Instead of the bright early morning sunshine that fills our room, there was a dull gray light, a thick dense blanket of acrid, black smoke that covered our neighborhood. I turned on the TV to find out the latest. The violence had spread throughout the entire city. I knew that the fires were spreading unchecked throughout our neighborhood. The density of the smoke suggested that few buildings were being spared.

Finally, I got out of the bed and decided to take a swim in our pool. I did about twenty brisk laps. The thought of losing everything haunted me. There was no escape.

After my swim, I went to the kitchen and got a glass of orange juice. I don't know why, but I felt compelled to turn on the television again, just in case I missed something important.

According to anchor woman Beverly Blue, from the beginning, the violence was never limited to South Central. It had fanned out across Southern California like wild fire, and to a lesser extent, across the country. There were protests in San Francisco,

Las Vegas and Kansas City that lead to scattered violence and hundreds of arrests. From the aerial shots, I saw the TV helicopters made last night, L.A. look like Dante's inferno. Over a thousand fires had been set, at least twenty-five people were dead, and hundreds were injured.

I turned the channel to one of those early morning news programs and they were in the middle of playing an interview with one of the jurors. Her face was hidden from the camera's view, but I could tell from the tone of her voice that she was a middle-aged woman. "They're policemen, they're not angels. They're out there doing a low down dirty job. Would you want your husband doing it, or your son or father?" Low down dirty job? That's what I call the change in venue to Simi Valley. Why did officers Powell, Koon, Briseno and Wind manage to get the opportunity that was denied other high profile cases like Charles Manson and the Hillside Strangler?

I was pissed off again and mad as hell.

How could that woman be so cold and callous? Even if she felt that way, with all that's going on, she should've just kept her mouth shut. I felt something in me die. Maybe it was that last flicker of hope that I held out for America, the part of me that wanted to believe that justice could be found somewhere in this land. I don't know what's going to happen now. But one thing I do know, burning down a community is not going to solve the problem. It's just going to make matters even worse.

five

All morning, the wave of anarchy, chaos and destruction engulfed the city. Fires burned out of control and people looted at will. It was a free for all. From the television reports, it was obvious that it's not only Black folk who are involved. I watched scores of Hispanics, whites and Asians taking part in this madness. I knew I needed to find out what was going on with Stewart Computers. I hoped and prayed that my building was still standing and I had to figure out a way to get to my office. I was really afraid that everything I had put together with my own bare hands, more than fifteen years of blood, sweat and tears, everything I've worked for had gone up in smoked, burned to a crisp.

I'm a take charge man and I had to find out for myself exactly what was going on. So I called up one of my buddies who worked in the mayor's office. Back in the seventies, Ron was one of the first brothers I met when I moved out here. He's been the liaison between the mayor's office and the police department for twelve or fourteen years. If anybody could get me into that war zone, I knew it was him. He wasn't at home or in his office. I tried to reach him on his cellular phone, but it was turned off. My last resort was to page him on his beeper. After doing that, all I could do was sit and wait for his call.

Knowing my wife, she was probably upstairs trying to figure out what I was up to. So when I walked into the kitchen, a few minutes after paging Ron, I tried to play it off, the best way that I could. She gave me her once over look of suspicion, as though she had already figured out my plans, as she stood at the stove, frying a pan full of bacon. When I kissed her on the cheek as I normally do every morning, she said, "I know what you're up to. I don't like it, and it's not going to work."

"What's not going to work?" I replied as innocently as I could.

"Honey, you're not going to get down to you office today, so you might as well take it easy and relax. Whatever is lost, it can be replaced. You've got good insurance," she said as she stirred the grits.

"I see you're cooking my favorite breakfast. Where's my stewed apples? And look at you!" I said bending over, cracking open the oven door. "You've even made fresh biscuits. I'm such a lucky man." I hoped the diversion would work.

"So you think you can change the subject, so I forget what you're trying to do? John, you should know better. It doesn't work like that." During the course of our marriage, I've accused her several times of reading my mind. I guess that's what happens to people after you've been together as long as we have.

"I know you. John, I repeat, you don't need to go down there. It's too dangerous."

I can't get away with anything, not around my wife. I replied with a growl, "Angela, what's a man supposed to do? Sit around and do nothing? My life is down there, and I need to know what's going on."

She stopped turning the bacon, turned the burner off, wiped her hands with a towel, turned in my direction, looked me straight in the eyes, put her left hand on her hip and at the same time pointed her right index finger at me and roared, "Man, are you crazy? Come here, let me turn on this TV, so you can see what's going on down in South Central this morning. It's complete chaos down there. Snipers are everywhere, burning and looting on every block, even the police can't control the situation. And speaking of the police, not only do you have to worry about the people who are rioting, but you have to be even more concerned about the police.

"Why do you want to risk your life? You could get arrested, shot or beaten. Better than that, as dangerous as that situation is, you could get yourself killed! There's nothing down there that can't be replaced, or that your insurance won't cover."

She placed her fork down on the stove, walked over to the kitchen table, where I was sitting, put both hands down on the table, leaned over toward me and said, "In the midst of all this madness, you need to check things out for yourself to make sure that it hasn't been burned to the ground. What if it has, what are you going to do? Rebuild it today, so it can be burned down tonight?"

"Angie, baby, you just don't understand what I'm going through. You don't know what it's like to sit around hour after hour, not knowing if your life's dream has gone up in smoke."

"Well, that may be true, maybe I don't know how you're feeling. But one thing I do understand is that we need you more than we need your little business. You don't know what our life would be like if you were unnecessarily taken away from us. You don't have to risk your life. It's not worth it."

"Little business?" I replied, unwrapping her arms.

"I can't believe my ears!" I said raising my voice. "After all that business has done for us and meant to this family. It's the reason we're living in this house, the source that pays all our bills, you have the nerve to call it a little business. Woman, you never cease to amaze me."

"John, it is a small business. And there's nothing wrong with that. Might I remind you that you are the recipient of a small business loan? Correct me, if I'm wrong, but Stewart Electronics is not a Fortune 500 company. Please hear me loud and clear. Honey, there's no business, no amount of money, nothing compared to your life. You are just that precious to me. Everything else pales in comparison to your life. I really didn't mean to insult your or any of your accomplishments. You should know by now that I am very proud of you. I just don't want you putting your life in jeopardy."

"You called it 'little' and there is a difference between little and small."

"What's the difference?"

"Little is smaller than small."

"Well excuse me for my mistake!" she huffed back to the stove.

How could she understand that my business is my lifeline? She's a woman, she doesn't have the same concerns that I do as a man. Over the years, I've given it everything I have to give, my blood, my sweat and my tears. That company is as much part of me, as my arm or my leg. I'm proud that I made it in a highly competitive industry in one of the most economically blighted areas of the city. I ran with the big boys and did a pretty good job if I do say so myself. I never wanted to leave the community, to leave behind the place where I made my mark. Angie suggested several times that it would be easier on me to have the business located a little closer to our home, but I wouldn't hear any of that. Man, maybe I should've listened to her.

I sat at the kitchen table stewing in my juices on the edge of my seat, staring at television, hoping that maybe I could get a glimpse of my building. The entire kitchen was filled with the fresh aroma of morning: bacon frying and coffee percolating. My stomach was churning with hunger. I hadn't had anything to eat since yesterday at lunchtime.

My wife was just being overprotective. I saw on television this morning plenty of people down there guarding their businesses. Nothing's going to happen to me if I go down there. If I lived through being shot at in Mississippi during the movement, I certainly can make out all right down in South Central. Angie will never understand how much I needed to know that I can continue to support my family. I've been a good provider and I've tried to give her and the kids the security and stability that I never knew when I was growing up.

My daddy was killed during the Korean war, leaving my mother to fend for herself and four children all less than ten years of age. Daddy was a war hero during World War II. After returning to the States, Momma said Daddy worked a lot of odd jobs to support our family, but couldn't find steady work in Cleveland back then. So when the Korean conflict happened during the early fifties, he felt that he had no choice but to re-enlist.

I barely remember my father, I was only six years old when he left for Korea. All I have are vague, fragments of memories of the presence of a strong and loving man. I can still feel him throwing me up in the air and horsing me around when I was very small, but that's it. I must have been no more than seven or eight years old when we got the word that my daddy was missing in action in Korea and presumed dead. His body was never found. According to the reports Momma received, he was lost behind enemy lines during a major battle. Most of his platoon was wiped out.

I do remember the day we found out my father had died. I got home from school and Momma was sitting on our big brown sofa in the living room crying so hard, I thought she was about to pass out. I didn't know what was wrong, but whatever it was, I knew it was something terrible. One of our neighbors, Mrs. Stinson, was standing over her, fanning her with a newspaper.

"Momma, what's wrong?" I pleaded, I was scared half to death with the way she was carrying on.

"Your poppa's gone, he was killed. We'll never see him again."

"No!" I shouted. "You're lying, my daddy isn't dead!" Because my father promised me he'd be home soon, I absolutely refused to believe that my father was dead. It had to be a big mistake or an awful lie. I didn't want to go to his funeral, but my Uncle Willie made me go. I held my hands to my ears throughout the entire service.

Each day when I came home from school, I'd go up the stairs of our brownstone, expecting that he had suddenly returned a hero from the war. But Daddy never came home. Only Momma was there, trying desperately to find her center again, to fill up the hole in her heart his death created.

A few months after we got word of his death, one of my daddy's buddies from World War II came to see us. They were in the same unit in the European theater. Mr. Marshall lived in Detroit, and had tried to get my dad to move to Detroit and get a job at one of the auto factories. "Mrs. Stewart, your husband Zeke was a fine man and a soldier's soldier. In fact, he was the bravest man I ever knew. You should be proud of him. He served his country with honor and distinction. Had he been a white man, he would've received several medals, including the purple heart. But you know how this country treats colored soldiers. But that never bothered Zeke, not like it did a lot of us. He knew better, not to expect much from this land we call our home

"When we were in the European theater, in Italy to be exact, your husband single-handedly saved our entire battalion. He was our leader, more so than our commander, and the commander knew it."

He turned to me and said, "Son, with your father gone, you are now the head of this household, and it's up to you to look out for your little sisters and brother. Young man, you've got some big shoes to fill, but I know you can do it. You've got your daddy's blood in you, and he was a strong man.

"I owe my life to your father. So young man, if you ever need me, I'm here for you. If it hadn't been for your father's bravery, I wouldn't be here today. The least I can do for the man who saved my life is to look out for his family."

Over the years, Mr. Marshall continued to stay in close contact with us. We received letters from him at least once every two or three months, and he usually enclosed a few dollars to help us out. He remembered all of our birthdays and even sent Mom a Mother's Day card. When I graduated from high school he was there, and he even made it to a few of my college track meets.

Once when he came to visit me at Howard, he said, "Son, you got plenty of talent. If you make it to the Olympics, I'll be there, too."

A few years ago he came down with cancer and died, and we all attended his funeral. I took the kids with me out to his home in Pittsburgh shortly before his death. I wanted them to know the man who had meant so much to me.

Momma had only a few pictures of my father. One taken on their wedding day; a couple of him in his military uniform; and one of me and him when I was a baby. My favorite is the picture in his formal uniform. He was a handsome guy. I favor him, but he was taller and thinner than I am. In the picture with his uniform on, he had a serious, determined expression. I knew he was a soldier who took care of business, and I wouldn't want to be fighting on the other side, not against him.

For years, I insisted that he was still alive and was coming home. I wouldn't let anyone, not even Momma speak of him in the past tense. I'm sure my refusal to accept my father's death probably caused my mother great pain. As a wounded child, I was too young and too hurt to see anyone's pain but my own. It took me years to finally accept, hope against hope, that my daddy wasn't coming home.

"My Daddy is alive!" I declared, whenever I felt the urge.

"No, he's not Johnnie. Your daddy is dead," Momma would whisper. She'd put her arms around me, and tried to hold me. But I'd refuse her touch and would always yank my body away,

"No, he's not! He's coming home. You just wait and see. And when he does, I'm gonna tell him how everybody except me said he was dead!"

Every day after school, I'd rush home to see if Daddy had returned, but he never did. So after school before I did anything, I would go in the living room and spend time with his picture. Sometimes I'd talk to him, and have a one-sided father/son conversation. I'd try to imagine what he might say to his first born son.

When he didn't come home, I became very angry. I was mad at him and the world for taking my father away from me. Why did he have to die? For a very long time, I held it all in. I was very pissed off at the world and at God. My grades suffered in school, and I know I was a challenge for my already beleaguered mother. But what was I supposed to do? I was just a little boy carrying the weight of the world on my shoulders. Eventually, my unexpressed grief turned to anger. I tried to stop thinking about him. But the harder I tried, the more he stayed with me. I quit looking at his picture, but his presence stayed with me. It refused to go away. I didn't know what to do. I was hurting, and couldn't express it. It was just too overwhelming for a ten-year-old trying to be a man.

"Why did you have to go off to some old Korea, and die?" The answers never came. I was mad and jealous. Jealous of my friends who had a father, and mad at mine who was gone. Why did my dad have to die?

My mother never put any pressure on me to help her out. But I knew that was what I was supposed to do. Mr. Marshall had told me so as well as dozens of neighbors and relatives. A couple of men did look out for me, tried to be surrogate fathers, but I pushed them away. I could not allow any other man the possibility of even thinking that he could take my daddy's place. I wanted him and nobody else.

I don't remember the precise moment when I finally realized that he was dead. Even today, I sometimes forget that he's gone. His spirit seems alive. Gradually as with all things, I faced the fact that he was not coming home and that I was going to have to fend for myself. I was going to have to be a strong man. It was just that simple. After that I grew up very fast.

Shortly after accepting Dad's death, I started having these vivid dreams about him. He was always wearing his drab green uniform. He would talk to me and share things with me. I didn't know what to make of it. Actually, I enjoyed them, and for a while I went to bed early. Momma didn't know what to make of my new found cooperation at bedtime. I never told her about the dreams. I don't know why, I guess I wanted to keep it to myself ,.

Then one day, the strangest thing happened, I saw him. I had never had anything like this happen before. It must've been on a Saturday afternoon because I was on my way outside to play a game of basketball with a few of my boys in the neighborhood. And there he was, a ghost, sitting in his favorite chair looking at me. I could see him, clearly as the light of day, but I could also see through him. He had on his uniform, a light beige shirt and pair of slacks. He looked at me, reaching out to me, desperately trying to touch me. I felt like he was trying to talk to me. But I couldn't hear him.

At first, I thought I was just imagining the whole thing. I turned my head, looked away and he was still there.

"Momma, come here quick," I yelled.

My mother rushed out of the kitchen, wiping her hands on a plaid green and white dish cloth and found me standing in the living room looking at the wing-tipped upholstered chair, next to the table containing his pictures.

"What's wrong?" she asked breathlessly.

"Momma, Daddy's here! I can see him, he's sitting right there. Can't you see him?" I asked pointing at the chair.

"Lord have mercy boy, I don't see nothin but an empty chair. You got a fever or something? Your father is gone with a capital 'G.' I know its hard for you and that you miss him an awful lot. But you're going to have to live with the truth that your father is dead and gone."

"But Momma, I know he's dead. I'm not lying; I can see him standing there!" I said while pointing at our fireplace. "He's a ghost." I insisted, "Can't you see him, too?"

"Boy that is just wishful thinking.

"Now you go on, get out of here and go play your games with your friends."

"No, I want you to see him."

"Boy, get outside, before I change my mind and send you to your room."

She didn't believe me, but I did see him. And from time to time for several years he would appear before me. He never said a word, at least not one that I could hear. But I know that he was there.

After my father's death, our living situation took a huge turn for the worse. Suddenly, without any money, we became poor. Momma refused to go on welfare. She was too proud for that and felt that it had a crippling effect on people that made it difficult for them to get off once they got on.

Momma used to say, "I'd rather work twenty-four hours, seven days a week, than have to depend on the government for handouts. They owe colored people more, a whole lot more than that.

"If the government wants to give me anything, they can pay me all the money my foreparents never got as slaves. They can pay me for three hundred years of free labor. That's what they can do for me."

Because our clothes were so old and a little raggedy, we were taunted daily by a lot of kids in our neighborhood. But Momma never allowed us the luxury of wallowing in shame. Her spirit was varnished with a fierce, unrelenting pride, born from the depths of her character and integrity. She didn't care about material things as much as she was concerned about the development of our character. Momma wasn't unique in terms of her thinking. There were a lot of Black people in my community who felt that way too. They were simply too proud to receive handouts.

"I better not ever catching you children being shamed 'bout what we have and who you are," she said. "All that you got, by the grace of God has been mine to give."

For years, I only had one black pair of Buster Brown shoes. Momma bought them two sizes larger than my foot, so I could grow into them. She would stuff tissue in the toes so I could wear them the first year. I had a few shirts, one pair of Keds sneakers, maybe three or four pairs of slacks and one gray suit that I wore to church.

Our clothes were always clean. No matter what I wore, my classmates taunted me with a cruel innocence, never thinking about the damage they could be inflicting.

"Hold your head up high," Momma would say. "You ain't done nothin to cause you no shame. Just as long as you know in your heart that you is livin an honest life and treatin people right you have everything to be proud of. In this life, it's what's in your heart that counts not what's on your back, or in your bank."

"This welfare mess is gonna be the death of a whole lotta folk, colored and white alike. The government is tearing families apart, making men leave their families in droves so their families can get a pitiful relief check, they ain't got enough money to last a whole month! That ain't right. There is somethin wrong, very wrong with this here plan.

"Mark my words, one day white folks will use welfare as one more reason to keep colored folks down. Not that they need another excuse."

Momma did the best she could with the little she had. Some nights we'd go to sleep with growling empty stomachs—full of nothing but moldy Cleveland air. We ate so much of it, I grew up thinking that Spam was a real part of a hog.

Much more than being hungry, what I hated was being cold. The heat in our apartment rarely worked during the winter and that piercing, ice cold wind rushing off Lake Erie would cut through you so fast it would make you want to cry. That's the reason I found sunny California so appealing and decided to move out here.

Mother worked three or four domestic jobs at a time just to make ends meet. Sometimes she didn't get home until midnight, after we were in the bed. Since I was the oldest, I had to take care of my younger brother and sisters.

When I was in the seventh or eight grade, I became very interested in sports. As I grew, my natural talent also sprang into a fuller expression. I liked track and football the best. Jesse Owens was my hero. I remember sitting in the balcony of the old Loew's movie theater, watching newsreel clippings of him winning his four gold medals at the Olympics in 1940. He truly embarrassed Hitler and made his racist theory of Aryan supremacy look very stupid.

Black folk back then were truly proud of him and Joe Louis. The folk in my neighborhood talked about them for years. In high school, I broke several records and lead my team to the school's first state championship. I received offers from several schools, but decided to attend Howard University because my coach at Clearview High, Mr. Francis, encouraged me to go there. He was an alumnus and felt that I could get a well rounded education in a nurturing environment.

I arrived at Howard in the late summer of 1961. It seems like as soon as I hit the campus, I got involved in the movement. That's what we called the Civil Rights Movement. Howard was a hotbed for variety of groups and organizations, more than I can remember. After meeting Angie, I joined the Student Nonviolent Coordinating Committee, "Snick" for short. My experiences in the movement were a life-changing experience. At a very young age, I was forced to confront my own mortality in a way that only men forty or fifty years my senior had to. I learned of lot a those values that are usually just religious concepts: courage, fortitude, faith and forgiveness. Not so much from what I saw in myself, as what I saw in others.

They were the bravest people I've ever known. The way they stood up to one of the most intractable systems of racism and oppression was awesome. And through it all, these proud, simple people possessed an unbelievable strength of character and dignity.

After receiving my degree in computer science from Howard, and working in the movement in Mississippi, Angie and I got married. My wife was two years behind me, so we remained in the D.C. area until she graduated. I received my master's degree at George Washington University in business administration.

When Angie graduated, we moved back to Cleveland. I took a job in the corporate world at IBM in their research and development department. I didn't stay there for more than three years, because Mayor Carl Stokes, one of the first black men elected mayor of a large city in the country, asked me to work in his administration. He said he especially liked my aggressive, go-get'em approach to life. The mayor often said I was a natural leader and had all the necessary ingredients to make it big in the world of politics with my personality, intelligence and charm.

For a while, I thought he was right, and with his encouragement and guidance I became very involved in local politics. But it just wasn't me. I didn't fit in—try as I might, there were just too many compromises, too much underhandedness and lying. I just wasn't comfortable being close to the glare of public life, much less having it pointed at me. The thought of putting my life on public display wasn't at all appealing to me. And although Angie was supportive and always encouraged me, I knew deep down inside that she wasn't thrilled with the idea either. Now looking at the way the media chews up and devours public officials, I'm glad I'm not subject to its ferocious scrutiny.

While living in Cleveland, I ran into a lot of people from the old neighborhood. Many, if not most them were still on welfare. Momma was right. That type of dependency had a lasting crippling effect on them. Robbed of their dreams, forced to be chronically dissatisfied with a few crumbs, they were lost souls, a broken people, trapped in a world of poverty that had slowly snuffed out their spirit. It was such a shame. I saw so much wasted talent that had rotted away, in those folk who were completely dependent on the welfare system. Now their children and grandchildren were lost on it, too.

For our family, education was our ticket out of our poverty. My brother Aaron graduated from Lincoln University in Pennsylvania, my sister Juanita received her degree from Ohio State, and my baby sister, Betty attended Smith College. After graduating, all of them returned home and are still living there and are doing quite well. Aaron is a high school biology teacher, Juanita a nurse at the Cleveland Clinics and Betty is a chemical engineer. Momma is doing fine. She's living it up in a home I bought her several years ago. She is the most fiercely independent woman I've ever known and simply refuses to move in with my brother or sisters.

About fifteen years ago, after deciding it was time to get out of Cleveland, we moved to Los Angeles. Cleveland was on a downward spiral economically and more than anything else, I wanted to live in a warm climate. Several friends out here were doing well and helped me get started. They provided me with great connections and the support I needed to get my business started. Owning a business had always been my dream since I was a little boy. My corporate experience was in software development, and I entered the industry just at the right time. I was fortunate enough to receive a few key government contracts, plus my contacts had a great network. It was hard in the beginning, and the cash flow was always difficult. Sometimes I didn't think it was going to work—I had enough doubts to fill a room—but even during the roughest of times, Angie never faltered, she never lost faith in me and my vision. She always believed that I'd be successful, most of the time she believed more so than I did myself.

Each and every night she used to whisper in my ears, before I fell asleep, "Honey, we're going to make it. Don't worry, I know we are."

"How do you know that?" I'd ask earnestly. I could never understand why she had so much faith in me.

She'd take my hand, kiss it and place it over her heart and say, "Because in my heart I know you can do anything you choose to do."

After seeing her faith in me, night after night, day in and day out, what else could I do, but succeed? And she was right. The success of Stewart Computers was beyond my wildest dreams. We've grown by leaps and bounds, and provide software technology to numerous government agencies and businesses across the country.

So here I am, after all these years, all the ups and downs, the good days and the bad days, the successes and the failures, waiting to learn my fate, while my wife and my children are carrying on as if it were just another day in L.A. This could be the end, the day when our world collapses. If my business is gone, so is everything else.

Our kids were downstairs in the family room watching television, while our homeless houseguest had yet to make an appearance. Angie walked over to the top of the stairs and called the kids, "James and Ashley, breakfast is ready, come on up."

"Okay mom, we'll be right up, just as soon as we finish this video game."

"Honey, why don't you use the intercom system? That's why it's there so you don't have to yell at the kids throughout the house."

She ignored me and replied indignantly, "Video games? You two are supposed to be down there watching the live television reports about what's going on with the state of emergency in the city, not playing Nintendo, or whatever else fits your fancy. Bring your two little behinds up here right now! Pronto!"

All I could do was laugh. At least my children had provided me with a brief moment of diversion from my worries. In a world where child rearing has typically become quite lax, my wife, the mother of my children, is a ripple in a pond, a wave going against the tide of parental behavior. Angie's a loving mother, but an exacting disciplinarian and doesn't play games with our children. The kids flew up the stairs, almost knocking each other over trying to get to the table first, and were sitting down in less than the time it takes to spell Nintendo. From the tone of her voice, they knew this was not a good morning to horse around with her.

"I can't believe you two. After all we've taught you and exposed you to during this very crucial time you are downstairs playing video games."

"Ah, Mom, we watched it a little bit," whined James, "but we got tired of watching all that burning and looting and all those white reporters talking about how bad the Black and Hispanic folks were and how we have no morals."

"James, I don't care what they said. That's no excuse for your behavior. If you are going to live in this world, you must learn how to make your own assessment of any situation."

Angie sat next to me down at the table, placed a platter filled with bacon and scrambled eggs with cheese, green peppers and onions in the center of the table, looked at him, pointed her right index finger at him and said, "I tell you what, 'Mr. Sensitivity of 1992' I want you to write me two papers. The first will be on the images of Black people in the media, and the second on the Watts riots that occurred during the sixties. I want ten pages on each paper. And they better be good.'

There she goes again, I chuckled again to myself, shooting off assignments like a Marine drill sergeant ordering push ups.

"Ma, why?" my son whined.

"Because I said so. You've got plenty of time on your hands, and you are not going to spend it having a Nintendo marathon. School is out, there's no telling as to when you'll go back. Plus you've got plenty of resources at your fingertips in our library."

"Why do I have to do that? Just because I didn't do what you wanted me to do? Mom, that's not fair."

"You know what?" she said quizzically. "You're right, it's not fair. But the sooner you learn that life isn't fair, the better it'll be for you. You don't realize how good you and your sister have it. You know your father and I have talked to both of you time and time again about our history and the obstacles our people have struggled against and risen above.

"We've worked hard. Your father and I have given you everything so you wouldn't have to go through all that we did to get where we are. Especially your dad. You know how hard he works each and every day to bless you with this home and the opportunities you have to do wonderful and meaningful things with your life. Your brothers and sisters down in South Central are not so fortunate."

"So if I'm so fortunate, why do I have to suffer and do this stupid paper?" he snarled, almost glaring at his mother.

"James, watch your mouth," I roared. "You know better than to be disrespectful to your mother. And if you do it again, it's me and you."

Angie continued, "Maybe this research will be just the beginning of your greater enlightenment. If not, then we'll have to look into other ways to restrict some of your options. Maybe we'll have to take away some of those video games and a few other of your treasured possessions like your designer gym shoes that cost me a hundred and sixty dollars, and replace them with books on African American history, that you probably haven't touched in months.

"Hear me loud and clear, and this goes for you too, Ashley, I am not raising a generation of video game knuckleheads, and the sooner the two of you learn that the better!"

"Mommie, why are you being so mean to James this morning? Are you stressed out or something like that?" pleaded Ashley.

Angela snapped her head in Ashley's direction, and with the scorn of an angry drill sergeant, replied, "And as for you, Miss Lady, I expect the same! Two reports, ten pages each."

All of the blood suddenly drained from Ashley's face. In a split second, she was pale and ashen. She took a deep breath and gasped, creating a noise that sounded like a death rattle. Had I not known better, I would've been tempted to call the paramedics to come and revive her. But I've seen my daughter's dramatic responses before.

After about five seconds, when it finally dawned on both of them that their mother was very serious and unrelenting, Ashley and James turned to me in helpless unison, like two lost puppies. Their eyes silently begged, pleading for my help.

A long time ago, they had mastered the art of looking like innocent fawns being led off to slaughter, seeking my fatherly influence as their last resort. When they were much younger, I used to easily fall for this little stunt. They seemed so innocent, so very sincere. I'd ask Angie, "How could they be pretending? Those are real tears." Now I see through their crocodile tears, and today, I'm not about to step into that field of manure. I learned my lesson, how masterfully my children can play the 'divide and conquer' game with their parents.

"Don't look over here for any help. I'm sorry kids, but your mother is absolutely right. You get so much from us, you don't know how good your life is. She's not punishing you. It's for your own good. We won't ever have to worry about catching you in the streets acting like two crazy people. Because when you know your history and you know it well, you know who you are."

Just as I finished my last sentence, we heard a voice from the lower level crying out, "Hep! Somebody please come and hep me."

"Did you hear that?" Angie asked. "Oh my goodness," she gasped while putting her fork, "I hope she didn't fall out of the bed."

"You mean our mystery guest?" I replied sarcastically.

Angie leapt from her seat and rushed across the room and downstairs to the guest room. Feeling guilty, I followed closely behind her. Before she hit the bottom of the stairs, she fired back at me, "John this is no time to be funny or sarcastic! She could've been seriously hurt."

As usual, my wife was correct. We found her sprawled on the floor like a bag of loose potatoes. She was mumbling what sounded like "Lawd have mercy, Lawd have mercy on me." I lifted her legs, Angie picked up her shoulders, and we sat her on the edge of the bed.

For a frail little woman, she felt like a ton of bricks.

Once we got her upright on the bed, Angie asked, "Ma'am are you alright?" She just sat there, staring directly ahead. Angie kept repeating, "Miss Zoli, are you alright? Is anything hurting you? Please tell us something."

She sat there on the edge of the bed in a daze. I wondered if she was drunk. Maybe she had slipped into our bar. Or maybe she's crazy. After a few moments, she finally came around or at least she noticed that we were in the room. It looked like she was finding her way out of a fog.

"Wheah is I? Whot place is dis?" She had the thickest Southern accent I'd ever heard. She sounded like she had just escaped from the deepest, darkest corner of the South.

Angie firmly held her shoulders upright to keep her steady, and replied, "Ma'am don't you remember me? You are in my house and my name is Angela Stewart. This is my husband John," she said pointing to me. "You met him last night. Ma'am, do you remember when I found you yesterday and brought you home with me?"

"I does a little bit. But not much. I remembas yah bringin me somewheahs in dat macheen dat ain't got no hoss or mule pullin it. Yeah, I remembas dat much."

I tried to read Angela's face for a clue concerning her true feelings about this strange old woman. I saw nothing but pure compassion.

"Well, now isn't that a major accomplishment, wouldn't you say so Angela?"

Angela straightened herself up, made sure Miss Zoli could sit up without her support, grabbed me by the sleeve and pulled me out of the room into the family room. "John, spare me the sarcasm. Can't you see how fragile she is? If you can't say anything nice, then why don't you just go on back upstairs and leave us alone?"

"I'm sorry. There's just something about that woman that isn't right. Look at her. She's disturbed. Can't you tell that? She doesn't need to be here. This woman needs to be in a hospital receiving proper treatment."

"John, we'll finish this discussion upstairs. Right now, Miss Zoli needs us. She could've seriously injured herself when she fell."

When we walked back into the room, she looked at me, pointed her bony little finger and said to Angie, "Who dat?"

"That's my husband John. You met him last night."

"Oh yeah? Tell me somethin—wheah is yoh massa an mistrus?"

"Excuse me?"

"Wheah is yoh massa an yoh mistrus? Tells me de truf!" she demanded, as if Angela was mocking her.

"Master and Mistress? Ma'am, I don't quite understand your question. My husband John and I live here with our children; we own this house."

Her face broke into a big smile. The loose skin and flesh around her eyes compressed together like an accordion. "Oh yeah? I done heard 'bout colored folks like y'all. I heard about some colored folks in Nah Leans like dat. Ain't dat somethin grand!" she said with a toothless grin.

"How many slaves, uh, I means servants does y'all has since de wah been ovah?"

"What did you say?" I asked, not believing my ears.

"I says, how many folk does yah got workin heah?"

"Well, ma'am, we don't really have any. I do have a lady that comes in a few times during the week and helps me with the cleaning and does a little cooking."

"Now it's comin back to me. Ma'am, yah gots a mighty fine 'tation heah."

"Tation—what's a 'tation' ?" I asked quite puzzled.

"Suh I is talkin bout a 'tation. I knows yah knows a tation, but maybe yah rich folks calls it somethin else. Ain't dat what dis heah place is?"

"No, ma'am it's not. We don't live in the country. This home is located in a city, the city of Los Angeles," Angie replied.

"Wait a minute, before we go any further. What is your name, and where are you from?"

"John, remember what I said, don't push her. We can find out all of that pertinent information later."

"Ma'am, dats alright. I doesn't mine answerin."

Suddenly the intercom crackled, Ash screeched. "Mom, Dad hurry upstairs! Daddy's office building is on television!"

I dashed up the stairs and a local reporter, Chris Walker, was standing in front of the building reporting. There were no signs of damage. Other buildings in the area were burning. Tears welled up in my eyes. I was so relieved to know that it was still standing.

Ash asked, "Daddy why are you crying?"

"Baby, don't worry. These tears are tears of joy."

six

In all of my life, I never felt so much joy and relief. I didn't know how good I'd feel seeing that small brown building still standing, unharmed and in one piece. It felt like my heart was going to jump out of my chest and take on a life of its own. I took a deep breath and sighed. I felt overwhelmed, profoundly grateful.

"See there," said Angela, her eyes glowing. "I told you everything was okay and that you didn't need to run down there in the middle of all of that madness. You didn't believe me."

"Yeah, it's okay right now, but that could change any moment."

"Honey what's wrong with you? What do you mean, for the time being? John, why don't you just relax? Don't you remember what you told me yesterday? You told me I was too pessimistic, now look at you. Your building is safe and you can't accept your blessing."

"I just don't know how long my luck will last. Angela, it's a free for all down there. You sound like Mayor Bradley. Last night he said that the situation was simmering down. Is the brother in this world or another? You and I both know this could go on for days. What I saw last night looks worse than anything that ever happened during the sixties. This is civil war, every man for himself. The police aren't doing anything to stop it. They should've anticipated this was going to happen. The situation is out of control."

"Okay Mister Black Bart. Don't let me stop you and your black horse from charging in there to save the day. Never mind the fact that you could go down there and get yourself killed. Maybe you got lost in a fantasy world too. I don't know, but you need to get a grip."

"I need to go down there every day and check it out for myself. I've gotta do it, for my own peace of mind."

"Peace of mind? What about my peace of mind? Maybe you don't care!"

"You know I do."

Ashley whined, "Daddy, I'm scared you might get hurt. You shouldn't go down there. It's too dangerous. I don't want you to go."

"Don't worry, baby, I'm not going to get hurt. Daddy can take care of himself."

I knew what they were up to. Angela and Ashley were double teaming me, trying to pull off an emotional TKO with a one, two punch.

James chimed in, "Dad, can I go with you? I want to go down there and see the action for myself."

"Son, this situation is nothing to play with. For the time being, no one is going anywhere."

"Dad you're always talking about what you did during the movement. And I just want to see some real action for myself."

"Your mother is right, it's dangerous down there. I can take care of myself, but I can't take care of you, too." He slumped into his seat, disappointed.

"Now back to that old woman. Don't you think there's something wrong with her. Isn't it obvious to you that she's got a real problem?"

"So you want to change the subject? And you're just going to do what you want to do, and to hell with what I feel?"

"I'm not discussing that issue anymore. What are you going to do with her? She needs to see a doctor."

"She needs a lot more than that. She needs our help."

"Look at her. Can't you see how disoriented she is? Didn't you hear what she said? She asked us who was our massa and mistrus! Come on, Ang, give me a break. Slavery ended more than a hundred and twenty-five years ago."

"Did you ever consider that she may be from somewhere in the deep South?"

"Angela, come on. She sounds like someone out of the dark ages. I don't like her being here, not one bit. I want to know more."

Since she knew she was fighting a losing battle, trying to regain her moral advantage, she gave me one of her how-could-you-be-so-cruel-and-insensitive looks.

I truly love her to death, but sometimes she can work my last nerve like nobody else. She gets so riled up and blinded by what she believes is right until I can't reason with her. She thinks she's right and I'm wrong about this woman and wanting to go down to South Central and check on Stewart Computers. I know why she brought her home, but that doesn't mean I have to be comfortable with what she did. I know she's going to want to keep her until we locate her real family, I can't see keeping this crazy woman in my house indefinitely, it's not right.

After all, I fell in love with her because she has such a good heart. My problem is that she didn't ask me or think through this whole thing before she dropped this woman into the lap of our life. I know she doesn't think about the effect it will have on all of us.

"What do you want me to do?"

"I want to know where she's from and how she got here. Plus her full name wouldn't hurt either." My wife didn't say one word, she was distracted by the presence of our houseguest at the top of the stairs. I don't know how long Miss Zoli had been standing there. I was so wrapped up in my conversation with Angela, I didn't hear her climbing the stairs. She stood there frozen, like a zombie. Her eerie presence made me feel very uncomfortable in my own home.

"Ma'am," Angie said nervously as she stood up. "Why don't you come on over and have a seat. Breakfast is almost ready."

No response. She just stood there.

"Daddy, what's wrong with that lady?"

"Hush, Ashley, and mind your manners, young lady. This is not the time to ask such a question," I replied sternly.

Angela rose from the table, walked across the room and gently touched her shoulder.

"Ma'am, Miss Zoli, come on over here and take a seat." She turned toward Angie. A faint glimmer of recognition appeared her eyes. She obediently followed my wife across the room to the table, dragging her right foot.

Oh no, here we go again, I thought to myself. This woman jumps in and out of reality like forty going north. Her mind must have an on and off switch for this reality and others.

"Wheah is I?" she asked, as my wife helped her into the chair.

"Miss Zoli, you're in our home, don't you remember?"

She sat for a few moments in silence. Finally she said, "I does a li'l bit. But not much. I remembas walkin aroune in dis strange place, an den I remembas when yah foune me an brung me heah in a machine dat ain't got no mule an no hoss pullin it."

"Well that's a major accomplishment, wouldn't you say so Angela?"

She snapped her head around glared at me, and said with her holier than thou attitude, "John please, can't you see how fragile Miss Zoli is? I asked you before to cool it."

"Miss Zoli. I'd like to ask you just one question, if that's alright with you."

"Yes, suh. It's alright wid me. What does yah wants to know?"

"I'd like to know where you're from and how did you get out here to California? Did someone bring you out here?"

"Miss Zoli, why don't you come on and eat first, aren't you hungry?" interrupted Angela.

"Ma'am, I doesn't minds. Not one bit. I is jist a little hungry and dem vittles sho do smell good. But I can ansah yoh husban's question."

"Well, suh-"

"Miss Zoli, you certainly don't have to call me 'sir' and my wife 'ma'am.' You could be my mother, and we always give our elders their proper respect. I apologize for not doing so before now."

"Well dats right kindly of you suh. But I is in yoh house.

"Suh, tah tell yah de truf, I doesn't quite knows how I gots down here," she said. I could see in her face that her disorientation had resurfaced.

"Well, can you tell us where you came from?"

"John, you said you only had one question."

"I doesn't mind tellin yah. I is from de Steadwell 'tation. Right outsidah Jackson, 'Sippi. Dats wheah I is from. Dats wheah I live mose of my life."

"I see," I replied. "So you lived on a plantation. Were you a sharecropper?"

"Sharecroppah? No sir. I was a slave, till de wah was ovah and de soldiers came aroune an tole us dat we was free."

"No, let me get this straight. You're telling me that you were a slave?"

"Yes suh. I sho nuff was."

"And you're telling me that you were set free after the war ended?"

"Yes, suh you is right 'bout dat."

"What war are you talking about? Vietnam? Korea or World War II when were you set free?"

"Suh, I ain't knowin nothin 'bout dem wahs dat yoh talkin 'bout. I ain't nevah heard ah no Vee-yet-nam or no Core-ee-ah. But as neah as I can recollect, doe I ain't sho 'bout dis, but it is my undastandin dat de slaves was set free rite aftah de wah 'tween de norf an de souf was ovah.

"When dem Yankee soldiers come aroune tellin us dat we is free, ole Massa Steadwell tried his best tah keeps us on de 'tation an away from our freedom. One day, I jist got up an walked away. I took mah freedom. But I hads to git up an outtah dat place. 'Cause I had tah fine my family."

"And what year might that be?"

"I thank it was 'bout eighteen-sixtee-seben." She said.

"Now let me get this straight. You were a slave on the Steadwell plantation."

"Yes suh, I was."

"And you lived there until after the war."

"Yes suh, yah 'zactly rite"

"Ma'am, do you know that it's nineteen-ninety-two?"

"No, suh, dis heah is eighteen an sixtee-seben."

"Ma'am, you're wrong. This is nineteen-ninety-two."

She looked up to Angela with utter disbelief. Her eyes became glassy as tears welled up in them. "Dat cain't be. Dat ain't possible. I knows dat just ain't right. I knows what yeah dis is, 'cause I in keepin track by countin de new moons. It's gotta be right."

"No ma'am, you are confused. This is nineteen hundred and ninety-two."

"Time out," barked Angela. "Let's eat. We've had enough questions. Now it's time to eat breakfast. John, let me get the orange juice before you say grace." Angela set a plate of steaming hot food on the placemat in front of our guest. "Here's your food, Miss Zoli," I said. "Go on and eat it while it's hot."

As Angela walked across the room Miss Zoli's eyes followed her. When she opened the refrigerator door to get the juice, Miss Zoli asked, "Whot's dat?"

"What's what?" I replied.

"Whot's dat big white box she ah goin intah?" she asked, pointing her crooked index finger.

"That is a refrigerator."

"Whot's a 'frig-ah-ray-tah?"

The children giggled nervously. Ashley chirped, "Haven't you seen one of those before?"

"Mind your manners young lady," Angela warned.

"But Dad—"

"I don't want to hear it, not this morning."

When I said the grace, Miss Zoli leaned over her plate of food, folded her hands, closed her eyes and softly mumbled a few words of grace to herself. The lines in her face seemed to soften while she ate so fast, slurping up the food, I thought she was going to choke. When she finished, she picked up the plate and licked it clean. I kind of felt sorry for her. Looking at her closely, I did feel sorry for her. I hadn't seen hunger like that since I was a kid.

"Miss Zoli?" I asked. "Would you like to have seconds? There's plenty more where that came from."

Her wrinkled little face crunched into a beaming smile. "Why thank yah, suh. That is so nice of yah. But I is fine. I don't need no moh food. My belly is full an it sho does feel good!"

"Thank you, Miss Zoli. That's such a nice thing for you to say," smiled Angela.

After breakfast was over, Angela cleaned off the table. While standing at the sink as she normally does, my wife turned on the little color portable television on the counter.

The noise startled Miss Zoli. "Whot's dat box?" she asked. "How did dem li'l peoples git in dat box?"

"Miss Zoli, that's a television."

"A tele whot?"

The kids giggled again. In unison, Angela and I gave them the warning look, letting them know they were treading on dangerous ground. They stopped and sat there, wiggling uncomfortably in their seats.

"That's kind of hard to explain. They're not really inside of that box, it's a moving picture."

"A tele whot? I doesn't undastands, I ain't nevah seen nothin like dis."

"Everybody has a TV," chirped in Ashley.

"Miss Zoli, please don't take me in the wrong way, but ma'am how did you get here from Mississippi?

"Well suh, I wish I knew dat," she said somberly. "All I knows is dat I been ah lookin for my husban and my chilrens for so long, such a very, very long time.

"Yah see, dey got sole away from me ah lon time ago I doesn't knows wheah dey is. An evah since slavery broke, I has been try'n tah fine dem. I been lookin each an ev'ry day. I jist been ah walkin an ah lookin, an ah lookin an ah walkin tryin tah fine dem all ovah 'Sippi. Dese ole tired feets must tah walked tin thousan miles since I bin lookin' foh dem."

"Wait a minute, Miss Zoli, I want to make sure I got this one straight. Your family was sold?"

"Yes, suh. You gots dat right."

"Where were they sold?"

"Back in Jackson."

"Sold to who?"

"Dat, I doesn't knows."

"You lived on a plantation?"

"Yes, suh I sho nuff did, all of mah life 'til de wah was ovah."

"Why do you insist that you were a slave?"

"Cause dat's de truf. I ain't bin free dat long. I was born a slave. I doesn't knows when an I doesn't knows wheah. An when I gots free de first thang dat I did was to go lookin foh my chilrens."

"Miss Zoli, slavery ended over a hundred years ago."

"Dat cain't be!" she replied, clearly becoming more agitated.

I couldn't believe my ears. This woman is more disturbed than I ever imagined. There was something seriously wrong with this woman. I'm no psychiatrist, but it's obvious to me that she's crazy and hallucinating. Talk about living in the past, I'm sure this is one for the medical record book. But I felt sorry for her. The little old woman looked so pitifully lost.

But the craziest part about this situation was my wife's response. Since this woman set foot in my house, Angela had pretended that everything was fine, and I had reached the point that I couldn't tolerate this charade much longer.

"Angie, can I speak to you in the library for a minute? Kids, you stay here and keep Miss Zoli company."

Angela, still putting away the breakfast dishes, walked over to the table, leaned over and said, "Miss Zoli, are you gonna be okay? I'll be back in a few minutes."

"Sugah, you go on. I be fine down heah, wid yah purdy li'l chilrens."

We walked into the hallway that links the kitchen to the rest of that level. Angie stopped several feet away from the door. "What's wrong with you?" she whispered in a demanding tone. "Can't you see she's very confused?"

"What's wrong with me? What's wrong with her is a whole lot more than confusion. Angela, you and I both know that she's crazy. Why is it so hard to admit that I'm right and you are wrong?"

"John, would you please hold your voice down. Why are you being so unreasonable? I've never seen you like this. What's up with you?"

"Unreasonable? Don't try to get me off the track. You can call me a lot of things, but when it comes to you and the kids—the safety of my family—I am not unreasonable. You're the one who's being unreasonable. I'm the one who doesn't understand you. You brought this crazy old woman into my home, and you expect me just to sit here and go along with your program. I don't understand you. You were talking just a few minutes ago about how I can't see the forest for the trees when it comes to my business. Well, Miss Sojourner Nightingale, you can't see the forest for the trees either, when it comes to your home missionary work!"

"Well, thank you very much for the backhanded compliment. And by the way, her name is Sojourner Truth."

"I know the woman's name. You're a combo of the two of them. Every since yesterday you've been acting like you're running Sojourner Truth's underground railroad and Florence Nightingale's hospital. That's why I decided to call you that.

"Look Angie, it's more than obvious to me that woman needs some professional help. And the sooner she gets it, the better it will be for all of us."

"Maybe you know something that I don't know. But I'd like for you to name one hospital, just one in Los Angeles that will accept a poor homeless woman today. She doesn't have a dime to her name or health insurance. In case you haven't heard the hospitals are overwhelmed with injuries, most of them are serious and the city has exploded into a civil war, and you expect me to waltz into an emergency room like they do on television and get appropriate treatment for her. You must be kidding me!

"She's not going anywhere because there's nowhere for her to go. If you could give me that name, I will gladly call them to see if they will evaluate and admit her."

Disgusted, I turned and walked down the long hallway that led to the front door.

"Where are you going? You can't leave, we haven't finished talking."

I stopped in my tracks, turned around to face her and said, "Oh yes we have. There's no need to talk anymore, you've already made up your mind. And you're not listening to me, so I'm outta here."

"Where are you going? I hope it's not to your office."

"I'm going to see Doug."

"How do you know he's home?"

"Who's left this neighborhood today to go work?" I asked while opening the front door.

"Remember there's a riot going on at the bottom of these hills."

Once outside I jogged across my parched yard. Blades of dry yellow grass crunched like old straw beneath my feet. Clouds of smoke blotted out the sun. As I trotted up the hill I could feel the soot burning my lungs. In less than five minutes, I had made my way up to the top of one of the highest hills in my neighborhood, and was out of breath. Panting, I stood in front of Doug's place, a huge spacious pink stucco mansion. He has a fine, gorgeous home, twice the size of mine. Doug Garrett was one of the first people I met when we moved into our neighborhood over ten years ago. He and his family have lived in the hills for almost twenty years ago. When we arrived with the movers, he was the first one to come down and welcome us into the neighborhood. Doug owns so many businesses 'til I can't keep up with them. I know he has at least three or four fast food franchises, a car wash, two cleaners, a hardware store, an appliance store, a couple of liquor stores and three grocery stores. About three years ago, he started buying real estate, apartment buildings, office buildings and a few more commercial properties.

Despite the fact that he is in his mid-sixties, he is the picture of good health and looks like one of my running partners. Most people think he's in his late forties. Looking at him today, tall, fit, lean and healthy with his jogging suit on, it's hard to believe that less than five years ago he almost died. Doug suffered a massive heart attack shortly after the death of his first wife, Lizzy, who was just like a grandmother to our children. She was the sweetest and prettiest gray haired woman I'd ever seen, and I used to call her the 'Silver Fox.' When we moved in they drove matching pink Eldorado Cadillacs. She and my wife were just as close as Doug and I were, and the kids adored their Momma Lizzy. Even though they had their own grandchildren, she had a special relationship with Ashley and James. It took all of us a long time to get over her death.

Doug took Lizzy's death very hard. For weeks he was so torn with grief and riddled by guilt, that he refused to get out of bed. I was very worried that he might try to take his own life. About four months after Lizzy's death, he finally returned to work. During that first week, while sitting at his desk and talking to his secretary he had a heart attack. Fortunately Doug's secretary knew CPR and kept him alive until the paramedics arrived. According to the doctor's that treated him, he was dead for at least an hour. My wife said that the had the heart attack because he was suffering from a broken heart. Although I disagreed with her, maybe she was right.

He met his second wife, Kathy Lee, while he was in the hospital. She was the resident in charge of his case. Sly old man that he is, Doug refused to let any of the other doctors touch him or make decisions about his case without consulting her. Even though Doug is almost thirty years older than her, they fell in love and got married less than six months after they met. Now they have a little two-and-a-half-year-old girl, Imani, our goddaughter and Kathy Lee is expecting another baby the end of August.

When Doug was released from the hospital he stopped smoking and drinking, lost about thirty pounds and started exercising. I didn't believe that he was serious, but he proved me wrong. Kathy Lee really turned his life around. Although she and Angie are now very close, it was a long time before my wife accepted her.

Before their wedding, which I almost had to drag my wife to, she began teasing me. "Are you going to do this too when I'm dead and gone?"

"Do what?"

"Find you a sweet young thing to rub your arthritic joints?"

"No, I don't think so."

"Honey, if you do decide to bring a child bride into my home when I'm dead and gone, I promise you I will return and haunt you and her each and every day for the rest of your life. So don't be surprised when she tells you that she saw my ghost. Miss Sweet Young Thing won't be imagining anything—she'll be seeing the real thing."

As time passed on, my wife warmed up to Kathy Lee. I don't know what happened but something changed her mind, and now they're the best of friends.

Doug is one of the most successful people I've ever known. He's a multimillionaire, but you'd never know how rich he is. He's very down to earth and has never lost his common touch.

"Hey brother, what's happening?" he smiled opening one of the two huge hand-carved ebony doors, covering two floors of his mansion.

"Not much. I guess I needed some fresh air. I just had to get out of the house."

"Well the air out here shouldn't be breathed by anyone on a good day, much less on a day like this. Come on man, you mean to tell me you have cabin fever already? What's up with you? You look worried."

"Man, where have you been for the last twenty-four hours, out meditating on life or eating some of those nasty tasting bamboo shoots? You know there's a riot going on throughout this city. Aren't you worried about your businesses?"

"Yes, I know all that, and I am concerned. But what can you or I do to stop this madness?"

"That's a good question, my brother, I wish I knew the answer."

We walked through the house to the pool. I sat there watching him drink some dark green concoction that he had made.

"Where's Kathy Lee and Imani?"

"In Denver visiting her mother. You know, I'm really glad they're not here, because she would be wanting to go down to the hospital and help out today. That is the last place a pregnant woman needs to be right now. It looks like there's a war going on down there."

"Yeah, man it sure does. You know my wife pulled a fast one on me. She brought this crazy old homeless lady home last night. She found her in the parking lot at the Center on her way home."

"And you're upset about it?"

"Damn right I am."

"Man, what are you so uptight about?"

"Uptight? Who's uptight? Not me."

"Now, I want to know who do you think you are fooling?"

"Alright, alright, hell yeah, I'm mad. I'm pissed off because my wife and I have this agreement. One that I might add that she concocted. We have agreed not to make any major decisions, one that can impact upon our family, without consulting the other partner first. Now she conveniently reneged on the deal. She says she didn't have enough time to call. She says it was a split second, life and death decision that she had to make without me.

"And then to add insult to injury, she could've called me to let me know what the deal was after she got home. Did she do that? No man, she waited 'til I got home to tell me."

"Well, if I were in your shoes, I would probably feel the same way that you do."

"Thank you man, I knew you would understand my feelings."

"However, I'm not wearing your shoes. The way I see it, Angie did do the right thing."

I jumped out of my seat and yelled, "Man I don't believe you! What kind of traitor are you siding with her like that?"

"Calm down, my friend," he replied in a soothing and un-ruffled voice. "One day you'll see for yourself that she did do the right thing. It's gonna be alright. Trust me."

"Well, anyway, that's not the reason I came down here," I said taking my last sip of orange juice that I'm sure he squeezed himself this morning. "Are you up to riding lookout with me? I'm going in."

"Going in where?"

"Down to my office."

"Man, have you lost your mind? Are you crazy, or are you suicidal?"

"You sound like Angela. No, I'm not crazy. I've gotta check out my building for myself. KABC did a live shot right in front of it. But it could go any minute."

"Look, John I'm getting a little too old for this. You know that I have a weak heart," he chuckled patting his heart with his left hand. "But, since I don't want your wife to become a widow, nor your children fatherless, I will ride down there with you."

"My man! I knew I could depend on you."

"And one more thing—"

"What's that?"

"I'll do the driving. You need to cool out. Looks like you're going to pop a blood vessel or two."

Doug finished his drink, and we headed through the garden to the garage. He walked toward his silver Mercedes sedan parked between Kathy Lee's red Corvette and his blue Lexus. I just stood there at the door watching him. As he put the key in the car door, I asked, "Man, how far do you think we'd get in this car on a day like this? I can just see it now. We get stopped by the police on the suspicion of theft, and instead of them arresting us, today they will shoot first and ask questions later."

"Yes, my brother, you're right. I just wasn't thinking. Let's go in the van."

We hopped into a rusty, battered old white van that was parked against the wall on the far side of the garage. He uses it to transport stock and supplies for his various businesses.

"Man, why don't you get a new van? I know you can afford it."

"You know why. I've had this old heap for almost thirty years, and it's been my good luck charm. I bought it right after I opened my first store. It reminds me of where I came from."

He slowed down the car as we approached my home, and asked, "Hey, don't you want to let Angie know where we're headed?"

"Not in this life. You know how she is. She went on and on this morning, and I don't need to hear any more of her mouth. I'm the man of the house, and I'm going to do what I've gotta do."

"Man, you can talk that stuff to me, but you know I know better. You don't know how lucky you are to have a woman who cares deeply about you. I know plenty of men whose wives are concerned about one thing. And that's about them bringing home the bacon. Otherwise they don't need 'em. There are plenty of people in this neighborhood like that. Do you think I'd be doing this if Kathy Lee was here? I don't think so. She'd yell and scream, just like Angie and threaten to go into labor. She's called me four times since yesterday when the verdict was rendered, just to make sure that I was okay. Even my two grown kids called, and you know how often they pick up a phone to talk to me? Once a year, maybe. But you better believe today Greg and Liz both wanted to make sure that their dear old dad was alright.

"You should be happy that you have a woman in your life who really cares about you. It's when they stop nagging you that you should get concerned."

"Well, I guess you do have a point," I reluctantly agreed. "But Ang just doesn't have a clue when it comes to understanding how important Stewart Computers is to me. That business is a part of me, like an arm or a leg, and I have to protect it. If it goes up in smoke, my life is over."

"John, why don't you give it a rest and calm down? I worry about you. If you keep this up I'll be visiting you in a cardiac unit. Trust me, I know what I'm talking about my brother, I've walked ten miles in your shoes."

At the bottom of the hill, as we pulled onto Martin Luther King Jr. Boulevard heading south toward Crenshaw Boulevard, it felt like we were passing through a force field that made my body tighten up. I'd never seen anything like it in my entire life. It was like a descent into hell, flames were bursting through the roofs of familiar businesses, shooting up into the sky, smoke billowing everywhere, people looting buildings, darting in and out of traffic,

carting off any and everything that they could. And the few buildings that weren't burning, most of them were being looted or had
been. My head felt like it was about to explode as it pounded louder
and louder. Fire, fire, fire. Higgins Furniture store was already
gone, destroyed beyond recognition. Even the sign was gone.
Brunetta's Hair Salon was blazing, Harold's Video store was going
up in smoke, too. A couple of blocks down the street, in the shopping mall, the Our Way grocery store must've had hundreds of
looters running in and out taking food. I even saw two-and-three-
year-old kids following behind their parents dragging boxes of dia-
pers. Most of the stores in the strip mall across the street were
burning. And where were the police? Nowhere to be found.

A few people were out guarding their buildings with shot-
guns and assault weapons and signs and placards that said, "Black
owned." The overwhelming destruction of my entire community
made me sick to my stomach. I looked at Doug. His face was filled
with disgust and he shook his head. I wanted to jump out of the
van, and make them stop. But I knew it wouldn't do any good, and
that I could get myself killed in the process.

It looked like these were the last days. In spite of all that I
saw on TV, I wasn't ready for this. Looters were everywhere, boldly
strutting across the street, stopping traffic. It was a street party,
as they carted off stereos on their shoulders, televisions in shopping carts, radios, computers, bags of food bursted at the seems,
arms full of clothing.

"Man, can you believe this?" asked Doug, still shaking his
head.

"No, I can't. I wasn't ready for this."

It seemed like the world had gone mad. I watched helplessly
as my community was consumed by its own rage. People roamed
the streets freely, without fear of reprisal, taking whatever they
wanted from the remaining stores that had yet to be torched by
fire. I heard last night some people said they were avenging the
death of fifteen-year-old Latasha Harlins, the child that was murdered in cold blood last year by a Korean storeowner over a bottle

of orange juice. She was shot in the back of her head. Even though the store's videotape clearly showed the ruthlessly brutal way she died, Latasha's killer was convicted of manslaughter and sentenced to several hours of community service—for cold blooded murder. I wondered how little Latasha would feel about people carrying on like this in her name.

"I saw Asians getting pulled from their cars last night and beaten, probably worse than Rodney King," I said.

Doug didn't respond, he probably didn't hear me. He was dazed, by what lay before him. If they thought they were harming only the Koreans, they were sorely mistaken. But now it looked like people just really didn't care. Any business was fair game. It was an opportunity to take, and that's what they were doing, until there was nothing left. Before my eyes, the entire economic lifeline of our community was being wiped out, going up in smoke. As if it needed any help.

He looked even more disgusted. Then he said, "What's gonna happen next?"

"I wish I knew," were the only words I could find. Why are we tearing up our own neighborhood?

"Man, are you sure you want to do this? We can turn around and go back home."

"No, let's get this over and done with. I have to make sure my building is secure."

"Last night I was listening to KGBF," he said slowly, almost struggling to find the words. "A minister called in. You know what he said? Man, it was profound. He said, 'That verdict rattled the bones of our mothers and fathers in their graves.'

"How can we go on like this? How can this injustice continue? Man, its gotta stop sooner or later! Something's gotta give. It really makes you wonder whether this little corner of the world has gone stark raving mad."

"Doug, when I was in the movement, I thought we stood a chance. Now I don't anymore. Now I wonder, if that was ever true. The changes I've seen during my lifetime in many ways are significant, now all of them seem to be very superficial."

"You may be right, but I know there are some opportunists out here to take advantage of the situation."

"No doubt about it, you are absolutely right."

As we traveled further along Crenshaw, the smoke got thicker, and breathing became more difficult. Both of us started coughing, choking on the poisonous smoke seeping into the van. Even though the air conditioner was on at full blast, I could feel the intensity of the heat from the flames.

"Man, this is absolute chaos. It just doesn't make any sense. This looks like Bosnia."

"In a way it's worse than Bosnia."

"You know this city has been on edge for a long time. That video of Rodney King getting beaten just helped to bring it to a head."

Block after block, intersection after intersection, cars were moving slowly, creeping along. The streets were packed, filled with cars. People leaned out of windows flashing the power sign, and shouting at one another.

"Man, this is worse than cutting off your nose to spite your face. What's going to happen when the fires are put out and the stores are gone?"

"Where is the National Guard? I thought they were supposed to be here by now."

"Oh yeah, like in the movies. The calvary always makes it there just in time. Well, this time the calvary isn't showing up."

"I heard this morning on the television that twenty five people had already been killed," Doug said, his voice filled with disgust. "Well brother, from what we're seeing now, that was just the beginning. Before it's over and done, there will be a lot more people hurting and dying."

The muffled sounds of gunshots ricochetted through the air. My body reacted instinctively and I ducked. We saw TV crews hiding behind police cars. "Man, Angie was right. It is dangerous out here."

"I was wondering how long it was going to take for you to figure that one out and finally admit the truth, but we'll be okay. And so will your business."

"How do you know that?"

"Trust me, I know. I have a gut feeling, and my gut is always right."

"What about your businesses? Aren't you concerned them?"

"You know I haven't really thought about them. I hope everything is okay. And if not, we do have insurance."

"Man, you need to get a grip. Everything that you've built could've gone up in smoke."

"Well if it did, at this ripe old age of sixty-three, I've finally realized there is more to life, a lot more, than making money and being successful."

"You know I know that."

"Do you really? It took me a long time, most of my life, to figure that one out. I did a pretty good job of pretending I did, fooling everybody including myself. I wasn't a good husband to my first wife Lizzy, God rest her soul, but she was a good woman. Sure, I provided her and the kids with material things, but I wasn't there for them. I didn't have any time to enjoy her. No, that's not true. I didn't make any time for her. I was so busy, running around being successful and making my mark during most of the years that we were together. Then one day she was gone. Man, I barely know my own children. They didn't have a father, 'cause I was never around long enough to be a father, I mean a real one. Not the one that shows up at the right times on birthdays, at graduations and on holidays, but the day-in-and-day-out father, the one that's there when you need him. Man, that wasn't me. I was too busy trying to make my first million to give my children what they needed more than my money. Even though I'm getting what I deserve from them, it still hurts."

"I know you've tried to make it up to them."

"Oh, sure I've tried to make my amends, but sometimes it's too late for a second chance, and you just have to keep on living. They rarely call and visit even less. I can count the number of times I've seen my kids on one hand since Lizzy died, and still have a few fingers left. I've got five or six beautiful grandchildren

I don't even know. The best I can hope to do is to try to not make the same mistake that I did with my new family.

"So use me as an example. Don't take your family for granted. Please don't make the same mistake that I did. You never know what tomorrow's going to bring."

"Yeah, you're right."

"Listen to me and listen to me good. You are one blessed man. Blessed to have a good wife and two great kids. You don't know how lucky you are. And there's nothing in your office that is as precious as them."

"Man, I know that my family is important. I'm looking out for their interests right now."

"I knew you were going to say that. Because that's exactly what I used to say to justify whatever I wanted to do. John, I'm a lot older than you. I've seen a lot and have made my mark in the business world. I've made more money than I'll ever have the opportunity to spend, and have more material possessions than I need. Even now sometimes I feel that my life is filled with too many things. Making money doesn't hold the excitement it once did.

"Trust me. I'm not crazy. I just don't want you to make the same mistakes that I did. Life is too short and so very unpredictable. You have to live your life the best way that you can each and every day. And I'm just telling you that you shouldn't get lost in your business. One day your behavior might come back to haunt you."

"I hear you, and I appreciate what you said. But I needed to get out of that house. That old woman gives me the creeps, I don't like her being there, not one bit."

"And that's another thing. What's with you and this old woman? This isn't like you to get so upset about something like this. You and Angela have been helping people for almost of all your life."

"I don't know, and I don't need to try to figure it out. I just want her out of my house."

"Where can she go? You can't just put her out on the street. Look at what's going on around you. How can you kick her out with all of this madness going on? Man, the poor old woman wouldn't stand a chance."

"Whose side are you on, anyway? I though you were my best friend, not Angela's."

"Why don't you calm down. All I'm saying is that you should just chill out and let her stay there, at least until the situation on the streets calm down."

"So she can harm my children or wife?"

"No, she's not going to do that. Everything's gonna turn out fine."

"Man, you sound like Angela. How do you know that for sure."

"I can't say. It's just another feeling. But like I know your business is fine, this situation at home is okay, too."

Doug looked out the window. I could see the side of his face turning into a grimace as we watched people pouring out of Bannister's Clothing store, carrying bundles of stolen clothes still on the hangers. "I wonder how I would feel if I had nothing to lose. Maybe I would do the same thing."

"I don't know. I can't say what I would do."

"Everything in this world is built on violence. What's the difference between war and what's going on down here?"

"The difference is, it's happening in our neighborhood." We both chuckled.

"Remember the song 'California Dreamin'?" I asked, as my mind flashed back to the summer of sixty-six when that song was a hit.

"Vaguely, I do."

"This is a California nightmare. I wonder if there isn't another way? A more effective way of dealing with anger and rage than just burning down your own neighborhood? And if so, what is it?

"Man, I felt so helpless, just sitting around the house. Thanks so much for coming."

"No, problem. You know I got your back."

When we turned the corner, I could see from a block away that the building was still standing, in one piece. I was filled with relief, as we got closer. A couple of blocks away buildings were burning out of control. I thanked the man upstairs for letting mine remain untouched, in the midst of all this madness. As we got closer, I noticed there was something different about the building. The windows were covered with plywood. "Black-owned" had been spray painted in big bold letters. The door was covered, too. I wondered who'd beat me to the punch.

Doug said, "Looks like someone is looking out for you."

"Yeah, it sure does. I wonder who did this."

When I got out of the van, Doug parked it on the side street. I heard someone yell, "Put your guns down! It's Mr. Stewart." I looked up and there were several of my employees up on the roof, guarding the building. We climbed the ladder, and there was Jackie, my office manager, Willie, Brenda, Bobby, Russell and Cornelius. "What are you all doing up here?"

"Mr. Stewart. We're here protecting the building," yelled Cornelius, my stock man. "Last night was crazy all over the neighborhood. This morning we saw the building on television and decided sort of on our own to come down here and protect it.

"You've been good to us, real good, and with all that is going on this is the least we can do. Plus, to be honest, we want to protect our jobs," chuckled Bobby, my shipping and receiving clerk.

"Why didn't you call?"

"We didn't want to disturb you," piped in Cornelius, a tall, lanky man. He looked more like a farmer wearing a blue jean cap and overalls. Only he was carrying an assault rifle, instead of a hoe. "Mr. Stewart. You been good to us, real good to us. You gave me a chance when no other business in town would talk to me. You helped to straighten out my life. I ain't had no steady job in ten years. Then you helped my boy get into Howard. And you never asked for one thing in return. You been good to all of us, treated us like family. Please, this is the least I can do."

I was stunned by their generosity. "I'm speechless. I'm overwhelmed. Thank you so much. But I should be down here."

"No, you shouldn't, you don't have to do that. We called some of the other guys, and they'll be down this afternoon. We'll be back at midnight. We're going to rotate in shifts, twenty-four seven, and stay down here as long as it takes.

"Like I said, I'm speechless." I looked to Doug.

He was standing smiling like he was about to burst. He looked at me and said, "Man, this is beautiful."

"Mr. Stewart—" I heard a faint voice calling me from the parking lot. I looked down and there was Mrs. Washington, one of my invoicing clerks. She's a tiny little old lady in her early sixties. Barely five feet tall, she was standing next to the ladder wearing a pair of fading overalls and a straw hat toting a double barreled shot gun. "I came down here on my own. Those boys didn't want me to be here. But since I came with my husband's shotgun, none of them would send me home. I'm staying just as long as you need me."

We all cracked up into laughter at the spry little woman.

"Let me go get you something to eat, that's the least I can do," I offered.

"That's not necessary Mr. Stewart. My wife is going to bring us lunch in a little bit."

"I really don't know what to say. Okay. Since you've got everything under control here, I might as well get on back home. Thanks so much, I'll be back in the evening to check on you."

"You don't have to do that, Sonny," said Mrs. Washington. "We've got everything under control."

"Yes, ma'am."

Doug turned the van around and started heading back home.

"Don't you want to check out any of your businesses?" I asked.

"No man, that's not necessary."

On the way back, I tuned out the outside world. My thoughts rested on the outpouring of loyalty I'd just witnessed, wondering what had I done to deserve this? I was overwhelmed by their generosity. They were risking their lives for me and my business.

"I don't know what I did to deserve such loyalty."

"Man, you are too much. You break your back, day in and day out helping people, who otherwise wouldn't have jobs, and now you're shocked when they return in kind what you've done for them?"

"I guess you're right. But they're risking their lives for me."

"You deserve it. So just be cool and accept your blessing."

We heard on the radio that the National Guard was finally rolling in, setting up guard posts at key intersections along Western, Pico and Crenshaw Boulevard.

"Doug, I can't thank you enough for riding lookout with me. Tomorrow I'll go alone."

"No can do. I'll be going, too."

It was around two thirty when Doug dropped me off. When I walked into house I headed for the family room. They were probably down there watching television or out by the pool. Angela was sitting in the kitchen on a stool next to the phone, talking and twisting the cord around her fingers. Her face was drawn, just about as twisted as the cord she was nervously wrapping around her fingers and arm. I guess she was worried and a bit pissed off about my absence. She looked up at me and rolled her eyes as I approached the refrigerator to get a glass of water.

I leaned over to give her a kiss on the cheek and she snatched her head away from me so fast she could've broken her neck "Listen Jay, I've gotta run. My husband just walked in the house and I need to talk to him. I'll talk to you later."

She hung up the phone and looked at me. Her eyes were glaring and her nostrils flared like an angry bull's. "Where have you been? she demanded. "You've been gone for hours."

"I was down at Doug's place. I told you I was going there."

"John, why do have to lie? Your mother called about an hour after you left the house. She was worried about us, especially you. I told her you were at Doug's and gave her his number. Before I hung up the phone good she called back saying that nobody answered. Then I called several times for hours, and only got the answering machine. I even walked up to the house.

"So where have you been? I've been worried sick that the two of you took off and went down into South Central, in the middle of that war zone. Do you know how many people have been killed? More than thirty since last night."

"Okay, so we got a little bored. We just went for a spin."

"A little spin you say? Man, do I look like an idiot?"

"Why can't you stop nagging me?"

She just sat there, rolling her eyes at me. I knew my strategy wasn't working.

"Alright, alright. I went down there. Listen, I'll talk to you about this later. I'm going to call my mother."

"You shouldn't have gone. It's too dangerous. You and Doug were lucky, very lucky that the two of you didn't get killed."

"I'm not arguing with you about something that's over and done with, that I felt I had to do. Like I told you before, a man's gotta do what a man's gotta do." I left her sitting there and walked into the library. Even though it was mid-afternoon, the room was very dark. I turned on the green banker's lamp sitting in the middle of my desk, and dialed my mother's number.

"Hello." Her raspy voice cracked with the presence of old age.

"Hi, Momma. It's your favorite son. How are you doing?"

"Johnny, is that you? Boy, where you been? I been worried sick 'bout you since I called this morning. Angie said you were at your friend's house. I called down there, got no answer. An I kept callin. Where were you? Out gallivanting around in that riot?"

"Momma, remember I am grown, been so for a long time. You act like I'm James' age."

"Well son, to do something as stupid as riding down into the middle of a riot, is something a sixteen-year-old would do. But to tell you the truth, I don't think that darling grandson of mine would do that, he's too bright."

"Mom, I went down there, alright. And I made it back in one piece."

"I am grateful to the Lord for that. Now promise me one thing. That you won't go back down there."

"Momma, I can't promise you that. I'll try not to."

"Now Johnny, you knows that your poor old mother has a heart condition. My heart has been beating like a horse. Do you want me to have a heart attack worrying about you?"

"No, ma'am, I certainly don't."

"So tell me something. Is it as bad as it looks out there?"

"Yes, Momma. It's pretty bad. Actually its worse than what you've probably seen on television."

"From what I see on TV, it looks like those Koreans are really taking a beating."

"We all are. A lot of Black businesses have been destroyed, too."

"I don't know why them Koreans are so mean to Black folk. 'Specially if it hadn't been for all of them colored men that died over there fighting for their freedom, like your daddy they wouldn't be here today. Seems like they forgot a big chunk of their history."

"You know what? Momma, you are absolutely right. I'd never thought about it quite like that."

"Johnny, I understand why our people are so upset about the way they been treated by them. But, that's no excuse to burn somebody's property down. All they have to do is boycott. That's the way to close a business down without breaking the law.

"Remember Marie, that old evil white woman, at the corner store and the way she tried to cheat me outta my hard earned money?"

"Yes, ma'am I do."

"Back then in fifty-seven she had the nerve to call me a nigga. To this very day she ain't seen hide nor hair of me or of my money. Something I never understood about my people, and still don't to this very day is why they put up with so much mistreatment. My Momma and Daddy, God rest their souls, didn't raise me to be mistreated. So I never would let anybody do me wrong. If they can't treat me right, then they can't have my hard earned money. Its just that simple.

"I don't know why everybody is so surprised over that verdict. Why did they expect any justice this time?"

"I think the videotape had a lot to do with that."

"Videotape my foot. Son, your memory must be fadin faster than mine. Don't you remember about eleven or twelve years ago when the Klu Klux Klan shot and killed those people in North

Carolina? They had those murders on videotape, and they got off just like the police out there."

"Yeah, Momma you do have a point."

Momma and I talked for may be fifteen or twenty minutes longer. I went upstairs and laid down across the bed. I was drained. I hoped my wife would let me rest in peace before I had to have another argument with her about the business. I wasn't up for another round of arguing. As soon as my head hit the pillow, my body collapsed into a deep and restful sleep.

seven

I don't know what's wrong with my husband. He waltzes out of the house and down into a war zone, like he's going to a picnic with his sidekick. Men! Sometimes he's too much for me to even think about handling. For the life of me I can't figure out what's so critical, why he has to risk life and limb to make sure that that stupid business of his is still standing. He's stupid—thought telling me that he was going to see Doug, made me believe that he changed his mind, and he's only fooling himself. But what could I do to stop him, call the police? Knowing Doug, he wanted to cruise on down there in his Mercedes, not realizing that car is a moving target on a day like this. I can just see the two of them now, both of them wearing their I'm a big, bad macho man masks to cover up their fears. He always says whenever we disagree, 'You don't understand, it's a man's thing.' What I do understand is that he's acting like he doesn't have the sense that he was born with.

Watching television didn't help any. I thought the riots during the sixties were bad, but what's happening now takes it to a new level. The bottom line is that this is more than a riot, it's a civil war, nothing short. Any time more than a thousand fires are set in one night, it's pretty bad.

I'm just grateful, very grateful that he made it back home safe and sound. Even though I was really pissed off, I must admit, I was very relieved to see him walk in the kitchen.

Miss Zoli had stayed in her room for most of the morning. After breakfast, she said she was sleepy, and her leg was hurting. I knew I needed to get her to a hospital, but we'd probably sit there for twenty hours or so waiting for her to see a doctor, if I took her to an emergency room.

This morning, after John left, I went out on the patio for a few minutes. The thick, acrid smoke rising from the floor of the city burned my eyes.

What am I supposed to tell my children? They keep looking at me, as if I am a vessel of deep knowledge that will give them something to hold onto through all of this madness. But I can't do that. I wish I could, but I just don't have any answers. I don't know what to tell them. When I was growing up we believed that things were going to get better. My mother used to say, "You're getting a chance to live in a better world, a world of opportunities I never dreamed of having and so will you children. Each generation of colored children will do more and more. Look at how far we've come."

During the sixties we truly believed we were on the brink of a new day in America. We believed that with moral persuasion and political action that the walls would come down and justice would flow like a mighty stream. Today those beliefs feel quite hollow.

When I thought about my friends, those who owned businesses down there, I wondered what's going on with them. Is everyone safe? Is Geneva okay? How are Bill and Georgette? I wonder if Doc Whitney is walking the streets trying to stop this madness. Is the agency still standing? What about our neighbors, our other friends? I even wonder if our church is still standing. I heard this morning that the library and post office had been burned down.

In my heart I knew that Stewart Computer's was safe, but I didn't feel that way about Chez Georgette's. I wondered if it was still there. My mind kept focusing in on that painting of the African warrior. I saw it burning, and the last things to be consumed by the flames were those mystical mesmerizing eyes of his. In the final moment of my vision, I saw one small tear emerging from the corner of his eye, rolling down toward his consumed cheek. I don't know what this means, or even if it does mean anything. But something was going on that was frightening me deeply.

Whenever I get scared, really scared, my mother comes to me. Although she passed away almost sixteen years ago, shortly after James' birth, not a day passes without me thinking about her. I still regret that she didn't live long enough to see her two grandchildren. She would've been so very proud of them.

I miss her a lot. For a woman of such a tiny stature, my mother was a spiritual giant. Momma was a resilient lady. Swathed in a fearless streak of determination, she wore it gently, like fine silk. She never took no for an answer—not from me, not from my father, my brother or anyone else for that matter.

I grew up like an only child. My brother Frank was twelve years older than me, and took off to see the world before I started school. He's still with the Navy. Now he's a commander stationed in the Philippines.

Momma used to tell John, "Don't you worry about making all that money. You just worry about making me some grandchildren." If she was alive today, she'd probably be on her way out here to make sure that we were all okay.

Finally, I'd had enough and decided to call friends and family who'd probably tried to reach us, to let them know that we were alright. I decided to call my father first. Actually, I was a bit perplexed as to why he hadn't called us to see how we were doing. He's still living at home alone in Milwaukee.

After forty years, Daddy retired about ten years ago from the beer factory, and has been living the life of Riley. I'm surprised he never remarried, as most men do, but he said to me, when he was out here visiting a few months after Momma passed away, "Angela, your mother was the best. Why would I ever want to settle for second best?"

I called Dad to let him know that we were okay.

"Dad, how are you?"

"Sugah, I'm doing just fine for a man my age. I been taking it easy the last few days, my arthritis has flared up on me."

"Oh, I see. I guess that's why you hadn't called us to see how we are doing out here since the verdict was rendered."

"Well, you know I had intended to call you today. I didn't hear about the verdict and all that's going on out there until this morning. Yes, I was a bit concerned about you all, but I know that son-in-law of mine is going to take care of you.

"Tell him I'm sure he's taking good care of my little sunshine, and those two grandchildren of mine. Where is he? I'd like to speak to him."

"Dad he's not here."

"Oh yeah? Knowing that son-in-law of mine, he's probably gone to check on his building. Isn't it down in the area where the rioting is going on?"

"Dad, you're absolutely correct."

"Don't worry darlin'. John's alright, he can take good care of himself."

"If you say so," I responded unconvincingly.

Trying to change the subject, I asked, "Dad, when are we going to see you again?"

"Oh, sugah, I don't know. You know I'm not one for traveling. Maybe this summer."

"We miss you, I hope you come out soon. The kids want to see you." Normally Dad comes at least two or three times a year, but we haven't seen him since last Christmas.

I tried to make a few more local calls, but couldn't get through. I guessed some of the lines were down.

Around noon, I let the kids go visit with their friends who live about five doors away. They had grown very tired of watching television and were getting very restless. The Williams' kids were their classmates at St. Ignatius. They hadn't been gone for more than an hour when I walked into the kitchen and found Ashley coughing, gasping for air. She hasn't had a bad asthma attack since she was a little girl.

"What's wrong, Ash?"

"Mommie, I can't breathe. I started wheezing on the way to Sean's house. After we got there it got worse."

"Why didn't your brother come back home with you?"

"I told him I'd be okay. I'm a big girl." I rushed upstairs to my bathroom and rummaged through the medicine cabinet. I keep an inhaler in the house, and usually it helped, but the air was so bad. I was sure smoke and soot triggered her attack. The inhaler didn't help her at all. The thought of taking her to the hospital worried me. Unlike my husband, I didn't want to be driving around in all of that chaos. But it looked like I didn't have a choice and if I had to do it, I would.

Miss Zoli stumbled into the kitchen. She looked quizzically at Ashley and asked, "Lord ah mercy me, whot wrong wid dat chile?"

"She's having an asthma attack."

"A whot?"

Ashley, gasping for air, replied, "I can't breathe."

She looked at me perplexed and asked, "Why cain't dat chile breathe?"

"She has a problem in her lungs. I need to take her to the hospital."

"Gonna do whot?"

"Take her to the doctor."

"Whot is yah gonna do dat foh, huh? All she needs is some hep to git dat burnin' outtah her. Befoh yah go runnin off, maybe dere is somethin dat I can do."

"That's awfully sweet of you, but I don't think there is."

"Does yah haf any of dat Castah Oil?"

"Yes, Ma'am I do."

"Go fetch it foh me." I obeyed her again, and rushed upstairs to my bathroom and got the bottle of Castor Oil that I keep in the house as a last resort laxative for John.

When I returned to the kitchen she was hovering over Ashley and rubbing on her back.

"Sugah, it's gonna be alrite. Jist gives me a minute an' we gonna git some aiah into yah."

I handed her the bottle she asked, "Can I haf a glass of cole watah?"

"Yes, Ma'am."

She took the bottle, pored some of the oil into the palm of her hand, closed her eyes, and mumbled a few words, as if she were praying. A few moments later she opened her eyes and rubbed the oil on Ashley's chest. Then she had her drink the glass of water that I was holding. "It's gonna be bettah, jist give it a minute." My daughter sat there still struggling to breathe. She looked at me with desperate confusion. I nodded my head as reassuringly as I could. Miss Zoli closed her eyes again and bowed her head once more, and rubbed Ash's back.

Suddenly something shifted. Ashley took a deep breath and sighed. Her eyes were suddenly gleaming, her labored breathing disappeared. "Mommie, I can breathe! The wheezing stopped!"

Miss Zoli opened her eyes and smiled. "See I told yah it would git bettah!" Ashley leaped out of her chair and hugged her. "Thank you so much Miss Zoli, I can breathe! My lungs feel so good."

I was stunned. I'd never seen Ash stop wheezing so abruptly before, and I didn't know what to think. "Thank you so much, Miss Zoli. What did you do?"

"I ain't do nothin but ease her burden by annointin her body with de palm of Christ and prayin foh her. Don't yah knows dat prayer changes thins?"

"Yes, ma'am we do."

In the twinkling of an eye, before my daughter could thank her, she blanked out on us, drifting off into another world.

"Miss Zoli, you made me feel so much better, my lungs feel so good. I feel this cool, fresh air inside of me."

She stood there unresponsive, staring straight ahead.

"Mommie, what's wrong with her? Can't you do something?"

"Ash, I don't know. I just think she's a little disoriented."

"Can't we do anything to help her?"

"I don't know what to do sweetie. Let's take her to her room and lie her down. Maybe a little rest will help her"

We took her by the hand and led her back to her room. Lifting her legs, I could see her socks were soaked, stained a pale, light yellow from the fluid that was oozing from the terrible rash that had invaded her skin. I went upstairs and got gauze to wrap her feet with. While applying the dressing, I wondered again where she was from. There was so much I wanted to know about her. She was confused, alone and fragile, like a delicate little flower blossoming in the desert. I wondered where her children were. I knew they must be worried sick about her.

For the rest of the afternoon, my daughter went on about her day as if she'd never had an attack. Normally an attack tires her out so much that she has to take a nap for at least an hour. Her breathing was fine, and she never complained again, even though the air quality continued to worsen as the day progressed.

Around noon, I was sitting in the kitchen when I heard the phone ring. When I answered I didn't recognize the voice on the other end.

"My sister, my sister how are you?"

"Who is this?"

"You don't know?"

"If I did, would I ask?"

"Does Vidaylia ring a bell?"

It was one of my dearest friends from Howard, one of my movement buddies, sister Soyini. "Soyini! Is that you?"

"In the flesh and at your service. What's going on out there? How are you all doing?"

"Aside from the fact that my husband is probably roaming around in South Central, and Ashley just had an asthma attack, as well as our unexpected, homeless houseguest, I'd say that everything is fine. How about you?"

"Sounds like you're in the middle of it."

"Girl, you just don't know how true those words are. But we're hanging in there. What else can we do?"

"I hear you."

"Listen, enough about me, what's going on in your neck of the woods?"

"No, no, no, Miss 'I am woman hear me roar.' Talk to me, tell me what's going on with you. I'm all ears. We haven't talked in months, and this is not like us. So I decided to call and make sure that two of my most favorite people were alright."

"That's really sweet of you. Hearing your voice is a breath of fresh air today. I'm just sitting around the house, watching television, listening to the reports, and trying not to worry about John."

"Is it as bad as it seems?

"It's worse. Soyo, I've never seen anything like this—what's going on out here now, makes the sixties look like a picnic."

"Really? Girl, you gotta be kidding me."

"Would I lie? Last night there were more than a thousand fires set."

"I wish I was there with you."

"That's so sweet of you. I wish you were too, but I'm glad you're not. You don't want to live through this. We'll be alright. Tell me what's going on in Manhattan? I heard there were tons of rumors flying."

"Yeah, girl, everybody is walking around here on pins and needles. I just heard from one of my friends who works downtown that white folk are packing up early and getting out of the city as fast as they can, and it's not even lunchtime. There may have been a few minor incidents, but nothing like what's going on out there. Who knows what's going to happen next? I'm still surprised that there were no riots after those brothers were murdered in Howard Beach and Bensenhurst."

Soyini ran an independent school in Harlem for over fifteen years. It had grown tremendously. By in large it had blossomed due to the sheer strength of her persistence and determination.

When we were in the movement, and talked about what we wanted to be when we grew up, she always insisted quite emphatically, "I'm going back home to New York to open a school for our children. Since I've yet to find a brother who can accept me and my independent streak that's as wide as the Grand Canyon for more than a couple of months, I know I'm not going to have any, the children in my school are going to be my own children. And I'm going to give them everything that's lacking in education:

love, warmth, a stimulating environment and a knowledge of themselves."

After the movement, before returning to New York, she took a three-year detour by way of Tanzania and lived there, working for the Nyere government. I used to receive long letters from her that always opened with, "Habari Gani, my sister, I bring you greetings from the Motherland." When she returned from Africa she opened the Imani School.

Imani means faith in Swahili. The school has been a great blessing to that community. She started the school in her extra bedroom with four or five students. When her landlord threatened to evict her, she found a space in a community center on One hundred and twenty-fifth street and Lenox Avenue. By the late seventies, she had more than two hundred students, converted an old community center and bought and rehabbed two brownstones for her adolescent mothers center. She's expanded to include a program for teenage mothers, substance abusers, job training, and a high school.

"You know after all these years there's one thing that remains constant?"

"What's that, Soyo?"

"Well, it's like what my dear old Mama used to say, 'The more things change. The more they remain the same.'"

"Girl, you can say that again. I'm so glad that you called me right now. I was down. I don't know what to do with myself. I just talked to Daddy, which cheered me up a bit, but I just feel awful, like something's eating my insides up."

"Well, you're pretty sensitive, and you're probably picking up on all the emotions, rage, fear, anguish and Lord knows whatever else. And with John out there makes you even more sensitive to the negativity. Your fear might be aggravating the situation."

"You could be right. But I think there's more to it than that."

"What else could it be?"

"This verdict, the response to it, have caused me to question things I haven't thought about in a long time."

"Like whether or not the movement made any difference?"

"You always know what I'm thinking."

"Don't praise me too much. I was wondering the same thing, too."

"How can you ask those questions? You've given so much, and you still are. I sometimes wonder—"

"If you should be ashamed of all the success that you and John have?"

"Sort of..... Yeah, you're right."

"Girl, you oughta quit tripping. I'm sure you're feeling guilty knowing that you have acquired so much, while others have received so little. That's not even an issue in my mind. If I had more financial supporters like the two of you, I'd have Imani University up and running with thousands of students.

"There's nothing wrong with material wealth. It's not what you have but what you do with what you have. The problem with this society is that everything is distorted to focus on materialism and greed in a way that is unhealthy and unholy."

"Yeah, but—"

"Let me tell you what a wise brother once told me. 'You reflect the tradition of the elders where greatness is measured not by what you have, but by what you give.' You and John are two of the most giving people I know. And your wealth rests in your hearts."

"Soyo, thanks, I really needed to hear that."

"It's only the truth, my sister. Didn't you just say that you have a homeless person staying in your house? How many people can you name that would do something that giving?"

"You do have a point there. But it's not without its consequences. John isn't too pleased with what I've done—I didn't discuss it with him first."

"You know how the brother is. He's going to be alright. His feathers might be a little ruffled right now. But let me say this— the beautiful part about John is that although the brother's male pride might be bent out of shape a bit, I know had it been him, he would've done the same thing. Your biggest mistake was not letting him take part in your decision. But as upset as he pretends to be, he's not going to make you put her out of your home."

"I hope you're right. He's acting so strange about this situation. He's extremely uncomfortable around her. I thinks she reminds him of a part of his life that he doesn't want to remember."

"What part is that?"

"How poor his family was when he was growing up."

"You could be right but who knows for sure? Come on Ang, give the brother a break. Look at the situation from his perspective. You might feel the same way if he had brought an old homeless man home. I'm sure you'd have some concerns that John is experiencing right now."

Our conversation ended with a firm promise to visit each other before the end of the year.

I hadn't heard a peep out of Miss Zoli in several hours so I decided to check her room again. She was sitting on the chaise lounge, facing the window, looking out staring into space. "Miss Zoli are you alright?" She remained unaware of my presence, her body in one world, her mind in another. As I sat on the edge of the bed watching her, I could almost feel her mind returning.

She looked at me and said, "Whot cha doin down heah?"

"Oh, nothing, ma'am, I just wanted to see how you were doing."

Her face brightened in response. "Dat's so sweet of yah. I jist wonts tah thank yah foh takin me in. I jist doesn't knows whot woudah come of me down theah in dat terrible place."

"Miss Zoli, can I ask you something?"

"Yah can axe me anythin yah wonts tah."

"How did you get to the place where I found you?"

"I doesn't rightly remembas. All I knows is dat I been walkin aroune down dere foh de longess time, tryin tah figah out wheah in de worle I is."

"How long have you been walking around?"

"All de day lon, since I woke up 'neaf dem trees wid de funny leaves."

"What do you mean? Had you been in another part of Los Angeles?"

"Whot's Los Angelees?"

"That's the name of this city."

"Can yah tells me how far away is dis heah place from 'Sippi?"

"Ma'am, I don't know exactly, but we're a long way, about two thousand miles away from Mississippi."

"How many walkin days is dat?"

"A lotta days Miss Zoli. Maybe three or four months."

"Dat cain't be. I was jist in 'Sippi, day befoh yestahday. Are yah sho?"

"Yes, ma'am, I'm pretty sure."

"Well den, how did I gits out heah?"

"Ma'am, that's what I'm asking you. How did you get to California? And how long have you been out here?"

"Dat I donno. Let me tells yah whot happen de bes dat I can. Yah see, I been lookin foh my husban an my youngins foh almose two yeahs now evah since I ran away. I bin walkin up an down de roads of 'Sippi, 'Bama, an parts of Louise-see-ana. Dats de last thing I wonts tah do, befoh I leaves dis here worle.

"So de nite befoh last I jist laid my weary body down 'neaf dis big ole purdy weepin willoh tree. I thinks it ain't too far from Vidaylia. Den de next mawnin I gits up, an Lawd ah mercy own me, I is in a diff'rnt worle. I doesn't knows wheah I is. Dis heah town is a beautiful place. I see dese trees like I ain't nevah seen befoh an dese colored folk walkin aroune lookin real good, bettah dan any of us slaves. Chile, I thought de Lawd had done come callin foh me an taken me tah heaven. I was walkin aroune axin folk wheah I fine Saint Petah, an dey was lookin at me actin like I was a crazy ole woman or somethin. Dey wouldn't tell me nothin. I ain't knowin whot was wrong in dis heah place. Den all of a sudden, I seen all of dese colored people outside runnin an ah screamin, I thought dey was gettin ready tah hurt somebody.

"An a few of dem ran off intah de store, an ran dese yellah folk outside, den dey started beatin' on dem. I ain't know what tah do, I gots real scared. I thought I was in heaven, den I couldn't believes I was in hell. Somehow I made it 'cross street, an to de bess of my recollectin dats when yah foune me."

"I see. Miss Zoli, you do realize that this is nineteen-ninety-two, don't you?"

"Dat ain't right, it cain't be. I tells yah, I knows whot I is talkin 'bout, its eighteen sixtee-seben. It ain't in no nineteen an ninetee-two," she said, her voice choking with anguish.

"Okay, calm, down, ma'am. I don't mean to rile you up. If you believe that, then I'm not going to argue with you."

"It ain't whot I believes. Dat's de truf."

"Look, why don't you lie down for a while. We call talk a little more later."

"Ma'am, I has jist one thang tah axe of yah."

"Yes, ma'am, what's that?"

"Can yah hep me tah gits back tah 'Sippi, tah fine mah family?"

"Yes, ma'am. I promised yesterday I'd do that, and I will."

I finally began to wonder—had I bitten off more than I can chew? I don't understand why she insists that it's 1867. Her behavior was so strange, it was as though she was getting adjusted to being in a world that was so radically different from what her mind was accustomed to. I wondered what type of environment she came from.

I knew she needed to see a psychiatrist and a medical doctor to take care of her infected foot. I had never seen anything like that rash. It gives me the creeps. I don't really know what a psychiatrist would be able to do for her right now. But since she's not a danger to anyone but herself, I don't care how John feels about this, I'm going to keep her here with us until we locate her family.

I went upstairs and turned on the jacuzzi's water. After the tub was filled, I lit a scented candle and turned on some soft, relaxing music, slipped into the tub, and took a few deep breaths to relax my troubled spirit. Slowly, my tension and stress floated away. Moments later, losing all awareness of myself, I felt like a little drop in the ocean, surrounded by peace.

Suddenly the memory of my first meeting with Dr. King flooded my mind. It was August 1957. I was eleven or twelve years old. Dr. King was well on his way to becoming the most famous colored preacher in the country. He was on a triumphant speaking tour.

"Angela Mary Lucile Johnson, you better hurry up and get down these stairs! I told you last night we had to leave for church an hour early, so we can get a good seat for us to see Dr. King."

Momma kept saying "I'm gonna make sure my daughter gets a chance to see him. He's the most famous man to ever enter our church, and we'll be there, sitting in a good seat."

We got up at five that morning and were sitting in our regular pew at seven o'clock. Momma and I wore yellow calico dresses with stiff slips, the kind that scratches your thighs and made your dress resemble a colorful lamp shade. Momma tied my plaited hair with yellow ribbons, and plastered enough Dixie Peach hair pomade on my hair that always made it and my face shine as well.

On the way to church, momma kept saying, "I'm gonna make sure my daughter shakes this great man's hand. This is important, this is history. One day you will tell your children and grandchildren about this."

It was so hot that day, it felt like my scalp was frying beneath the hot sunlight that filtered in through the yellow and purple stained glass windows. Streams of melted Dixie Peach trickled down my forehead and neck. Throughout the service, I constantly wiped the grease off my neck, ears and forehead, with a pink-laced handkerchief momma gave me.

Even my Aunt Alice came to church for the first time in years with my Uncle Pete to see Dr. King. They sat a couple of rows behind us. I remember turning and seeing her fanning her face beneath her floppy white hat with a gaudy clump of flowers, desperately trying to cool herself in the face of the blazing heat.

As it turned out, I was the only one to shake Dr. King's hand. Daddy wasn't too excited about standing in the long line, but momma and I stood waiting for more than a half hour. When it was finally our turn, she was so excited and busy talking to him while making sure that I shook his hand, until she forgot to do it herself.

He shook my hand, and gave a big wide grin, saying, "Young lady, I hope you know all the work that we do and plan to do is for you."

"Thank you, sir," I replied barely louder than a whisper as my mother nudged me.

Suddenly my mind shifted to the Lorraine Hotel in Memphis. I could see him preparing to walk out of his room. His face was strained and tired as he looked around, then stepped outside. A few people were on the balcony, bending over to talk to the people in the parking lot. Suddenly a loud boom raced through the air. A bullet collided with the side of his face which erupted like a volcano. He lay there, sprawled on the floor. One side of his face was normal, while the other was an explosion of ruptured flesh and pieces of bone, gushing out in a river of blood.

My mind drifted away from Memphis and map of the United States slowly took shape. I saw fires sweeping across the country, consuming the major cities. Then I began to see faces of old people in torn, raggedy clothing. They looked at me as if to ask why? What are you doing? What's going on? Slowly their faces melted into a dark void. Finally, I returned to a place of peace again, floating in silence.

When I got out of the tub and returned to the kitchen, I wondered about the meaning of all that I had seen. I looked at the clock. It was two-twenty five. I jumped when the phone rang, thinking it might be John. On the other end was Jay, one of our neighbors.

A few moments later, I heard John's heavy footsteps entering the kitchen. Even though I was angry with his sudden disappearance, I was relieved to know that he was back home, safe and sound.

eight

When I opened my eyes, the room was pitch black. I lay there for a minute, trying to get my bearings straight. I fumbled around trying to turn on the lamp on the nightstand, and noticed that the alarm clock next to it was out. It took me a few seconds to realize that our power was gone. Shuffling through my nightstand's drawer I found my trusty flashlight, stumbled down two flights of stairs, to the family room. Angie and the kids were quietly sitting in the middle of our black leather couch. My wife's favorite thick white candles were burning on our coffee table, filling the room with an eerie, incandescent light.

"Why didn't you wake me up?"

"Mom wouldn't let us. She said you needed your sleep," replied my son.

"How many hours have the lights been out?"

With her voice still carrying a trace of this morning's sarcasm, Angela replied, "A couple."

"Why are you all sitting around here in the dark like you're at a seance or something?"

"Because it's so peaceful down here, daddy. Why don't you come over and sit with us? We've never done this before. This is fun."

"So you think having no electricity is fun?"

"Daddy, Mommie said it could be worse," Ashley replied. "We could be homeless."

"John, the phones are out, too. Fortunately for the time being your cellular phone is still working."

"Let me go and turn on the generator, so we can get some light in this place." Shortly after we moved in, I bought a generator, in the event of a natural disaster. It never occurred to me that the first time I'd need to use it would be during a riot.

"It doesn't work, we tried to turn it on," Angela said with a smirk.

"Maybe I can fix it."

"Good luck."

"Can I help, dad?"

"Sure you can."

Doug's words of wisdom popped into my thoughts, "You don't know how lucky you are to have a wife that cares."

It was considerate of her to let me sleep instead of waking me up when the lights went out. But I'm sure she was still mad at me for my little excursion down into South Central. And knowing Angie, she isn't about to let me forget that anytime soon. James and I tried to get that damn thing started for over an hour with no luck at all. The only thing I accomplished was to sweat a lot. When we walked back into the family room, Angela and Ashley were still sitting in silence.

"No luck? Don't say I didn't warn you," Angela smiled sarcastically.

I turned to her and said as sincerely as I could, "I'd like to thank my beautiful and supportive wife for that big vote of confidence."

The kids fell into laughter, while she rolled her eyes at me. She turned to them, with the same expression and froze their laughter into silence.

"Okay kids, it's almost ten o'clock time for bed."

"But mom, we don't have to go to school tomorrow. Why can't we stay up?"

"Son, go on and do what your mother says."

"Daddy, can I tell you what Miss Zoli did for me before we go?"

"Alright Ash, as long as you don't stretch it out too long. I know storytelling is your best stalling technique."

Her eyes were gleaming against the darkness of the room. "Daddy, after you left this morning, my chest started hurting really bad. Mommie said it was hurting because of all the smoke and soot that was in the air. Then I started wheezing real bad. It was scary, I could barely breathe. Even the inhaler didn't help. So Mommie said she was going to take me to the hospital.

"Then Miss Zoli came upstairs. She saw how hard it was for me to breathe, and she told Mommie to get some castor oil. Daddy, when Miss Zoli rubbed that oil on me, in just a couple of minutes, I could breathe just like normal. She stopped my asthma attack."

"That's a very interesting coincidence, baby. Now you and your brother get on upstairs."

"But, daddy, don't you think it was a miracle that mommie didn't have to take me to the hospital?"

"I don't think so baby. I think it was a coincidence, and I'm glad you're feeling better. But I want you to go to bed."

"But Daddy—"

"No buts. I want you to give me a hug and go to bed." She gave me a half-hearted hug, and walked reluctantly upstairs, as if she was on her way to the gallows instead of to her room. James trailed behind her.

"What's she talking about?"

"It happened exactly the way she described it—Miss Zoli healed her asthmatic attack."

"So now I'm supposed to believe that this crazy homeless woman can cure asthma? Come on Angie, give me a break! I'm glad my baby girl is feeling much better, but that one little incident doesn't change my mind. Miss Zoli is crazier than a bed bug, and doesn't need to be in my house."

"Shh, she could walk out of her room at any moment and hear you."

"So what if she does? This is my house. She needs to know exactly how I feel."

I didn't feel right about the way we were treating each other because we argued so rarely.

"John, it looks like the only thing we've been doing for the last two days is arguing. We're both stressed out. So can we hold off on talking anymore about Miss Zoli and your voyage down into South Central until the morning? I'm not up to arguing with you anymore tonight."

"You're right. This can wait until the morning. Let's go to bed."

A few minutes later, I rolled over in our bed and said to my wife, "Baby, I understand your good intentions, I really do. But there is something about this woman, I can't put my finger on it. She's too close."

"Like I told you, I don't want to argue. Let me just say this and I'm through with the subject for the time being—but I feel the exact opposite. She wouldn't hurt a fly, and for me, there is something very special about her that makes me want to keep her close. I can not and will not send her away until we locate her family."

I just couldn't figure out why we saw this woman so differently. Normally we agree on the important things, but this time we didn't, and I didn't know why we're on opposite sides in this situation.

"Okay you're right. We can talk about it in the morning." I leaned over and kissed her on the cheek, and fell into another deep sleep. I woke up a couple of times during the night. Angie was sleeping peacefully. Since the electricity was off, and our alarm system was out, I got up and checked on the kids and our houseguest. Everyone was sleeping quietly.

The next morning when I woke up, Angie was sitting up in the bed carefully studying me.

"Preparing for your next strategy?"

"No."

"Well then what's going on?"

"I had these awful dreams last night that everything on Crenshaw and King Boulevard was burned down. It was like a no man's land. The streets were filled with these lost spirits roaming through the burning buildings and all of the rubble left behind."

"I hate to tell you this, but from what I saw yesterday, sounds like your dream is pretty accurate. Its terrible down there. The place looks like its in the middle of a war zone."

"Is it really that bad?"

"I wish I could tell you that it wasn't, but it is."

"You aren't going down there today are you?"

"Angela, don't start. Can't we wait at least until after breakfast to discuss this?"

"You said last night that you wanted to talk this morning."

"But that was about your houseguest. Are we getting Miss Zoli to the hospital today?"

"No, I don't want to go down there."

"I'll take her on my way to the office."

"No, I can't let you do that." She grabbed my hand, squeezing it, trying to plead her point. "We can't abandon her like that, drop her off at the hospital like she's at the lost and found."

"I don't feel safe or comfortable with her here in my house. I don't like it one bit. It's not right for her or safe for us."

"She's okay, I know that in my heart. Look at how she helped Ash."

"That was just a fluke, a coincidence. You should know better than that, instead of letting Ash think that this woman healed her."

"That's exactly what happened."

"Now you sound like those folks talking about those televangelists. I thought you knew better than that."

"And you know what? I am grateful that she was here to do that. I was so relieved that she was here to help out, since I really didn't want to drive down there through all of that chaos. But since you were out gallivanting around with your buddy Doug, I had no other choice."

"You're acting like I left knowing that my baby girl was going to get sick. You know better than that. I left because I had to."

For several moments, she didn't say a word. She just sat there staring at me again.

"John, you know what I think?"

"No, what do you think?"

"I think the reason she makes you so uncomfortable is that she reminds you of when you were poor."

"Angela, please. Give me a break. You're pulling at straws. If I had a problem with being around poor people, I most certainly wouldn't have my business in South Central. If anything is a bit strange, it's your behavior.

"Can you explain why you want to keep her close to you? In my humble opinion, I think she reminds you of what you don't want to be in your future, and your rescuing her is an attempt to get brownie points. You're very afraid of growing old all alone."

"John, that's a low blow. How could you say such a thing?"

"You know it's the truth. How many times have you told me that you're afraid you'll be sent to a nursing home like your Aunt Bertha was by her mean and uncaring children? You remember your dear cousins, the ones that she sacrificed and cared for when her husband left her for another woman."

"You're wrong!" she yelled.

"If I'm wrong, then why are you so upset? I don't know why it's so hard for you to admit the truth, when it's slapping you in the face."

She paused again falling into a brief, deep thought. "I know what you're doing. This is your typical way of getting out of discussing something difficult. You divert, or as the saying goes, 'the best defense is a good offense.'"

I got up, threw on my bathrobe and walked through the hallway. The electricity was still off. I went back down into the generator room, trying to get the thing to work, I must've messed around with that thing for two hours or more. It sputtered and churned from time to time, threatening to start, but refusing to comply with my needs.

Looking outside, I could see the sky was filled with even more smoke than the day before. A huge black cloud covered the entire sky over Los Angeles. Only a few rays of sunlight penetrated through the dark blanket of smoke. It looked like it was twilight. There must've been hundreds of fires still burning out of control.

Again, I felt the weight of the world resting on my shoulders. It was worse than I ever imagined. I knew by now that many of my friends' businesses had been destroyed. I didn't want to call them to find out how they were doing. I wondered how many of Angie's clients had lost their homes.

Not wanting to be in the dark about what was going on in the city, I went into the garage and turned on my car radio. On KABC, a reporter stated that in less than thirty-six hours more than three thousand fires had been set. On a good day, the fire department couldn't manage a fraction of that number. They called in backup from the surrounding areas, but that still wasn't enough to make a dent on what was happening in the streets. To add insult to injury, the extremely overworked firefighters were getting shot at. A few had already been wounded, and there were unconfirmed reports that one had been killed. I hoped my employees made it safely through the night.

The National Guard hadn't done anything to stop the rioting. Yesterday, I heard Governor Wilson might ask the president to deploy the Army or the Marines.

At breakfast, my family's mood seemed to reflect the dark clouds of smoke hovering over the city. Everyone seemed to be a little on edge. Since we had no electricity, Angela did the best she could with preparing breakfast. She concocted a fruit salad, orange juice, granola and wheat bread with strawberry jam. It wasn't what we normally ate, but it was enough to fill us up for the time being.

James asked, "Dad, do we have to watch it today? I had dreams about our house catching on fire last night."

"No, son, you can't today. Remember we don't have any electricity. But you still have to do your paper."

"Daddy, he asked you that because his TV works. It runs on batteries."

"Big mouth, traitor," snapped James.

"Son, watch your mouth. I've told you about calling your sister names. I better not hear that again. Understand?"

"Yes, sir."

"Daddy, my chest is hurting. I can hardly breathe," whined Ashley.

"Go on upstairs and get your inhaler Ash, you know what to do," interjected my wife.

"Um-hmm. Mommie, it doesn't hurt like it did yesterday. It hurts because I'm real scared. I'm scared somebody's going to hurt you. Daddy, please don't go down there today," she pleaded, wrapping her arms tightly around my neck.

My little girl's concern was touching. "Baby, that is really sweet of you. But you don't have to be worried about me. Your old man can take care of himself. Don't you worry your pretty little head." I could hear my wife's sigh of disgust leap across the table at me.

"Dad, can I go?" asked James. "I still want to take in some action."

"James, maybe I can't keep your father from playing Russian Roulette with his life, but I can certainly stop you. You can go only under one condition."

"Oh yeah, what's that, mom?" he asked with a big grin.

"You can go over my dead body." And on that note, we quietly finished eating breakfast.

After finishing breakfast, the kids left us alone. "Why are you planning on going back to this office today?" Angela asked.

"I need to check on everybody. See if they need anything."

"On who? What are you talking about?"

"Some of the staff took it upon themselves to guard the building round the clock. I need to check on them, see if they need anything. Since they're risking their lives, that's the least I can do for them."

"Oh John, that's so thoughtful of them. Why didn't you tell me?"

"Because you were mad at me yesterday, you didn't want to hear anything I had to say."

"Honey, you know I'm worried about you, and you don't need to take any unnecessary risks, like going down there. Especially since there are people there looking out for your interests."

"Baby, you don't understand, do you? If my staff can risk their lives for me, how do you think they would feel if I didn't show up? What would they think about my commitment to them?"

"Well, you do have a point there. I just don't want to see you getting hurt, that's all."

"I'll be careful. You know I don't take any unnecessary risks.

On my way out the door, she rushed from the kitchen to the front door and said, "Honey, I don't want you to think I'm a nag. I just worry about you. You and Doug be careful and hurry home."

"I promise, I will."

I tried calling Doug on my cellular phone, but didn't get an answer. So I hopped into our Volvo and drove up the hill. I found him sitting by the pool eating breakfast. "If there ever was a way to do a riot, you do it quite well."

"Looks can be deceiving, my brother. Looks like you are ready to make your daily trek down into the 'hood." Doug said peering up at me. He seemed so calm and relaxed sitting there.

"Man, I don't get it. What is it with you? Why are you so calm? You're acting like you're on vacation instead of living through a riot. You stand to lose more than I've ever had. What gives?"

"Sooner or later you're going to get it through your thick skull that there's more to life than these material possessions that you seem to cherish. And what I have doesn't worry me. Whatever goes up in smoke is gone, and my worrying about it won't stop it from happening or bring it back."

"Okay, if you say so. Did you talk to Kathy Lee last night?"

"Yes, I did. As a matter of fact the phone was ringing when I walked in the house yesterday, after dropping you off. She had called several times while we were out and she wanted to know where I had been."

"Did you tell her what we did yesterday?"

"Hell, no! I'm not that crazy. I told her that we were working on the van."

"You know when she gets back her good buddy is going to tell her the truth."

"I know. I'll cross that bridge when she's here. I don't want her out there in Denver worrying about me in her condition. Man, she worries about everything.

"What did Angie have to say when you got home?"

"Not much of anything. She was very pissed, and I wasn't up to getting into another argument with her. So we didn't really talk until this morning. And I just explained to her that I have to do what I have to do.

"Look man, you were good to go yesterday. Are you ready for some more today?"

"To keep you from doing something stupid? I guess so," he replied.

"Fine, after we look in on mine, think we should go check out some of your businesses, especially those in the Mid-Wilshire district."

"You know that's not necessary."

"If you say so."

We hopped in the Volvo and headed down the hill. "I heard on the radio that disturbances have broke out all across the country, San Francisco, New York, Atlanta, Las Vegas," I said.

"Yeah, it's bad. But it still doesn't make any sense to me. I heard a rapper on television last night saying that he's happy, very happy that 'the people spoke.' Well, I have news for the brother. This is like watching your mother getting beat up, nearly half to death and a son saying, 'Now my mother knows what so and so was thinking.'"

When we reached the bottom of the hill I felt my body grow tense again. I felt even more disgusted today than I did the day before. As we moved slowly down the street, instead of the raging fires, today most of Crenshaw Boulevard and King were charred remnants of war. Block after block, businesses were gone. It was unreal. Where were all of the familiar sites in my community? Gone, all gone. I felt disgusted, sick to my stomach. My throat was choked up, not from smoke but strangled by all that I saw. It really looked like a bomb had been dropped, and reminded me of footage I've seen showing war zones. Twisted wreckage stood everywhere. The place looked like a ghost town.

"Man, this is worse than yesterday," I said shaking my head.

"Yeah, man, this is too much."

"How can we ever hope to recover? This is the last thing this community needs. Thousands of jobs have gone up in smoke in less than forty-eight hours. It just doesn't make any sense. Why is this going on? Even during our darkest moments in the movement, I never felt this hopeless."

"That, my brother, I wish I knew. You know, I look at all that's going on down here, and it just doesn't make any sense to me. Truth be told, my father and his generation had a lot more to deal with than us. They knew who they were, beyond the way that white folk treated them, and they didn't expect a lot from this society.

"It seems like all that we have put up with over the last four hundred years is finally coming to a head. But I'm not surprised. Look at what's going on all over the world. There's so much warfare and ethnic strife in every corner. People are killing and destroying each other for all sorts of stupid reasons."

"Doug, I hate to admit it, but man, you're probably right."

"I get no pleasure out of talking like this. But I think we should be realistic."

For the rest of the ride we didn't talk too much. I guess both of us escaped into our own private worlds.

Along the way, we passed several barricades set up by the National Guard. When we finally reached my building, everything appeared to be intact. There were several more familiar faces guarding the building today. At least half of my thirty employees were present.

"Mr. Stewart, I mean no disrespect, but yesterday we told you you didn't have to come down here and we meant that."

"But Junebug, I have to come, just to let you know how much I appreciate what you're doing for me."

"How's it going? Any problems?"

"No, not really. The police came by last night and tried to make us leave. But we told them we were staying. We told them straight up the only way we would leave would be for them to arrest us. And since they had no cause, not to say that fact ever stopped the LAPD from arresting anyone, they decided to leave us alone."

"I hope you don't mind, but we took turns sleeping on the couch in your office."

"Are you kidding? It's no problem. Man, I don't mind at all. Can I get you anything?"

"No, we're fine. You just go on home and we'll take care of the situation down here."

"You don't know how much this means to me, risking your lives to protect my business."

"You don't know how much you mean to us."

Back in the car, I headed north up Vermont Avenue toward Wilshire Boulevard where Doug had a few businesses. The police and National Guard hard cordoned off several sections of the street. There were too many fires to count that were burning out of control. As we got closer there were people everywhere in the streets.

"How's your houseguest?"

"She's still there."

"You don't seem to be as upset today."

"Looks are deceiving my brother. I still don't want her in my house. But I know I can't get her out, not right now anyway without a lot of commotion. I've never seen my wife like this before. She's so wrapped up into this old, homeless woman that she never laid eyes on before. For the life of me, I can't figure out why. If I didn't know better I'd swear she was one of her long lost relatives."

"Man, I still think Angie is doing the right thing."

"I do too, I just don't want her to do it in my house. You know I've always supported her work."

"John, she's doing this from her heart. Just like people who have risked their lives over the last couple of days to save those in distress. Last night, I saw the four young people that rescued that truck driver and saved his life. Two of them were sitting at home and watching his beating live on television, and decided to go out into that crazy crowd and save him.

"Then they showed a young woman from Belize who saved another young man's life. He was on his way home from work, in his own neighborhood, and a crowd mistook him for being white, he was just another light-skinned brother. While they were beating him, she jumped onto his jeep, and got him out of there. She could've been killed herself.

"Angie is a hero in her own right, and you need to accept that."

"Gimme a break. I don't care what you say, I still don't like that woman in my house. She gives me the creeps. And nothing you can say will make me change my mind."

nine

When I got home Friday afternoon, I tried for several hours to fix the generator. I was determined to get the damn thing working. Finally around seven thirty I got it started. Ashley rushing into the room, screaming "Daddy you did it! You fixed it. The lights in my room came on."

James and my wife rushed in a few seconds later.

"Dad, I told you I wanted to help."

"I know you did son, and I apologize for not asking you."

"Honey, I don't know what to say."

"You could eat your 'good luck' words from last night, Miss 'Ye of little faith 1992.'"

The kids chuckled and Angie pecked me on the cheek with embarrassment smeared across her face.

"Kids, even though it's back on, we have to keep the lights, radios and TVs off!"

Around four in the morning the helicopters overhead rattled me out of my sleep. Something made me get out of bed and go downstairs and check on Miss Zoli. Yesterday, she had stayed out of my way all day long. I found her in the family room feeling her way around the curtains that cover the glass wall that leads to the patio. The room was pitch black. The heavy blue draperies blocked out any light from the outside, not that there was a lot that could get in on a night like this anyway. She could hurt herself. That's why she needed to be in a hospital, and not in my house.

She was mumbling, "I wonts tah gits home. I wonts tah fine mah chilrens."

"Miss Zoli is something wrong?" No response. I flashed the flashlight across her face, she didn't miss a beat. She kept moving slowly along the curtains, feeling her way around like a blind person, searching for a doorway or a way out.

I touched her wrinkled, leathery hand. She pulled away from me as if it she'd been burned by a hot iron. I touched her shoulder. She struggled away dragging her heavy foot. Angela told me she can't bear weight on it because it's severely infected.

Looking at her helplessness, I felt kind of sorry for her. I still didn't like having her here. Finally after several minutes her mind returned to her body.

She looked at me and said firmly, "I wonts tah go home. Can yah hep me gits outta heah?"

"Miss Zoli, you don't have a home. Where would you go?"

"I wonts tah gits back tah 'Sippi. I ain't got no place wheah I can call home. Mah home is wheah evah my chilrens is. As long as I knows dey ain't too far away. Can yah hep me please, suh?"

"Yes, ma'am. I'll do whatever I can to help you."

"Thank yah, suh. De Lawd is gonna bless yah in a mighty fine way. I knows day he is."

"It's no problem at all, ma'am. But it's gonna take a while. A few days at least. We have to wait for things to return to normal."

"Whot is yah talkin bout?"

"There is a riot going on and we can't help you until it stops."

She looked at me then she took a deep look into my eyes. When she did that she gave me the creeps. "I knows what yah feelin."

"What's that?" I replied trying to hide the fact that she had disarmed me.

"I knows dat yah wants me tah leave."

"No, ma'am, that's not true."

"Suh yah ain't 'pose tah lie like dat. I can sees it in yoh eyes, an I can feels yah in mah spirit. Me bein heah bring out a troublin spirit. I can sees it all aroune yah. I is sorry. Dats why I knows I gots tah git on mah way."

For the first time since she's been in my house, I really felt guilty, like I did when my mother caught me doing something I knew I had no business doing. I felt like a heartless heel that didn't have any home training, who wanted to put this helpless old woman out onto the streets.

"Miss Zoli. Don't worry. Everything is going to be alright. Come on, let me help you lie down and get some sleep."

"Yah knows I used tah gits up real early in de mawnin, an look up at de stars, befoh de light of de sun would block dem out of de sky. I did dat ev'ry night an ev'ry mawnin, since I can remembas, since dey took my first youngin away from me."

I didn't know what to say. She looked so sincere, as if she was experiencing something that really happened. I'd never seen anyone as confused as she was.

"Yah ain't believin me is yah?"

"Ma'am, what I think really isn't important. You need help."

"Yoh right. I needs some hep tah gits back tah 'Sippi."

"No, I didn't mean that. You need to see a doctor."

"Foh what? I ain't nevah seen no doctah befoh."

"Miss Zoli, your mind is not well. I know I shouldn't be talking like this to you but you need to hear the truth."

"What yah tryin tah say? You be thinkin dat I is crazy. Well let me tells yah somethang. Momma Zoli ain't no crazy woman. I knows 'zactly what I be talkin bout, an I is tellin de truf!"

"Alright, alright. Ma'am, I didn't mean to rile you up. Why don't you calm down and let me help you get back into the bed."

"If yah needs tah knows one thang 'bout Momma Zoli, it's dat she ain't be tellin no lies."

"Yes, ma'am, I understand."

"Yah jist bein nice. Yah don't believes me."

"Miss Zoli, I just want you to calm down."

She didn't hear a word I said. In the twinkling of an eye, she was gone again. I took her withered, leathery hand and led her back to her room. As I helped ease her down on the bed, her nightgown slipped from her shoulder and I saw these awful, thick, nauseating scars covering her shoulder. I wondered what caused these raised strips of flesh, but didn't have the heart to listen to another distorted answer. By the time I got her back in the bed, I decided to lay on the couch and wait for sunrise to come.

After breakfast, I heard that President Bush had ordered in troops on Friday night. The marines were expected to roll in from Camp Pendleton sometime today. Sooner or later order was going to be restored in this city.

I don't relish the thought of sitting around the house all day doing nothing.

"What are you doing today, Daddy?"

"I plan to go down to check on my office this afternoon. Why do you want to know?"

"We want to go to the cleanup. I heard on James' TV that people were going to go down today and help clean up the stores and buildings that have been burned out. Can we go? I want to help."

"I don't know if that's such a good idea. It could be dangerous down there. This city hasn't calmed down yet," Angela replied.

"Angela things have quieted down considerably. The troops from Pendleton should rolling through the streets any minute. I think it's a great idea and I'm proud of our children for making the suggestion. After all, they're only following our example, especially yours, bringing Miss Zoli home the way you did.

"Why don't you go too?"

"Someone needs to stay here with Miss Zoli."

"What about Ashley's asthma? It could flare up again, around all of that soot and debris."

"Daddy, I promise, I'll be fine. Please let me go. I've been breathing okay ever since Miss Zoli fixed me."

"Let me think about it for a few minutes. I'll check and see if Doug wants to go."

"Can I speak to you for a minute in the dining room?" Angela asked.

We stepped into the doorway between our kitchen and the dining room, a good little distance out of our children's listening ears.

"You're not serious are you?" she asked sternly.

"Why not? It might be a good experience for them."

"But John, I think its still very dangerous out there."

"You're the one always talking about practicing what we have been preaching for years. Don't you think this would be an excellent opportunity for them? Aside from that, they've probably got cabin fever, they haven't left the neighborhood since Wednesday."

"I don't know if it's a good idea. I don't want them to get hurt."

"Angie, we need to be consistent. You know I'll never intentionally place our children in harm's way.

"Alright, alright. Maybe I'm just being overprotective, but after all that's happened, who wouldn't be?"

"Wait one minute, Mrs. Stewart," I said grabbing her wrist as she turned to walk away from me. "I know what's really going on here, you're afraid to see what's going on down there. You don't want to face all that's happened."

"What on earth are you talking about?" she replied coyly.

"You don't want to face it. You are afraid to go down there."

"John, don't be silly. No, I'm not," she said with an edge of anxiety lacing her voice.

"Okay, well you should come along, too."

"I can't leave Miss Zoli alone, there's no telling what she might do to herself."

"You can bring her, too."

"Get serious."

"I am."

"You and I both know that she's in no condition to leave this house."

"I'm not going to get into the fact that you and I finally agree on something about her. For the time being I'll leave it alone.

"And one more thing. Sooner or later you're going to have to face what has gone on down there. And the sooner you do it the better."

"John, you're wrong. I'm not afraid."

"If you say so. But remember, I know you."

"Okay, kids you can go. Just be careful." I knew that she knew I was right. That's why she changed her mind and agreed with me so quickly.

The kids and I threw on some old raggedy clothes. We hopped in the Volvo and picked Doug up.

"Uncle Doug, have you ever lived through a riot before?" Ashley asked.

"Well, sort of."

"What do you mean sort of?"

"When I was just a baby in Oklahoma, there was a riot, where the Black folk, we were colored back then, were attacked. There was a very prosperous business section, and for a flimsy reason, like a man allegedly touching a white woman's dress, the Black part of town was destroyed. The businesses were burned down after bombs were dropped from airplanes. That was the only time that bombs have been dropped on these United States. It was terrible. Some people lost everything, all of their worldly possessions. A lot of them were forced to live in tents for years. My father moved us to Texas and never went back. I don't remember, but they talked about it so much, it was as if they transferred their memories into me."

"Why did they bomb the people?"

"Because they didn't want the Black folk to have anything."

"Did any of the people go to jail?"

"No."

"Why not?"

"Because that's just how evil some people can be."

"But there's one thing you need to understand, this country and most of the world has a history of resorting to violence to solve a number of problems, and race is just one of them. There have always been wars. And it doesn't look like that fact is going to change anytime soon. Even though this riot is bad, it is not the worst in terms of the loss of human life. In the 1860s, after the war was started, more than a thousand people were killed in a riot in New York City. The Yankees didn't want to be drafted into the army to fight against the Confederacy."

"That's when Momma Zoli said she came from. She said the last thing that she can remember is that it was eighteen hundred and sixty-seven, and that she was somewhere in Mississippi looking for her family."

"Listen, baby, what she's telling you isn't true. I'm not calling her a liar. You've gotta understand that she's extremely confused, and the woman has a mental problem. You can't believe what she's saying. She lives in a fantasy world."

"You don't believe her, daddy?"

"No, not for one minute. What's she's talking about is not possible."

"Are you sure?"

"Trust me, kids, I know what I'm talking about."

"But maybe isn't there just one in a million chance, a little itty bitty possibility?"

"Ash, why are you being such a big baby? Dad already told you 'no', but you can't take no for an answer cause you want to believe her."

"Daddy, you aren't going to make her leave our house are you?"

"Why do you ask me that?"

"I was just wondering. You don't act like you like her, and she seems to be scared of you."

"No, I'm not going to do that."

"Are your sure? Please don't make her be homeless again. She seems so sad and all she wants to do is to find her children."

"Did your mother put you up to this?"

"No, we just like her. Go on and tell him what you said James."

"Dad, all I said was that it was kinda nice having her around. Like we had a grandmother living with us."

Doug just gave me, the I-know-you're-losing-this-battle-look.

When we reached the bottom of the hill, the children abruptly stopped talking, stunned by the onslaught of destruction that stood before them.

"I can't believe it. Everything is gone. This looks like somebody dropped a bomb down here," said James.

A distressing silence filled the car. Through the rear view mirror I could see Ashley sitting behind me, shaking her head. James' face seemed to be stuck to the window. I felt sorry for them. They weren't prepared and I didn't know what to say to them to help them to understand the destruction of our community that was still perplexing to me.

Driving down Crenshaw Boulevard, there were people everywhere. Some were obvious store owners sifting through the rubble, while others appeared to be scavengers looking for whatever was left in the burned out and looted remains.

"Daddy, why did they burn down everything?"

"I wish I could tell you I knew all of the reasons. I guess the verdict was like the straw that broke the camel's back. People were very angry and frustrated, and expected for justice to happen. When it didn't, they reacted."

"How soon will the stores open up again?"

"Ashley, if it ever happens it's gonna be a long time, maybe years before our community is back to normal."

"Daddy, why if white and Hispanic people are burning down buildings too, why do they only show mostly us doing it on TV?"

"Because the unspoken number one 'Racist Rule of Order' is to blame every problem on Black people. We are the most convenient scapegoats in town."

"What do you mean?"

"Well, for example, you guys are well aware of the fact that there is a recession going on, and that a lot of people are out of work. First of all, some people would like for us to think that the problem is due to lazy Black people, and the affirmative action movement has hurt white men. I wonder what they would do if they ever turned Black?"

"Why is it like this? Dad, do you think it will ever change?"

"I used to be very hopeful, but now I don't know anymore. Maybe in your lifetime it will; I don't expect it to happen in mine."

"What do you think, Uncle Doug?"

"Oh, I think your dad is right."

"Dad, what's going to happen next?"

"It's hard to say, son. We'll have to wait and see."

I decided to take the kids to the burned out area near my office. There were a lot of people out there. I figured that would give them a chance to see close up how blessed we were. On the way, we saw the troops rolling into the city. A squadron was set up only a couple of blocks away from my building, which made me feel a lot more confident that Stewart Computers was going to weather the rest of this storm in one piece.

A couple of blocks away from my office, I saw Mr. Rogers slowly sifting through the rubble of his destroyed hardware store. I'd known him for years. He was planning to retire this summer and turn the store over to his son and move to Guadalajara, Mexico, with his wife. I pulled over to the front of his store and got out of the car.

Ashley asked, "Where are you going, daddy?"

"I need to speak to Mr. Rogers for a minute. I'll be right back."

Sifting through the wreckage of his once thriving business, he wasn't aware of my presence as I approached him. "Mr. Rogers, I'm so sorry this happened. Is there anything I can do to help you?"

I don't think he heard me, he continued to mumble to himself, "This just doesn't make any sense. It ain't right." When I touched his shoulder, he turned to me with a dazed expression.

"What you doin heah, John?"

"Is there anything I can do to help you?"

"No, it's too late. Everything's all gone. I shoulda sold it last year when I had the chance. But I didn't want to do that. I had to stay here one more year before I turned it over to my son. Now everything is gone."

"Your insurance policy can replace all of this."

"Nope, that ain't gonna happen, 'cause I don't have no insurance. I did for a long time, but the last few years have been pretty lean, and I cut corners."

"I know you and Bobby can rebuild this business. If anybody can do that on this street, I know it's you."

"That's an easy thing for you to say. You're a young man. I done seen the best years of my life a long time ago. Georgia wants us to get out of this city and move back to Louisiana. But I don't have enough money in the bank to do that now. I don't know how we're going to live off my social security check and the little savings I done stashed away."

"Mr. Rogers, if there's anything I can to do help, just let me know."

I got back in the car, shaking my head. I don't know what I would do if the same thing had happened to me. As I turned on the car, Ashley reached from the back seat and grabbed my shoulder.

"Daddy, he looks so sad. Why don't we stay and help him?"

"Ash, I don't know if that's such a good idea. I think he needs to be alone—"

Before I could finish my sentence, Ashley bolted out of the car and ran over to Mr. Rogers. She exchanged a few words with him, and she ran back to my window with a big wide grin and said, "Daddy, he said it's okay for us to help him clean up his store."

I looked at Doug. He shrugged his shoulders and said, "This must be the place."

We unloaded the car with all of the equipment I had assembled, shovels, brooms, plastic bags and started cleaning. About an hour or so later, two car loads of people from Santa Barbara joined us.

Mr. Rogers wandered around for a couple of hours through the debris, trying to find something to salvage. I finally sent him home shortly after noon. I felt sorry for him. The loss had wiped him out and more than anything else, trying to find something salvageable, he was getting in the way of the cleanup. He didn't want to go at first, but I insisted, and he finally relented.

We worked for hours without stopping. Only a few things were salvaged from his entire inventory. The street was filled with clean up crews and a full assortment of volunteers from all walks of life. Trucks came by to pick up the debris, and some people came by distributing sandwiches and lemonade to the volunteers.

I'd never seen my kids work so hard. They really got into it. I had to make them stop and take a break.

Toward the end of the day, Doug came over to my section and said, "Man, you should be proud of your kids. Look at them, they are working their little butts off."

"Yes, they are. And I'm very proud of both of them."

It was close to four o'clock when we finally finished cleaning up. All of us were pretty tired from a hard day's work.

"Dad, my muscles aching all over."

"Hard work is good for you, son. You better be glad you didn't have to grow up on a farm. You'd be doing more of this each and every day. But you'll be fine. When we get home, you need to soak in the tub. And as young as you are, you'll be good as new."

On the way home, I realized I needed to get some gas. The lines were unbelievably long in South Central at the stations that hadn't been torched, five and six rows deep, a half a mile to a mile long.

I headed for Culver City to fill up and pick up a few groceries I know we needed.

"Uncle Doug, can I ask you something?"

"Sure son, what is it?"

"What do you think about what Rodney King said yesterday?"

"I didn't hear, what did he say?"

"He said that the rioting wasn't right, and 'Can't we all get along?'"

"I don't know what to say about that James. I guess in light of the situation, what else could he say?"

He turned to me and asked, "What do you think Dad?"

I saw a report on him Wednesday night. He'd been in hiding, and was very depressed about the verdict. He locked himself in his room, his friends and advisors were concerned that he might harm himself. The whole incident had disrupted his life. I read in the paper that he was yelling and screaming so much that a psychiatrist was brought in on Wednesday night to calm him down. I wondered what I would say if I was in his situation.

"James, I think it's good to be forgiving, but it seems to me that Black folk are the most forgiving people in the world. And since we've been in America, our forgiving nature has worked to our disadvantage."

"But what could the brother say? Burn, baby, burn?" asked Doug.

"I don't think so. But I would've hoped he could've said something a little more observant about the conditions that led people to do what they did."

When we got to the grocery store, while walking down the aisles, I noticed that the white folk in the store were watching us a lot more than usual. They looked frightened, as if I they thought we were going to jump on them. I know with all of the soot covering our clothes that we were an awful sight, but I didn't care.

"Is it me or them?" I asked Doug.

"It's them," he replied. "You gotta remember it's paranoia time. They're probably thinking that we've come over here to burn this store down."

'Man, you're probably right," I replied. I found Ash and James and made them stay with us. I didn't want anybody messing with my kids.

"Dad, I can handle the situation. Nobody's going to give me or my sister any trouble."

"Son, I'm glad you think you can take care of yourself, but until we get out of this store, the two of you are going to stay with me."

After we paid for the groceries and I put a full tank of gas in the car, I turned on the ignition and headed home.

ten

After John and the kids left for the cleanup, I spent a little time straightening up the house, and threw a couple of loads of clothes into the washing machine. Mrs. Henderson normally comes in on Monday and Thursday to help with the cleaning and cooking. I hadn't heard from her since the verdict. I hoped that she and her family were alright. She has lived in Watts for nearly forty years, and from what I had heard, she was caught in the middle of this madness. During the afternoon, after finishing all of my chores, I didn't know what to do next.

I thought about Kathy Lee and Imani. I miss them alot, but I'm grateful they didn't have to live through this nightmare. It's so frightening not knowing what's going to happen. It felt like our world was sinking in quicksand. K.L., that's what I call her sometimes, is such a dedicated doctor. She doesn't need to be worrying herself about doing her part down at King Hospital. She'd work herself into premature labor like she did when she was carrying Imani.

Miss Zoli was very quiet throughout most of the day. During breakfast, she was as quiet as a little church mouse. She did her best to avoid making any eye contact with John and quietly left the table. I guess my husband wasn't up to starting anything this morning. Aside from speaking to her when she sat down at the table, he left her alone. For whatever reasons, it seemed that her room was becoming her cocoon. I had checked in on her a couple of times today, and she was usually sleeping. Once, I found her sitting on the bed, appearing to be in that same state of suspended animation she was in when I first discovered her. I checked the lock on the glass door in the family room to make sure she couldn't wander outside by the pool.

As I was sitting at the table in the kitchen, I heard her slowly climbing the stairs.

She limped toward me, at the table and said, 'cuse me ma'am, can yah hep me?"

"Miss Zoli, is something wrong?"

"I wonts tah go home. I wonts tah fine my chilrens an my husban."

While stroking her frail hand, I said, "Miss Zoli, you can't go home, not yet, but I will help you get there."

"But yah husban said he would hep me." Her frail eyes were pleading for help.

Considering his belligerent behavior, I was quite surprised to hear that John had said he would help her. Maybe his statement was just another hallucination. "When did he say that, Miss Zoli?"

"He tole me dat early dis heah mawnin."

"I see. Are you sure my husband really said this?"

In a split second her eyes became very glassy, like a sheet of thin ice as she drifted away once more into her twilight state. Then suddenly, she seemed to snap out of it. "Who is yah?" she screeched pulling her hand away from me.

"Miss Zoli, don't you know who I am?" As I touched her hand again, she flinched again.

"No, gits away from me!" She struggled away from me, dragging her diseased foot, into the center of the kitchen. "I doesn't like bein heah in dis heah house. It's got too many haints runnin aroune in it." She squinched her eyes at me, and the flesh surrounding the outer corners contracted like a fan, accentuating her eyes overflowing with fear.

"Shh .... shh," I said calmly, with a softer voice, as if I were talking to a frightened child. "This house isn't haunted, its a safe place for you. This is your home until we find your children."

"Yah gots haints ev'rywheah! No, I doesn't likes it heah," she screamed, pulling away from me again. "Yah gots all dese strange 'traptions livin up in heah. Cold food in dat big ole box and den dat othah box wid de haints dat be lookin likes li'l peoples movin aroune it. I is scared yah gonna hurts me when I is sleepin an—" she stopped dead in her tracks in the middle of a sentence. She became frozen again, lost into another world.

I tried to imagine where she had lived before and what caused her bizarre behavior. Who knows? She's such a sweet old lady when her mind is clear.

I reached out and touched her hands with both of mine and stroked them gently. "Miss Zoli," I whispered, "Would you come with me please?" She followed without resistance, still lost, perhaps not even partially aware of my presence.

I helped her downstairs to her room, sitting her down on the bed. I wrapped my arms around her and rocked her. I sang a song my mother used to sing to me, "I am Waiting for My Child to Get Home." The words and melody seemed to soothe her, as her shoulders relaxed and melted into mine.

She began to murmur, "I jist wonts tah fine mah chilrens, I jist wonts tah fine mah chilrens."

A few minutes later when I gave her a hot cup of chamomile tea with honey, she drank it quietly. I pulled back the covers for her to take a nap. She looked up at me and said, "Thank yah so much foh bein nice tah me. I knows dat I is a burden on yah an yoh family. I is so sorry foh dat.

"I donno whot's de mattah wid me. I is heah in dis heah worle, den I is in 'Sippi, back on dem roads jist a lookin foh my chilrens like I bin doin foh yeahs. But I keep on comin back tah dis heah place, an I doesn't knows why."

"Miss Zoli, everything is gonna be alright."

"Is yah sho bout dat?"

"Yes, ma'am, I am."

"Is yah heppin me likes yoh husban said he wood?"

"Yes, ma'am I will. But for the time being, the only thing I want you to worry about is getting enough rest so you'll be strong, and to eat enough food to fatten up those little bones of yours."

She smiled, her face shriveled into a beaming light, radiating joy through the cracks and crevices of her skin.

By the time I reached the top of the stairs, John and the kids were coming in through the garage entrance that leads directly into the kitchen. It was almost dusk, and they looked exhausted, more like coal miners than anything else. Their clothes, faces and hands were covered with layers of soot.

John was bending his body to slip into a chair at the table, when I caught him in mid air. I yelled, when he was threatening to plop his filthy body into my clean chair, "John Henry Stewart, freeze! You should be ashamed of yourself, as dirty as you are. All of you, before anybody makes a move, I want you to go back into the garage, and take off those dirty shoes, get a plastic bag from the cabinet for your clothes, and I want each of you to shower for at least twenty minutes! You are filthy, you should've had a change of clothes in the garage."

"Baby, give us a break! We were out doing our civic duty, cleaning up our community. And now you're treating us like we're part of the dirt brigade!"

"Well, that is what the three of you look like," I laughed. "I don't care if you got a Nobel Peace Prize for you efforts, you are not messing up my house!"

"Mommie, you didn't even ask us if we had fun."

"Did you?"

"Yes, we did. Well, it was sort of fun."

"What do you mean?"

"I got a good feeling helping people out. But it's kinda sad, too. Mom, a whole lot of businesses were destroyed and there's a lot of people upset about losing everything. I'm glad daddy's building is safe."

"Plus, Mom," piped in James, "there were all sorts of people out there—African Americans, Asian Americans and European Americans. I've never seen so many people working together like that. And they came from all over, from Beverly Hills, Santa Barbara, Marina del Ray and Malibu.

"People brought a lot of food and clothing at the churches. It was great to see how so many people cared."

On her way to the garage, Ashley turned around and asked, "Mommie, are we going to church in the morning?"

In light of all that had happened, I hadn't given going to church a thought. "If it's still quiet, sure we can," I replied hesitantly.

When I woke up Sunday morning, it hit me that I hadn't left the house since Wednesday evening. As I got up, I saw John sitting on the edge of his side of the bed. His folded hands were swaying nervously and hanging between his knees. His face was stained with worry. "Honey, what's wrong? Why are you looking so serious this early in the morning?"

He sat there for a moment, surrounded by deep thought. As I walked past him, he took me by the hand, and I sat down next to him. He held my hand for a few minutes, studying it, looking at my wedding ring, with deep intensity. "Honey, are you going to tell me what's bothering you?" I asked.

With an uncomfortable intensity, he looked deep into my eyes, searching them, as if he was looking for an answer. "Angela, I'm not sure if you're ready for this—"

"Ready for what?"

"Ready to see for yourself how bad it is down there."

"Oh John, come on now, don't be silly," I replied chiding him. "Your concern for me is very sweet, but I'm a big girl now. I've lived through the sixties and that was a similar situation."

"I don't think you get it, Angela. It's gone. Just about everything in our community is gone. You saw how it affected me and the kids. Or maybe you didn't notice. You've been so wrapped up into Miss Zoli that I don't think you realize how bad it is down there. I just want you to be emotionally prepared for this," he said, still desperately clinging to my hand, swinging it back and forth. It felt like he was trying to will some of his strength into me.

"Whatever you think you understand by what you saw on television, it's ten times worse. It's a holocaust. Ang, just about everything is gone. It looks like a war zone down there. I wish I could spare you, because I know you and how extremely sensitive you are. And I just want to brace you for this experience. It's something you've never seen before. It looks like another world down there."

I leaned over and kissed him on the cheek. "You know that's what I love about you the most. You are so very protective of me, and I'm grateful for that, especially since I haven't been the easiest person in the world to live with during the last couple of days. And in spite of that you are still looking out for me. But I know I can handle this, trust me. So let's get this show on the road!"

"Alright, if you say so. You might be ready intellectually, but I'm not so sure that you are emotionally."

"Trust me, I'll be fine."

I hurried down the hall, woke up James and Ash, rushed downstairs, woke up Miss Zoli, and made a quick breakfast. I'm not afraid to go out and see what happened. I don't know what's wrong with my husband. Sometimes his protective nature goes a bit overboard and he can't see the forest for the trees. If I lived through the movement, why does he now think that I might wilt up like a dainty little flower?

Miss Zoli wore a pretty pink and white floral dress with a matching pink hat that my Aunt Minnie had left during her last visit. I had never gotten around to shipping it back to her. Finally, she told me to keep the dress out here, since she was planning to return this fall. I gave Miss Zoli a pair of my soft soled white leather moccasins with pink and blue beading to wear. To be extra careful, I gave her two pairs of white socks to wear, so the fluid wouldn't seep through.

For the last three and a half days, I felt like I was wrapped up in a cocoon that was holding me at bay, hidden from the world. Now it was time for me to see for myself. We loaded up and got into our family car, the silver Volvo that we usually drove on weekends.

As I got in the car, John looked at me over the roof, studying me again. "Relax," I said patting his hand. "I'll be alright."

"If you say so," he replied, with a tinge of disgust, while turning the ignition key.

"Mommie, it's really bad down there, you're in for a big surprise," whispered Ashley into my ear.

"Yeah, mom, it looks like there was a war down there."

Miss Zoli sat quite peacefully between the two of them, looking straight ahead. John drove slowly, he seemed to be stalling for time. Normally, he breezes down this hill. As we approached the bottom of the hill at Martin Luther King Boulevard and 39th street, he turned on his blinker to make a left turn, to head toward the freeway. "I think I'll take the expressway, the Harbor Freeway is open now."

I touched his hand on the steering wheel and said, "No, don't do that on my account. I want to see it. We can take the streets."

"Okay, if you insist. But don't say that I didn't warn you."

As we drove down there, I couldn't believe my eyes. I was overwhelmed. Everything was gone. Charred, burned out remains, now stood where there was once a row of thriving businesses. There was nothing left but a few walls. It looked like a ghost town.

"This looks like 12th street in Detroit in 1967."

"Mom, most of the streets look like this."

"James, aren't you exaggerating a bit?"

"No, he's not, Angela. I took the kids around most of the area yesterday, I wanted them to see for themselves, I want them to remember this for the rest of their lives."

John was right. Nothing prepared me for what stood before me as we drove down the streets that have been at the core of my world. He had tried to warn me, but I cavalierly ignored him. I thought he was being too overprotective. My wise husband was just being honest—and realistic. Maybe John was right. I probably didn't want to think about it. I'd been so caught up with Miss Zoli and keeping order in our home, that the thought of what really happened down here never occurred to me.

When I was finally confronted with the awful, overwhelming reality of exactly how widespread and devastating the rioting had been, I was engulfed by a deep, aching sorrow. I felt the pain of all those who had lost their dreams, jobs and lives. Very little had been spared. The tears of a thousand dreams that had gone up in smoke rolled down my cheeks.

It seemed like most of the important landmarks in my world had suddenly vanished, gone with a flaming, destructive wind. It had been a holocaust prompted by rage allowed expression in only the most violent forms. We were now living in a hurting and deeply wounded world. For the first time in my entire life, I wondered: Can this world be saved? In the face of all this destruction. I didn't know, not anymore. In my heart, I wanted to believe that America would one day do right by us, but that belief seemed to roll up in its own dark plume of smoke, leaving me empty and in greater despair. The ancient wounds that had been suppressed from one generation to another had once again seen the light of a destructive day.

The very fabric of my world lay desperately unraveled before my eyes. In my heart, I knew, our lives would never be the same. All of the important landmarks, the touchstones were gone. My spirit was withering up, like a piece of parchment paper consumed by a flame, running away from this reality.

Everywhere I looked as we proceeded along Crenshaw Boulevard heading south I saw destruction. Gone was the Aquarian Bookstore, opened fifty years ago, the first Black bookstore on the west coast. Since moving to L.A., it was my favorite place. I bought dozens of books to read after we first came out here. I found children's books for Ashley and James there, books that I longed to read as a child with Black images and role models, and African fables. Gone was Broadway Federal Savings and Loan, the oldest Black savings and loan company in the city. We opened our first savings account after moving out here. Broadway gave John his first loan, the seed money he used for Stewart Computers. When our children were born, we opened accounts for them there, too. Gone was Evers Furniture, where we bought the bulk of the furniture for both of our homes. Where would I buy groceries, get

James' haircut, go to the doctor's office, find a pharmacy? It was not the lost of the physical, but the sudden disruption, the severing of those meaningful relationships that had been an important part of my life. Its one thing to imagine destruction, while its another to see it, to be there, present in the midst of such unbelievable despair and horrific devastation.

I wanted to scream, "No, no. This cannot be!" John continued to watch me. I couldn't bear to look anymore.

Convoys of National Guard and Marines moved up and down the street, in jeeps and armored trucks. What was there to guard? Just about everything was gone. Along the way, they stood guard at several major intersections. They looked tense, anxious and weary. At the last intersection before reaching our church, a young Black soldier holding a rifle looked into my tears and glimpsed my anguish. In a split second, he lowered his rifle and waved sorrowfully at me as if to say, "I'm sorry." But it wasn't his fault. Whose fault was it?

I heard Miss Zoli whispering to James, "Whot happined? Was dere a wah down heah?" My son didn't respond. Neither did anyone else in the car. I guess we didn't know what to say. When we finally pulled into the parking lot of out church at Manchester and Vermont, I wasn't sure if I could get out of the car. And more than anything else, I was surprised to see the building was still standing.

By the time John parked the car, my body felt like a instrument composed of a thousand taut strings, all at their breaking point. I was utterly devastated.

John walked over to my side and opened the door. "Come on, baby, let's go in church," he said softly. "I know it's hard for you to take all of this in, but at least the worst is already over." Hot, steaming tears slowly trickled down my face as I shook my head and replied, " I wish that was true. The worst has just begun."

As we walked to the church from the lot, James came over to me and gently placed his arm around my neck, "Mom, don't worry, it's gonna be alright."

"Yeah, mommie it is, we promise," replied Ashley.

My children were something else, I didn't have to say a word. They knew how heavy my heart was. The questions continued to haunt me. How will our community ever be the same? How can we overcome this overwhelming destruction? Is it possible?

I looked at the huge brick edifice shaped like an arc, noticing the huge stained glass panels at the bow, standing before me. It looked the same, but something about it was different. I wished for this nightmare to be over. My body felt like a bowl of loose jello as we walked into the sanctuary. James and Ashley held Miss Zoli's hand and closely followed behind us. She seemed to be cooperating quite nicely. Other members were entering the church in their own encapsulated world of silence. Since our church is located on Vermont near Ninety-ninth Street in South Central, many of our members lived nearby. I'm sure their lives had been a living hell for the last three and a half days.

Usually our church overflows with joyous celebration, filled with many smiles, happy chatter, joy filled greetings and bright exchanges. Today, it felt like we were attending a funeral. The only thing missing was a corpse. The few members I noticed seemed to be stunned, their faces carried sullen expressions, stripped of any light. The sanctuary was so quiet you could almost hear a pin drop. A nervous, anxious hush penetrated the entire sanctuary.

Finally, the choir marched down the sanctuary's center aisle to, "We're Marching Up to Zion." They were also subdued in their white and gold trimmed robes. Their voices were dull and hollow, free of the exuberant, joyful harmonies they normally created, resonating throughout the entire building, waking up dozing members and bringing the rest of us to our feet. Our minister, Reverend Elijah Knight, says our choir would wake up the dead. As the choir continued down the aisle, the somber atmosphere seemed to be loosening its grip a little bit, as their voices began to harmonize, "We're marching, we're marching up to Zion that beautiful city of God, We're marching, we're marching up to Zion that beautiful city of God."

Reverend Knight stepped to the pulpit after Deacon Green gave a somber invocation and said, "We are all deeply hurt, we are all weary, but we all know that those who wait on the Lord shall renew their strength; they shall mount up on wings like eagles; they shall run and not be weary; and they shall walk and not faint.

"Breathe the fresh air of new life, of faith of hope, and of love upon us dear Lord. Give us the breath of life, free of anger, relieved of haunting memories, released of the anguish from our past. And now let us bow our heads in prayer.

"You, oh Lord, God our father, the God of Abraham, Issac and Jacob, the God of our weary years, the God of our silent tears, the God who has brought us thus far on our way. It's been a rough week. Oh, Lord. This is a difficult and trying time. We waited on justice and justice did not come. Once again we have seen our people treated in an unjust and ungodly fashion, but we know it is you who metes out the true justice, based on divine law rather than man's infirmities and prejudices.

"There are many gathered here today who have lost their homes, lost their jobs, their businesses gone up in smoke. Dreams of a life time destroyed in the twinkling of an eye. There are some here who have lost a loved one in the wake of all this destruction that has fallen upon our community. There are those who don't even know if their son or daughter, husband or wife is dead or alive."

The moaning sounds of the congregation responded like body of instruments disharmonious yet in unison, "Yes, Lord," "Yes oh yes," "Thank you, Jesus."

"Lord, hear me today. There are so many of your children in pain. So many needs, so much trouble, so much pain. And, Lord, I must admit, that I, too, have lost my faith. I, too, did not know where to turn or what to do. But you showed me the way. Your loving grace and mercy wrapped itself around me and gave me the peace that passes all understanding."

"This is not our darkest hour, this is not our bleakest moment. We have survived far greater tragedies. Because on Christ the solid rock we stand. We have faith in things hoped for in the evidence of things not seen, and like the Phoenix of the ancient, myth I say to you members of Trinity, my brothers and sisters in Christ, that we shall rise again."

The rest of the service moved along quite briskly. The spirit of the congregation seemed to be getting lighter as the songs and hymns of praise one by one seemed to lift the heavy burdens we carried.

Out of the corner of my eye, I caught a glimpse of Miss Zoli a few times during the service. I hadn't payed a lot of attention to her since the service began. It seemed like she was enjoying the service. I wondered when was the last time she was in church, as she sat quietly between my children. At the beginning of the service, she smiled throughout most of the opening hymn, nodding her head to the beat of "We're Marching Up to Zion."

After the offering, Reverend Knight began his sermon. He looked troubled. He was a tall, middle aged man, who had pastored our church for almost twenty years. During his tenure, the membership has grown from sixty to over five thousand. "We all know the verdict was wrong and that those four policemen are guilty. They beat Mr. King unmercifully and unjustly. Anyone with eyes can see the truth for themselves. The hypocrisy of this system, the blatant injustice and disrespect for Black people, is more than apparent to righteous thinking individuals not only in America, but throughout the world. We remember Emmett Till, we remember the Scottsboro boys. Clarence Thomas said his was a high-tech lynching, but I say to you today that the only thing missing on that videotape was a rope and a tree. And because of the years of injustice that have been heaped upon us, many reacted in a violent way. We have experienced a spiritual death, a social death. What are we to do? Many of you are wondering, which way do we go from here, as Doctor King asked more than twenty-five years ago. Which way do we go, chaos or community?

"Are we to believe all that the world says is true about us? Are we to accept the notion that we are nothing more than a collection of irresponsible men and women? Thieves, murderers, arsonists and welfare recipients?

"In spite of my wife's objections, I walked the streets of this community every night since the verdict was rendered. I saw the good and I saw the bad in my people. The bad has been reported and acknowledged. The good has been ignored and silenced. I saw people risking their lives to save a stranger. I saw an old couple at the gas station just two blocks away carrying a young Asian man to the hospital who had been shot and beaten. I heard about the people who took a young reporter into their home who had been shot and got him safely to the hospital. I saw those four young people on television who risked their lives to save Reginald Denny. Two of them left the safety of their home, after watching his beating on television to rescue him. But the world would have you think that the residents of South Central L.A. are nothing more than a band of common criminals. How much longer will we believe the lies that we have been told?

"All of our hearts are laden with heavy burdens. But I am here today to tell you that He can and will make your burdens light. We are a community twice devastated by the law and by the response of our brothers and sisters, and others who invaded our community to take advantage of a bad situation. I know there are some of you gathered here today who may have participated, or who know people who did. We are not victims but victors. We have won so many battles that we have forgotten all that has gone on before. This is certainly not the first time, nor will it be the last time that America will slap us in the face. We shall not be moved. Victory is mine sayeth the Lord.

"Hold your head up high and keep the faith. We have the capacity, we possess the means and have the talent of untapped human potential to rebuild our city out of the devastation of injustice and violence. I say to you on this day, we shall rise again."

His sermon was accompanied by shouts of, "Amen, Rev, tell the truth..."

"I know many of you have lost businesses, a few of you have

lost loved ones. Some are homeless who have never known what it is like not to have a roof over your heads. Many have loved ones in jail, and you can't get to the bank to withdraw the needed money to make bail because your bank has either been closed or burned down and you can't find a gas station in your neighborhood to provide you with a full tank of gas, gas you so desperately need to make a trip. Again I say, this is not our darkest hour, nor our bleakest moment. For the children of the people who survived the middle passage, the God of our weary years, the God of our silent tears, the God who has brought us thus far on our way did not bring us this far to leave us."

"Well, well, well."

"Amen, Rev. Tell the truth."

"But I say to you on this the day the Lord hath made, I say to each and every one of you, the Lord will make a way somehow. Justice shall prevail, it will roll down like a mighty stream. He will make you stronger. I am a witness to that. The doors of the church are open, for anyone needing prayer."

"Yes, Lord! Thank you, Jesus! Thank you, Jesus!" shouted Mrs. Washington, who was sitting on the second row from the altar.

When I stood up for altar call, my knees were unsteady, and my head was still swimming around in a pool of disorienting misery. The brutal reality of all that I'd seen had settled into my bones. John leaped up and grabbed my hand and said, "I'll go with you." We left the children and Miss Zoli sitting on the pew. He led me holding my hand down the center aisle. By the time we reached the altar I felt a little stronger. Yet, I couldn't hear my minister's prayers. On bended knee, holding my husband's hand to my right and an older member, Mrs. Yates, to my left, the sounds of destruction and images of devastation surged again in my mind. Over and over, images of the destruction I'd witnessed surrounded me. My head felt like it was about to explode, crammed tight with overflowing memories. I felt vulnerable. I realized there is no safe haven to be found. Suddenly, I was lost in another river of tears.

John leaned over and whispered in my ear, "Baby come on, its time to get up, the prayers are over.

"I can't move."

"Yes, you can. I'll help you."

In spite of my tears, as we left the service, I felt replenished and relieved. On the way out, we shook the pastor's hand. "John, I need to talk to you as soon as possible. Can I give you a call tomorrow?"

"Yes, reverend, you most certainly can. I'll be in the office."

On the way to the car, John said," Let's go get something to eat at the Crenshaw Cafe."

"Honey, I don't know. My head is killing me. I'd like to go home and get in the bed and take a nap."

"Let's do it, Mom. We didn't have much for breakfast. And you need a break," pleaded James.

"Please Mommie, can't we do that? Please," begged Ashley.

"Oh, alright. I guess I'm outnumbered. You all have triple teamed me again."

When we arrived at the Crenshaw Boulevard Cafe, the parking lot was full. Inside, there were several people standing in line, waiting for a table. I took Miss Zoli back to the car so she wouldn't have to stand for a long time.

Once we were back in the car, she said, "Now I wonts yah tah tells me somethin—how does dis funny lookin thin git aroune without no hosses or mules?"

"It has an engine."

"Like what make a steamboat or a train run?"

"Yes, ma'am, that's right."

"Dis heah sho nuff is a strange, strange worle. I ain't nevah seen or heard ah nothin like it. Please ansah me a question. What yeah is dis?"

"This is 1992."

"I don't undahstands. Dat cain't be!"

"Yes, it is. I can show you a newspaper that has a date on it when we go back inside."

"Dat's alright."

"No, ma'am, it's no problem."

"Sugah," she replied, bowing her head in shame, "I cain't read."

"I'm sorry, I didn't mean to embarrass you."

"Can yah read?"

"Yes, ma'am. Excuse me, did you grow up on a farm that didn't have a school nearby?"

"A whot?"

"You know, a school, a place where children learn how to read."

"Chile, what's got in yah? Don't yah know dat it was agin de law tah teach slaves how tah read?"

"Yes, ma'am, I did know that. But Miss Zoli, slavery ended over one-hundred and twenty-five years ago."

She drifted away again, into her solitary world of confinement, blocking the outside world out of her consciousness. I didn't know what we were going to do with her. I hope we can help her to find her family. I just didn't understand why she believed she was a slave. This just didn't make any sense to me. We had to hurry up and find her family soon before my husband pops a blood vessel.

We finally got a table and as we ate, I could see John's face was finally beginning to look relaxed. I hadn't seen him like this in almost a week. He was frequently tense, and anxious, but the strain of the riots had taken its toll on his face. He looked like he had aged five years in less than five nights.

We didn't have much to talk about during breakfast, although there were several lively conversations going on at tables adjacent to ours. These bold souls had ventured out of their homes to try to regain a bit of normalcy by having a bite to eat. Most of them were probably still without electricity, and low on food. We were lucky that John had finally fixed the generator and restored our electricity.

When we got home, I led Miss Zoli downstairs to change into a sweatsuit.

"Tells me somethin."

"Yes, ma'am. What would you like to know?"

"Wheah all of dem fine lookin colored folk come from?"

"Who are you talkin about?"

"Dem people at yah church."

"Most of the people live near the church in the neighborhood."

"Well, dey sho nuff is some fine lookin colored folk, if I do say so myself. It was such ah site tah see."

"Miss Zoli, tell me something. When was the last time you were in a church?"

"Now dat I cain't reckon to be telling de truf. We al'ays had service in de woods, not in no big ole buildin like dat one. De church was foh de Mass and de Mistrus. But I can say dis foh sho, I ain't nevah seen no colored folk dat looked so good in all my days. Dey sho is high fallutin an very fancy."

She studied me for a few moments while I watched her. "I knows yoh wonderin agin whot is wrong wid me. I can feels dat way down deep in mah bones."

"No ma'am, I really don't think that. I just feel that you're a little confused."

"Whot dat means?"

"That you don't really don't remember how you got to California or who brought you out here, and where you were staying before I found you. And that's okay. Being more forgetful can happen as you get older."

"Forgittin? I ain't forgittin nothin. Does yah heahs me? I remembas each an ev'ry las thin dat is 'potent to me. I remembas de las time I kiss an touch each one of mah youngins. An dat was way back. Foh I gots most ah dese heah gray hairs on mah head."

"Yes, ma'am. If you say so."

"I told yah how I gots heah. I woke up an I was heah. Nobody brought me tah dis here worle. Yah keeps tellin me bout dis heah yeah bein a long time aftah my recollectin. I knows dat cain't be. I knows how lon I bin a free nigga, an it ain't bin lon 'nouf. So I wish yah would stop foolin me an tells me de truf—"

"Miss Zoli, everything we have told you is true."

"Well dat cain't be. It ain't possible foh me tah be so fah away

from home an way pass de time I knows is rite. Dat jist ain't possible."

James' voice crackled through on the intercom. "Mom, you
got a phone call."

"Who is it?"

"It's Doc Whitney."

"I'll pick it up in the family room. Excuse me, Miss Zoli."

"Hi Doc, how are you?"

"I'm here." His voice sounded drained and heavy. I almost
didn't recognize it. "I just want you to know that the center will be
open tomorrow for business as usual."

"Alright," I sighed. "I'll be there." Click. He had hung up the
phone without saying good bye. I can only imagine what he's gone
through in the last five days. He and his wife live within walking
distance of the center. They were caught right in the middle of
wall of fire that destroyed our community. I'd never heard him
sound so distraught before.

Maybe tomorrow our lives would return back to normal. Maybe
tomorrow.

eleven

I wish somebody would hep me tah git outtah dis heah place an back on mah way tah 'Sippi. Dis is a strange worle an I doesn't like bein heah. It ain't like nothin I ain't nevah seen befoh an I jist cain't git siteeated an feels right bein heah. Dis place riles me up. I feels funny walkin aroune dis big ole house wid all ah dese strange thangs.

Dey gots thangs aroune heah dat I ain't nevah thought couldah been made. Dey got watah runnin insidah de house, an de outhouse is insidah de big house. An dere's a whole heap of 'em, not jist one. Dey gots light wid out no candies, calls it 'lectricity', an big ole cold closets wid food in 'em. Dat dere hot box in dey kitchen wheah yah put food on a plate ain it come out hot enuf tah burns yoh skin, befoh yah can lickity split it across de room. Ain't dat somethin? Hot food in de twinklin of ah eye!

An I still ain't gots no ways ah knowin how I gots heah.

But dis heah place is funny tah me, ain't somethin rite bout me bein heah. Dere is dis, Lawd have mercy on me, awful feelin dat I gots, like I is in de middle of ah wah, wid all dis fightin an killin goin on. But I ain't seen too many soldiahs. I seed a few ah 'em when dey took me tah church dat mornin. From all dat I could see, Lawd ah mercy me, I thinks dere mustah bin a wah down heah. Dat mustah bin goin on de firs day dat I woke up in dis place. An de funny thin 'bout it is dat de wah went on foh only a few days. Maybe its gonna start up agin.

I thanks sonethiin ain't right wid de whole heap ah dem. Dey keep ah tellin me, tryin tah makes me believe dat dis is nineteen ninetee somthin. Dat ain't right, dat cain't be, cause I knows dat is a lon, lon time from eighteen hundred an sixtee-seben. Yah means tah tells me dat Momma Zoli done gone tah sleep foh dat long? Dat cain't be true. I knows de Lawd ain't gonna do no thing like dat tah me. Dey say dey is gonna takes me tah some doctah. I ain't needin no doctah. What I needs is tah be own mah way back home.

I ain't nevah heard ah no place like dis heah worle. De air is brown, an it hurts tah breathe, I feel like somebody done put a fire down insidah me. An everythin heah is brown. I ain't seen no fields wif no crops heah, I wondas wheah all dese peoples be gittin dey food from. Dere ain't too many trees wid leaves, not like de ones back in 'Sippi. I remembas de beautiful 'nolias back in 'Sippi. I misses dem so much, dey is so pretty. I knows I'll gits back tah seem dem one day.

Dey jist don't wants tah believes dat I is tell'n de truf 'bout who I is an wheah I is from. Sometime I don't knows wheah I is. Sometime I is dis heah worle, den sometime I is back on dem roads in 'Sippi, jist like I ain't nevah left. I jist don't knows how dat can be. But when I is in 'Sippi, I is but I ain't. It's like I is dere, but part ah bein dere feels like ah dream. Sometime I knows somethin ain't right, I don't knows what's wron wid me, I jist don't knows. I wish I could gits on back home tah wheah I is 'pose tah be. I wonts dese chilrens tah hep me gits back tah mine.

Dey keepah axin me tah tell dem everythin dat I could remembas 'bout mah life. But when I did, I could see it in dey eyes, dey look at Momma Zoli, an dey ain't believin me. Dey still thinks I is some kine ah crazy ole woman, who don't knows de truf. But, if its one thin dat I knows is de truf ah who I is.

All ah mah life I bin a slave. I doesn't knows wheah I was born, an I cain't say when cause I ain't nevah seen, not even one time, de face ah mah mammy or mah pappy, not tah remembas dem. I ain't nevah knows if I gots any brothas or sistahs. Dem ole slave tradah took rne away befoh I could hold onto de sweet recollectin ah dey face. I caint' remembas anythan 'bout mah mammy. I misses huh moh dan anybody else. All ah mah life I has carried dis heavy saddness dats bin wid me most ah mah days, an ah knows its 'bout missin mah family, specially mah mammy, from bein in mah life. I used tah have dreams 'bout huh when I was a l'l girl, but I could nevah see huh face.

'Cordin tah Aint Bertha, de woman dat raise me, I came tah de Steadwell 'tation when I was 'bout three or foh yeahs ole. Aint Bertha, she treat me good, an' all dem yeahs til dey day she close huh eyes foh dey las time, she treat me like I was huh own flesh an' blood. An who knows? Maybe I was. Dey way dem tradahs be takin way peoples, breakin dem away from dey family, she coulda bin some kin tah me, an we jist didn't knows it. Much as dey sole an swap niggas aroune we all gots some blood from each othah. So womin took in chilrens an treat dem like dey was dey own, cause most of 'em had lost some ah dey own youngins in de same way.

Aint Bertha tole dat dey bought me to be a playmate foh Massa Steadwell's daughta, Miss Stephanie. She was his only girl chile, so when she say she needed a n'ga wench tah be wid huh. But all dat time when we was li'l guls she nevah took tah me, an' I ain't take much of a likin tah huh eitha. She was a mean ole haint. Had a mean streak wider dan de 'Sippi rivah, an she used tah take a heap ah pride in hurtin an beatin own me when we was growin up.

Foh all ah my life, til de niggas got free, dat dere Steadwell 'tation was de only home dat I knows. Most ah de time aftah I gots big enuf, I was workin in de big house, in de spinnin room, makin clof. Sometime I cooks but I like workin on dem spinnin wheels an sewin up purdy new cloves.

Dey raise ah whole heap ah crops on de 'tation. Mostly cotton an indigo. Ah nevah worked in de fields.

When I was grown up, I marries dis big ole buck dat live own de 'tation name Andrew. We had seven chilrens, five boys and two guls. I loved dem chilrens wid all ah de heart dat I gots. An one by one dey grew up an dat ole evil Massa Steadwell sole dem off. It hurt me somethin so awful.

An each time it hurt me moh an moh. Til by de time dey stole my baby boy from me, I thoughts dat I was gonna die. Massa

Steadwell promise me dat he would nevah takes Jeremiah away from me, but he did. An den he say, "I ain't nevah tole no nigga no such thing! You is one lyin nigga wench an I is gonna make sho dat yah ain't lie on me agin." Den he beat me till I couldn't bleed no moh. An tah make it even worser dan dat, he sole mah husban away from me.

Mah husban took good care ah me, done de best dat he could do as a slave. An he was a good man. Wid a tenda heart dat he done try tah hide. I knows it hurt tah have his youngins sole away from him, too. But dat was de way de Lawd let owah life be, an we made de bess ah a bad siteeation.

Sometime I wondas whot would happin if I foune one of dem. I wondas if mah boys will remembas em, dey poh broke down motha? Aint Bertha use tah tells me dat yah al'ays remembas yah mammy, an a mammy always knows who huh youngins is. I knows dat mah time on dis here earf is runnin out, I is gettin tah be a purdy ole woman. I bin prayin an prayin, axin de Lawd tah let me live jist long enuf tah see freedom foh mahself. I jist want tah see whot it be like tah be free from all de misery dat had been own me foh all ah mah life.

Niggas was al'ays talkin bout bein free. I knows dat when de wah got start up dat somethin good was gonna come outta all dat fightin an killin, we was gonna be free. I could jist feel it runnin through mah bones.

But, when I was back in 'Sippi lookin foh mah loved ones, I ain't see dat freedom doin much foh us dat ain't nevah bin free befoh. All I wonts tah do now is git own back home.

I once was lost,

but now am found

twelve

When I woke up Monday morning, it felt like I hadn't been to work in years, instead of the four days that had actually passed. Looking out over my balcony, I could feel an invisible cloud of darkness billowing over my city. I wondered how long this painful presence would be with us. Days? Weeks? Months? Who knows for sure?

John rolled over to my side of the bed and snuggled his body next to mine. He touched my shoulder gently, yet purposefully, and whispered in my ear, "Before you get up, I just have one question—"

"What's that?"

"What are you going to do with Miss Zoli today?"

"Nothing," I replied, as I turned my head toward him.

"Come on, Ang, you can't leave that woman alone in the house."

"I didn't say I was going to do that."

"Then what are you going to do?"

"Hopefully Mrs. Henderson will be here this morning."

"And if she doesn't show up? What are you going to do then?"

"I'll take her to work with me."

"Right," he replied sarcastically. "Ang, I still don't get it. What's up with you and this woman? You're acting like you're responsible for her and you're not."

"John, why is it so hard for you to understand that I just feel sorry for her? She's all alone in this world right now. We're not going to abandon her. Not until we find her family."

For once, he didn't have anything more to say. I was glad we didn't fall into another argument. I wasn't up for that this morning. I hopped into the shower after waking up the kids. Before I made breakfast, I checked on Miss Zoli. She was fast asleep, like a baby. Her face was softer, covered with a sweet half smile that almost looked like a sigh. As I stood there in the doorway of her room, I wondered where her children were. I knew they must be frantic, trying to find her. They were probably wondering if she was dead or alive. Or maybe there is some truth to her story. Perhaps she's experiencing some type of partial amnesia. Maybe she grew up in Mississippi and is blanking out the most recent part of her life.

During breakfast, I sensed that my children, especially Ashley, were feeling a lot of anxiety about returning to school. Normally, they're quite talkative and high spirited in the morning, full of chatter about the day awaiting them. Today, they were somber. I didn't know what to say or do to make them feel any better. After all that we had been through, I was at a loss for something soothing to say to make them feel better. Maybe John could console them today, better than I. He was sitting at the table smiling and happy. He appeared to be ready and willing to sink his teeth back into work. I don't think he noticed how mournful our children actually were.

"Okay kids, it's back to school, back to our normal lives. Are you ready to get back into the swing of things?"

"Daddy, I'm scared. How do we know for sure that the rioting is over?" Ashley asked.

John's expression suggested that her question had taken him by surprise.

"Listen, baby. You don't have anything to worry about. The worst is over."

"But, daddy, I don't want to go to school."

"Ash, you have to."

"What happens if the kids start fighting at school?"

"I'll come and get you if anything happens."

"You promise?"

"You know I do. You can always reach me on my cellular phone. You know that."

"But, daddy, I really don't want to go to school. I might start wheezing again and have to go to the hospital."

"Ash, you're such a big baby," snapped James, hungry for attention.

"James, leave your sister alone. She has every right to be afraid considering all that we've been through," John said. Then he turned to Ashley, "Ash, if it will make you feel any better, I'll take the two of you to school."

"Will you pick us up, too?"

"Sure, I will."

"Dad, you don't have to do that. I can take care of my baby sister."

John turned to James and said with a fatherly smile, signaling his pride, "Son, I'm proud of you. I know you can take of your little sister if anything happens at school."

"Thanks, Dad."

"So why don't we compromise? I'll drop you off. And if all goes well, you two can come home on the bus, like you normally do. Is that okay?" They both nodded in agreement.

John and the kids left the house shortly after breakfast. I stayed behind and waited for Mrs. Henderson. Fortunately, she arrived on time at eight-thirty. I didn't know what I was going to do with Miss Zoli if she hadn't shown up.

"Mrs. Henderson, you are certainly a sight for sore eyes! It's so good to see you. I was worried that you might not be able to make it in today."

"And it's real good to see you, too. You know you can always depend on me."

"Don't take it the wrong way. I know I can depend on you. I just didn't know if your circumstances was going to allow you to get here today. That's all."

"Well, I can understand why you would wonder about that. But I was determined to get here. Lord knows, there were more times than I can count last week that I thought my house was going to go up in flames, with me in it. I ain't never seen nothin' like that in my entire life. You know I lived through the Watts riots, back in sixty-five, and I thought that it was bad back then. But now I know what I lived through then was a little Sunday afternoon picnic compared to all that I done seen and lived through last week. It was a living hell. All of that fighting, and killing, burning, shooting, and stealing, in each and every direction.

"I thank the good master that all of my children are safe. But my husband lost his job at the garage. You know he was planning on retiring this summer. But that's the way things happen sometimes, I suppose."

"I'm sorry to hear that."

"Thank yah, but sugah, we're gonna be alright."

"If you say so."

"Is there anything special that you want me to do today?"

"Yes, as a matter of fact, there is. You must've read my mind. There's someone I want you to meet."

"You do?"

"Um-hmm, we have a houseguest. But let me be very honest with you. She's not a typical houseguest. I found her Wednesday in the center's parking lot, next to my car. She's been living on the streets for a long time."

"I see. That was awful nice of you to take her in. You know that the Lord is going to bless you in a mighty fine way."

"Well, there's more," I said hesitating a bit. "Not to alarm you, but you need to know that she goes in and out of hallucinations. Don't worry. I'm sure she wouldn't hurt a fly. And most of the time she's keeps to herself."

"I see. I'm sure we'll be fine, Mrs. Stewart. You just go on to work."

"But there's more to her story. I told you she hallucinates from time to time. You need to know that they are quite bizarre. She thinks she's a former slave from Mississippi."

"Mrs. Stewart, don't you worry. I been around crazy folk before. This ain't nothin new to me. When I was a little girl growing up in Texas my Uncle Hezekiah lived on the farm with us, and as long as I can remember he thought that he was a horse. It was something. We kept him around, 'cause there was no where else he could go."

"Thank you," I replied, with a deep sigh of relief. "I wish my husband felt the way you do. He's been very upset about Miss Zoli being here. But what else could I do? I couldn't leave her down there in the middle of all that madness. And I can't abandon her now."

We walked down to the first level to her room. As we entered, she was slowly approaching the door, still wearing her nightgown. "Miss Zoli, I want you to meet..." Again she was in a walking daze, I pretended not to notice, hoping that my voice might bring her back. "This is Mrs. Henderson. She's going to stay here with you until we come home."

Mrs. Henderson extended her hand in Miss Zoli's direction, "Hello, Miss Zoli, how are you today?"

I was stunned when Miss Zoli looked into her eyes and replied, "I is fine, thank yah."

"Miss Zoli, I'm going to leave you now. I'm sure you and Mrs. Henderson are going to be fine. The two of you have a lot in common. She has six children."

"You does?"

"I most certainly do. I have four sons and two daughters."

I left the room, knowing the two of them shared a bond that perhaps would allow Miss Zoli to connect with us.

Miraculously, thank God, the center was still in one piece when I arrived. As I pulled into the parking lot, I could barely recognize what was left of a once familiar neighborhood. The emptiness across the street where the strip mall once stood took my breath away. Even the rubble had been taken away. I was so overwhelmed by the changes, that the absence of those familiar surroundings made me feel sick to my stomach. I thought about the people at the stores in the mall that I'd become friendly with over the years. Mr. Kim the grocer, Mrs. Washington who owned the cleaners, the Jamesons, who lost their life's work when their video

store went up in smoke, a Korean family had just bought the electronics store less than a month ago, now all of that was gone and
their livelihood destroyed.

Wrapped around the building was a line of at least two hundred people waiting for the center to open. My heart sank even
deeper with the realization that the people who needed our services were even more desperate than ever before. How could we
do it, I wondered. We were already stretched beyond our service
capacity before last Wednesday, now it seemed impossible for us to
meet the overwhelming need.

Once inside the building, I noticed a few staff members in the
hall whispering nervously to one another. I looked into their eyes
on the way to my office and saw fear and anguish.

Being back at work made me feel even weaker and depleted
of energy than I had felt on my way to work. I just sat at my desk
in a state of suspended pain, burrowing my shoulders and back
into the center of the black leather chair. I wondered through my
numbness what we were going to do next? Our staff was already
severely overextended in terms of the caseload that we handle.
How could we take on anymore? I sat there in a fog, lost in my
thoughts and fears as they raced across my mind. Where do I begin today? What to do first? I just didn't know.

Dora buzzed me on the intercom. "Excuse me, Mrs. Stewart,
I have Mr. Stewart on the other line. He said he needed to speak
to you immediately. He sounds pretty upset, and says that it's an
emergency."

I picked up the other line, "John, what's wrong?" I asked.

"You're not going to believe this." I barely recognized his voice,
distorted by pain as he spoke. He sounded like a wounded, lost
little boy.

"I'm not going to believe what? What's wrong?" I begged. My
heart was racing, my stomach churned and I felt like my whole
body was about to burst.

He paused for a moment, I could hear him breathing heavily.
"It's gone."

"What's gone? John, what are you talking about?"

"I told you they were going to get me, but you refused to believe me. Woman, I told you that my life was going to be destroyed and it happened. We thought it was over, but we were wrong. Last night they burned my building down. It's over, Angela, everything is gone."

"What do you mean, everything is gone? Honey, that's not possible. I thought that your employees were guarding the building?" I gasped, feeling his pain flow into me. I couldn't believe my ears.

"Last night I told them to go home to get a good night's sleep. There were at least twenty marines stationed a block away.

"What do you mean you sent them home? Why did you do a thing like that?"

"You know why, because we all thought that the worst was over. Remember hearing on the radio that Bradley was lifting the curfew last night, because the troops had finally regained control over the city?

He paused for a moment, I could hear his heavy breathing, his choking voice, trying to stop his tears. "Angela, do you realize what this means? It means that everything is gone, I've lost everything. Everything I ever hoped for and planned to be, went up last night in a cloud of black smoke. Now all that's here is a pile of worthless rubble."

"Honey, please calm down. You're wrong. The worst is over. We're safe. We have each other, and you know that's the most important thing in life. We can rebuild the business. We've done it before, and we can do it again, only this time we can do it faster. You've got insurance, and they'll pay for it."

"I don't want to do it over again. I can't do this, not now, not at my age. I'm tired of always being behind the eight ball. I told you this was going to happen. But you didn't want to believe me."

"Honey, I'm so sorry, so very, very sorry that this happened," I said with tears streaming down my face. "Where are you right now?"

"I'm in the middle of all this rubble. There's nothing left. Do you hear me Angela? Everything's gone."

"Listen, don't leave. I'm on my way over. I'll be there in fifteen or twenty minutes. Is there anyone there with you?"

"Yeah, most of the staff is here, sifting through the rubble, trying to salvage whatever they can. But there's nothing left. I know that. They're going through the motions to make me feel good," he said. Then he simply hung up the phone without saying another word.

When I hung up the phone, I felt a force strike my stomach and knock the wind out of me. It had to be a mistake. I didn't want to believe that Stewart Computers was gone, that it had actually been destroyed. That seemed impossible. I just sat there focusing on my husband, and what he must be going through now. My heart was numb, I couldn't think about my personal loss, it was too much of a burden to bear.

"Dora, there's an emergency and I'm going to have to leave the office. I'm not sure if I'll be back today."

"Mrs. Stewart, what's wrong? Is there anything I can do for you?"

"No honey, your hands are full. Mr. Stewart's building burned down last night, and I'm going over there to be with him. Please inform the rest of the staff that I will be in tomorrow." On my way out I said, "I'm going to stop by Doc Whitney's office and let him know what's going on."

"Yes ma'am. Mrs. Stewart, tell Mr. Stewart that I'm sorry."

"Thanks, honey. That means an awful lot to me."

I rushed into Doc's office, his secretary wasn't there. I knocked on his partially closed door, and his deep resonating voice replied, "Come on in." When I entered the room, he was sitting at his small round conference table in the middle of a conversation with a well-dressed and important looking middle-aged man.

"Doc, I apologize for disturbing you, but I needed to talk to you before I left."

"No problem, Angela, please have a seat," he replied, waving me into the room. I sat down next to this man. "Mr. Jamison, this is my director of family services, Angela Stewart. She is one of the best, if not the best social workers I've ever worked with in my forty years of being in this business."

"Mr. Jamison is part of the Rebuild L.A. committee. He's representing the construction industry and is doing a detailed needs assessment survey of the social service agencies to identify the need. They want to focus on rebuilding the social service and medical offices first."

"Doc, I didn't mean to interrupt your meeting." I said. "But, I wanted you to know that I have to leave now. And I'm not sure if I will be back today or not. John's building was burned down last night, and he's pretty devastated by it."

"Angela, I'm so very, very sorry to hear that," Doc said, shaking his head with disgust. "I know that's a tremendous loss to John. He's put so much into that business. And John is such a fine young man. I can only imagine what he's going through right now. It must be a terrible burden he's carrying now."

"Mr. Jamison, this family is a perfect example of how devastating, how destructive this riot has been. The loss of this business is another tremendous blow to our community. I call it a riot, because that's exactly what it was. I know there's a lot of discussion going on right now in our community as to whether or not what happened was a riot or a rebellion. A rebellion is a political force that directly confronts a system of oppression. What happened here was a violent free-for-all, an undirected and very misguided venting of pent up anguish. It was the closest thing to a civil war this nation has seen in a hundred years. Six thousand fires in three nights? Sounds like a civil war to me.

"And anyone, any business, any man, woman, boy or girl, who stood in the way of this wave of madness that swept through our community was harmed. It didn't matter if you had given your life to this community. It's a sin and a shame. What happened in Watts thirty years ago was bad, and a deep blow to our community, but this most recent riot could be the death blow." He looked at me with sadness, while his face filled with fresh sorrow.

"Angela, go ahead, it's no problem. And take a few days off if you need. Leave. Tell John if there's anything I can do, to please call me. He's been good to the center in terms of support, not only lending his wonderful wife.

"Be sure to tell him that we're one hundred percent behind him, and we'll do anything that we can to help him rebuild."

"Thank you, Doc, I really appreciate it."

They both rose as I stood up. I shook Mr. Jamison's hand. "It was a pleasure meeting you, Mrs. Stewart. I'm sorry it was under such an unfortunate circumstance."

"Thank you, Mr. Jamison."

"Here's my card. If there's anything I can do, please have your husband give me a call." On my way out, I glanced at it. The card had his name and a 'Rebuild L.A.' logo. I smiled as I thought to myself, that this brother works pretty fast.

Outside, the line of clients had swelled. In less than a half hour it looked like the lines had quadrupled. There were close to a thousand people waiting for assistance wrapped around the building.

I looked across the street again and thought about what Miss Zoli said about her experience in the Korean store that was now gone. She blamed herself for something that was beyond her control, something that had nothing to do with her at all.

I couldn't believe that after all we went through, that this could happen. Perversely, I wished it had of burned down during the first night. Then we wouldn't have to go through what were facing today. I knew I was going to have to put on a good, strong face for him. I cried and cried not so much for the loss of the business, but what this loss means to my husband. He's put so much of himself into it.

Now I finally had to admit, at least to myself, that my husband was right. All last week, he was so worried about losing his business, I thought he was just being paranoid. But maybe he knew something was going to happen. And when we finally took a deep breath thinking it was all over, his worst possible nightmare happened. Just last night before we went to bed, I asked him if he felt silly for having been such a worry wart. He finally sighed and smiled, and admitted that I was right. Yet, now I can't help but feel guilty for trying to reassure him that everything was going to be alright,

Maybe I shouldn't have tried to minimize his fears. But what else was I supposed to do? How could life be so cruel?

When I reached the building, I couldn't believe my eyes— everything was gone. There was only one wall standing, the one along the back. The rest was smoldering embers, strewn about like it had been hit by a smartbomb.

In that moment, I knew our lives would never be the same. Suddenly, hard as it was for me to believe, I felt more pain today than I did yesterday. I was lost in a maze of devastating emotion. I found my husband walking around through the rubble, his shoulders hunched over, kicking a can, looking like a lost child. He didn't hear me approaching or feel my presence. I touched his shoulder. He turned to me, his eyes red, burning with pain, anger and the shadow of tears. "I told you, I told you this was going to happen," he cried. "I told you if I had stayed down here I could've stopped this from happening. But oh, no, you wouldn't let me."

I felt guilty, almost as if he were blaming me. "Honey, calm down, this is like crying over spilt milk."

"There you go again. How can you compare Stewart Computers to spilt milk? Woman, don't you know what this means? Everything is gone. What about all of my employees?"

I stood there, frozen in pain. I couldn't respond. There were no words, no answers. Nothing. Nothing but his pain and mine, in the midst of all that we had lost.

"How did this happen? The marines were a block away. Why didn't the fire department come?" my mind begged silently as I watched my husband trapped in the shadow of his sorrow.

Finally, I found the strength to say, "Honey, we still have each other, and that's the most important thing. We can build it again. You've done it before and you can do it again."

"No, I can't. Ang, I don't have it in me. I'm too old to start all over again."

"Yes, you can. You're only forty seven. You're still a young man." As I spoke my heart sank deeper into the darkest space I'd ever known. I'd never actually considered the possibility of losing our business.

The words from a conversation we had over twenty years ago echoed in my heart.

"Ang, I'm tired of this. I want to be my own man, and start my own business."

"You do?"

"Yeah, I've been thinking about putting a little computer firm together."

"I thought everything was going pretty well for you at IBM."

"You're right, but you never know what's going to happen next in the corporate world. Baby, I want to run my own show. I know I've got what it takes to make a go of it.

"Ten, twenty years from now, I don't want to look back and think about what I could've done as my own man." He wanted so desperately to make his mark in the business world and he did. He was a pioneer at IBM, one of the company's first Black managers. And my husband wore his success well. Yet, it took its toll. At age twenty nine, he had an ulcer and severe anxiety that he tried to hide from everyone including himself.

Now that his dream were gone up in smoke, it was time for me to help to pick up the pieces again, collect the fragments of his shattered ego and find his wholeness all over again.

And to add insult to injury, I knew he was going to want me to get rid of Miss Zoli even more so now. But I can't, and I don't know why. I can't abandon her, and in my heart I knew she needed to stay with us until we located her family.

Jim, one of John's oldest and most trusted employees, was walking around, putting out a few of the smoldering flames with a garden hose. John turned his head, as if to reject any notion of Jim's presence.

"Look at that sign," John said, pointing to the fallen logo that rested at the front of the building. "It says 'Stewart Computers.' Can you tell me where it is? It's a joke, it's gone."

For nearly a half hour, I stayed there. I tried to console him several times as he wandered around, lost in the midst of his destroyed dream. But I couldn't pull him out of it. He put up a wall and simply refused to let me in. My own frustration led me to talk to his staff, and comfort them. Their situation was far more desperate than ours. Yet, despite their sudden loss of income, they were far more concerned about my husband's welfare than their own. John wandering through the rubble aimlessly and grumbling to himself, "I should've stayed. I should've stayed."

I could tell that his behavior was starting to get to those who were present. I could tell by the way that they moved, that they were becoming increasingly distressed by his anguish. As they reached out to touch him, he shunned their offer and pushed them away. I wanted to wrap my arms around him and ease his pain.

"Mr. Stewart, I'm awful sorry that we didn't stay," said Mr. Brown, his security guard for more than ten years.

"Man, it's not your fault. I should've stayed the whole time this riot was going on and guarded it myself. It was my business."

"And what good would that have done, sir? Somebody could've hurt you real bad, or killed you. It's our fault. We shouldn't have let you talk us into going home."

"Would both of you stop blaming yourselves!" I cried. "This doesn't make any sense. It's nobody's fault. This is something that happened that we have to deal with and move on. Assessing blame is not going to bring Stewart Computers back."

"Angie, you're a woman," John replied shaking his head. "You just don't understand."

"What I do understand is that it's a blessing that neither you nor any of your employees were harmed. That's what I understand and that's the most important thing."

"Blessing?" his yelling startled me. "Woman, have you lost your mind?"

"I know you're upset. But you don't have to take it out on me."

"Yes, I can. I can do whatever I choose, since this is all your fault!"

"My fault?" I cried. "Now I know you're losing it." I turned and walked away.

"Where are you going?"

"I'm going home. Yes, you've lost your business, and I'm terribly sorry that happened. You don't know how much this hurts me. But I don't have to stand around here and take any abuse from you. I haven't done that before, and I'm not doing it now."

"So you're deserting me in my time of need?"

I almost laughed, but I knew that he was serious. I stopped, turned and faced my husband. "John, you know I am not deserting you. I'm just going home to get out of your way. I'm so sorry that we lost Stewart Computers last night. But I'm not going to stand here and let you blame me or anyone else for that matter. We just have to move on and begin to rebuild"

"Will you be home when I get there?"

"Of course I will. Where else would I be?"

"You have no reason to stay with me. I have nothing more to give you since my business is gone."

My heart sank even deeper as I stood there facing my husband. I couldn't bear to reply. I wondered who this stranger was standing before me, and what had happened to the man that I loved for so many years. After all that we've been through, I'd never seen him like this. Tears streamed once more from my eyes, as I walked to my car. Today, not only did something die within me, I realized a big, precious, chunk of my husband had gone up in smoke with the destruction of his dream.

thirteen

It was all gone. All gone. What a dirty, low down trick to play on a man like me. I've done everything that I can do according to the rules of the game. I worked hard, took real good care of my family. I go to church, I am a decent man. Why me? I even tried to help people around me. How did this happen, and why did it have to happen to me? What did I do to deserve this? How is it possible that the marines were only a block away, and they let my building burn down to the ground? Did they set it on fire? And if they didn't, why wasn't the fire department here?

Everything that I've done, everything that was important to was gone. My life was over. I got the kick in the teeth of a lifetime. I'm no good for anybody right now. They might as well put me six feet under.

Just when I finally relaxed and cooled out, thinking the worst was over, believing that I could take a deep breath and go to my office today like it was going to be just another normal day, I got here and there was nothing left. On Sunday night, while on my way home to my daily check on the building, I heard on the radio that the mayor was planning to lift the curfew in Monday. I thought that my life was getting back on track, and that come Monday morning we would be back to business. I knew that it wouldn't be business as usual, but I did know that my doors would be open.

The marines and the National Guard had finally regained control of the city, even the hardest hit areas. When I got there last night, I told Johnnie, Paul, Anthony, Frankie, Butch, Franco and Spencer—the crew that was duty that evening—to go home. They didn't want to leave. "Are you sure about this, Mr. Stewart? We really don't mind staying."

"No, you can go home , you've already done so much, more than I ever expected," I told them. It meant an awful lot to me, their dedication and the way they risked their lives for me and my company.

When I turned the corner this morning, I thought my mind was playing games with me. I couldn't believe my eyes. How could this be? I've worked too hard for this. It's too bitter a pill to swallow. Everybody was talking on the radio and on the television about how much the Koreans were suffering. How about a brother like me? What was I supposed to do now, now that my dream was gone? I might as well crawl up in a hole and die.

For ten years straight, Stewart Computers was listed on Black Enterprise's top one hundred business list. I had the world on a string, or so I thought. The Black business magazine called me, "A bold, successful and daring entrepreneur. A man willing to take the necessary risks to make it to the top." I had a name for myself in the most competitive business this nation can still claim to be a leader in. Black man, self-made millionaire, a leader in his community. I loved to see the looks of subtle shock, the hush whispers of secretaries and executives when I entered the corporate suites to do business.

Sure, I had plenty of doors closed on me. I heard more, "No thank you, we're not interested," than I care to remember. But that was okay because each time that I heard no, it was just fuel I needed to make me stronger.

And now everything was gone. When I saw what was left of my building, I think my mind must've blanked out for a moment or two. I still don't remember calling my wife, and telling her what had happened, but she said that I did. I told her that this was going to happen, but little Miss Pollyanna didn't want to hear any of it. "Everything is going to be alright, I don't know what you are worrying about." But I was right. I knew in my gut that this was going to happen. And what makes me so mad is that I listened to her and let her convince me that everything was fine, when I knew that I should've stayed down here.

Now what does she have to say? "It could be worse. You could've been killed." She kept going on and on about how we have so much to be grateful for, and that at least we have each other and a roof over our heads. Doesn't she understand that most of me died last night in that fire? I had nothing to live for. Everything was gone. I was a fool to listen to her and my staff about my own business. I should know better. I should've done what a man is supposed to do.

Julius was walking through the rubble, looking more dazed than me. "Julius, what happened?" I asked.

"I don't know, Mr. Stewart. I decided to come in a little early this morning around seven, and when I got here, the building was ablaze. No fire trucks were in sight. I called 911, but nobody ever came. I ran down the street to the Marines, and they didn't budge, not one inch. They said they had to stay to their assigned patrol site to maintain the peace. I'm awful sorry that this had to happen. You're a good man and you deserve better. I know what this company means to you and how hard you've worked all these years. I been with you since the beginning, and I know how bad this is.

Wihelmenhia, my secretary, made it to the building about fifteen or twenty minutes after I arrived. The loss stunned her, too. She was sobbing. All I could do was put my arms around her. "Mr. Stewart, I can't believe this. I'm sorry. I wish I could change this, but I can't. You have been so good to me and my family. This was more than a job to me. This place was my second home."

I didn't know what to do. I didn't want to go home. I couldn't face my family. What could I say to them? How could I ever make up for letting them down and being such a failure? I couldn't provide for them anymore. How could I look into my children's eyes and expect them to respect me? How was I supposed to act? What was I supposed to do, now that everything's gone?

My wife kept harping on the brighter side. Where was it? Couldn't she see there was no brighter side? How could she be so optimistic? She made me sick to my stomach. I didn't need to be patronized. That was not helping me one bit. It just made me feel worse. How could I be thankful, when there's nothing to live for anymore?

Life wasn't that simple. I had seen plenty of men lose their jobs, and their marriage went down the tubes. Women didn't stand by their men too long anymore when the money stopped coming in. And I knew it could happen to me. Even though Angie's been very supportive of me, deep down inside I knew she wasn't going to hang around waiting for me to become productive again. I knew I had got plenty of money in the bank, but that isn't going to last forever. What was going to happen to happen when the money ran out? What was she going to think of me then? And what were my children going to feel about their old man, who couldn't support them anymore?

After I got home, Angela had even called my mother because she said I was out of control. How was I supposed to act? What was I supposed to do? Walk around here as if nothing's wrong? All day long the only thing that kept coming to my mind was all of those hungry days and ice cold nights I lived through when I was just a kid in Cleveland. I never wanted to feel that kind of hunger again, but here it was. Suddenly, I was sitting on the edge of returning to poverty.

And what does my mother know about what I'm going through? She should know how I feel, but what does she say? "Johnnie, calm yourself down. There's no need for you to be acting like this. I know you don't want me getting on a plane to come out there and straighten you up. Do you?"

She didn't even tell me she's sorry I lost my business. You know the one that's been supporting her more years than I can count. Everybody just thinks I go out and pick money off a tree? Hell no! I work for it, and they know how hard I work to make all of this happen. But nobody wanted to talk about that. They just wanted to make me feel bad for being upset.

After dinner, I stayed out of everybody's way. I knew they didn't want to be around me; I could see it in their eyes. So I camped out in my office for the rest of the evening. I didn't feel like talking anyway. Finally after everybody had gone to bed, I went down-stairs to the family room to watch the eleven o'clock news.

I turned on the television and was flipping through the chan-nels with the remote control when Miss Zoli appeared at the edge of the sofa. I wasn't up to talking to her, so I hoped she was just wandering around in one of her dazes.

"'Cuse me suh. Is something wron?"

"No ma'am. Nothing wrong."

"Well den, why is yah down heah sitting all by yohsef like somethin mighty terrible done happined?"

"Miss Zoli, I don't mean to be rude, but you won't understand, and if you don't mind, I would prefer to be alone."

"No, de spirit is ah tellin me dat dere is somethin wrong wid yah."

"What does the spirit have to do with anything?"

"De spirit gots somethin tah do with ev'rythang. It's dah spirit dats bin guidin me all my life."

"Well, what does the spirit have to say about how to find your children?"

"Dat ain't bin 'vealed tah me as ah yet. Don't yah knows dat de spirit don't tells me ev'rythin? But when it tells me somethin I make sho dat I is listenin tah whot its got tah say tah Momma Zoli.

"Yes, suh, it woke me up outtah my dreams. I was in dis heah beautiful place, kinda like bein in heabin, ah whole lot prettier dan dis heah place."

I didn't want to go off on this crazy old woman. There's no telling what that might do to her. So I decided to kick back and let her run her mouth, hoping that she would get tired of me and go back to bed.

"I sees it. Yes, I does," she said pointing her crooked brown finger at me. "Yoh sufferin 'bout thangs dat ain't mountin up tah nothin. Don't yah knows dat all dat is impotant is de blessings yah gots in yoh life?"

"What are you talking about?"

"Yah gots so much tah be thankful foh, dat you ain't knowin it de way dat yah should. Chile, yoh sufferin ovah whot yah thanks yah done loss. Thangs dat ain't yohs tah keep in de firse place."

"Miss Zoli, I don't mean to be rude, but why should I listen to anything you have to say? You don't even know how you got here!"

"It's not foh yah tah believe me," she said while her piercing eyes seared mine. "But foh yah tah believe de spirit. Ah is only de spirit's messenger. I knows I is ah brokin vessel, but son, yah bettah listen tah what de spirit gots tah say.

"Doesn't yah knows how blessed you is? Yah gots dis heah beautiful family dat ain't nobody takin away from yah. Yah gots two good chilrens, and a fine wife."

"Has my wife been talking to you?"

"No, dat sweet chile ain't said one word tah me 'bout yah."

"Then who told you?"

"Is yah listening tah me? I sees yah sittin out here painin so much, ovah somethin dat ain't impotant."

"You wouldn't understand."

"I does bettah dan yah thinks. Dis heah siteeation is causin yah a heap ah sufferin an eatin yoh insides up like maggots eatin up a slab ah rotten meat on a hot 'Sippi day. But ain't y'all bin tellin me dat yah was born free in dis heah worle? You doesn't knows what it's like tah loose precious thangs, dats closer tah yah heart dan it's own beatin."

Tired of her ramblings, I interrupted and said, "Miss Zoli, ma'am, could you please tell me what you are trying to say?"

"Ain't it plain? Can't yah see? Whot I is trying tah say is dat you doesn't knows in yoh heart how lucky yah is. Yah bin spared whot darkies like me had tah live through in 'Sippi."

"What have I been spared?" I don't know what was wrong with me. Why was I continuing this idiotic conversation with this crazy old woman?

"Yah been spared," a glassy layer of tears suddenly covered her eyes. "A whole lot moh dan yah can evah knows. I cain't talk 'bout all dat Momma Zoli done seen an live through."

"What can't you talk about?"

"Bout how it feels tah lose a chile. How it feels tah have yah own flesh an blood snatched away from yah an yah can't do nothin but cry. Yah cain't knows how it feels in a mothah's heart tah lose each an ev'ry one of huh youngins, one by one tah dem ole evil men. An yah cain't even do nothin 'bout it. Dat's a hurtin pain like yah ain't nevah seen, an it's somethin dat yah nevah gonna forgits, foh de rest ah yoh life. It's gonna be wid yah till de day yah goes tah de grave." Tears were racing down both her leathery cheeks, toward her jagged jaw.

"Are you talking about losing a child to death?" I asked. "I know that feels, a lot more than you think. Angela had six or seven miscarriages, more than I can count before James was born. It hurt me so bad, 'til I got numb inside. I stopped wanting to have children."

"No suh, I ain't talkin 'bout dat, losin a chile tah de Lawd foh natu'al reasons. I is talkin 'bout losin yoh own flesh an blood, when dey is sole away from yah. Dere is no place in yoh heart dat is evah ready foh dat, an it eats yah up and tears up whot evah is left behine.

"Yah knows yah cain't be dere tah hep dem make it through anothah day. Yah cain't be dere when dem evil white folk be doin whotevah dere wicked minds be tellin dem tah do."

"What evil people are you talking about?"

"Don't yah knows? I is talkin 'bout dem evil ole slave tradahs." Her tears continued to flow as she sat there rocking herself. I didn't know what to do. I thought she was about to go off the deep end. "Yah see, I doesn't knows if mah children is livin or dead. I lost dem, one by one tah de slave tradahs. No mattah how much I begged dat evil ole man, Massa Steadwell, he did whot he wanted tah do, he took mah babies away from me. An each an ev'ry time dat dey did, dey yanked out a piece ah mah heart. I got weaker an weaker, til I thought I wuz gonna die.

"I axed de Lawd tah let me live lon enough tah see de day ah freedom when I could takes it upon mahself tah fine each an ev'ry one ah dem. An I is gonna do jist dat, befoh I lay down dese old bones foh de last time. I gots tah fine my chilrens an my husban. So if de Lawd done seen fit tah spare yah dat misery yah shore is a mighty lucky man. Yah ain't nevah gonna knows how terrible dat is. Nobody can come an snatch up dat purdy li'l gul ah yohs or dat fine strappin boy. Cain't nobody do dat, an yah blessed.

I didn't know what to say. For the first time since she invaded my home, I felt sorry for her. I've seen a few crazy people before, but I've never heard of anything like this. She was living in the most bizarre world of hallucinations—one that was beyond my understanding. I had never heard of anything like this before. Because her hallucinations were so vivid in detail, she even took my mind briefly off my catastrophe. I was more convinced now than ever before that we had to get her out of the house and into an institution that could help her.

"Miss Zoli, I want to thank you for your advise. I'm going to turn in now. So why don't you lay down, too? Get yourself a good night's sleep and I'll see you tomorrow."

"Yes, suh, yoh rite, I do needs tah git some sleep. I ain't slept on no bed like dat. I's used tah sleepin on de groune."

"Well, goodnite suh. An please let yoh heart remembas whot I said."

"Yes, ma'am, I will."

She rose slowly from the couch, and dragged her right leg across the floor to her room.

I still don't know what to make of all this. I've heard of people believing that they are someone famous, but why would an old Black woman ever want to believe she was once a slave? It just didn't make any sense to me. She blew me away because she was so convincing. If I didn't know better, I'd swear she was telling the truth. Maybe the stories were passed on to her by her family. She was probably old enough to have known former slaves, maybe when she was a young girl growing up. All I knew is that she was definitely crazy and I wanted her out of my house, and far away from my family. She gave me the creeps.

When I got in the bed, Angela was already asleep, or doing a good job pretending. Even though I knew that old woman was clearly a mental case, her words kept running through my mind. "Yah jist doesn't knows how lucky you is. Yah jist doesn't know lucky yah is."

I tossed and turned for hours. It took me hours to asleep. When I did, I was in a strange, eerie place. I saw an old wrinkled-up white man wearing a wide brim straw hat, with a black band wrapped around it, a dingy suit and a string bowtie. His eyes had a funny gleam, and he wore an evil smirking smile. He had my children chained together and was loading them onto a horse-drawn cart. They were frightened, scared to death, begging and pleading to be set free. I could hear my little girl screaming, "Daddy, please save me! Please help me!" My son tried desperately to free himself from his chains, but couldn't. The shackles seem to swallow his arms. I tried to reach out and rescue my children, but I couldn't move. My hands and feet were bound by heavy black chains as well. I tried to tear the chains apart but I couldn't. I stood there, helpless, like a child, as he unhitched the horses and began to ride away from me. I tried with all my might, every ounce of my being, to break away but I couldn't. Then my back pierced with an overwhelming pain. I turned around, and saw another white man holding a lash over me. As my children moved away from, I struggled desperately to stand, and run after them, but I couldn't. I slumped helplessly in a puddle of cold mud. The last thing I remember was the sheer terror on both of their faces.

I woke up in the middle of the night, in a cold sweat, panting and gasping for air. The sheets surrounding my body were drenched in sweat. I couldn't breathe. My heart was pounding so rapidly, for a moment I thought I was going to die.

The brutal dream haunted me. Even though I was awake, I could still see those awful images of my children being torn away from me, and my impotence in failing to save them. I knew Miss Zoli's words had sliced into my mind and into my dreams like a hot knife cutting soft butter. I sat in the bed wondering what I would feel if someone actually took my children away and I couldn't do a damn thing to stop them. That old woman just spooked the hell out of me, and I wanted her out of my house faster than I did before.

"Nobody can steal yoh youngins form yah ... Yah bin spares a lot moh dan yah can evah knows."

"Angela," I called out. No response, she was dead to the world. I shook her, calling her name again, this time a bit louder. "Angela, wake up." Still no response. I continued to shake her until she woke up. Finally she opened her eyes, looked a bit confused and asked, "What's wrong? Did something happen to one of the kids?"

"No," I replied. "We've gotta do something about that woman."

"John, for God's sake! Why did you wake me up in the middle of the night to talk about Miss Zoli?"

"Because I want her out of my house!"

"So what else is new?" she said yawning.

"Angie, I don't want her in my house talking out of her head about being a slave. She's crazy and I'm tired of her nonsense. Tomorrow you find her a place to stay."

"Where am going to take her? Do you know how many people lost their homes last week? There were thousands."

"I don't know, you're a social worker. Just find her a place. I want her out of my house."

"What's gotten into you? You're not telling me everything."

"Like I said, just do it."

She rolled over away from me, and said nothing for several minutes. "John, this is not like you. I know you're upset about losing Stewart Computers, but why are you taking your frustrations out on a poor, helpless woman?"

"I want her out of my house."

I couldn't get that dream out of my mind. It was too real, too frightening. I could feel the chains that trapped my hands, preventing me from rescuing my children. But I realized it was stupid to spend my time on a silly dream. I had had too many other things to contend with—like finding a way to support my own family and keep it together after losing my business. Having made my point with Angela, I turned over and fell back into an uneasy sleep.

At breakfast, Angie started before I could get a work in edgewise. "I don't know what your problem is, but then again maybe I do."

"What are you talking about?"

"I know what's disturbing you about Miss Zoli being here."

"What is that oh wise one?"

She rolled her eyes at me like I was a disobedient child and said, "Like I told you before, you're intimidated by her presence because she reminds you of your past. You're worried that you might end up penniless like her, especially since Stewart Computers was destroyed.

You are a good man, and I know you have a heart that's much bigger than the one you're showing right now. You don't really mean it when you say you want her out of here today, because you know there is no place for me to take her. She's not leaving this house."

"You're disobeying me?!"

"I'm what?" she snapped. "Man, have you lost your mind? What do you mean 'obey?'"

"You heard me. Angela, you know exactly what I am talking about."

"Obey, let's see. Is than an African word similar to Omowale? You should know after all these years that I have never been into obeying you or anyone else for that matter. I think you're the one who's losing touch with reality."

"You know exactly what I mean. You're not giving me any respect, going against my wishes for some old homeless woman who's never done a damn thing for you."

"John, I'm not going to start my day off with another argument. I've got too many other things on my mind."

"Yeah, and everyone else is more important than me."

"Like I said, I'm not going to stand here and argue with you about her. You don't have to worry about her being here in the house all day alone. I've made arrangements for Mrs. Henderson to be here every day."

Angela turned her head, and saw Miss Zoli standing in the middle of the kitchen without our noticing her presence, until it was too late.

"I needs tah say somethin tah both of yah," she said looking at me. "Yah bin so good tah me, treat me like I was a part ah dis heah family. But I doesn't wonts mah bein heah tah cause yah no troubles. It was so kine of yah tah take me in, but I best be's on mah way. I gots tah gits back tah 'Sippi, an I might as well begins dat journey rite now.

"I jist wannah thanks yah for all dat yah has done foh me. I knows dat de Lawd will be bringin a heap ah blessings on dis heah house."

"Miss Zoli, you can't leave. Where would you go?" Angela asked.

"Sugah, I will goes wheah evah de spirit of de Lawd sends me."

"Do you know how far away Mississippi is?"

"It don't mattah. If yah has walks as fah as I has since freedom broke, yah would knows dat dese feets could walk aroune de worle if I had tah, tah fine mah chilrens."

"Mommie, Daddy we don't want Miss Zoli to leave," cried Ashley rushing into the room.

"Yeah, dad, that goes for me too," interjected my son, as he followed her.

Angela looked at her and said, "Miss Zoli, we really don't want you to leave. There's no place for you to go right now. You need to stay with us, at least for a few more days, because you could get hurt in the streets."

"I knows yah wonts me tah stay, but I knows yoh husband don't wonts me heah, an I knows why. So I'll be own mah way."

She put me on front street. What could I say to make this situation right? "No, ma'am, that's not exactly true. I hope you'll stay because I don't want my wife and children out on the streets looking for you, and I don't think you need to be out there yourself. Angie's right, it's still very dangerous out there. So you better stay put, here with us."

Miss Zoli looked to Angela for help. She was standing there smiling, vigorous nodding her head with approval.

"I'll give it some thought, but I ain't makin no promises. De only thang dats own mah mine is gettin back, jist a little closah tah de place wheah mah chilrens is."

Angela smiled and said, "Okay, enough of all this talk on empty stomachs. Let's sit down and have breakfast.

"Miss Zoli, are you hungry?"

"I sho nuff is."

Miss Zoli and the children sat down at the table. Ashley looked at me with a frightened expression on her face, "Daddy, I'm scared."

"Baby, what's wrong now?" Are you still worried about going to school?"

"No, I had a scary dream last night."

"What did you dream, baby?"

"That a mean old white man with big green eyes put these heavy chains on me that hurt my hands and feet. He took me and James away from you and Mommie, and put us in this old cart. When we got to this town, they took off my clothes and made me stand in front of all these people naked. It was so scary—I've never had a dream like that before. Then this other evil looking man brought me and took me to his big old house."

"Dad," James interrupted, "I had a dream just like that, too! The only difference was that I fought back and tried to save me and Ash. But they beat me so bad, I couldn't do anything."

My wife and I just stared at each other. I'd never heard of anything like this before.

"I don't know what it means, son. I have to tell you I had just about the same dream last night."

"You did?" asked Angela. "Why didn't you tell me that's what made you so upset?"

"Did you have it too, mom?" asked James.

"No, honey, I don't think so. I don't remember dreaming last night."

My mind was still reeling with all of this. It made no sense to me at all. "This is all very strange." I wonder why we all had the same dream.

Miss Zoli looked at me and said, "De spirit is tryin tah sho y'all somethin."

"Show us what?"

"It's showin to you how blessed yah is tah have yah familee togethah." Suddenly, her face was drained of emotion, and a blank stare settled in. Her eyes drifted into the place that was beyond our world. And we all sat there around the breakfast table, uncertain and puzzled, not knowing what the significance of this old woman's presence in our lives really meant.

fourteen

What has happened to my husband? Why is he being so mean and unreasonable? In my wildest dreams, I never thought he'd react like this. I knew he was hurting, but why did he have to take it out on me? It was only a business. The world wasn't over. We had so much to be thankful for, that his pain wouldn't let him see. The most important thing was that as long as we had each other we could face anything that came.

I cried all of the way home. The tears just wouldn't stop. I wanted to be there for him, but he pushed me away and said it was all my fault. Doesn't he know that I'm hurting, too? Stewart Computers was a part of me, just like it was a part of him. I'd been there from the beginning, and did everything I could, devoted a big part of myself—encouraging and helping him in any way that I could. I didn't want this to happen. But I'm so thankful, so very, very grateful that John wasn't around when it did. He could've been killed.

When I got home, I headed straight for his office, and began looking for his insurance papers. That was the least I could do. After that, I found Mrs. Henderson and Miss Zoli in the laundry room. Mrs. Henderson was loading clothes in the washing machine, while Miss Zoli sat watching her attentively.

"Mrs. Stewart, what are you doing home this time of day?" Mrs. Henderson asked.

"I had an emergency and had to leave the office."

"What kind of emergency are you talking about? By the look on your face, it seems mighty serious. What in heaven's name is wrong?"

"It's John."

"Did he get hurt?"

"No, he's alright," I replied slowly. The words seemed to get caught in the middle of my throat. I finally blurted out, "Stewart Computers was destroyed in a fire last night."

"Oh, my Lord," she replied dropping the washing machine's lid. The sound startled Miss Zoli, and caused her to almost fall from her seat. I leaped over to her and caught her by the shoulders.

"Miss Zoli, are you alright?"

"Yes, I is. It's just all ah dese 'traptions aroune heah gots mah insides all riled up."

"It's going to be alright. Sweetie, you're going to be fine," I said as reassuringly as I could.

"Mrs. Stewart, I'm so sorry to hear that. Is there anything that I can do?"

"No, ma'am. I'm afraid there isn't. John's taking it pretty hard. For the time being, I don't know what any of us can do."

I went upstairs to my room, fell across the bed and cried. My husband's words continued to haunt me, racing through my mind. "So you're deserting me right now? How could you do a thing like that in my time of need? ... Will you be home when I get there?"

I remembered my pleas falling on deaf ears, "John, please don't do this. Don't do this to us."

He had turned and walked away from me, as if I had already abandoned him and our life together. His angry words pierced my heart again, "You're going to leave me. I can see that in your eyes. You have no reason to stay. The business is gone, I have nothing more to give to you."

I was sure he knows better than that, but the severity of his pain created a cold barrier that prevented the warmth of my love and support from reaching his heart, and touching the place from which healing springs.

When the kids came home from their first day back at school, they found me sitting in the breakfast nook looking out over the backyard remembering all of the good times we had down there.

"Mom, what are you doing home so early?" asked James.

"Mommie, what's wrong?" asked Ashley.

"It's been a rough day. Did you two have a good day at school?" I asked, trying to figure out the gentlest way to tell them what had happened to our family business.

"Yeah, we did. But mom, what's wrong?" asked James.

"Sit down, I have something to tell you." They sat down slowly, continuing to carefully examine my face much more closely than they normally do. I took a deep breath that rattled against my empty stomach, still lacking the words to soften the blow of what I knew would have a profound impact on their lives. Most of all because of the way it was affecting their father,

"Stewart Computers was destroyed last night."

"Oh, no!" screamed Ashley. "Where's my daddy?"

Before I could answer, James pounded his hand on the glass table and demanded, sounding more like his father than ever before, "How did that happen?"

"We don't know for sure exactly what happened, or who set the fire. But you need to know that everything was destroyed and that your father is okay, but he's taking this very hard. He's very upset."

"Did daddy cry?"

"Yes, Ash, he did."

"How did it happen, mom? I thought dad had everything taken care of at the building, He told me last night that everything was fine and he couldn't wait to get back to work this morning," said James.

"Honey, that's what we all expected. Nobody thought that this was going to happen now."

"Mom, what's going to happen next?"

"I don't know for sure. We have to focus on the positive side of things. We still have each other, a roof over our heads, and enough money in the bank to last us a long time—long enough for your father to get the business up and running again. He's been very wise with our money and I don't want you worrying about this. We're going to be fine."

"Mom, if that's true, then why are you so worried?"

"James, more than anything else, I'm worried about your father's reaction. I have to warn you that he's not going to be very easy to get along with for a while, because he's so upset. He might say things that he doesn't mean to you. We have to be supportive and help him get through this time in any way that we can."

James managed to muster up a smile and said, "Mom, I know what I'm going to do."

"What's that?"

"I'm going to help dad rebuild Stewart Computers."

I don't know why, but my child's words touched my heart so deeply, that before I knew what had happened, I broke down in tears. Both of my sweet children came to me, wrapped their arms around me and wiped away my tears.

"Don't worry, mommie," sighed Ashley. "Everything's going to be alright."

John came home shortly before dinner. I was in the kitchen warming up dinner when he swept into the room in a gust of seething anger. His eyes radiated a wild, ferocious rage. My heart throbbed and pounded at the sight of him. I could see that his pain was eating him up, rapidly devouring his spirit and ripping him apart. For the first time since I'd known him, I was afraid of him. I had no idea what he might do next.

Without saying a word, he raced across the kitchen, snarling at me. He grumbled a few inaudible words to himself and left the room. I turned on the intercom, and heard him in our room screaming at the top of his lungs, "Why me? Why me? Why did this happen to me? What did I ever do to deserve this?"

Miss Zoli must have sensed something was wrong. She was smart enough to take a nap shortly before dinner. When I checked on her, I didn't have the heart to wake her up.

John ate dinner in complete silence. My stomach gurgled and burned while I picked at my food. The children wiggled uncomfortably in their seats, playing with the strips of turkey, clumps of dressing, mounds of yesterday's collard greens, corn and black-eyed peas instead of eating them. Everyone was on edge, anticipating my husband's volcanic eruption.

"Eat your dinner," he said harshly to the children. "Sit up in your seats and stop playing with your food."

"John, you don't need to speak to the children in that tone. They're not eating because they're worried about you."

"They better eat up while they can," he snarled at me. "James, what's wrong with you? Why aren't you eating?"

"I guess I'm not hungry, dad," he replied huddling over his food, speaking into his plate. His elbows burrowed into the table while his fork dangled from his hand like a pendulum, swinging back and forth over the corn and black-eyed peas he had yet to touch.

"Well, you better eat that food. There's no telling how long your gravy train is going to last." John's brown face was flushed with streaks of anger.

I wanted to shake him back into his right mind, and scream at this stranger, "Give me my husband back," but I knew my John couldn't hear me, his spirit was too far away to know how to return home.

"Dad, why are you acting like this?" asked James. "You know it's not the end of the world. I want to help you rebuild Stewart Computers."

"Don't be stupid!" he bellowed at my son. "What do you know about rebuilding anything, when you haven't done a damn thing in your life!" His words sliced through my heart. I didn't know what to do. I felt his pain, and now the deeper pain he'd inflicted upon my son.

"John, don't talk to him like that," I said firmly.

"Shut up!" he yelled, looking at me.

"Daddy, why are you being so mean?"

He turned and glared at Ashley, the former apple of his eye, with utter contempt. Ashley started crying. "Ash, honey," I said in as soothing a tone as I could muster up. "Shh, shh, it's going to be alright. Daddy is just a little upset right now."

"What are you trying to do now? Put words into my mouth? I suppose the next thing you'll be up to is trying to support this family."

"John," I said looking him straight in the eye, "I know you're very upset about losing Stewart Computers, but that gives you no right to act like you've lost your mind. I won't allow you to take out your frustrations on me or the children. You need to calm down and get a grip."

"Shut up!" he yelled, even louder than before. His thunderous roar seemed to fill the kitchen with rage. "Shut up!" he yelled again. "Or I'll" he said, springing from his seat and raising his hand in my direction.

"Or you'll do what?" I demanded, as my pain turned to anger. "Or you'll do what? Hit me? If that's what you think you need to do, you go ahead, my brother, and give it your best shot. But I want you to know it will be the first and the last time you ever lay a hand on me. I guarantee you that!"

"Woman, I ought to put you in your place once and for all!" he screamed.

"Put me in my place? How dare you! If you think you've got trouble now, you don't know what trouble is. How dare you even think about raising a hand to me!"

"Mommie, Daddy! Please stop," screamed Ashley.

I was so pissed off until I could only see red. I knew I surprised him, because he stood there studying me in a similar fashion to the way that I had studied him.

"And let me tell you one thing, John Stewart. Hear me good. If you ever lay a hand on me, if you do it today, if you do it tomorrow, or if you do it twenty years from now, I promise you on my mother's grave it will be the first and the last time you ever do such a thing. Do you hear me?

"On the day that you do, I will call the police and they will take your black behind to jail so fast that it will make your head spin. And when you make bail, you can rest assured that my relatives will be waiting for you to make sure that you never strike me again!

"Do I make myself clear? You know I don't tolerate any suggestion of violence, not in this house. I never have and I never will."

Ashley burst into tears, while James leaped to his feet and shouted, "Mom, dad, please stop it! You don't have to treat each other like this."

John hovered over me, suspended in time and space. He looked at James, turned and stalked out of the kitchen, headed downstairs. Before he landed on the first level, I had picked up the cordless phone resting on the counter next to the stove and dialed ten digits

"Hello,"

"Momma Mae-"

"Yes, baby. How are you doing?"

"Not too good right now," my voice trembled with an mixture of rage and fear.

"What's wrong? I can hear it in your voice. Did something happen to Johnnie or one of my grandbabies?"

"No, ma'am. John is acting like he's losing his mind. We lost Stewart Computers last night. I've never seen him like this before. He even threatened to hit me."

"He what?" she asked, her voice saturated with shock. "Put him on the phone."

"But Momma Mae-"

"Angela, I said, put him on the phone right now."

I walked downstairs. Through the glass wall I saw him on the patio, pacing in front of the pool. I walked over and handed him the phone.

"I don't want to talk to anybody."

"It's your mother."

"I don't want to talk to her either."

"Well, you'll have to tell her that yourself," I snapped, placing the phone on the small black lacquer table standing between us. I turned and walked back into the family room. I knew as soon as I was out of sight he'd pick up the phone. If anybody could cool his jets, it was certainly his mother.

A few minutes later, he rushed through the kitchen like a tornado, his unbridled rage swirling across the room. He refused to look at me or the children.

"What have I done to deserve this?" my heart cried out. I didn't know what to do next. The children retreated to their rooms, and I sat there all alone.

I tried calling Doug, not that he could do John any more good than his mother, but Doug wasn't in. Maybe he'd gone to the airport to pick up Kathy Lee and Imani.

After doing the dishes and straightening up the kitchen, I went downstairs to the family room and watched television for a few hours. Then I checked on Miss Zoli. She was still dead to the world, and I thanked God that at least she had been spared John's wrath. I don't know what that would've done to her fragile state of mind.

I wondered where she's lived all of her life to have been deprived of not only the conveniences of the twentieth century, but the knowledge of these conveniences. That's almost impossible, but she's living proof that it wasn't.

Before I went upstairs to bed, I checked in on her one last time. She was sitting by the window peering out of her curtains into the darkness.

As I entered her room, the words from last night's conversation suddenly rushed into my mind. "Dis heah house is sho nuff a palace. It's purdier dan any 'tation I done evah seen in mah life. It be fit foh kings an queens. It's bin nice stayin heah, but I gots tah be on mah way. I gots tah gits back tah 'Sippi tah fine dose dat I loves. I 'preciate yoh mighty fine hospitality. I ain't nevah step in no bed like dis. I is used tah sleeping on straw and maybe a few chicken feathers. But dis heah room dat I bin stayin in is beyon mah dreams."

She smiled when she saw me entering the room, and said, "I axed dat little gul ah yohs tah open dese here purdy yellah curtains so I could see outside.

"I wont yah tah tells me somethin."

"Yes, ma'am. What is it?"

"Wheah is de stars? I cain't see none of dem from dis heah windah. Can I go outside an see dem?"

"No, ma'am, you can't."

"Why cain't I? Yah don't wont me tah go outside?"

"No, it's not that Miss Zoli. Even if you went outside, you still couldn't see any stars."

"Why not? I ain't nevah seen or heard ah no sky dat ain't got no stars. Looks like somebody done suck up all ah de stars from de sky."

"It's because of all the pollution and the street lights. The stars are still there, you just can't see them. I haven't seen any in years. You have to leave the city to see them."

"Whot's po-loo-shion? Wheah did dey go? Did dey fall from de sky?"

"They're still there. It's just that the air is filled with dirt, like a blanket, and it blocks out the light from the stars."

I took her by the hand and led her out to the patio. "See, you can't see them out here either."

"Lawd a mercy on me. I ain't nevah seen nothin like dis. How long it bin like dis?"

"As long as we've been out here."

"What's dat down dere?" she asked, pointing at the city. "It looks like de stars done fallen down from de sky."

"No, ma'am. Those are just electrical lights. That's all."

"My Lawd, my Lawd," she said. Her eyes were filled with a confused awe. "It seems like I is lookin ovah de valley ah dry bones. Dis heah place is a dyin worle. When I was back in 'Sippi ev'ry night before I went to sleep, I'd look up at de stars and say mah prayers, axin de Lawd ta shine His light own mah husban and mah chilrens, wherevah dey might be. I felt bettah knowin dat at lease we was 'neath de same stars and de same sky. Now I doesn't knows dat, not no moh. I ain't nevah seen no empty sky like dis."

"Miss Zoli, we're going to help you find your family. I promise you that."

"How is yah gonna do dat?"

"I don't know for sure. But we'll get to working on it in the next day or so. I will help you in any way that I can, but you've got to help me help you. Do you remember your last name?"

"It's Steadwell. Ain't I done tole yah dat befoh? I lives on de Steadwell 'tation foh mose ah mah life, evah since I can remembas. An de Steadwell 'tation is right outsidah Jackson."

"I see."

"Why don't y'all believes me? You an 'specially dat husban ah yohs keep ah lookin at me like dere is somethin wrong wid me. Momma Zoli gots plenty ah good sense."

"Yes, ma'am. I know you do," I replied, trying not to sound patronizing.

"But Miss Zoli, it's impossible for us to believe that you came from Mississippi in eighteen-sixty seven." As soon as I said that, I knew I had made a big mistake. She got riled up like fireworks on the fourth of July.

"I ain't arguin wid yah. I knows whot yeah dis is."

"Is that right?"

"It sho nuff is. But I knows whot yah is thinkin."

"What's that?"

"Dat I is crazy."

"No, I don't."

"Yes, yah does. Chile, you cain't lie wid no straight face. I can see it in yoh eyes, an de way yoh husban keep ah watchin ovah me, like I is gonna hurt somebody. But let me tells yah somethin. I ain't crazy. I ain't nevah bin, an I ain't nevah gonna be. I gots de sense de Lawd done birthed me wid.

"Let me tells yah what crazy is. I guess you ain't nevah seen it scratchin across somebody's face if you think I gots it own mine. De only crazy person dat I has evah known gots tah be crazy cause ah whot dey did to huh an huh chile. Iola, dat was huh name. She was workin out in de fields in de late spring. It was a vary purdy day, jist befoh de first harvest ah cotton was 'bout tah come in. She had one little boy, Benjie. He was only 'bout two yeahs ole. When dat poor chile got back tah huh cabin in de evenin she couldn't fine him wid de rest ah de chilrens dat de ole womins was 'tending to. She ran all ovah de slave quarters lookin foh her baby boy. Den she ran up tah de big house lookin foh him. I was in de kitchin when she hit de dooh rushin in wid wile eyes bout tah pop outtah huh head. 'Wheah's mah baby? Wheah's mah baby boy?' she kep axin ev'rybody.

"'Chile, calm down,' I says. 'I doesn't knows wheah he is. I ain't seen him.' Den ole evil Massa Steadwell comes in de kitchin. I guess he heard all ah de commotion Iola was makin.

"'Massa, wheah is mah boy? Has yah seen him?' He jist stood dere an looked at huh. Didn't even open his ole mean mouth. Den he turned away from huh an on his way outtah de dooh, he said, 'Ah gave him tah mah niece. She needed a chile foh her boy tah play wid.'

"'Massa, please give me back mah baby. He too young tah be wid out his Ma.'

"Dat ole evil man says, 'I cain't do dat I is ah man ah my word. Any way dey done gone tah Kentucky, an I cain't gits him back, even if I wonted to. He already gone.' De poh chile hit de floor like a rock. I thought she done dropped dead. Den she started hoopin an hollerin up somethin terrible. I ain't nevah seen nothin like dat befoh. Den ole evil Missus Steadwell come in talkin 'bout, 'Yah ole nigga wench, yah bettah stop cryin or we gonna sells yah off too. Yah bettah stop yoh cryin ovah dat picanniny. He ain't worth nothin noway.'

"De poh chile start screamin even louder an foamin at de mouth. I seen lotsah womins and men lose dey chilrens tah de slave tradahs. But I ain't nevah gonna forgits de look on dat chiles face. She looked like de livin dead. All de life was gone outtah huh. When me an Bessie Mae finally got huh up, she was gone.

"Befoh de chile had a chance tah say 'Good-bye' tah huh own flesh an blood, dey had taken away huh only baby. An de pooh little chile couldn't take it. It was somethin terrible. Mose times dey don't sell off no youngin til dey is at least five or six yeahs ole.

Takin away huh baby boy knocked de wind outtah huh heart, an she weren't nevah rite agin.

"Dey tried everythin tah bring huh back. Dey tried beatin huh and starvin huh. Dey even pulled out huh tongue an she still ain't do nothin. Lawd ah mercy on me whot dese eyes done seen. Chile, I tells yah, I seen moh dan I can evah tells. Momma Zoli ain't like dat. Momma Zoli is alrite. De only thin dat is wrong wid me is dat I needs tah gits back home tah 'Sippi tah fine mah familee."

That night, alone in the silence of our bedroom, I began to cry again. I knew that something had forever changed between me and my husband. I couldn't put my finger on it because it was beyond his threats, past his pain. Maybe, after all these years, it was the loss of that final thread of innocence that binds a relationship and buoys it through the darkest of times. Today, I looked into the eyes of a man that I did not know. I saw something that I'd never seen before—a clump of my husband that was been hiding in a deep crevice of his being. I knew that it existed, even got a whiff of it from time to time, but never saw it in full measure. My entire body was flooded with the pain of deep regret. I still loved him, and I loved him deeply. Nothing would ever change that. But somehow, after today, I knew that we would never be the same.

Sure, we've had our ups and our downs, and a fair share of heated arguments, just like any other couple. That's a natural, unavoidable part of any marriage. But I never, not in my wildest dreams, ever thought that he would react with such overwhelming rage and anger to his loss. I also knew this was the way divorce begins, a little conflict, a minor problem that's blown out of proportion.

As I lay there soaking in a pool of my own pain, he slipped quietly into our room. I almost didn't hear him come in. When I did, my body froze as I closed my eyes, pretending to be asleep. He went into the bathroom, changed his clothes, and carefully slipped into the bed. I could hear him grinding his teeth across the expanse of pain that separated our hearts.

I wanted to turn to him and say, "John, I know this is very hard for you. I know you're bleeding, 'cause I'm bleeding, too. You've lived your life with almost one mission: to be able to take care of your family. And baby, you've done that and you've done that well. Honey, there's no need for you to twist yourself into this rage that is tearing us apart. Please stop this madness. We have two beautiful children. How did you forget how much we've been through, how far we've come?"

He turned on the light and leaned over my body to see if I was still awake. I continued to play possum, pretending to be asleep. He sat down on the edge of the bed. I could hear him crying. I wanted to reach out to him, like I had done so many countless times before and tell him that it was going to be alright. But I couldn't move. Trapped in a thick sheet of frozen fear, I did the only thing I could do. I prayed, asking God to ease his pain and to give me my husband back, the one that I knew and loved. All I could do was wait for his return.

fifteen

This morning Angela and everybody else around here was walking around the house on egg shells, looking at me like I had gone crazy, while they were treating this crazy old woman like a queen. I didn't get it. After all that I've done for them, they really don't care about me. I might as well be dead. Sure, they want to pretend like they really care, but the bottom line is that all I am to them is a meal ticket.

I was running low on cash and I tried to call a couple of my bank's branches, but the lines were busy. Then I tried calling Pacifica International Insurance, but their lines were busy, too. I guess they had hundreds, if not thousands, of clients who'd probably lost their businesses and homes that were trying to get through. For the entire morning, my finger lived on the phone's redial button.

I sat in the library trying to figure out what to do next. What in God's name was I going to do with my life? And I couldn't see anything, not a damn thing, except flashbacks from yesterday's fire. I even fell asleep for a minute and started dreaming about the fire. I was trying to put it out with firehoses, but nothing would help. It just kept burning and burning, until everything was gone. I woke up remembering how I felt, walking around my destroyed dream. As I looked at all of the piles of destroyed inventory—computers melted into unrecognizable globs, mounds of software charred beyond recognition—a wall had wrapped around my heart.

My nerves were fried to a crisp. How could I ever start all over again? I was twenty years older than I was when I first started out. I didn't have the strength or the energy to even think about doing this again. It might kill me. I heard Bob Noles on the radio this morning talking about how he was determined to build his business again, and to tell you the truth, I felt sorry for him. How stupid could he be? If he rebuilds, the same thing could happen again.

I wished somebody would tell me, what I was supposed to feel? Happy that I lost everything and look on the brighter side of nothing? I don't think so. How am I supposed to be thankful, when I have nothing left to live for? Ever since I found out that everything was gone, memories reappeared of how hungry I felt going to sleep on a fairly empty stomach after my daddy died. I didn't ever want to feel that hungry again.

"I've been here since the beginning. I've watched you make your dreams come true. We can rebuild, I know we can." My wife's words haunted me. I don't see how she can ever believe in me again.

Sometimes, my wife's bright and cheery outlook got on my last nerve and wore it thin. I didn't need her patronizing optimism. Life just isn't that simple. I've seen plenty of men lose their jobs or their businesses, and before you know it their marriages have gone up in smoke.

Doug stopped in around noon. "What are you doing at home?"

"What does it look like? I'm working. How did you know I was here?"

"I just had this feeling that you were in the house."

"And what else did you feel?"

"Nothing in particular. Man, what's going on with you?"

"Nothing. Not one damn thing."

"Well, man, what gives? Why are you looking like you lost your best friend?"

"No good reason. I just didn't feel like going in today."

"No, no. Short of you having a heart attack or a stroke, you are always down at Stewart Computers by this time. So what gives?"

"Nothing, man. Remember, I'm the boss, and I can go to work when I feel like it."

"No, I'm not buying that. Last week, you had risking my life after all hell had broken lose, and now that everything's quiet, you're working at home? That doesn't make any sense."

I didn't say another word. How could I tell my best friend that I lost everything and that my business was gone?

He sat there studying me for a moment, and said, "Man, did something happen to your building?"

"No!"

"Okay, if you say so. But whatever is gnawing away at you, I hope you take care of it soon, my brother. In the meantime, since you're not doing anything, why don't you ride out to LAX with me? I'm on my way to pick up Kathy Lee and Imani."

"No, man, I don't think so. I'm not up for it right now."

"Okay, well, I'll check with you later when we get back home."

"Yeah, later."

I was glad he was gone. I couldn't tell him how much a failure I was. He wouldn't be my friend anymore. He'd just hang around out of pity for me, and I can't think about that. Doug has to respect me as a man. Otherwise, I didn't need him in my life.

sixteen

I couldn't get to work fast enough on Tuesday morning. It was a relief to get back to the mountain of problems I had to face there. When I pulled into the parking lot, there was an even longer line of clients than the day before. A few of our satellite facilities had been damaged and the overflow came here.

Dora informed me that we had a meeting scheduled for the entire staff this morning. According to a memo, the meeting would focus on mobilizing and coordinating the relief effort. An accompanying preliminary report clearly outlined the overwhelming need facing our community. It was worse than I could've ever imagined. Thousands were without electricity, food and shelter. They needed clothing and assistance to put their lives back together again.

To make matters even worse for us, several staff members were homeless, a few were injured. I heard a couple were in the hospital, while many had relatives who were in jail, and one lost her son. Even Doc Whitney, who is normally the epitome of patience and calm, seemed to have been distraught and overwhelmed at what happened. Today's L.A. Times had a report about how one of our sister centers, another large social-service agency, was brunt to the ground on Thursday, by a mob of Black and Hispanic people.

It seemed like a lifetime has passed since I last set foot in this conference room. In truth, it had only been a few days since we last met here. Doc Whitney entered the room with a gruff burst of energy. I was sure, considering all that he had been through, he was trying to muster up the strength and wit to rise to this tremendously difficult occasion we all faced. His face was a drained, sallow brown, instead of its normal rich brown hue. Slumping be-

neath the weight of last week's destruction and this week's new
and insurmountable burdens, his sagging face revealed the signs
of rapid aging. He looked at least ten years older than he did only
a few days ago.

"Let's get started," he said impatiently. "We have a lot of work
to do. Our communities needs are enormous. There are thousands
of people who need our help." As my eyes scanned the room I could
see the staff wiggling uncomfortably in their seats, deep tension
in their expressions.

"Certainly, I'm not suggesting that we can handle this job
alone. It is clear to me that we cannot. The task at hand is far
greater than anything little David ever had to face with Goliath.
However, we must do everything that we can to help those who so
desperately need our services.

"I had a meeting last night with the directors of several to
pool our resources. We will coordinating our efforts with over fifty
churches and agencies in the area, including F.A.M.E., St. Ignatius,
Bethel A.M.E. and Tabernacle. Our initial focus is to find shelter
for those who are homeless. We are going to devote our energies to
that one particular aspect of the tragic situation. Therefore, for
the time being, all other activities will be indefinitely suspended
or severely limited."

"But Doc," asked Jerry, one of the younger social workers.
"What about food stamps, day care and senior-citizens programs?"

"As I said before, they will be suspended until further notice.
There are people living on the streets, in places that are not fit for
human habitation. We must do our best to place them immediately in adequate housing. When that task is done, then we can
return to business as usual."

"But Doc, how am I supposed to turn my clients away who
need food stamps?" insisted Jerry.

"I know it's hard," Doc replied, his eyes strained with sadness. "Trust me, this was a very difficult decision. But housing is
going to be our top priority until further notice. We are going to do
what we have to do."

Across the room, my eyes met Geneva's. I hadn't notices when she entered the room. I was relieved to see her. Yet, there was something different about her presence. Despite her smile, her face carried the weight of last week's trauma.

My mind drifted away from the conference room. How was I going to do this? How would I find the strength to do all that I had to do at home and at work? As if I didn't already have enough to worry about in my life: the business was gone; John was going crazy; he didn't want Miss Zoli in the house; the center was overwhelmed by the need in the community. My cup is full, I had too much to bear.

I still needed to hire an assistant and ten more staff people. Who in their right mind would take a job down here at this time? Yet, I couldn't help but feel a little guilty as I sat there. Sure my family lost our electricity for a few days, and our business was gone. But we still had more than we'll ever need.

I was so tense, but I didn't want my husband to know, then he would feel even worse. This was a mess. The children were hurt and confused by all that they've seen since last week—especially James. Even though John and Ashley are closer, James is more sensitive to John's moods than Ash is when it comes to the issues of being a father and the man of the house.

MY nerves were getting bad, I felt like smoking a cigarette and I hadn't had one in years. I didn't know what I was going to do. I wish momma was here. I knew if I could talk to her I'd feel much better.

Mrs. Pugh sat in my office. I had to pitch in because Dalilah, one of my case workers, hadn't returned. Her husband was caught in cross fire while on his way home from working the midnight shift early Thursday morning and suffered a gunshot wound to the chest. He lost a lot of blood waiting for the paramedics. Finally, a family member took him to the King Hospital. He was still in the intensive-care unit in critical condition.

However, while I was trying to help out her clients, every thing that I had been running away from finally caught up with me. In the middle of my conversation with Mrs. Pugh, trying to figure out how I was going to help her find a place to stay, I burst into tears.

"Mrs. Stewart, what's wrong?" she asked.

"I'm sorry. I didn't mean to do this," I replied sobbing. "This is so unprofessional of me. I've never done this before." Mrs. Pugh got up form her seat, walked around my desk and put her arms around me.

"It's alright, you can cry. There are a lot of people pulling at you, pleading for help. I know that's a burden too much for anyone to bear. Go ahead, just let it all out."

"It's not just that. My husband lost his business yesterday. He's so stressed out, I'm afraid he might have a heart attack. The only good thing is that he is in pretty good shape for a man his age. Otherwise, I know he could've dropped dead from the way he's carrying on."

"Yes, sugah, you do have a lot on your mind."

"Let me stop. I need to get myself together so I can help you."

I went into the women's employee washroom, and while drenching my face with cold, refreshing water, Miss Zoli's words came to me: "Dis heah place is a strange, strange world." I didn't care how crazy we thought she was, she was right about that. Her words contained an awful lot of painful truth. It seemed like up was down and down was up.

Somehow, I regained my composure, and returned to my office. Mrs. Pugh was still sitting there. "I decided I was gonna wait til you came back to make sure that you was alright before I left," she said.

"Thank you for being so understanding, you're such a sweetheart," I replied as I kissed her on the cheek and hugged her.

"Honey, we're all we got. Us colored folks kindah got away from that. When I was growing up back in Arkansas, all we had was each other. We held each other up like one big family, kept each other strong, looked out for each other and helped to raise each other's children. Now, we done got so high fallutin', livin' in these big cities, that we done gone off and forgot who we is and how we made it over a mighty long way."

"Yes, ma'am, you are right about that."

"Maybe one of the blessings that will come out of this hell is that we'll find a way to come together again as one family."

"I hope so," I said with tears still streaming down my cheeks. "You're so right about that. We truly need each other."

"We always have and always will. We just forgot that, tryin' to be so fancy in this here modern world."

"Yes, Mrs. Pugh, you can say that again. I wish you could talk with my husband. He needs something to stir him up. Look at you, you've lost all of your worldly possessions, the roof over your head, but you're holding up."

She smiled and said, "Yes, I have been through a lot, but praise God, I've been through a whole lot more. One thing you gots to understand about your husband, sounds like he's got a heap of pride stirring up in him. A kind of pride that women don't have or understand.

"It's the way he's looking at what he done lost. It's not so much what you lose as it is how you see what you done lost."

"You may be right, but it's awful hard right now."

"Not much in this life is easy. All us Black people ever had that we can count on is one another. I know I can count on you all, you've been so good to me over the years. The least I could do is to give you a shoulder to cry on when you needed one."

"But we still have to find you a place to stay."

"No you doesn't. I decided to go to stay with my sister. For the time being, I can go over there and help her out with her grand-children."

"Are you sure?" I asked, feeling even more guilty.

"I'll be fine. Don't you worry your pretty little head about me. You've got other things to contend with."

I hugged her again, her plump little arms felt like baby fat, reminding me of the way Ashley felt when she was a plump little baby girl.

A few minutes later, Geneva poked her head into my office, "You sure are a sight for sore eyes. Darlin', where have you been?"

"Gen, I called you on Thursday, then our phones went out on Friday."

"I've been trying to reach you for days, but I couldn't get through either. I figured your line was down. We left the city and went to my daughter's place in Riverside. And to tell you the truth, it wasn't much better out there. You and Abe were right. I don't think anybody was prepared for what happened after the verdict. It was too much for my little heart. I thought Abe was going to have a heart attack as upset as he was after the verdict." I could see that Geneva was still not back to her normal self. She was too subdued and a bit edgy.

"I need to get out of here. Let's go and get a bite to eat," I said.

"Where do you want to go?"

"The usual."

She looked away from me as if she didn't want me to see her expression. "I guess you don't know. Chez Georgette's is gone. I drove past there Monday morning on my way in, just to see for myself if it was still standing, and the only thing left is that big yellow sign with the blue letters in the parking lot and the two walls that run the length of the building. It's such a shame. I guess they cleaned out the rubble over the weekend 'cause nothing else is left."

"No, I didn't know." My heart was pierced again with a numbing pain that quickly flooded the rest of my body.

"Not only that, I found out that Bill was shot by the police. They though that he was trying to break into his own restaurant, so they shot him first and asked questions later. Then, later that night, the building was looted and burned down. Fortunately, he's doing okay. He's over at Freeman Hospital. I think the injury wasn't too bad."

"When is all of this madness going to stop?"

"I heard about John yesterday, Doc Whitney told me after you left. I'm so sorry. How's he doing?"

"Not well. He's not talking this loss well at all."

"But John is such an enterprising young man. He'll rebuild that company in a flash, in no time flat."

"I don't know, Gen, I've never seen him like this."

"He'll bounce back, just you wait and see."

"I hope you're right. He's devastated, a destroyed man. I never knew how much of him was wrapped up in Stewart Computers. Oh, there have been times when I was worried that he was over-doing it, but I never had a clue it was to this extent. He's vested so much emotion that it's as if his whole life had been destroyed. That business was his whole life."

"Yes, sugah, I know. You know how men are, especially our men. Sometimes they're like little boys. They can get so focused and shortsighted that they literally can't see the nose on their faces. They can get lost."

"But Gen, what am I going to do?"

"Just give him time, he'll pull out of it. Let it go."

"I don't know. I just don't know anymore."

"Angela, what's gotten into you? The best thing I can tell you is to give it to the Lord."

Lunchtime rolled around and I didn't know what to do with myself. I decided to go home and check on John, Miss Zoli and Mrs. Henderson to see how they were doing.

John was in the library on the phone when I arrived. "I tried calling this damn insurance company and I can't get though."

"Did you try calling your agent?" I asked.

"Yeah, but no one is answering. You know his office is on Pico Boulevard, so he might've been burned out, too. Only in L.A.," he smirked.

"Well just calm down, I'm sure you'll get though."

"Don't think I've forgotten what I said this morning."

"About what?"

"You know what I'm talking about—Miss Zoli. She needs to go."

"Why didn't you say that this morning when you had a chance to tell her and the kids?"

"Because you boxed me into a corner."

"I what?"

"You know you want me to come off looking like the heavy. And I'm not falling for that. We can handle this matter discreetly. The children don't have to be involved in this. This is none of their business."

"John, I know you're having a bad day. I am, too. And I'm not up to getting into an argument with you right now. I came home to get something to eat, since our favorite restaurant is no longer in existence. I will talk to you later about Miss Zoli."

"What do you mean? Did they burn down Chez Georgette, too?"

"You heard me. Plus, not only that, Bill was shot."

"What?! Man, this shit is crazy."

"I told you we should count our blessings. He's alright, according to Geneva. I'm going to try to call the hospital and find out how he's doing.

"Have you talked to Doug?"

"No, why?"

"Just wondering. I have a feeling he lost some of his businesses, too."

"Why didn't you have a feeling that I was going to lose mine?"

Without saying another word, John walked out of the room. I didn't have the strength to finish the conversation. Instead of following him, I checked on Miss Zoli and Mrs. Henderson and then returned to the office and finished up the rest of my day as best as I could. The burden was overwhelming. I tried calling Bill at the hospital several times but the line was busy. Finally, I decided to send him a bouquet of flowers.

seventeen

Angela came home from the office in the middle of the afternoon. I thought she had come home to give me a hard time because of what I said last night. She told me that Bill was in the hospital because the police shot him, and that Chez Georgette was destroyed. Man, when was this madness going to stop? Maybe Angie was right, even though it didn't feel like it. I guess it could be worse.

To add insult to injury, Doug showed up again this afternoon when I was on my way to the hospital to see Bill.

"Hey, man, what are you still doing home?"

"I told you I didn't feel like going into the office today."

"Why not?"

"Just taking care of a few loose ends. Where are Kathy Lee and Imani?"

"They missed their flight. They'll be in this evening."

I knew he didn't believe me, but I didn't care. Angela doesn't understand why I wouldn't tell him, especially since he had lost a couple of businesses too. It's a man's thing. Doug has already made his mark on the world. I was still spawning mine.

"Man, I know."

"You know what?"

"I know what happened to Stewart Computers."

"What are you talking about?" I replied trying to act perplexed.

"Man, why don't you quit playing games? I know what happened. You lost your business."

"I don't know who told you that. But it's a lie. Listen, if you don't mind, I've got a lot of things to do."

"If you say so, but I thought I was your friend. Why are you pretending? I drove past the place this afternoon. I saw it for myself," he said putting his hands on my shoulders. "I know nothing's left."

"Man, I don't want to talk about it now. I've get to get to the hospital to see Bill."

"What are you talking about? What happened to him?"

"Angie said he got shot last week."

"Want me to go with you?"

"I need to make this run on my own." I didn't know why I lied, and I really felt bad after he left.

When I got to the hospital the receptionist said that Bill had just been transferred from intensive care to a private room. When I walked in the room, he was laying on his back smiling as he hung up the phone. He looked like he was stretched out on a beach somewhere in the Caribbean. He looked so good I almost missed seeing his right leg dangling above him in traction. Georgette was sitting on the edge of the bed, watching him with doting eyes.

"Man, what are you doing in a place like this?"

"I guess you could say it's the luck of the Irish."

"Well, I see your bad sense of humor has gotten worse."

I kissed Georgette on the cheek and shook my partner's hand. From the strength of his handshake, I would never have known that he was in the hospital.

"Georgette, you're getting prettier with each passing day. You look like a beautiful magnolia tree on a sunny Louisiana day."

"John, you always know the right thing to say. I bet you could charm a dead woman in her grave," she said blushing like a little girl.

"All I want to know is why you didn't call us and let us know what had happened to you? Man, it's a damn shame for you to be laid up in the hospital without your friends knowing that you were here."

"John, Georgette did try calling you, but we couldn't get through. I figured your phones were out." Georgette sat there holding his hand, nodding her head.

"You're right. That did happen. Sorry, I stand corrected. Man, how did this happen?"

"Bill was being hardheaded. John, I told him not to go. But he insisted. You know how foolish and hardheaded you men can be. He said he had to check it for himself. So you see what he got for being the concerned businessman? He go shot. Lord knows he could have been killed."

"Sugar, you need to clam down. Worrying over this is like crying over spilled milk. It'll raise you blood pressure high enough to cause you to have a stroke," Bill said stroking her hand.

"Spilled milk, you say? How can you ever call getting shot spilled milk? Johnnie, that's what I love about this man. Here he is laid up with a bullet wound in his leg, fresh out of intensive care, and is worrying about me. I think this man must've suffered some kind of brain damage." She leaned over and kissed him on the cheek.

"John, being a businessman yourself, you know how it is. Chez Georgette was my baby. And I couldn't sit around the house without doing anything. So on Thursday night, after I heard on television that there were several fires in the area, I set out to see how she was doing. Just when I was unlocking the door, two trigger-happy cops came by. I explained to them that I was the owner. They cursed at me, with several words I dare not say before my wife, and as I attempted to pull out my wallet to show them who I was, they shot me.

"Said I was going to pull a gun on them. Had it not been for a couple of brothers in the 'hood who saw everything that happened, and risked their lives to get me to the hospital, I know I wouldn't be here today.

"I lost a lot of blood. The bullet cut through the biggest artery in my thigh, and it hit my hip bone. So I'm going to be out of commission for a while, but thank God that I'm alive."

"Man, this world has gone stark raving mad. When a brother gets shot by the police for protecting his property, you know there's something seriously wrong. I've seen things I never imagined seeing. People are arguing about whether or not it was a riot or a rebellion. What difference does it make considering all that's been destroyed? Man, that was a civil war, and nobody wants to admit it. I heard the mayor on the television, just a few minutes ago, announcing the Rebuild L.A. program. That's a joke."

"Johnnie, I've seen so many terrible tragedies in this hospital," Georgette said with tears in her eyes. "More tragedies than I can count, or ever care to remember. What Bill didn't tell you was that by the time he got to the hospital, not only was he in shock, but he was in a coma. Lord knows, I thought the worst had happened. I'm just extremely thankful that he's alive."

"I know this must've been a living hell for you."

"John, I tell you, I just don't know what this world is coming to. There are people in this city whose loved ones are maimed, missing or dead. L.A. is full of people in such deep pain," Georgette said.

"You know I know. I lived through the sixties in the Midwest, and I saw firsthand how little was rebuilt after the riots back then."

"Who in their right mind really wants to rebuild and run the risk of having their business destroyed again?" asked Georgette.

"Yeah, I wonder," I said thinking about my own situation.

"But my darlin, we have no choice but to rebuild."

"Bill, I told you before, and I'm telling you again, after all that we've been through, my heart's not in it, not anymore."

"So what are we supposed to do?" Crawl under a rock and hidden from the rest of the world?" I don't think so."

"Well, let me say this," I interjected. You've got plenty of time to decide your next move. Man, you've got to hurry up and get well."

"I know I'm no spring chicken, but I'll be walking again in no time flat. The doctors can't believe that I've progressed as much as I have in a few days. When they brought me to the hospital, I was in shock. They thought that they might have to amputate my foot. When I came to, I told them there was no way in this world that I was going to be a one-legged old man. Hell, it's hard enough being an elderly man, senior citizen, whatever that's supposed to be."

"See what I mean, John? He's just pigheaded."

"Pigheaded or not, I guarantee you that I'll be up and walking in a few more days."

"John, I don't know what I'm going to do with him!"

"Angie probably shares the same sentiments about me."

"How are Angie and the kids?"

"They're all fine. Very overwhelmed down at Bethune, but Angie's handling it. I'm sure she'll be by to see you."

"And how's Stewart Computers?"

"Everything is fine down there, too. As a matter of fact, I need to be getting back to the office. You know how it is. When the cat's away, the mice will play," I said. I didn't want to weigh him down with my burdens.

"Yes, I do. Well, thanks so much for stopping by to check in your old friend. I'll be out of this place in no time."

"Well, until that time, you do whatever it is your doctor tells you to do."

I left the hospital and headed for home. Somehow the visit with my old friend had made me feel better. I couldn't believe how high his spirits were. For a while, thinking about Bill helped me forget about my own trials and tribulations. Suddenly, my troubles seemed a lot smaller. As soon as I walked out of the hospital, I felt overwhelmed again but not as much as before.

I didn't have much to say during dinner and everyone was pretty quiet trying to keep from making eye contact with me. Afterwards, I was exhausted. My body was completely drained of any trace of energy. It felt like I had worked for two days straight. Later that evening after dinner, I sat out on the patio. I seemed like I hadn't been out there in weeks. It was quiet, the air was cleaner than it had been in months. The sky was clear and a full moon was my only companion.

As I sat lost in thought Doug joined me. "Hey man, what's happening?"

"You got it," I replied sarcastically.

"What are you doing out here?"

"I'm just thinking." I replied dryly.

"What's on your troubled mind?"

"Everything and nothing."

"How's Bill?"

"He's going to be alright."

"I see you're not up to talking right now. Is that because you don't want to admit the truth to me, about what's happened to you?"

"What are you talking about?"

"Don't play dumb on me, I'm you best friend. Man, desperation was written all over your face this morning."

"You don't know what you're talking about. I was worried about Bill. I told you I was going to see him."

I felt someone's eyes resting on the back of my neck. For the first time since this woman had invaded my home, I was more than thrilled to see Miss Zoli standing at the patio's entrance.

"Miss Zoli!" I almost sprung out of my chair to greet her. "Where have you been all day?"

"'Scuze me suh, can yah hep me?"

"That's alright. Come on over and have a seat with me and my friend. I'd like for you to meet him because he's heard alot about you."

I took her by the hand and led her over to a chair. "Wheah is yah takin me?"

"Shh, don't worry, I just want you to come over here and have a seat with me and my friend."

"I needs yoh hep. Will yah hep me gits outta dis place an back tah 'Sippi?"

Before I could respond, she looked and Doug and screamed, "Who dat?"

"Calm down, Miss Zoli. This is my friend, Doug."

"Are yah sho? He look like dat mean ole nigga drivah Willie who used tah beat niggas jist foh de fun ah it."

"No, ma'am, I assure you that's not me," Doug, almost laughing.

"Well, yah sho does looks alot like him. Maybe yah is some kin. Don't take no offense tah dis, but I don't wanna be aroune yah. Yah looks to much like dat evil ole nigga." Miss Zoli got up from her chair an hobbled back inside.

"Listen, man, now that you've exhausted all of your options of diversion, I want to talk to you about something."

"About what?"

"I don't know why you don't think I know you well enough to know what's going on. I told you—I know Stewart Computers was destroyed."

"So what! It's none of your business. Don't give me any of your pity. I don't need it."

"Why are you so set in going it alone? I lost a few of my businesses, too. What do you need friends for it you can't be honest and tell them the truth?"

"Listen, I can stand on my own two feet and do what I have to do. I don't need your sympathy."

"Good, 'cause I am not here to give it to you. I'm here for another reason."

"What's that?"

"I have a proposition for you."

"A what?"

"An offer I know you can't refuse."

"Let me hear it."

"You know, after I found that your business was gone, I got to thinking about a plan that could benefit both of us," he said. Excitement burst from his huge frame, as he was about to leap from his seat.

"I talked this over with Kathy Lee and she agrees with me."

"She agrees with what?"

"I want you to take over my business interests. I've laid a good foundation for you. Man, I'm tired of this day in and day out grind. I want to enjoy the rest of the years that I have left with my wife and children. I've got a little girl and another one on the way. I want to be a real father, too. Can you help me?"

"Doug, I'm not your man. I'm not up to being anyone's employee, not even yours. I've gotta have my own thing, you know that."

"You didn't let me finish. I want to sell you all of my business interests."

"Man, are you crazy? I don't have that kind of money!"

"I'm not talking about anything that you can't afford."

"Then what are you talking about?"

"You can give me your insurance, whatever that amount is to buy me out."

"What's wrong with you? Do you know what you're offering me?"

"Yes, I do," he said with a stupid grin. "Man, we've got plenty of money on the bank, a nice trust fund for the kids. And like I said before, I want to be free of the day-to-day hassles of being an entrepreneur. I've had enough, and now it's time for me to go. So what do you think?"

"I think I can't accept a handout or your pity, and you should be embarrassed to have made such a ridiculous offer."

He looked at me with disbelief as if I was kidding. "Are you out of your mind?" he replied raising his voice. "This is a chance of a lifetime, and you're treating me like I've insulted you."

"You have insulted me. A man does not make such an offer to a man he respects. He gives handouts to punks!"

"I think you are the one who needs to see a psychiatrist instead of Miss Zoli because you're crazy. Cutting off your nose to spite your face. I can't believe it."

"Well, believe this: The answer is no."

"Man, you're more pigheaded than I thought, You can't accept a gift as an opportunity. No, you're too much of a man to do that. You would rather sit around this house licking your wounds and wallowing in your stupid pride."

"You don't have to insult me in my own house."

"What are you saying? Are you asking me to leave?"

I yelled, "Damn right I am!"

"You don't have to 'cause I'm outta here."

"Good riddance! And don't come back!" I yelled.

I followed him upstairs and yelled, "Get out and stay out!" Angie and Kathy Lee looked surprised when we got to the kitchen.

"What's wrong with the two of you?" Angie asked. Neither of us answered her question. We didn't stop yelling.

"Get out of my house!" I yelled.

"What's wrong with the two of you?"

"It's your husband's fault. He must think I'm a fool."

"Enough already! What's gotten into the two of you? You're out of control! You are the best friends that either one of you has ever had, and here you are acting like two five-year-olds. Whatever is wrong, it's not enough to act like this, yelling and screaming to thy kingdom comes. We could hear you in the kitchen."

"Then you must've heard your pigheaded husband."

"Shut up both of you!" screamed Kathy Lee at the top of her lungs. "If the two of you keep this up, I'm going to drop this baby right now!"

eighteen

When we first moved into the neighborhood, Doug's wife, Lizzie, quickly became a second mother to me, and the kids even called her 'Nana Lizzie.' After she passed, it took me a long time to get used to her absence. And then when Doug started seeing Kathy Lee, I was extremely suspicious of her intentions. I didn't like her at all. I thought she was just another gold digging sweet young thing.

For the life of me, I couldn't figure out what an attractive, bright young woman like her would want with a half dead, burnt-out man like Doug. Unless, of course, it was his money. Even though she was a doctor, her age aroused my suspicions. She looked ten years younger than her age, and most people probably thought she was his granddaughter. Maybe she just went to medical school to find her a rich old sugar daddy. Of course, John didn't have a problem with the relationship and thought she was the best thing since hot coffee.

"I don't know why you got your dander all riled up about Kathy Lee, she's a nice kid."

"That's exactly my problem, she's a child."

"Angie, give her a break! You're exaggerating. Doug seems to be happy. So why aren't you?"

"Because I don't like her."

"You don't like her because you miss Lizzie."

"That's not true. I just think he needs someone a lot closer to his age. What do they have in common?"

"I don't know, but it's enough for him to ask her to marry him."

"He what? You mean that old fool is going to marry some sweet young thing he hasn't known for more than four months?"

"Yes, he is, and I'm happy for him."

"I bet Lizzie is turning cartwheels in her grave."

"Lighten up, baby. You're acting like you're turning over in yours."

"Well, let me tell you a thing or two, Mr. I'm-tickled-pink-for-my-friend Stewart. You're happy, because given the same situation, you'd do the same thing, too, and make an old fool of yourself. And one more thing, if I die before you do, you have my word of honor that I will come back and haunt you and your sweet young thing each and every day that you're together. You can bet your bottom dollar on that."

Needless to say, my darling husband didn't have much of a response to that statement, and never whispered another word about Kathy Lee's youth again.

Shortly before their wedding, she cornered me in Doug's kitchen. I'm sure she knew how I felt. I missed Lizzie, and I didn't want someone younger than me taking her place.

"Angela, can I ask you a question?"

"Go ahead, what is it?"

"Why don't you like me?"

"Who said I didn't?"

"You don't have to. The way you treat me says everything. You can barely stand to be in the same room with me. Angela, I know what you're thinking. All I ask is that you give us a chance."

"How do you know anything about my thoughts? I didn't think you were trained to be a psychologist," I said sarcastically.

"Why can't you be honest? You're a pretty straightforward woman. I know that you think I'm out to get his money."

"So what if I do?"

"You're wrong."

"If you don't want his money, then what do you want from Doug? He's old enough to be your father and he is extremely vulnerable right now. He lost his wife less than a year ago, and he is very lonely."

"Angela, all I ask is that you give me, give us a chance. When I met Doug, dating him was the last thing on my mind. But as I got to know him, I found that we had an awful lot in common, and I liked him. I've been in L.A. almost seven years, since coming out here to go to medical school. The men out here are a trip! The ones I run into that are in my age group are suffering from a syndrome I call 'Testosterone Toxicity.' Their hormones are in overdrive. They're running around looking for a starlet or a groupie, a twenty-year-old weighing ninety pounds, with a weave and no brains.

"They need to wear a warning label that says, 'Warning! This man may be hazardous to your emotional health.' I can't handle it. Angela, you are very fortunate to have a good husband, and not to have to deal with the dating scene. All that I've experienced has taught me how to appreciate life. Taking care of dying and critically ill patients, day in and day out has made me very appreciative of my time. I'm not wasting his or mine.

"And I guarantee you, before it's said and done, you'll see for yourself that I am sincere. His money is not important to me, his kindness is.

"Doug told me that you and Lizzie were close. But Angela, Lizzie's gone, and she's not coming back. I hope one day we can be friends."

"Don't count on it," I replied as sarcastically as I could. I was so mean to her.

I still wasn't convinced. John had to beg me to go to the wedding. I just didn't want to be a part of it. And regardless of what I did, Kathy Lee refused to dislike me. I'd ignored her, barely spoke to her, dismissed her kindness as meaningless attempts to try to make me like her. On their wedding day, it was only when my daughter pulled my coattails that I started to calm down.

"Mommie, why don't you like Kathy Lee?"

"Who told you that I don't like her?"

"Mommie, I can see it. You treat her so mean. You act like her, but I don't think that you really do. You never say anything nice about her.

"Don't you think Nana Lizzie would want Uncle Doug to be happy and for you to like Dr. Kathy Lee?"

"Maybe."

"I think she would, so why don't you try a little harder?"

I was stunned and embarrassed. I couldn't say another word because my daughter was right. I knew then I had to finally put my indignant behavior to rest, for my children's sake. Ash had done what no one else could do. She showed me the face of my own hypocrisy. My daughter shamed me into being more accepting of Doug's choice.

When I finally let go of my reservations, Kathy Lee proved me wrong, made a liar out of me, and in the process became my dearest friend. Now, she's like the little sister I never had.

I'm so very grateful that she forgave me.

As their relationship progressed, Kathy Lee had such a positive effect on Doug, it gave him a new lease on life, something to live for I couldn't deny. As their bond strengthened, Doug seemed to be growing younger with each passing day.

When the door bell rang earlier this evening, the kids flew up the stairs from the family room to answer the door. I guess they had missed seeing their little godsister, Imani, and were happy that she was back in town.

Kathy Lee waddled into the kitchen, behind Doug as he carried Imani, looking like she was about to deliver at any moment.

"Girl, you know that you two are a sight for sore eyes?"

"And what about me?" asked Doug jokingly.

"You can go on downstairs and hang with your homey."

"Well, if that's the way you want to treat me, I guess I have no choice."

"Oh, Doug, why you gotta be such a typical man?"

"He can't help himself, Angie. But I love my sugar anyway."

"Auntie Angie, I'm home!" squealed Imani. Her warm brown eyes were like those of a small doe, surrounded by honey brown skin. She planted a kiss on my cheek while James and Ashley fussed over her.

"Hi, sweetie, it sure is good to see you."

"How was Denver and your mom?"

"Better than what you guys had to deal with. How are you? I understand you've been through a lot."

"Girl, you said more than a mouthful. Where do I begin?"

"How's John?"

"He's not handling things well right now. I don't know what I'm going to do."

As usual, our conversation was beginning to bore the children. They left the room and took Imani upstairs.

"Now, tell me about this homeless woman you've found."

"Where do I begin? I found her next to my car last Wednesday when all of the fighting began. She's very disoriented. She says she is from Mississippi, but thinks the year is eighteen sixty-seven instead of nineteen-ninety two. John's worried that she's going to harm one of us. But I don't think so, and with everything else that is going on around here, I haven't had time to begin looking for her family. It's been one thing after another, and I am stressed out. I don't know what to do next."

"Have you called the police?"

"No. With everything that's going on I haven't had the time. Girl, we just got our phone and electricity turned on."

"Has she seen a doctor?"

"No, not yet. She definitely needs to see one. Her feet are covered with this God awful rash."

"You want me to take a look and see what I can do?"

"K.L., you're a life saver. Lord knows my husband wants to get her out of this house as soon as possible."

"Well, I can understand him being uncomfortable having a stranger in his house."

"You know, that's the funny thing about this situation. She doesn't feel like a stranger to me. I feel like I've known her all of my life. Maybe she reminds me of my clients, or someone from my childhood that I can't remember, I don't know what it is. But what I do know is that she's staying here until we find her family."

"If you say so, but Ang, don't let this situation get out of hand, and become a major bone of contention between you and John."

"Okay, I hear you. But I'm worried more about John than her. K.L. I've never seen him like this before, He's losing it."

"Well, maybe Doug can help him. You know he lost the convenience store on Western and the one on Wilshire."

"Wait a minute—you know, don't you?"

"Yeah, Doug already told me."

"How did he know? John's trying to keep it a secret. You know how it is. His pride won't let him tell his best friend what's happened."

"Doug drove by the building yesterday and saw it himself. But you know how intuitive he is. He said he knew Sunday night that something had happened."

"Well, John needs to lighten up and realize how blessed he is. You know Bill over at Chez Georgette?"

"Urn-huh."

"Girl, he's in your hospital, with a gunshot wound in his thigh, inflicted by one of L.A.'s finest, I might add. We should be grateful to be alive and in one piece. Doug and John are so different. You know from the way he sounded on the phone today, I wouldn't have suspected that he lost anything."

"Ang, don't be so hard on John, he's been through a lot. Doug is older and he feels like he's lived his life."

"Well, since you're so understanding, he can be your husband this week. He's making my life miserable. Worrying me to death about this business. And for what? We've got plenty of money in the bank. You know I think that he never got over his father's death, and the effect it had on his family. He can't relax and enjoy his accomplishments, he's gotta keep on doing instead of just being happy."

"Don't worry Ang, I think Doug has something up his sleeve that will help to work this thing out."

"What are you talking about?"

"I can't tell. Doug made me swear that I wouldn't tell you until he and John worked it out."

"Come on K.L. Can't you spill the beans? You know you want to."

"Okay, okay. He wants John to take over his businesses. No, actually he wants to give them to him."

"What? Are you serious?"

"He's serious as a heart attack. I couldn't believe my ears."

"How do you feel about that?"

"If that's what he wants to do, it's fine with me. We've got plenty of money and managing all of the businesses has become more of a hassle than anything else.

"Doug wants to give it to John straight up, but he said, knowing your husband, 'That negro is going to kick this gift horse in the mouth.' So he is going to ask John to give him the money from the insurance claim for the rest of his businesses and call it a day."

"I can't believe my ears. I haven't heard such good news in days. You two are too much!"

I heard Miss Zoli slowly struggling upstairs, dragging her foot. When she reached the top of the stairs, I walked over and greeted her.

"Miss Zoli, I want you to meet someone."

"Yah do? Can dey hep me git back tah 'Sippi?" Her eyes sparkled briefly.

"No, ma'am, I'm afraid not."

"Chile, yah knows I gots tah gits back tah 'Sippi."

"Yes ma'am, I know. And I promise to help you do just that. But in the meantime, Miss Zoli, this is Kathy Lee. She's my best friend."

"Hi, Miss Zoli, how are you?"

"I is alright foh ah ole woman. I'd be bettah if I could git back home."

"Ma'am, can I take a look at your feet?"

"Chile, dat ole thang done been on mah feet foh so lon dat its like a part of me. It ain't nothing to worries about. It bin like dat foh yeahs. Sometime it gets worser, sometime it gits bettah. It ain't dat bad rite now. Why does yah wonts tah see it?"

"Ma'am, I'm a doctor. Maybe I can help."

"Yah is a whot?"

"I arn a doctor."

She looked at me perplexed. "Whot kinda worle is dis? I ain't nevah heard of no colored doctah, an I ain't even heard ah no woman bein no doctah."

"You haven't?" Kathy Lee responded with honest surprise. "Well, here I am in living color. And I'm not the only one. There are probably over a hundred Black woman doctors in Los Angeles."

"Lawd ah mercy, Jesus, I ain't nevah even seen no doctah in my life. An now yah gonna tells me dat I is gonna have a colored woman doctah lookin at me? I wish somethin was wrong wit me."

"Why don't you just let me take a look at it and see for myself."

"If you say so, I don't mean to be disrespectin yah."

Very gently, I removed my old pink houseshoes and white socks from her feet and unwrapped the gauze. Kathy Lee gasped.

"Ma'am, how can you walk? I've never seen anything like this before."

"Oh, it ain't dat bad."

Kathy Lee turned to me and said, "Ang, she needs to see a dermatologist as soon as possible. This is the most severe fungal infection I've ever seen."

"Dat ole thang, ain't nothin' to worry 'bout. I done had it foh years. It makes my feets a little sore. But I has learned tah live wid it."

"Miss Zoli, these germs could get into your blood stream and kill you. Ma'am, where are you from?"

"Foh most of my life I lived outsidah Jacksun on de 'Steadwell 'tation."

"What did you do there?"

"I worked in de kitchen, an' sometime in de fields."

"Do you know what today is?"

"No, ma'am, I doesn't off han."

"Do you know what month it is?"

"I thank it's somewheahs aroune April."

"Do you know what year it is?"

"Las time I knew anythang, it was eighteen hundred an sixtee-seben."

"How did you know that?"

"Cause I bin free foh two yeahs, an' de slaves was set free in 'sixtee-five."

"So you're telling me that you were a slave?"

"Yes, ma'am, I sho nuff was."

"How did you get to Los Angeles?"

"I doesn't knows."

"Do you know who's the president?"

"Yeah, I thank it's dat Mr. Lincoln, de one who started de wah."

"What war are you talking about?" asked K.L. looking at me in utter disbelief.

"De wah between de Norf and de Souf." K.L. looked at me very concerned.

"I know yah is thankin dat I is crazy," Miss Zoli said.

"No, ma'am. I don't think that."

"Well, den does yah believe I is tellin de truf? If yah do, yoh de firs one in dis heah place dat does."

"Ma'am, what I think isn't important right now. I'd like to take a look at your feet."

"I ain't worried 'bout mah feet. I ain't got long tah las heah on dis earf, an I gots tah fine my chilrens. Can yah hep me? I needs tah gits back tah 'Sippi."

"Calm down, Miss Zoli, you know I gave you my word that I would help you get back home."

"Yah sho nuff did, but when is yah gonna do dat?"

"We're going to do it soon."

"Yah promise?"

"Yes, ma'am, I do."

"Dis is sho nuff somethin, seein a colored doctah."

Kathy Lee and I stepped out into the hallway. "What do you think?"

"She's clearly hallucinating. The confusing thing is that's she so rational in her delusions, she could be psychotic."

"Why do you say that?"

"Because she thinks it's 1867."

"To be fair, she is aware that this is 1992."

"Angela, you're splitting hairs. In my opinion, she needs to get some help. I'll see what I can do to set up an appointment for her to see a psychiatrist."

"K.L., I know she needs help. I'll do whatever you say."

"It's more serious than that."

"What do you mean? Can't you see that she's harmless?"

"Girl, you better get a grip. This woman is disoriented, and she could harm herself as well as you and your family."

"You sound like John."

"Well, maybe he's right. Ang, you have someone in your home that you know nothing about in terms of her past psychiatric history, which would give you insight about her behavior. I've never heard of anything this bizarre. Mind you, I'm not a psychiatrist, but I am a pretty good judge of character. And this notion about her being a slave worries me. It worries me a lot."

"So what am I supposed to do? Put her out on the streets?"

"No, you're supposed to get her some help. She needs to be hospitalized, to help her get back to this reality."

"I thought you were on my side."

"Angela, what's gotten into you? You don't know this woman from Adam. You're not responsible for her. Honey, lighten up."

"But K.L., you should've seen the way she looked when I found her. She was the most helpless and frightened human being that I've ever seen. I felt so sorry for her. There's no way I'm going to abandon her now. What would happen to her?"

"Like I said, she's not your responsibility."

"K.L., I don't care what you say. She's staying here until I find her family."

She looked at me, inspecting me as if I were a specimen or a patient she was evaluating.

"Now you're wondering if I need to see a psychiatrist, too?"

"Why are you taking this to the extreme?"

"Because I care."

"Is that all?"

"It most certainly is."

"If you say so. I do see your point, and I admire you for that. I just don't want anything to happen to you, the kids or John. I just want you to know how concerned I am that you have this severely disturbed woman in your house."

"When do you think you can get her an appointment?"

"I'll check on it first thing in the morning."

"Thanks, I appreciate that."

"No problem kiddo, that's what friends are for."

From downstairs a storm of yelling crashed into the kitchen. Doug rushed up the stairs like a typhoon smashing ashore. His face was flushed red as a beet.

Before we could open our mouths, he looked and Kathy Lee and yelled, "Come on we're outta here!"

K.L. asked, "Honey, what's wrong with you?"

"It's not me," he replied spitting his words like bullets. "It's that crazy husband of yours," he shouted, pointing his finger in my direction. "That man is out of his mind!"

"Doug, would you just calm down, and tell us what happened?" I pleaded. I was taken aback, I'd never seen him like this. And in all of the years that I'd known him, he and John have never had anything more than a minor disagreement.

"Angela, that man needs help! He needs to see a psychiatrist as soon as you can get him in! As a matter of fact, I'd go for an emergency consultation. Why don't you take him over to Freeman's tonight?"

"For the last time, Doug. What is wrong with you and John?"

"Nothing is wrong. He just needs to get out of my house!" yelled John as he bounded up the stairs. "Get out!"

"You don't have to tell me that again, I'm out of here!"

"Wait one minute," I said, holding out my hand and blocking the hallway entrance with my body. "Nobody is going anywhere until we get this situation straightened out. You two care too much about each other to be acting like two spoiled brats. What's got you so upset?"

"Ask him, let your husband tell you how stupid he is to kick a gift horse in the mouth."

"John, what is he talking about?"

"Let him tell you."

"Angela, I know what's wrong with these two ignoramuses," Kathy Lee interjected. "Doug came over here to ask John to take over his businesses."

"And what's wrong with that?" I asked.

"He wants me to take a handout!" sputtered John.

"How's taking over his business a handout?"

"I should've known you'd be on his side."

"Honey, be reasonable. You know I'm always on your side. What's wrong with that?"

"Then why do you want me to take a handout?"

"John, tell me what's wrong and why you're so upset. This isn't a handout, it's a wonderful gift."

"You just don't get it, do you?"

"Get what?"

"He's insulted my manhood by offering me something he knows I can't afford to buy on my own."

"See how crazy he is," yelled Doug. ,I give him a chance of a lifetime, something that would benefit me and him, and he slaps me in the face, and tells me to get out of his house!"

"John, you didn't tell him to get out?"

"Damn right I did! I don't want nobody pitying me in my house."

"Wait one minute!" shouted Kathy Lee. "Both of you are acting like you don't have the sense you were born with. I want you to apologize to each other. I don't care who started it, I'm finishing this one. If the two of you keep this up, I'm going to drop this baby right now!"

"I have nothing to apologize for. It's all his fault for being so ungrateful. The man's a lunatic," Doug said, pouting like a ten-year-old.

"Now, Doug, you stop name calling. There's no need for that," K.L. said sternly.

"What he needs is to find some other lacky. 'Cause I'm not his boy," said John.

"Same goes for you, John. You and your male pride. It's too much this time," I interjected.

We all stood there in absolute silence.

John finally said, "Alright, I'm doing this for you, Kathy Lee. I don't want be blamed if something happens to you and your baby tonight from all of this stress. Then he mumbled something that no one else could understand.

"What did you say?" I asked.

"I said I'm sorry," he mumbled.

"Yeah, I'm sorry too—that you're so pigheaded," Doug replied.

"Doug, that's enough," said K.L. "You're two of a kind. That's why you get along so well, most of the time. You can't make him take a gift. I told you that before we got here. You make the offer, then it's up to him to decide, and he obviously doesn't want to accept. End of story."

"See there, I always knew that K.L. had more sense than you."

"John, give it a rest and cool your jets," I said sternly. "You know righteous indignation gets very old, very quickly. Doug was kind enough to make an exceedingly generous offer to you. You are fortunate to have such a good and dear friend. Most people I know would leap at this chance."

Fuming at both of them, K.L. said, "You two have been the best friend that the other has ever had, and you're trying to destroy something that is very important to both of you. Both of you are wired and about to explode. And you've got this pigheaded male pride that can't let you see beyond the end of its nose. So let's call it a night. And go home and get some rest."

"Okay, baby, let's go home."

Was blind, but now I see

nineteen

When I woke up the next morning, I found a note on my nightstand.

> Honey, you were sleeping so peacefully this morning, I didn't want to disturb you. Please call me when you get up.
> Love, Angie

Translation: I didn't feel like talking to you this morning. So don't call me, I'll call you.

I'd overslept, it was almost nine. I turned on the radio to hear the morning news. Of course, the first report heard was about the aftermath of the riots. All of those depressing statistics that I didn't need to hear this morning—fifty-three people dead, more than six thousand fires and a half billion dollars in damage. The reporter mentioned that it was going to take several years for Los Angeles, especially South Central, to recover. But I didn't let it get me down, not this morning. The only good thing about Doug's insulting offer is that he made me mad enough to want to rebuild Stewart Computers.

I'm going to rebuild my company if it was the last thing that I do.

My growling empty stomach took me by the hand and led me to the intercom in search of Mrs. Henderson. "Mrs. Henderson—"

"Yes, sir."

"I overslept a bit this morning. Could you fix me something to eat?"

"Yes, Mr. Stewart, just as soon as I get Miss Zoli out the tub."

After I took a quick shower and soaked in the jacuzzi for the first time in weeks, I felt refreshed and ready to deal with the world. When I made it down to the kitchen, I grabbed the pitcher of orange juice out of the refrigerator. Just as I was about to pour a glass, a loud screeching voice came over the intercom and half of the juice ended up on the counter.

"Mr. Stewart, I'm in Miss Zoli's room. I need you!"

I ran downstairs and heard Mrs. Henderson's voice crying desperately from the guest room. "We're in the bathroom!"

Miss Zoli was sprawled on the floor in the bathroom between the door and the tub. Mrs. Henderson was in the doorway between the bathroom and the bedroom trying to pick her up. Miss Zoli was writhing around in pain, screaming out of her head. I saw streaks of blood on the floor.

"What happened?"

"I don't know. She must be having some kind of a fit or a seizure and she fell. She's bleeding."

"Bleeding from where?"

"From her back."

I looked down at her half clothed body. She was writhing around having a seizure, mumbling inaudible words. When I leaned over her body, I was shocked with what I saw. Blood was gushing from all over her back. Her entire back was covered with huge, gaping, diagonal, open wounds, that were streaming with blood.

"Stop it! Stop it! You is killin me!" she pleaded, writhing around on the floor like she was being beaten.

"Miss Zoli, please—it's okay, calm down. You're fine, nobody's hurting you. You're okay." I really felt sorry for her. She was so out of it, I knew she didn't hear a word I said.

Oblivious to her surroundings, she continued to scream, "Please stop beatin, me, Massa please, yah is gonna kill me."

"Mr. Stewart, what's wrong with her? I've never seen anything like this."

"I don't know, I just don't know." I was downright confused, and didn't know what to do. So I just held onto her while Mrs.

Henderson covered her body with towels. I didn't know if she was going to bleed to death. Most of the bathroom floor was covered with blood. Miss Zoli writhed around in what appeared to be excruciating pain, and finally after several minutes, she finally calmed down. Somehow, I managed to get her up and on the bed.

"I tried to give her a sponge bath, but she wouldn't let me touch her," Mrs. Henderson said nervously. "Said she could do it herself. And the next thing I know, when I turned my back, just a minute later, she fell down and started acting like she was having a fit.

"Lawd have mercy on me!" Miss Zoli moaned. "Make dem stop doin dese thangs tah me!"

"Miss Zoli," I whispered as I gently touched her shoulder. She flinched away in pain as if she'd been burned.

I turned to Mrs. Henderson, "What caused the bleeding?"

"I don't know. She was bleeding when I got in the room. I've never seen anything like this, Mr. Stewart, what are we going to do?"

"I'm going to take her to the emergency room." I tried to sound like I was in control and knew what to do next, but I really didn't.

"Don't you think she needs an ambulance?"

"No, we can handle this. We'll get her there if you help me."

Miss Zoli continued to moan and groan as if she was being attacked by some invisible assailant.

Mrs. Henderson wrapped a yellow terry cloth bathrobe around Miss Zoli, while I steadied her and grabbed a few towels. I picked her up as her arms flailed around and slapped my face a few of times. I made it to the car with Mrs. Henderson trailing me.

I put her in the backseat, then helped Mrs. Henderson get in the car next to her. As I raced down the drive headed for King Hospital, I called Angela. She wasn't in her office. I told Dora to have her call me on the car phone as soon as possible. Then I called Kathy Lee at the hospital. She was in with a patient. Just my luck, I didn't know what to do next.

"Mr. Stewart, I have never seen anything like this," repeated Mrs. Henderson. The backseat of the car was filled with blood. I guess I was so worried about Miss Zoli that the sight of the blood didn't really bother me.

"That makes two of us."

On the way to the hospital, Miss Zoli kept on mumbling, "Massa, please stop beatin me. Massa please."

I pulled the car up to the emergency room entrance. Fortunately no ambulances were at the entrance. I hopped out of the car and ran inside to get help. I leaned over the registration desk and said to the young woman sitting with a bored look lacking concern, "I have a sick woman in the car."

"What's wrong with her?"

"She's bleeding and I think she's having a nervous breakdown. Can you get someone to help me bring her in?"

"Just a minute," she replied. She appeared unmoved by my anxiety.

"Look, lady, she needs help right now. She might not have a minute."

"Yeah, right," she replied sarcastically, rolling her eyes upward.

She leaned over into a small mike stationed in front of her and shouted, "Get me a gurney to the entrance—stat." In less than ten seconds, a couple of young orderlies appeared and I lead them out to the car. Miss Zoli was still writhing in the backseat, blood was everywhere, and most of her yellow terry cloth robe was now a drenched blood red.

The orderlies followed me out to the car and gently eased Miss Zoli onto the gurney and strapped her down. "Please stop, Lord have mercy on me. Somebody hep me," she screamed.

As we entered the emergency room, I whispered in her ear, "Miss Zoli, don't worry, you're at the hospital and everything is going to be alright."

It didn't make that much of a difference, she continued to squirm around on the gurney in deep pain, lost to the presence of this world. They wheeled her behind the two large swinging white doors. I tried to follow behind her, but a nurse stopped me. "Sir, you'll have to wait outside, until the doctor sees her."

"She's very confused and disoriented. I think I need to be there with her."

"I'm sorry, you can't go back there. Just take a seat. I'll be with you in a minute."

Mrs. Henderson and I sat down in the waiting room. Everything in the room was gray. Gray wall, gray vinyl chairs, gray tile, gray signs, the people even looked like they had a gray tint. The room was filled with people seeking medical attention. Women with babies, teenagers, old men who appeared to be lost in drunken stupors.

"Mr. Stewart, what do you think's wrong with her?"

"I don't know, Mrs. Henderson, I just don't know. I've never seen anything like this before. The way her back opened up and started bleeding. I wonder what could've ripped her back apart like that."

"Excuse me sir," another clerk stood before me. She was a young woman, probably no more than twenty-five years of age, but her demeanor was stern and severe, making her appear to be much older. Peering over her glasses, like one of my old school-teachers, she looked at me and said, "I need you to come with me and register the patient."

I followed her to the front desk and asked, "What do you need to know?"

"The patient's name—"

"Zoli."

"Zoli what?"

"I don't know."

"Sir, we can't register her without a full name."

"Okay, put down Zoli Stewart then."

"Is that her correct name?"

"No."

"Then that's fraud, and I can't do that."

"Look, this is a homeless woman that my wife brought home a week ago on Wednesday. You might remember that night when the riot started?"

"Yeah, so what do you want, a medal?" she said sarcastically.

"Whatever the circumstances may be, it doesn't matter, I still need her full legal name."

"Can't you get it through your head that I don't know her full name!" I roared.

"Sir," she replied with venomous sarcasm, "all I'm asking for is her last name."

"And I don't have one," my voice grew louder.

"Sir, this is simply hospital policy. I need a full name."

"You mean to tell me that when somebody rolls into this emergency room with a gunshot wound that you stop and get all of this paperwork done first before you treat them?"

"No, that's an emergency."

"She's an emergency, too. Anyway, she's already in the back getting care."

"Well, that may be true. But you better believe if she isn't properly registered, she won't get a bed in this hospital."

"What else do you want to know?"

"Her social security number."

"Did you hear me the first time? I told you that she's a stranger to me. I have no idea as to what her social security number is."

"Do you know if she has any insurance?"

"Listen to me young lady, and listen carefully." I leaned over the counter only a few inches away from her face and said softly, "You don't have to be a rocket scientist to figure this one out. If I don't know her last name, if I don't know her social security number and I told you she's a homeless person, chances are that she does not have health insurance and if she did, I wouldn't know that information either!"

"Sir, I'm just doing my job."

"Well, I have to give you one thing. You do know how to follow instructions to the letter, regardless of how ignorant they may be."

"Thank you," she said with a smirk

"If it weren't for that I could only conclude that you are brain dead!"

"Sir, you don't have to get raise your voice and if you continue, I will be forced to call security."

I couldn't take it anymore from Freeman Hospital's Miss Procedure and Policies 1992. "I need to go to make a phone call." I said as I walked away.

"Do whatever you wish, but she still has to be registered, according to our procedures and policies."

I found a pay phone down the hallway. I decided to call Angela first. At least fifteen or twenty minutes had passed, since the first time I tried to reach her. She'd finally returned from her break. "Where are you?"

"At Freeman Hospital," I replied.

"What's wrong?"

"Something's wrong with Miss Zoli—"

"What happened to her?" she asked. I knew she was scared, the pitch of her voice always gives her away.

"I don't know for sure. She's bleeding, her back opened up like somebody beat her."

"I'll be right over."

"No, I can handle this. You need to stay at work."

"Call me just as soon as you hear something."

"Okay, baby, I will. Don't worry. She's going to be alright."

"If you say so."

I walked back down the hall to the waiting room. The burning, putrid hospital odor filled my nostrils. It was an awful smell, a mixture of antiseptic and germs up your nose that made you not want to breathe.

"Mr. Stewart, you want to walk down to the cafeteria, and get a bite to eat?" Mrs. Henderson asked.

"No, that's okay."

"But you said you were really hungry this morning, and you haven't had a bite to eat yet."

"I guess all of this excitement made me lose my appetite. I forgot all about being hungry, with Miss Zoli in the shape she's in."

"Poor thing. You know I really feel sorry for her. She's lost, confused, doesn't know where she is, doesn't know how she got here, and doesn't know where her family is. There's no telling how we're going to leave this world, or what's going to happen to us when we're old."

"Yes, that's true—but you know she's very lucky to have you all looking out for her."

"Yes, you're right about that. If it wasn't for my wife's heart of gold, there's no telling where she might be."

"I wasn't just talking about Mrs. Stewart, I was talking about you. If you hadn't been home this morning, I don't know what I would've done. She could've bled to death."

"I can't take any credit for that. I just did what I'm supposed to do."

"Mr. Stewart, you shouldn't be so hard on yourself. You're a good man to let Miss Zoli stay in your home."

"I think she needs help, and a lot of it."

"I agree with you. I just hope they can help her here. Mr. Stewart, what do you think caused her to bleed like that?"

"I was getting ready to ask you the same thing. I've never seen or heard of anything like this in my whole life. She's probably going to require hospitalization."

"Yes, she does need some help."

"So you agree with me? I wish my wife would. She's putting our whole family at risk by allowing this woman to stay in our house."

"Mr. Stewart, I really don't know what to think. I agree with you that she needs help, but I agree with Mrs. Stewart, too"

"You do?"

"Yes, I do. I know you think she's crazy, but there's something very real about what she says. Maybe the circumstances are mistaken or exaggerated, but there's something to her story. Perhaps she and her family were lost or separated by some unforeseen circumstance. I don't know, and I can't put my finger on it. Plus, she and your wife have a very special bond."

"What do you mean?"

"I don't know. But there is a special caring that your wife has for her. It's really something to see."

"We'll just have to wait and see what happens."

I hated being in hospitals, they gave me the creeps. I remembered all of the times I sat in waiting rooms when Angela lost the babies. It was the hardest thing I ever had to do. I had to sit in waiting rooms, helpless, not being able to help save my babies. It was the worst feeling I had ever had.

It tore me up. But I never told Angela. I didn't want to make her feel any worse than she already did.

Waiting. More than anything else, I hated waiting. I hated the suspense of not knowing what was going to happen next. It unraveled my nerves. But for the time being, that was all we could do as we watched the steady stream of emergencies that flowed in. Gunshot wounds, stabbings, car accidents, people yelling and screaming, pleading for relief from their pain.

I hope Miss Zoli is okay. I hope she doesn't die on me. If she does, I'd never forgive myself.

twenty

Sometime I is in dis strange worle heah, sometime I is back in 'Sippi a lon, lon time ago. I doesn't knows whot's wrong wid me. Some haints must be trickin mah mine or somethin.

All of ah sudden I was back in 'Sippi an dat ole evil Massa Steadwell was beatin me wid a whip cause I didn't stop cryin when he sole mah daughtah Eula away. He beat me til I ain't feel no moh pain. De Lawd jist took me away from dat place, an de next thang I knows is dat I is in dis heah room, back in dis strange worle, an peoples is runnin aroune doin all kines ah things to mah body.

Maybe I is crazy or maybe dis heah place is jist one lon, lon dream dat I cain't wakes up from. I remembas dat happinin tah Aintie Bertha when she died. She went into a dream dat she nevah woke up from, an den she died. Maybe dat's whot be goin on wid me. I is probably still undah dat weepin willow tree an I jist cain't wakes up. I gotta do dat, foh I die, cause I gotta fine mah chilrens.

Somethin jist ain't rite 'bout dis place. I feels like I is in de valley. De valley ah dry bones. Dere is somethin wrong wid de air. Not jist all dat brown smoke dat be burnin me up when I breathe, but dat funny feelin I gits whenevah I goes outside. It feels like death is all aroune me, an I doesn't likes it, not ah t'all. I jist wonts tah gits back home, even though I ain't got no roof ovah mah head.

But dere be some thangs dat I do be likin a whole lots 'bout dis place. Lawd ah mercy me, dese colored folk be livin like kings an queens. I ain't nevah seen or heard anything like dat. An I likes de runnin watah, an de nice hot bath I can takes whenevah I wonts tah. But I still misses de fresh air, an all de green trees an flowahs in 'Sippi. I misses dat big ole 'nolia tree dat sits out on de side ah de 'tation. Dats de only thin I be missin bout de Steadwells. I don't miss dem mean an evil ole massa and mistrus, dat treat me an mah youngins worse dan dirt. But dat tree was awful beautiful. I wish I could sees it agin. So I would knows dat I is alright, an dat ev'ry thang is gonna be fine.

I bin axin de Lawd tah lets me wake up, so I can be on mah way tah fine dem chilrens dat I done loss a lon, lon time ago. I hopes dat he sees fit tah ansah mah prayahs very, very soon.

twenty-one

After waiting over six hours, Dr. Jonas finally came out to talk to us.

"Give it to me straight doc, what's wrong with her?"

"Physically, she is fine. I know this may be hard to believe, Mr. Stewart, but once we evaluated her she was stable. Psychologically, I think she's hallucinating, perhaps a borderline psychotic. Unfortunately, we're not equipped to handle her condition here. She's quite bizarre. I've never seen anything like it myself. She really believes that it's eighteen-sixty seven."

"Are you going to admit her?"

"No."

"Why not?"

"We don't have any beds."

"How can you send a bleeding woman home?"

"She stopped bleeding shortly after her arrival. But what makes this very peculiar from a medical point of view—her back is filled with scars instead of the open wounds that you saw."

"How can that be? She was bleeding profusely just a few hours ago. Now you're telling me those wounds have scarred up that quickly? Isn't that more than a little strange?"

"You're absolutely correct. Her presentation is quite unusual and very interesting.

"Very interesting?" I said stymied by his casual attitude. "Doctor, what do you think triggered the bleeding?"

"I'm not certain, Mr. Stewart. But there are reports in the medical literature of 'stigmata'?"

"What on earth are you talking about?"

"There are cases where people bleed spontaneously, typically from the palms of their hands, very similar to the way that it's recorded in the Bible that Jesus bled."

"Wait a minute! Are you telling me what I saw today had something to do with the Bible?"

"No, I'm not. I'm just using that as an example. What I'm trying to explain to you, Mr. Stewart, is that people can have spontaneous occurrences of bleeding that may be induced by some religious or spiritual belief."

"Is that the case with Miss Zoli?"

"I'm not sure."

"Can the bleeding start again?"

"That's always a possibility, but I don't think it will."

"Doc, am I hearing you right?"

"Yes, sir. You most certainly are."

"Well, would you mind explaining to me why you're so nonchalant about the whole thing? Have you ever seen anything like this before?"

"No, I haven't. We ran extensive tests on her and checked her blood. Everything came back within normal limits. There's no sign of any bleeding abnormality. Her kidneys, liver, blood, mineral balance are all fine. In addition, we X-rayed her chest and did an EKG. Everything came up normal. So there's no need to keep her here. Yes, she's quite an unusual presentation, but she's fine now."

"How could that be? She was bleeding profusely for at least a half an hour. I have blood all over my house and car."

"I know this might sound strange, but it's the truth, Mr. Stewart."

"Let me make sure I got this straight—you mean to tell me that there are no signs of bleeding? When I brought her here her back looked like someone had ripped her wide open. Now you're telling me that there's nothing wrong with her?!"

"The only thing present on her trunk is a network of leathery old scars. Several physicians examined her. Aside from her disorientation, she's physically intact."

"What do you think caused the scars on her back?"

"That I don't know. She says she was beaten, and that is a possibility. What do you know about her?"

"Not much aside from her name is Miss Zoli and she's looking for her family. My wife found her in South Central in her office parking lot last Wednesday, shortly after the verdict was released.

"Doesn't she needs to be hospitalized for her mental problem?"

"I'm not certain if she needs to be admitted, but she most certainly does need to be evaluated by a psychiatrist, and we'll make a referral for her."

"Doc, I don't mean to question your judgment, but I think she needs to be in the hospital. The woman is clearly crazy, and I think she could harm either herself or someone else."

"Mr. Stewart, even if I thought she needed to be admitted, I couldn't. All of our psychiatric beds are full."

"Can't you transfer her to another hospital?"

"No, I'm sorry but I can't. Due to the riots, bed space is at a premium throughout the city. "

"So what am I supposed to do?"

"Take her home. I wish I could suggest something to make this easier for you. But, I'm sorry, I can't be of greater assistance to you."

"I don't mean to sound sarcastic, Doc, but thanks for all of your help, I appreciate it." I'd spent most of the day in the hospital, hoping that maybe we could find her some help, and the only thing I knew for sure was that she really needed psychiatric care that this hospital couldn't provide. Her bleeding stopped, but no one knew why or how it happened. Her open wounds were now old scars, and the doctor couldn't figure it out, and didn't seem to care.

On that disgusting note, Mrs. Henderson and I collected Miss Zoli.

"Come on, Miss Zoli, let's go home."

She looked at me like an abandoned child and asked, "Why did yah brings me heah foh dem people to be pokin an prodin all ovah me like I was some ole pin cushion?"

"They were just trying to help you and figure out what was going on."

"I jist wonts tah gits back tah 'Sippi. I doesn't likes it heah."

On the way to the parking lot, she grabbed my hand and begged, "Can yah tells me whot happined to me?"

"Miss Zoli, you were bleeding this morning, and I thought you were having a nervous breakdown or something like that, so we brought you to the hospital."

"Sweetie, you were in pretty bad shape, don't you remember anything?" asked Mrs. Henderson, while holding her hand.

"I doesn't remembas much 'bout dis mawnin. It seems like sometime I be back in 'Sippi, and den sometime I be heah. But I ain't really back dere, it jist don't seem rite. Like my mine is playin tricks on me, cause I be knowin dat I ain't really dere."

On the way home, I called Angela but she'd already left the office. When I got home, I called Ron at police headquarters and asked him to help find out if anyone fitting Miss Zoli's description had been reported missing. He called back later, and said no one in their current missing person's file fit Miss Zoli's description. He said he'd also checked with the Mississippi State Police, and they didn't have a match either.

My wife got home around a half hour after we returned. Miss Zoli was taking a nap and I was eating a sandwich when Angela came in. "John, why didn't you call me? Where is she? You didn't leave her there, did you?"

"Ang, give me a break. I've had a long day. I know you don't think much of me right now, but I brought her back home. I even called Ron. There's no missing person's report that comes close to fitting Miss Zoli's description in California or Mississippi."

"Why didn't you call me?

"Baby, I'm sorry, but you know how I feel about hospitals. I got out as soon as I could. The place gives me the creeps."

"What did the doctor say?"

"Not much of anything. Just that he doesn't know what caused her bleeding. All of her test results were normal, her back is now filled with scars. He mumbled something about 'stigmata' and that she needs to see a psychiatrist."

"Slow down, you've got me on information overload! Actually, I'm surprised you brought her back home, and didn't leave her down there. I figured that's why you didn't call."

Ticked off, I yelled, "Will you give me a break? I just spent most of my day down there with a stranger, trying to help her out. And this is the thanks I get. You don't know what I've been through today."

"Honey, I'm sorry."

"You should be," I snapped. "Do you know how hard it was to get her registered without insurance, a social security number or a full name?"

"I can imagine."

"No, you can't. You needed to be there for yourself to fully appreciate all that I went through to get her some help."

"Thanks for taking her to the hospital."

"Have you seen the scars on her back?"

"No, I haven't."

"When you get a chance take a look at them. This morning they were bleeding like an open faucet, and a few minutes later they closed up into old leathery scars. Even the doctor says he's never seen anything like them in all of his years of practicing.

"What did Miss Zoli say caused them?"

"She didn't. You need to ask her. Maybe she'll tell you the truth."

During dinner, James asked, "Dad, are you going to let Miss Zoli stay with us?"

"Son, she needs help. She needs to be under the care of a good psychiatrist."

"I believe her, I think she's telling the truth."

"Son, you're young and very naive. There is no way that she could be telling the truth. You've got to learn that you can't believe everything someone tells you. The woman has a serious mental disorder."

"Daddy, I believe her, too!" pleaded Ashley. "You promised not to send her away. Are you going to keep your promise?"

"Baby, you, your brother and your mother are my first priority. I have to make sure that your safety in our home has not been compromised by Miss Zoli. I don't know if she's harmless. And in spite of what all of you may think, nobody knows for sure what she is capable of. I'm just going to play it by ear." I said that praying that the psychiatrist would admit her to a hospital for treatment, and then finally she would be out of my hair, so I could get on with my life.

That day couldn't end soon enough. I'd finally decided to get back on the stick and start rebuilding Stewart Computers, only to have my efforts thwarted by the urgency of Miss Zoli's condition. I hoped tomorrow would be a better day for rebuilding my dream.

twenty-two

I hadn't wanted to leave home this morning, I didn't know why. While sitting in my office surrounded by a ton of work, I couldn't get Miss Zoli out of my mind. I didn't know why, but something just felt different.

In spite of my husband's feelings, I knew she needed someone like me and the safety of our home until we located her family. If she was placed in a shelter, she could get lost in the system and fall through the cracks, and end up homeless again. I didn't care what John or anyone else for that matter had to say, she was not a dangerous person. That was simply not in her nature. I didn't care if the world's most brilliant psychiatrist felt the same as John and Kathy Lee, in my heart I knew she was not going to hurt anyone.

Geneva stopped by my office around nine thirty in the morning. "Girl, let's get a cup of coffee like old times."

"Sounds like a good idea to me."

"A penny for your thoughts," said Geneva.

"Oh, Gen, I don't want to worry you with my problems."

"What else is a good friend for?" she asked, touching my hand across the table.

"Well, I just don't know what to do about Miss Zoli."

"What do you mean?"

"John and Kathy Lee both insist that she needs to be hospitalized. They're worried that she might hurt one of us. Kathy Lee specifically said that her condition is dangerous and that she shouldn't be in our home."

"Well, my dear, you never know. You can't be too careful when it comes to your family. They could be right."

"So what am I supposed to do? Just abandon her? Gen, I can't do that."

"Angela, you've already done more than your share. You're not responsible for her."

"Yes, I am. Don't you get it? The problem with this world today is that we only feel responsible for ourselves and a tight little circle of people we claim as immediate kin. No one gives a care about anyone else. How did we forget so easily that Black people didn't get this far by looking out for number one?"

From across the room, a voice with a distinctive Jamaican melody interrupted my speech, "Leave her alone."

"Excuse me?" replied Geneva.

"I said, leave her alone." It was Jacqueline, one of our social workers from Jamaica. She's a tall, lanky, mysterious woman with piercing eyes. Jacqueline moved to the melody of her own song.

"Dere is no-ting wrong wid dat woe-man."

"Jacqueline, what are you talking about?"

"I see her, wid my own eye," she said smiling, pointing to the middle of her shiny brown forehead. "Girl, you're saying here dat you wants tah get rid of dis woman, but de spirits tell me dere is no-ting wrong wid her. To leave here exactly where she is."

Geneva, stunned by the interruption, said, "Where's your home training? We weren't talking to you! And aside from that, how could you possibly know anything about her?"

"I do know, de spirit knows everything. So you bettah hear me and hear me good. Leave dat woe-man alone! She be fine. No problem at all. I know what I hear the spirits tellin me, an dat, my dear, is what dey whisper in my ear."

She gracefully rose to her feet still staring directly into my eyes, and walked out of the room.

I didn't know what to say. I was flabbergasted.

Geneva said, "The nerve of her! I don't believe that woman and the way she butted into our conversation without being invited. You know how those people from the islands are, always sticking their nose into places where it shouldn't be. You know she's always been a little off. Like one taco short of a full platter. I never understood why Doc Whitney didn't fire her years ago. Just ignore her."

"But I can't. Maybe she's right."

"Angela, what is wrong with you? You just said that Miss Zoli needs help. And that's exactly what you should do."

Geneva left and I stayed in the break room, as my mind wandered, trying to figure out what all of this meant. From day one, Miss Zoli has been a mystery, an enigma that I had refused to let go as if I owed her something. How can that be? She was a perfect stranger. I knew she wasn't crazy, just very confused.

Somehow, I knew Jacqueline was right to the extent that there was really nothing wrong with Miss Zoli that couldn't be corrected. And once she found her family, my heart told me she would be fine.

When I returned to my office, Dora was away from her desk, and there was a note on the door:

Call your husband on the car phone. Emergency!

Oh, my God. What happened now? I called his car phone and there was no answer, then I called home, and the answering machine was on. Maybe Mrs. Henderson had taken Miss Zoli out on the patio.

I waited half an hour on pins and needles to hear something. I continued to call but there was still no answer. Finally John called and said he was at the hospital with Miss Zoli and something strange was happening to her. I wanted to rush over there, but John said he could handle it and I shouldn't leave my job.

As I hung up the phone I wondered, what was going to happen next? What could be wrong with her? But I knew John was right. I had been in and out of the office for so many days. I should stay here and let him handle Miss Zoli.

I thrust myself back into work so I wouldn't spend my time worrying about my husband and Miss Zoli. I hoped she was alright. And I also hoped he didn't find a way to get rid of her. Knowing him, he's going to try to get her admitted to the hospital.

Around noon, Dora poked her head into my office. I looked up and she was beaming. "Mrs. Stewart, you're not going to believe this. I just heard on the radio that the Crips and the Bloods are going to sign a truce."

"You've got to be kidding me."

"No, ma'am. That's the word on the streets, and I hear there's going to be a press conference today or tomorrow announcing the truce."

Could this be true? How could this be happening? For years, the daily warfare between the two largest gangs in the city had taken a deadly toll in our community. A week didn't go by without at least one young person, usually a young man, getting killed. As the violence escalated, more and more innocent people were killed. Often I worried about my safety. I had heard that several community leaders had been workin on a truce for over a year. Perhaps the fruit of their labor was finally being born. If this was true. But the proof was in the pudding. We'd have to see what was going to happen on the streets in the days and weeks to come. The thought of a gang truce kept my mind off Miss Zoli for the rest of the morning.

I called the hospital at lunchtime, but there was no word. I continued to see clients, processing requests for housing and doing things I hadn't done in years. The lines had shortened, but there was still a tremendous need for help and relief from the devastating toll the riots had taken on the lives of those in South Central Los Angeles.

It seemed like I held my breath most of the day, waiting to hear something, but John never called. I left the office and stopped by the hospital. The clerk said they'd left, but I didn't know if John took her home or to another hospital.

When I got home, John was sitting in the kitchen nonchalantly eating, as if nothing had happened.

"What happened? Why didn't you call?"

John tried to explain, but his explanation didn't make any sense to me. I rushed down to Miss Zoli's room to find out what was going on.

twenty-three

"Miss Zoli are you alright? How do you feel?" After leaving John I went directly to her room, and found her lying in the bed, staring at the ceiling.

"I is fine. Jist a little tired."

"What happened to you this morning?"

"De only thing dat I remembas is dat I was heah, an den de next thing dat I knows, I is back in 'Sippi gettin de beatin of mah life. It hurt so bad, I jist wanted to die."

"You mean that you had a flashback?"

"What's dat?"

"When a bad memory suddenly returns to your mind and you relive the moment, the same way you did the when it really happened."

"Yah doesn't undastands, I was dere, gittin de life beat out ah me."

"That's what happens when you have a flashback."

Her eyes were shadowed with the same confusion I saw the day I found her. "I doesn't knows what's wrong wid me."

"Don't worry, Miss Zoli, everything is going to be alright."

"How can yah say dat?"

"It's just a feeling that I have. Miss Zoli, how did you get those scars?"

"Yah means tah tells me dat yah don't be knowin?"

"No. ma'am. I don't."

"Yah ain't got none yohself?"

"No, ma'am, I don't"

"I cain't believes dat. I ain't nevah seen no nigga dat ain't bin beat."

"Are you telling me that somebody beat you?"

"Dey used tah beats me when I was a chile jist foh practice. But mosta dese heah scars, I gots dem 'em when dey be takin mah youngins away from me," she said with tears welling up in her eyes, and sheer terror settling in the crevices of her face

"Listen, you don't have to talk about it right now. I can see how much it is upsetting you."

"Dey took me tah see de doctah, I ain't likes bein down theah at dat place."

"You mean the hospital?"

"Yes, ma'am, I ain't like it not one bit."

"You and John have that in common."

"Yah gots yah a good husban. He a good man. He was vary kine tah me today, an I knows dat he don't wont me heah. He be doin what he thanks be right. Dats all. I don't faults him none foh not wontin me aroune."

"How do yah know that?"

"Don't get riled up, he ain't nevah said nothin tah me dat be mean and honery, but I can tells by de way dat he be lookin at me, studyin me, like I is gonna hurts him. Momma Zoli ain't nevah hurt nobody on dis heah earf. And he ain't gots nothin tah worries 'bout in dat regards. I ain't gonna bring no harm tah de peoples dat tooks me in."

"Would you like me to bring you something to eat?"

"Dat is very kine of yah, but Momma Zoli, aftah all she bin through tahday, needs tah gits her some rest."

I called K.L. and she was kind enough to call a couple of her friends and set up an appointment for Miss Zoli to see an internist and a psychiatrist in the morning.

Before I went to bed, I checked on Miss Zoli again, and found her looking out of the window.

"Miss Zoli, what are you doing? Why aren't you asleep?"

"I cain't sleep. I was wonderin 'bout mah chilrens."

"I'm so sorry. I know it must be hard for you to be away from them. I know you miss them."

"Been away so long, I might not know dem if I seen dem tahday. But I thinks I would knows in mah heart.

"Mah husban, Andrew, he used tah git mad at me cause I would stay up late as much as I could."

"Why did you do that?"

"I stay up late lookin at mah youngins. So I could remembas dey faces, remembas as much as I could 'bout dem. Cause I knows dat one day dey gonna be sole away from me," she said with tears streaming down her face. "I remembas what dey look like when dey was young. But now dat dey grown, I doesn't knows."

"Miss Zoli, it's gonna be alright. I promise. We're going to find your family, if it's the last thing I do."

"God bless yah, chile. De Lawd is really gonna take care of yah foh bein so good to me. All I wonts tah do is be wid mah familee befoh I closes mah eyes foh de las time."

"You really love your family, don't you?"

"Yes, I does," she said as a glow filled her eyes.

"You and John both have a lot in common. He loves us very much."

"Can I axe yah somethin?"

"Yes, ma'am. You most certainly can."

"Wheah did y'all gits de money from tah hold on tah dis heah house?"

"We earned it."

"How?" she demanded. "Yah ain't talkin 'bout workin in no fields is yah?"

"No, ma'am, I'm not."

"Y'all ain't got no farm?"

"No, ma'am, we don't have one. My granddaddy did."

"Was yoh mammy an pappy slaves?"

"No ma'am, my great-grandparents were."

"Dey was?" her eyes twinkled. "Wheah?"

"In Mississippi."

"How did so many colored folks gits out heah? Ev'ry wheah I looks when I is out, I ain't seein nothin but darkies runnin aroune."

"They came out here from the South. Did you say darkies?"

"I sho nuff did. Dat's what dey is. What do yah call dem?"

"Black or African American."

"Black?" she screeched. "Dem is fightin words. Don't yah knows dat?"

"They used to be a long time ago, but not anymore."

"Yah evah bin tah 'Sippi?"

"Yes, ma'am, I have."

"Will yah takes me back dere?"

"If we can't find your family out here, then we'll have to look for them in Mississippi."

"When de last time yah was dere?"

"Oh it was long ago maybe, twenty-five-years ago," I answered. "Miss Zoli, now I have something to ask of you."

"What dat be?"

"May I see the scars on your back?"

"Why yah wont tah see dem?"

"I'm just curious."

"What yah mean curious? Does yah wonts tah see how bad I gots beat? Is dat it?"

"No, ma'am, it's not, and I'm sorry, I didn't mean to get you riled up."

"Yah, jist don't undahstands, does yah?"

"Understand what?"

"What its like tah gits beat? Why ain't yah been born no slave?'

"Because slavery ended more than a hundred and twenty-five years ago, and I have no direct knowledge of it."

"Dat cain't be. Dat ain't possible. I knows wid all my good senses dat dis heah yeah is eighteen hundred an sixtee-seben. I ain't been free moh dan two good yeahs. I knows dat," she repeated.

twenty-four

The next morning I went to Miss Zoli's room to help her get dressed. While slipping on a pair of my old shoes, she peered into my eyes and asked, "Wheah is yah takin me?"

"We're going to see a doctor who's going to help you."

"Yah ain't takin me tah fine mah chilrens?"

"No, ma'am we have to get you to the doctor now."

"Why? I done seen ah doctah when yoh husban took me tah dat place wid all dem peoples. Why ain't yah takin me back tah 'Sippi tah fine mah chilrens?" she pleaded, with a desperation that sank my heart into deeper angst.

"Miss Zoli, please don't give me a hard time today," I pleaded. "You know John checked with the police yesterday, and there's no record of a missing person fitting your description in the state of California. He also asked his friend to check with missing persons in Mississippi, but that might take a few days."

"How is mah chilrens suppose tah know dat I is missin? I ain't seen dem in yeahs."

"Miss Zoli, I just think you're a little confused."

"I ain't 'fused 'bout who I is. I done tole yah an yoh husban an ev'rybody else dat gots ears tah heah dat I is Zoli Steadwell, dat I is from de Steadwell 'tation jist outside ah Jackson and dat I bin lookin foh mah husban an mah chilrens since de day I gots set free. So why cain't yah believes dat? I is tellin de truf!"

Once again, I didn't know what to say. I couldn't respond. The details of her hallucinations amazed me.

"I knows from yoh eyes dat yah still doesn't believes me when I tells yah de truf. But I cain't lie, an I cain't tells yah somethin I done made up tah makes yah believes me. Maybe one day when I gits back tah 'Sippi yah will knows de truf for yohself."

"Yes, ma'am. Maybe you're right. I'm sorry, I didn't mean to rile you up so much," I said with a soft, soothing tone. I reached over to stroke her hand, but she pulled away from me.

"I is tired ah bein heah in dis place, I jist wonts tah gits back tah 'Sippi. Cain't yah jist hep me do dat?"

"Okay, I'll tell you what, after we leave the doctor's office, we'll go looking to see if any place around here looks familiar to you. Maybe that will help to stir up your memory."

We must've sat in the crowded waiting room, filled mostly with older women, for over an hour. Finally, the nurse called us in. "Mrs. Stewart, Dr. Kathy Lee told us that you were coming. It's so good to see you," she said with a bright smile as she led us into a small examining room. "And this must be Miss Zoli. Come on in. The doctor is in with a patient but should be coming out shortly."

I nodded my head, while I led Miss Zoli through the door that led to the offices. We entered the small, white examining room. I helped her get undressed. For some reason, she didn't mind me helping her today even though she had objected so strongly to my removing her clothes on the day that I found her. I gasped when I saw the huge leathery scars which tracked across her entire back that John had told me about. These mounds of flesh looked older than the deep wrinkles covering her face and hands. The sight of the scars made me sick to my stomach. So very little of her normal skin remained untouched.

Dr. Goodard entered the room. He was a strikingly handsome man, probably in his mid-thirties, with a very gentle bedside manner. His charming smile and gentle voice immediately soothed Miss Zoli, and made me feel that she was in good, capable hands. He talked to her for a long time, asking a variety of questions about her medical condition.

"Miss Zoli, how are you feeling now?" asked Dr. Goodard, with comforting sincerity.

"Ah is feelin fine rite now. I jist wonts tah go home."

He laughed, in a most disarming way, and replied, "You'll be out of here before you can whistle Dixie." His interview continued for several minutes. Most of the questions he posed to her she couldn't answer.

"Now, I need to examine you." He untied the back of gown. His face winced, repulsed by the unexpected discovery of the horrid tracks of scars covering her back. "What happened to your back? What caused these scars?"

"Dem ole evil slave drivers, Massa Steadwell, and his mean ole wife beat me. She was mean as a poison snake."

He continued his careful, gentle examination. "Doctor, she also has a rash on her feet. Would you take a look at it?"

"Certainly."

"Miss Zoli, how long have you had this rash?"

"Oh dat ole thing? Foh a lon time. Since I was a young woman. Yah see back on de 'tation dey gib me dese heah li'l bitty shoes dat don't fits mah feets, an it make it raw. Den when mah feets gits wet, dese heah funny spots come up on it, and it jist kept on gittin worser an worser. Sometimes it hurt me tah walks, but most ah de time it don't be botherin me much."

"This is the worse fungal infection I've ever seen. She needs to be hospitalized for treatment. I'm surprised the ER physician let her go home with an infection this severe."

"To be honest, I don't know if they even looked at her foot. My husband didn't mention anything about that."

"Wheah is yah gonna takes me?"

"Miss Zoli, the doctor says you need to be in the hospital."

"Is yah goin tah stay dere wid me?"

"No, ma'am I can't."

"Well den, I ain't goin cause I ain't leavin yah tills I fines mah chilrens. I don't like bein in dis heah worle in de first place. But bein wid yah makes it a little easier tah bear. So I ain't goin nowheah, an yah cain't makes me do dat!"

"Miss Zoli, calm down. It's gonna be alright. Dr. Goodard can I speak to you outside?"

"You most certainly can."

"I know you want to put her in the hospital. But, first of all, she has no insurance. And secondly, I think that if you did, it would do her more harm than good."

"Mrs. Stewart, I appreciate your concern. But in my medical opinion, she needs to be hospitalized. She's needs powerful drugs that can only be appropriately administered intravenously. So she needs to be admitted. That infection in her foot could very well kill her at any moment."

"She says she's had it for years. How did she manage to live with it for that long?"

"That's a good question. But the fact remains she needs intravenous antibiotics for at least a week in order to prevent that fungus from spreading into her bloodstream and throughout her entire body.

"And aside from that, Mrs. Stewart, I'm not a psychiatrist, but she clearly needs help. She's quite hallucinatory."

"I know she needs help, but she's harmless. Doctor, can't you make an exception? How would you feel if this were your mother and she was lost? Would you want her to be thrown in the hospital against her wishes?"

"Trust me, Mrs. Stewart, I sympathize with you. I see your concern about Miss Steadwell's well being, and that's quite admirable. But there's things that we can do at the hospital for her that you simply can't do at home."

"Are you going to admit her to your hospital without any health insurance?"

"I'd like to, but I don't think that'll be possible. I can try to make arrangements for her to be admitted to the county hospital."

"Can't you at least try her on some medications for a few days, and then see if that will help this infection?"

"I could. But quite honestly, I'm not comfortable at all with that idea. Yet, I guess," he said with a sigh, "I have no choice."

"Mrs. Stewart, you're quite persuasive," he said with his a charming smile. "You should've been a lawyer."

We left the office with several prescriptions and instructions for the care of her infected foot, and headed for her next appointment.

While heading for the elevator, she turned to me and pleaded, "Wheah is we?"

"Honey, don't be afraid, we're in the building where your doctor's offices are located."

"I ain't nevah seen nothin like dis befoh."

When the elevator arrived she looked at me, and asked, "What's dat?"

"That's an elevator."

"Look like a big emptee pantry tah me."

"No, ma'am, it's not."

"Yah wonts me to git in it?" she asked perplexed again.

"Yes, ma'am. We're both getting in."

"Why? Who gonna let us out?"

"It's taking us upstairs to Dr. Wellington's office."

"How it gonnna do dat?"

"It will, just trust me."

After we got on and the door closed, she grabbed my hand and said, "Y'all got some ah de strangest 'traptions in dis heah worle! How dis thin be movin?"

Before I could answer her question, the door opened, "Who open dat doh?"

"Miss Zoli, it's alright. It opened on its own."

"Yah sho ain't no haint doin dis?"

"No ma'am, I'm sure."

"I doesn't undastands, why yah is so used tah dese thangs."

"I guess because I've been around them all of my life."

"Den what wrong wid me?

"What do mean?"

"Why ain't I in 'Sippi? Why cain't I remembas how I gots heah? Please heps me gits back home."

"Miss Zoli, maybe the next doctor can help us to figure out what's going on."

"I hope so."

Fortunately ,Dr. Wellington's waiting room was empty. I didn't want anyone else being subjected to her questions. That could make an unstable person even more uncomfortable. While registering Miss Zoli, I discreetly asked if I could speak to the doctor alone.

While sitting in the small, but tastefully decorated examining room, I recalled my last conversation with John. "Baby, can't you see how disoriented she is?"

"But she's getting better."

"Better? Better compared to what? She needs help, she needs to be in a mental institution."

"But she could be lost to her children forever if we don't keep her."

"Woman, you're too much. I don't know what I'm going to do with you. Love you to death, or put you over my knees for frustrating the hell out of me and keeping your loved ones at God knows what kind of risk. I don't care what that psychiatrist says, she's crazy."

"Honey, she's not going to hurt anyone, I promise you."

"I hope for our family's sake that you're right."

Finally, about an hour later, Dr. Wellington decided to see both of us together. She was an attractive, sophisticated ebony-hued woman, possessing a warm, nuturing aura. She was the antithesis of everything I'd thought about psychiatrists.

"I understand Miss Steadwell was referred by the emergency room. Dr. Garrett called me last night. What's the problem?"

When I looked at Miss Zoli, I realized she'd escaped to her other world again. So I felt comfortable talking about her.

"Dr. Wellington, I found Miss Zoli last Wednesday on my way out of South Central. She was quite disoriented for several days, her mind has come and gone of its own accord, as you see she is right now."

"When she's lucid, what does she say?"

"She says that she's looking for her children."

"That's not unusual for a homeless person to want to find his or her family."

"No, doctor you don't understand. Miss Zoli believes it's eighteen sixty-seven and that she's a slave who has been free for two years. She says she's been in search of her seven children and husband across the south for two years."

"This is quite fascinating," she said as her eyes brightened.

"Fascinating? Doctor, don't you think all of this is a little bizarre?"

"I've heard of a lot of hallucinations, but this is the first time I've ever heard of a person believing that she is a slave. What does she talk about?"

"Not a lot. She has briefly talked about her world, describing the Mississippi of eighteen sixty-seven. Oh! one interesting thing is that she has these severe scars on her back, which she says are the result of several beatings. Yesterday, they opened spontaneously and began to bleed, which is why she ended up in the ER.

"And according to my husband the doctor said the bleeding stopped as suddenly as it began and calls it 'stigmata.' Does this make any sense to you?"

"Not quite. I need more detail, she may be a reportable case."

Suddenly, Miss Zoli returned to our world.

"Wheah is I now?"

"Miss Zoli, this is Dr. Wellington. I was just telling her about how we met, and what's been going on since you've been staying with us."

"Can she hep me?"

"I think I can, Miss Steadwell."

Her eyes gleamed. "Yah mean dat yah can hep me git back tah 'Sippi?"

"No ma'am, that's not what I'm talking about. I'm talking about helping you with your mind."

"Dere ain't nothin wrong wid me. I ain't crazy. I jist needs tah git back home."

"Can I ask you a few questions?"

"Yes, ma'am yah can."

"What year is this?"

"Dis heah is eighteen sixtee-seben."

"Where are you?"

"I is dis heah strange worle called Lost Angeles."

"Do you know your full name?"

"Zoli Steadwell."

"Very good. Mrs. Steadwell, how did you get to Los Angeles?"

"Dat I doesn't knows. All I remembas is dat I was in 'Sippi, an de next mawnin I woke up in dis heah worle."

"What's your husband's name?"

"Andrew."

"How old is he?"

"I cain't remembas. I ain't nevah knowed."

"How many children do you have?"

"Seben."

"What are their names?"

"Why is yah axin me all ah dese questions? I knows dey names, even though I ain't seen dem since dey was youngins an sole away from me."

"What do you mean sold away from you?"

"Yah ain't nevah heard ah no niggas havin dey youngins sold away from dem? Chile wheah yah bin?"

"Miss Steadwell, that happened a long time ago during slavery."

"Ain't bin dat long ago. I only bin free foh two yeahs!"

And in the twinkling of another eye, she was gone again.

"Mrs. Stewart, she is quite unusual. I think she is a very interesting case of delusional psychosis."

"Is she dangerous?"

"I don't think so."

"My husband is quite worried that she might harm me or one of the children."

"While it's always a possibility with anyone who's psychotic, I don't think that she is going to harm you."

"The fascinating aspect about her case is that she's created an elaborate hallucination about a world that once existed over a hundred years ago. Most hallucinations are far more recent.

"Does she get agitated or violent?"

"Sometimes she is startled by things in the house."

"Like what?"

"The television, the lights and the refrigerator. It's as if she's never been around these things. She says the house is 'full of haints."

"I see. Perhaps the excess sensory stimulation is overwhelming her. When she's cogent, she carries out the role of a person from the past. This is all quite fascinating."

"Doctor, I must ask you. Does she need to be hospitalized?"

"No, I don't think so. As long as she's not violent. Being in a warm, loving environment, such as the one you're providing her will, in the long run, help her more than being in the hospital.

"In the meanwhile, I'm going to give you a prescription for some medication, in case she becomes agitated, and I'd like to see her back in two weeks."

As we drove through our neighborhood filled with burnt-out buildings, Miss Zoli looked at me and asked, "It shore do look like theah was a wah down heah"

"Well, people were very upset about the verdict."

"'Bout what?"

"You know the Rodney King trial. When the police beat up the Black man."

"How come yah keeps callin niggas an colored folk black?"

"Because that's what we African Americans are."

"Look at me!" she yelled, pointing to the skin on her wrinkled hand "I ain't black! I ain't nevah bin black an I ain't from no Africa. I is born heah in Americuh. I ain't wanna to be knowin nothin 'bout no Africa!."

"But Miss Zoli, that's where our foreparents came from. There's nothing we have to be ashamed of. We were lied to about our history to make us believe that we were supposed to be slaves."

"Dere is no buts! Dat place it ain't got nothin but heathens runnin aroune like monkeys. An if it ain't den why was we slaves?"

"Miss Zoli, if we were meant to be slaves, then why are we free? There's nothing wrong with being called Black. The color of our skin is beautiful."

"No it ain't. It's ugly. Dat's why de Lawd done cursed us tah be slaves. An chile let me tells yah somethin," she said pointing her index finger at me. "As long as yah lives on dis heah earf, yah bettah nevah forgit dat." After her speech she escaped back to her other world.

I knew John wasn't going to be pleased with the psychiatrist's opinion.

"What did the doctor say?"

"She said Miss Zoli has delusional psychosis, but doesn't think she'll harm anyone."

"What did she say about putting her in the hospital?"

"That as long as she's not violent, she didn't need to be hospitalized. And being in a warm, loving environment will do her more good than being in a hospital."

"And what if what the good doctor thinks turns out to be wrong?" he asked sarcastically.

"She's not wrong. I know it. John, Miss Zoli isn't going to hurt anyone."

"You better hope that she doesn't. If she does, you're going to have to live with that for the rest of your life."

twenty-five

"You want me to do what?"

Doug said with a silly smile, "Go to the luncheon with me."

"I don't think so. I don't have the time to waste. Especially not with a room full of Korean businessmen."

"Come on, man, you know you need to go. You've been pushing yourselves too much these last few weeks. Man, you need a break, it'll get your mind off yourself. And even more importantly, its a chance for us to open the lines of communication with the Koreans. Something needs to be done before this situation gets even worse."

"Why should I want to do that? I don't have the time or the energy to spend this afternoon breaking bread with any Koreans; I've got enough on my mind."

"Look, man, we're all in this together, and this is a chance for us to build bridges, and to create a meaningful link between two communities that don't need to be fighting one another. Do it for me, I'm your friend and I'm going."

"Man, you know for a fact, I've had more than my share of run-ins with Korean storekeepers. I go out of my way to avoid giving them any of my hard earned money. They're rude, arrogant, condescending, treat most Black folk like a piece of trash. Just look at what they did to little Latasha, shot the child in the back of her head. It was cold-blooded murder. And what did her murderer get? Probation. That could've been Ashley."

"All of them aren't like that."

"Don't tell me, you're going to say, that some of your best friends are Korean?"

"Do you want your children growing up in a world filled with more hate and animosity than there is now?

"No, I don't."

"Well, if you don't, then you need to do something about it."

I paused for a moment and for some reason I looked at him and said, "Okay, man, I'll go. "

"I knew you would say yes," he said patting me on my back.

Even after I said yes, a gnawing feeling ate away at the pit of my stomach. "Doug, I don't get it, man. Here we are—you've lost three businesses, two others are seriously damaged, everything that I've ever done in terms of what I can call my own is gone, and now you have us headed for a meeting with some Koreans? You've gotta explain this one to me."

"Well, what would do me some good would be for you to take over my businesses. I'm serious about my offer. I am ready to retire, and I know if you take over that it will be in good hands."

"Man, I ain't no insurance company. You gotta do better than that. How many times do I have to tell you that my first priority is to rebuild Stewart Computers as fast as I can? Breaking bread with the Koreans is not on my top ten list of things to do.

"And aside from that Doug, who do you think you're fooling?"

"What are you talking about" he tried his best to look like an innocent, confused child. But I saw through his facade.

"Man, maybe you thing you can fool Kathy Lee with that 'who me?' Look. I know better. I know exactly what you're up to."

"What's that?"

"You weren't serious about your offer. You did it to piss me off enough to get me off my ass so I would start rebuilding Stewart Computers again."

"Who me? I'm not that smart," he replied chuckling.

"Yeah, you. Man, you oughta quit. You can't even keep a straight face."

"Okay, you're right. It was a ploy to get you back up to speed. You were too busy wallowing in your own self pity to pull yourself out of it."

We arrived at the Hotel Escada on Wilshire Boulevard a few minutes after noon. As we entered the small banquet room, I felt trapped and restrained by an invisible vice. I felt a chill race up and down my spine that let me know this was not going to be a pleasant experience. Beneath the superficial smiles and pleasantries, I could feel the room was about to explode. I knew that this was not the place for me to be, but I didn't want to leave Doug hanging.

People had already started eating. There was clear segregation along racial lines at most of the tables in the room, . There were only a few tables composed of brothers and Koreans seated together. The room was filled with nervous chatter, complemented by the noisy clanging of forks and knives against the plates. Doug and I grabbed seats at an empty table in the back.

I noticed the centerpiece was a drawing of a dark brown hand shaking a light yellow one, surrounded by a circle of doves, with "Unity & Peace" inscribed at the bottom of the drawing.

A Korean man sitting at the dais looked over at us and rushed over to our table. "Doug, it's so good to see you," he said with the slightest hint of an accent. "Thanks for coming, I know this is a difficult time for you, I heard you lost a couple of businesses. I am very honored that you accepted my invitation and I appreciate you taking time to come and be with us today."

"No problem, Charlie, it's my pleasure. I want you to meet my best friend, John Stewart. John lost his business last week, too."

"It's an honor to meet you, Mr. Stewart." He bowed slightly while extending his hand. "Same here," I replied. For a small man, the strength of his handshake caught me by surprise. He possessed a strong and deliberate grip.

"Please make yourself at home. We are all very excited with this opportunity to get to know one another better.

"Please excuse me," he said bowing slightly again. "I must go and begin the program."

Charlie walked up to the podium and stood there for a few moments observing the audience. Then he began to speak slowly and deliberately. "Good afternoon, and thank you for coming," he said. "I am Charlie Kim, president of the Korean American Chamber of Commerce. My good friend, Jeff Green, is the cosponsor of this get-together and president of the African American Businessman's League. Jeff, would you please say a few words?"

Our paths had crossed many times. Jeff is also a very successful entrepreneur, the way I used to be.

"Thanks, Charlie. And welcome. This gathering was born out of the ashes of the destruction that rampaged through our city just a few days ago. Charlie and I had been talking about having this event for a long time, and as the tension has escalated between our communities, we decided we must act now. It is imperative for our common good to find new ways to communicate and understand one another.

"This is the first of a series of ongoing luncheons so that we can dialogue and improve relations between the African American and Korean American communities. We want to break the barriers that have separated us for too long. We want to be a conduit for change and healing in our community. We have so much more in common than the differences that the media have chosen to exaggerate.

"I'd like to thank you for coming. We must begin to get to know one another as friends instead of adversaries."

Following Jeff's words, Charlie returned to the podium and said, "It is our hope that efforts like these will help to foster a better understanding and friendship in our respective communities. There is no need for us to fight one another. Today, we plan to dialogue, to open our hearts to one another."

Why did I let Doug talk me into doing this? This was a waste of my time. These guys weren't really sincere, otherwise they wouldn't have waited for a riot to meet. I leaned over and asked Doug, "What took them so long to do this?"

"Better late than never."

"Koreans would never, not in a thousand years, treat white folk the way they treat us, and you know I'm right. They should've come over here humbly instead of arrogantly, mistreating Black folk in our own community."

"You're only saying that because you don't want to be here. Man, just chill for a minute. This is important."

Charlie smiled and looked in our direction. "Doug, I see the brother, Mr. Stewart, sitting next to you is quite engrossed in conversation, would he like to open up the dialogue?"

"No, I would not, I don't have anything to say."

People looked around nervously at one another, hesitant to speak. Instead of getting better, the tension was growing worse. At the table adjacent to ours, an elderly distinguished looking black man rose and said, "I came here today for one reason. The only thing I want to know is what do any of you here have to say about Latasha Harlin?"

The room collapsed into a dead, anxious silence. No one said a word.

Finally, a young Korean man, sitting at the table adjacent to ours, got up and said, "I think what happened when that little girl was killed was wrong. That woman, I don't care what color she was, was guilty. And they had it on tape to prove it."

From across the room, an older Korean man yelled, "You all kill one another, but nobody talks about that."

"And you beat your women, so what's the beef?" snapped a brother sitting at a table adjacent to the man's. "Black folk are being blamed for all that damage in Koreatown and I know for a fact, since I have a business there, that there were plenty of other people doing the burning and looting, as well as black folk."

"Yeah, but you all have done enough," shouted a young Korean man from the back of the room.

Near the entrance, a bespectacled old Korean man rose and said, "We don't need to feel guilty about anything. We have done nothing wrong."

"What's that supposed to mean?" grumbled a brother near me.

A young tall Korean sitting next to the bespectacled one jumped to his feet and said, "I've been in this country for over eleven years. I came here with nothing and me and my family, we worked our way up. We lived in apartments filled with roaches, rats and all sorts of awful things. I wish I could tell you all that I feel today about you people, but I can't because it's too painful. The day the riots started my friend's mother showed two Black men an apartment. Do you know what those two black animals did to her?

"They raped her and left her for dead. No, I'm wrong, you Black people are worse than animals. We are far more American than you! Why? Because we earned it. What have you done? Nothing. All you do is moan and groan about the way you've been treated. You do that because you're jealous of us. You animals! If you don't like it here I help you find a big boat to take you back to the jungles of Africa where you belong."

Suddenly, something swept over me like a tidal wave. My head was pounding like a drum, about to explode with anger, while a boiling, red hot rage raced through my body like wildfire. Without thought, I bolted to my feet and shouted, "You don't treat people right, and you've got a whole lot of nerve coming over here, fresh off the boat, barely speaking English to treat us the way that you do in our community. I don't patronize Koreans stores because it doesn't matter if I have on my three piece Italian designer suit or my sweats, I get the same treatment. I'm not going to have you disrespect me, my wife or my children. I have a fourteen-year-old daughter, and it's nothing but the grace of God that it wasn't her that was shot instead of Latasha Harlin.

"And, as for you," I said turning and pointing my finger at the angry young man, "Believe me, I am very sorry about what happened to that woman. What happened to that woman was beyond being despicable. No one deserves to be treated like that. From the bottom of my heart, I am sorry that happened to her." My rage began to settle.

"You niggers are still animals!" He screamed and spat on the floor. "I spit on your grave."

"You arrogant son of a bitch! You call us animals because you can't tell the truth if it was slapping you upside your stupid little head!" I said angrily. "You don't have a right to treat people the way that you do. How many of you Koreans are over forty?" Most of the them raised their hands. "Well, then you really don't have any excuse in terms of the way you treat black people. You should know better."

"But you kill each other more than we hurt you," yelled the angry young Korean.

"That's not the point!" I responded, pounding my fists on the table. "You forgot the truth. Just a few days ago, my mother reminded me that had it not been for the thousands of men like my father who laid down their lives so you could be free, none of you would be here today. And now you want to yank that page out of the history book and pretend that it never happened, simply to justify the way you treat us. Well, I'm not going to stand by and let you get away with it.

"It pisses me off to hear one of you stand up and have the nerve to say, 'We are more American than you, because we earned it!' For over four hundred years my ancestors helped to build this country and got nothing but a living hell in return. You need to turn black and walk in my shoes for a week. You don't understand, you have no idea how it feels to be a stranger in your own land. I'm hated and feared by everyone, including your people who just arrived here, and can't speak one word of good English."

"Each and every time this country goes to war, thousands of Black men go off and fight, laying down their lives for somebody else's freedom—Korea, Vietnam, the Persian Gulf. You get your freedom and we get the bullets. You are reaping the fruits of freedom in a way that the Black men who died for you and their children could never dream of. And then you come over here into our communities with contempt and disregard for our lives.

"How dare you! How dare you! My father is gone because of you ungrateful bastards, and you have the nerve to tell me that we don't deserve to be Americans. Spitting on you isn't sufficient, because that won't bring my father back. I'm sure he's turning over in his grave."

No one said a word. No nervous chatter, no whispering, no throat clearing, no clanging of utensils. Even the waiters removing plates from the table stopped, dead in their tracks. It even seemed to me as if everyone had even stopped breathing

"If I sound angry, it's because I am. If I sound outraged, it's because I am. I am pissed off! As soon as you get to this country, you believe everything that white folks tell you about us to be true, and you treat us like you think you are white. Don't you know that they would treat you just about as bad as us, if we weren't here?

"I don't remember hearing any outrage coming from your community when that woman got off for killing that little girl in cold blood. It was still business as usual. How would you have felt if a Korean teenager had been killed by a Black store owner? Then you have the nerve to talk about reparations. Black people ain't been paid reparations yet for over three hundred years of free labor. If you want money, you've got to stand in line, behind us."

Doug used all of his strength and pulled me down into my seat. I sat there for no longer than a second, threw my napkin onto table, and walked out. It felt like my head was about to explode.

I ran down the hallway into the lobby. My chest was tight, my heart pounded, so much that it made me gasp for air. Doug was following like my shadow right on my heels.

He put his hand on my shoulder, the way my father used to and said, "Come on, man, let's get out of here. Are you alright?"

"Yeah," I replied loosening my tie. "I'll be fine, I was just blowing off some steam." My head pounded with rage. "I'm outta here."

"Man, you did the right thing," he said.

"I needed to speak my peace. I've been holding this inside of me all of my life. I didn't see how it's been gnawing away at me. The nerve of that M.F. to call us animals. I've had it with each and every one of these foreigners who are fresh off the boat, trying to put us down. Like we're not even humans, treating us like a piece of shit. When is it gonna stop?"

"You need to calm down. At the rate you're going, you might pop a blood vessel or something. Man, I'm sorry for asking you to come, I didn't know it was going to be like this. "

"I can't figure you out. You don't let anything burden you. You take everything so calmly. Aren't you mad at what he said?"

"It did disturb me a bit, but I saw beyond his words. I know he's in a lot of pain."

"There you go, forever being the forgiving nigger. If you tell the truth, deep down inside, you're pissed off, too.

"No, I'm not. "

"You never cease to amaze me. You're too damn peaceful for your own good. Doesn't anything ever rile you up?"

"Sometimes."

"Man, where's your pride? I know it gets to you, too, so why do you play off your anger trying to be so calm?"

"I'm calm because it truly doesn't bother me. I know who I am and I really could care less what others think of me or call my people. "

"That's a punk response, and you and I both know it. "

"Call it what you like."

Charlie came rushing into the lobby yelling, "Mr. Stewart! Mr. Stewart! Please don't leave. I'd like to ask you to come back in so we can finish our meeting on a positive note. "

"No, I've had enough."

All the way home, neither one of us said a word. My head kept pounding, while my stomach boiled like acid had been poured into it. Doug finally turned to me and said, "You spoke your piece. You shook everybody up, and maybe that's what they needed.

"I'm your friend, and I'm on your side. And to answer your question about my being at peace, I am. I understand that others opinions of me are not important, because they're none of my business."

"Man, I told you this meeting was a waste of our time. Those Koreans are no different from white people. As soon as they get here, they get infected with the same racist attitude about us. Actually, it probably happens before they even leave Korea."

"You know, John, one day you're going to take a good took at whatever is eating you up. I don't know what it is, but whatever the case, you're either gonna have to deal with it or it's going to kill you."

"You are sounding more and more like Angela. What's your problem?"

"You've boxed your entire life into a corner about what you believe you can do. Your view of life begins and ends with Stewart Computers, and that's very dangerous. Actually, it can be deadly."

"So what am I supposed to do? Sit around the house and meditate all day long?"

"You'll have to find the answer in your own way," he replied, with a twinkle in his eye.

"Yeah, right. You're like the IRS. You never give up, do you?"

Questions without answers whipped across my mind. I asked Doug, "Why does everybody else get more chances than we do, and we built this country?"

"We know why."

"I guess we do. But do you ever think it'll change?"

"I don't know, man, but for our children's sake, I hope so. I know we won't be around to see it, but maybe our grandkids will live in a fairer world. One that doesn't judge them at all."

"I hope you're right. I think it's going to take longer than that."

I took a nap, and didn't eat dinner. A few minutes after I woke up, Angie found me watching TV in our room.

"Why didn't you wake me up for dinner?"

"Honey, you were dead to the world. I figured you needed the rest. Doug called to see how you were feeling. He told me what happened."

"What did he tell you?"

"That you were very upset, and it brought up a lot of old pain for you."

Suddenly, from the open balcony window I heard a loud splash from the pool, then someone screaming, "Hep! Hep! Somebody hep me please!"

I rushed downstairs, and out to the pool. Before I dove into the pool, I saw Miss Zoli, fighting at the deep end to keep her head above the water.

When I reached her and grabbed her shoulders, she slapped me in the face, striking my eye. She was fighting me, the water and even the air. "Miss Zoli, Miss Zoli, let me help you get our of the water," I cried. It took me several minutes to finally pull her over to the edge of the pool, and get her out.

She was choking, gasping for air, crying. "Lawd hep me, I is gonna die. "

"No, you're not. You're going to be alright. "

Angie rushed out of the house with several towels and covered her with them.

The kids came out to the patio. "This poor old woman could've drowned because of someone's carelessness. I told you something like this could happen. Who left the patio door unlocked?" I demanded.

Neither one of them said a word.

I yelled, "Did you hear me? Who left the door unlocked?"

"Baby, calm down. Everything is going to be alright," pleaded Angie, as she lead Miss Zoli back into the house.

With his head hanging like a convicted criminal, my son stepped forward and mumbled with deliberate calm, "Dad, I did it."

"How could you do such a stupid thing?"

"I don't know," he replied, shrugging his shoulders. "I guess I wasn't thinking."

"Wasn't thinking?" I yelled. "What kind of excuse is that? Don't you realize that Miss Zoli could've drowned?"

"No, I just forgot to do it when I came in. "

"Son, what's gotten into you? You're not that irresponsible. I'm extremely disappointed in you. "

"I don't know, dad. I just forgot," he replied nonchalantly.

"Just forgot? Well this is one thing you won't forget. You're grounded for the rest of the summer!"

"Dad, that's not fair. This is only May. "

"I know that."

"But Dad, it's—"

"I don't want to hear another peep out of you or you'll be grounded until nineteen ninety-three. "

He turned and somberly walked away. Ashley was crying.

"What's wrong with you?"

"Daddy, why did you have be so mean to him?"

"Little girl, this is my house and I make all of the rules."

Angie must have stayed in Miss Zoli's room for at least half an hour. When she finally came upstairs, I was sitting on the edge of the bed, still very upset about what had happened. I was exhausted from the long, difficult day, and hadn't planned to end it by pulling that old lady from the pool.

"I told you something like this was going to happen. Can't you see how dangerous it is for her to be here? Ang, she almost died tonight."

"But you saved her life."

"Don't go trying to make a hero out of me. I just did what I'm supposed to do. "

"Honey, don't you think you're being a little hard on James? Did you really have to ground him for the entire summer?"

"I'm not being hard on him. Miss Zoli could've drowned."

From the corner of my eye, I noticed Ashley was standing by the edge of the dresser in her pink pajamas. I turned to her and asked, "Baby, what's wrong?"

"Mommie, daddy, I have something to tell you," she replied, sounding like a five-year-old.

"What is it?" asked my wife.

"I left the door unlocked. James didn't do it."

"You what?" I yelled.

"Yeah, daddy, it was me. James was covering for me."

I couldn't believe my ears. "Why didn't you tell me the truth downstairs?"

"I was scared. And you were really upset. I didn't know what you were going to do to me."

"Go get your brother. I want to speak to him. " She scurried out of the room,

"You know why he said he did it, don't you?" asked Angela.

"No, I don't."

"Man, are you blind and in need of a seeing eye dog? He was doing it because you're always leaning on him about protecting Ashley."

James and Ashley stood at the entrance of the room, afraid to come too close. "Son, why did you lie to me?"

"I don't know, dad," he said shrugging his shoulders. "I did what I was supposed to do."

"What are you talking about?"

"You're always telling me to look out for my little sister. And that's the least I could do."

"When I said that, I meant for you to protect her from others. I never told you to lie."

"But, dad, as mad as you were, I didn't know what you might do. So I thought I could take the weight better than Ash could. She just made a mistake. You didn't need to treat her like a criminal."

"Listen, son. In a way, I am very proud of you for acting like a man. But on the other hand, I'm even more concerned about your lying to me. So I'm not going to keep you on punishment for the rest of the summer. Just a month, and that goes for you too, Miss Ashley. "

"But daddy, that's not fair!" pleaded Ashley. "Why are you making him pay for what I did? It was my fault. He was only looking out for me, and that's not fair. "

"Fair? Fair?! Your mother and I keep telling you that life isn't fair. And the sooner the two of you learn that simple fact, the better you will be."

After the children left the room, like they had been sentenced to a life of imprisonment, Angie turned to me and said, "John, don't you think you're being a bit hard on them?"

"No, I don't. And I'm not discussing it anymore. "

Early the next morning, I was awakened by the worst pain I've ever felt in my entire life. It felt like an elephant was sitting in the middle of my chest. I could barely breathe. When I sat up in the bed, the pain slapped me back down flat on my back. I shook Angie's shoulder, as hard as I could, with the little strength that I had.

"What's wrong?" she rolled over and asked in a groggy, half-awake, half-asleep voice.

"I don't know, I can't breathe."

She sat up in the bed and took a good look at me. "You're flushed, your face is as red as a beet, and you're sweating like you've been working out. I'm calling Kathy Lee."

"No, don't bother her. It's too early in the morning."

"I'm not arguing with you, I'll either call her or an ambulance. Take your choice. "

"Okay, you can call the ambulance. " I'd never felt like that and I didn't know what was going on. She picked up the phone and dialed 911. "Yes, that's 2842 Vallejo Drive. Please hurry. "

I thought the pain would go away in a few minutes, but it only got worse. Then I panicked. Maybe I'm dying. I thought about all the guys, acquaintances of mine that had dropped dead of a heart attack. Some of them were younger than me, in their thirties and early forties. It was scary. I never thought my body would betray me like this.

Angela sat nervously on the edge of the bed. "You want some water? Let me go get you something to drink."

I shook my head no. A crushing bolt of pain struck my heart. I couldn't say a word. James walked into the room and asked, "Mom, where's breakfast?"

When he saw me lying on the bed, he suddenly became frightened and asked, "Dad, what's wrong?" James stood over my bed looking more like a man than I'd ever seen before.

"Don't bother your dad, he's a little sick."

"He looks very sick to me."

"Here, honey, drink this water. "

As I reached for the glass, I tried to sit up, but couldn't.

A few minutes later, Ashley wandered into our room.

"Daddy, I'm scared," cried my terrified little girl as soon as she saw me.

I didn't want her to see me like this. It hurt so much, I was afraid. I didn't know for sure if I was going to live or die.

I whispered to my baby girl with all of the strength that I had, "Don't worry, baby, I'll be alright. "

We waited for a half hour and no one came. Angie called 911 several times. They kept saying, "The ambulance will be there shortly, ma'am."

Forty-five minutes had passed and the pain seemed to be getting worse.

"Looks like the paramedics aren't coming. "

"It does appear that way," replied Angela. "I guess we're going to have to take you to the hospital. "

"James, I need you to help me get your father in the car. Get his robe, and we'll take him downstairs. "

"Okay, mom. "

Miss Zoli stood at the entrance to our room. "What's wrong? My spirit tole me dat somethin was wrong with somebody in de house."

"Yes, ma'am, John needs to go to the hospital."

"Can I talk to him?"

"Miss Zoli, I'm sorry, but he's very sick right now, and we don't have time. We're waiting for the ambulance to come and take him to the hospital."

"Baby, it's alright, let her come in," I said, with sweat trickling down my temples, trying to put on a good front while my chest felt like it was being crushed beneath the weight of some invisible object that refused to move and relieve me of its intense presence.

She struggled over to the edge of the bed. "Suh, you is gonna be alright."

"I am?"

"Yes, suh yah is. Yah needs tah jist stop all dat worryin 'bout all dem things dat is clutterin up yoh heart an yoh life. Yah saved me last night an I know dat all of yah strainin is hurtin yah heart. But yoh a strong man, jist like a buck. Yoh gonna be alright. Now if yah don't mind befoh yah goes, I'd like tah say a little prayer foh yah."

"Miss Zoli, we really don't have time for that," interrupted Angela. Her voice was so strained it sounded like she was about to burst.

"Ang, its okay." A huge surprise lit up Miss Zoli's face. She looked at me with a calm certainty—unlike anything I'd ever seen her express before.

"Oh Lawd, please haf mercy on your chile. Make his body strong, an let him come back home safe an soune. In de name ah Jesus we pray. Amen."

I wanted to thank her for her prayer, but I felt so light-headed, all I could do was give her a faint smile. After she left the room, I tried to stand up.

"What are you doing?" Angie asked.

"I need to go to the bathroom before the paramedics get here."

"No," she replied forcefully. "You're not moving without our help." I tried again to lift my body up, but another wave of pain struck me down again.

I didn't want to admit it, but maybe she was right. Just the thought of trying to get up made the pain worse.

Finally, the paramedics arrived.

"Daddy, I want to go with you," pleaded Ash.

Before I could find the strength to reply, Angie turned to her and said, "You kids stay here with Miss Zoli. Your father's going to be alright."

The ambulance ride was like riding a wild horse as it raced down the hill and onto street. The paramedics wouldn't let Ang ride with me, so she followed behind in her car. In spite of the ride, by the time we got to the hospital, I tried to convince myself that I was feeling much better.

They rushed me into Freeman's emergency room—the same room Miss Zoli was taken to. The nurses scurried about hooking me up to monitors, while a bleary eyed resident fired questions at me like I was being cross-examined.

The nurses hooked me up to several monitors and gadgets that made the most irritating noises I've ever heard. I must've stayed in the emergency room for at least two hours. I quickly grew tired of all the poking and prodding that seemed to last forever..

When I finally asked one of the nurses, "What's wrong with me?" she looked like she was about to cry.

"I don't know sir, we'll have to find out. The doctor will be here in a few moments."

The doctor, a short diminutive Indian man, came in a few moments later, asked a few questions and listened to my heart.

"Do you know what's wrong with me?"

"I don't know, I don't know," he replied with a thick accent.

"Can you give me a hint?"

"We are trying to ascertain, sir, whether or not you had a heart attack. Please let me return to my work."

"Thank you for those kind words of encouragement. "

After drawing my blood at least three or four times, they finally let Angela into the room. She looked terrified, yet tried to put on a good front for me, trying to pretend that everything was okay.

"How do you feel?" she asked while kissing me on the cheek.

"I'm okay."

"No, you're not. You're sick."

"The pain's getting better."

Tears began to stream down her face.

"Hey, what's wrong with you?" I asked.

"I'm sorry. I hope you'll find it in your heart to forgive me. It's all my fault that you're here."

"Sorry for what?"

"You've been under so much pressure and I haven't been a good wife to you. I've been caught up in so many other things, doing what I wanted to do, and now you're here. Will you ever forgive me?"

"Baby, what on earth are you talking about?"

"Miss Zoli. I know that's why you're here. You didn't want her in the house, and if I'd done what you'd asked, you wouldn't be here."

"Alright, Angela, I want you to stop talking like that right now, or you're going to really get me upset and I will be sick. Baby, I'm going to be alright, and this is nobody's fault. Like I told you before, I love you because you are so generous and giving. Yeah, I don't like her being around, but we'll work it out. This is not the time to be talking about her. "

"He's right, Ang. " I turned and looked, it was Kathy Lee, sticking her head through the drapes.

"What are you doing here?" I asked.

"What do you think? I came to check on my pigheaded big brother. You know the guy who's been like my big brother. Do you know where he is?"

I started laughing, and the pain in my chest caught me off guard. I winced a little, trying not to let either one of them see how much pain I was really in.

"As if I didn't have enough patients to worry about. Here you come in complaining of chest pain. How are you feeling?"

"Good enough to go home."

"Kathy Lee, would you try to talk some sense into his thick head? He's serious, he feels better so he's ready to leave. You know he has to rebuild Stewart Computers. Heaven forbid it wait a few days. "

"Now listen to me, John Stewart, this is nothing to play with!" Kathy Lee said sternly. "Dr. Bajari says he's very concerned about your condition. I'd advise you to go on and be admitted and let us get to the bottom of this. "

"No can do."

"You could drop dead."

"Why you have to say it like that?"

"'Cause it seems as if you can't get it through that thick skull of yours any other way."

"Alright, alright. If you put it that way, I will stay for a day or two. But no longer than that. "

"Well, at least we don't have to commit you to a psychiatric ward."

"No, I know someone else who needs that."

"We are not yet certain what's wrong with you, Mr. Stewart. There are some concerning signs on your EKG that you may have had a heart attack. But your blood tests are negative. You have a very rapid heart beat, and your blood pressure is markedly elevated. We need to do additional tests, and possibly administer medication, if it is a heart attack. I would like to admit you to our cardiac intensive care unit for observation.

"What? Is that really necessary?"

"Yes, I'm afraid that it is."

"Dr. Bajari, I need to get home. I have things to do, a business to rebuild. I can't be sitting here in this hospital wasting my time and yours."

"John, you need to do what the doctor is suggesting. You know you thought that you were having a heart attack this morning. Now you're lucky. Think about all those people that we know who have dropped dead from a heart attack. Just let him do what's best for you," Angela said.

"I know what's best for me."

"Obviously you don't. Otherwise you would be cooperating."

As they rolled me out of the emergency room, I turned to Angela and said, "Do not call my mother. I don't want her to know about this." She softly nodded her head. She was so scared, at least for the moment, that she accepted what I said without resistance.

"I'll call the kids and let them know what's going on."

"Don't bring them down here. I don't want them to see me like this. "

"But John—"

"No, buts, I'll talk to them on the phone, but I don't want them seeing their old man being wheeled around this place like some cripple. Are you with me on this?"

"Okay," she replied sullenly. "If that's what you want. But there's no phones in the ICU."

"Bring a tape recorder then. "

I don't like being here, it gives me the creeps. It made me appreciate my family. I missed them even though the last few days had been rough, I needed to have them around. That night I couldn't go to sleep. The unit was filled and there were nurses running around left and right. The noise was enough to drive you crazy, all of the buzzers and alarms going off, just about every other minute, as the respirators breathing for the people. It felt like I was in a room filled with haunted computers. I tossed and turned for hours, I just couldn't get comfortable.

It must've been after two a.m. when I was finally tired enough to drift into a deep, dark sleep. I was in that twilight state when I felt something hovering over me. The room was dim; I guess the nurses had turned off most of the lights, and only a few beepers were making any noise

A flash of brilliant light caught the corner of my eye, as I saw something move at the foot of my bed. I looked up and saw the hint of a figure; a ghost, a spirit. When my eyes finally focused, I saw a man. As the features of his face became more distinct I realized it was my father. I couldn't believe my eyes, I hadn't seen him for years. He was standing there in his full military regalia.

He just stood there solemnly. Watching me.

For the first time in many years, I realized how much I missed him. He looked older and more distinguished. I felt like he was trying to tell me something.

Eventually he smiled, but it wasn't a big wide grin, it was a strange, almost eerie kind of smile. Then he waved his hand good-bye and vanished.

I didn't know what to do.

twenty-six

"Mommie, is daddy going to die?"

The piercing intensity of Ashley's question sliced through the core of my being like a hot knife cutting butter. Stunned, I didn't know what to say. Words clumped together in the middle of my throat like a pile of rocks blocking the flow of a trickling stream of water. I wanted to cry, but I didn't want my children to see how afraid I was.

"I don't think he's going to die anytime soon," I replied slowly, trying desperately not to stumble over my words. "But Ash, you have to realize that one day we're all going to die."

"I know that, mommie, but I'm scared," she cried.

"Mom, I just don't want him to die right now," asked James, his voice taunt with fear.

"I understand, I'm worried, too. We'll just have to pray and ask God to help daddy get well and to come home soon."

"Mom, when can we go to see dad?" asked James.

"I'm not sure, honey. We'll have to wait and see."

"I wanna see him, too! I miss him already," whimpered Ashley. "Can we call him on the phone?"

"No. He doesn't have a phone in his room."

James, perhaps sensing my own fears about John, turned to me and with a voice full of authority, said, "Don't worry, Mom, Dad's going to be alright. And until he comes home, I'm the man of the house."

I didn't mean to let it happen, but I broke down and cried like a baby in front of my children. They wrapped their arms around me and we shared the same tears.

I wasn't prepared for my husband's sudden illness, or the howling vacuum his absence created in my life. Before today, the notion of his mortality had never occurred to me. I knew he was a bit high strung and the last week or so has taken its toll on all of us. I never realized that it was affecting him as much as it had, almost killing him. He looked so helpless in the bed this morning; his body drenched with sweat, and his face flushed a bright beet red. I was terrified, afraid that he might die before we got him to the hospital.

Maybe this was the price I paid for casually suggesting to him last week that I would be a merry widow spending all of his money. What if he died? I didn't know what I would do without him. The memories of all the funerals I've attended rushed in my consciousness from the deep, dark wells of my memory. During the last five years, friends of John's, most of them in his age group, a few younger, and those husbands of my girlfriends who suddenly dropped dead, usually died of a heart attack. I used to sit there feeling sorry for them, never imagining for one moment that I could be wearing their shoes.

Throughout my life, I've never been sheltered from death's sting. I remember the time one of my first grade friends was hit by a car and killed. My mother and father took me to the funeral home to view her body, while most of my classmate's parents refused to let them see her. I remember crying over the loss of my friend. Momma wrapped her plump golden arms around me and let me cry in the softness of her breasts. She always did that when someone died, except when I was ten and her father died. Then it was my turn to comfort her.

When momma passed away, her absence left a big gaping hole in my life that was never filled. I missed her each and everyday of my life.

I didn't know what I would do if I lost John. He was too young, he was in good health, great shape, and I just didn't get it. I thought heart attacks happened to couch potatoes and those who ate and drank a lot. He has always been the picture of good health. He rarely got colds, and when he did he shook them off in two or three days.

During a very solemn dinner of leftovers, Miss Zoli asked, "How is dat husban ah yohs doin?"

"We don't know for sure. The doctors are running tests."

"He gonna be fine. Watch dese words, de spirit is ah tellin me dat he will be alright."

"Thank you, Miss Zoli, that's very sweet of you."

I felt guilty, very guilty. Maybe if I hadn't insisted that she stayed here, my husband wouldn't have ended up in the hospital.

Later in the evening, I called Bill, a few of John's friends, and in spite of his request, I called his mother. She'd never forgive me if I didn't tell her that something happened to him.

"Momma Mae, I have something to tell you."

"What is it, sugar?"

"John's in the hospital."

"Lord, have mercy on me. What's wrong with my child?"

"He woke up having chest pains this morning and we had to take him to the hospital."

"Did he have a heart attack? The way he's been running around and working himself to death, I told him that he was going to end up in the hospital."

"The doctors are pretty sure that he didn't have one. They're running tests."

"Well then, Angela, can you tell me what's wrong with my son?"

"No, ma'am I'm sorry, I can't."

"Well, do I have to get on a plane and find out what's going on?"

"Now, Momma Mae, calm down. You don't have to do that, I will keep you posted."

"Alright, I expect you to do that, Angela," she said with a firm voice.

"Yes, ma'am"

"And if you don't, I will be on the next plane out there."

Talking to her really didn't make me feel any better, I should've done what John asked me to do and not let her know what had happened to him. After talking to Momma Mae, I called the cardiac unit. The nurse said John was stable and resting comfortably. She promised to let him know that I had called.

By nine o'clock I was exhausted. My body felt so heavy, carrying all of my fears that I could barely get up the stairs. I took a hot shower. Afterward, as I sat on the edge of our bed, I couldn't get in. I'd never felt so lonely and frightened, not even when my mother died. John had been away so many times that for a while it had become a routine. But this time it was different, very different. How will I go on if he died? I'd always taken for granted that we would grow old together, now nothing seemed certain anymore. I wanted to call someone, but I couldn't think of who to call. I didn't know who would understand how I felt. How could I ever live without him? For almost thirty years, he had been the very the center of my life, my one and only love. To see him critically ill and frightened, while trying to put up a good front, was too much for me.

Without his anchoring presence I felt lost like a small piece of drifting wood on the waves of an angry, unmerciful sea. I desperately ached for the warmth of his body beside mine. When I finally got into the bed, fear and gloom descended upon me. I tried to convince myself that I was acting silly, being unreasonable, and overreacting, but I couldn't.

Reflecting over the events of the last few weeks, perhaps it was my guilt that stoked the flames of my fear. Guilt for not considering his feelings. Guilt for not paying attention to the warning signs I now clearly saw. Guilt for being so irritated with him since the loss of Stewart Computers. Guilt for not being more supportive. Guilt, guilt, guilt. Nothing but guilt visited me.

I wanted to cry, but couldn't. The pain was too severe. I begged and pleaded with God to spare my husband's life and not take him away from me. We had so much more living to do. Finally, after hours of this terrifying reality, my consciousness fell into the darkness of sleep.

twenty-seven

What am I supposed to think? How am I supposed to feel? Why did I see him now? After all of those years of not seeing him, why did he decide to reappear in my life now? I didn't get it. Why did he go away when I was a little boy? I finally had convinced myself, thanks to my mother, maybe a year or so after the last time that I saw him, that he was just a figment of my imagination. But in my heart, I always knew better.

I was trying to forget about what had happened last night. Even though I was happy to see him, it really gave me the creeps. Maybe he was showing up now because I was dying. I had heard stories about people seeing their long lost-loved ones at the time of death. I didn't know what to think.

Dr. Bajari came around to see me shortly after eight in the morning. "Well, Mr. Stewart, you seem to be making good progress."

"Yeah? Can I go home?"

"Not so fast, sir," he replied. "We have to run some additional tests to see what's causing your heart to beat so rapidly."

"Couldn't it just be case of bad nerves?"

"That's a possibility, sir, but we have to make certain that your heart is functioning properly before we send you home."

"Did I have a heart attack?"

"Your preliminary reports appear to be within normal limits, and your heart rate has slowed down significantly. Before I send you home, I want to make certain that your heart is functioning normally."

The morning moved by quickly. I went from one test to another—treadmill, breathing test, ultrasound, thallium scan—then they put another monitor on me. They came by and drew more blood at least twice that morning. Then they did an very painful test called a blood gas, where a needle was stuck down into my wrist like it was a pin cushion.

When I returned around lunchtime, my nurse said, "Your wife came by while you were in the cath lab. She said she'll be back around noon with your children."

"She what? Can you call her for me? I've got to stop her."

"Why?"

"Because I don't want my children seeing me look so helpless."

"Mr. Stewart, there's absolutely nothing wrong with your children coming by to visit you. I can't tell you how many people pass through this unit, and nobody ever comes to see them. You are really lucky to have a family that loves you. You know you men and your fragile egos ought to quit."

Kathy Lee stopped by just before noon.

"Can you tell me anything?" I asked.

"We're fairly sure that you didn't have a heart attack, but we're trying to ascertain the cause of your arrhythmia."

"Give it to me straight, K.L. Tell me the truth and skip the medical mumbo-jumbo."

"Man, must you be so melodramatic? It could be a lot worse."

"Easy for you to say."

"Listen to me, John Stewart, and listen to me good. I had a good friend, who was more like the brother I never had than a friend. We grew up together, three doors apart. Herman was an only child, and a year younger than me, and a year older than my sister. After his dad died, when he was about seven, my daddy kind of adopted him. When Herman finished Harvard Med School, he went to Sloan Kettering and did his residency there. And if that wasn't enough, he went on and got an M.B.A. from Wharton."

"Kathy Lee, I don't have all day."

"Yes, you do. Negro, if you don't act right, you might have all year in this place.

"Anyway, he was in town for a convention, maybe a couple of months before Doug and I got married. I went to dinner with him, and dropped him off at his hotel. Do you know that I was the last person to see him alive? He died in his sleep that night. He was just like you, an overachieving workaholic, and a wonderful man. Don't be another Herman. We can help you, if you let us."

"Okay, you sure do know how to lay on a heavy guilt trip."

I was dozing off when I heard Ashley scream, "Daddy, I miss you!" as she leaped into my arms. "When are you coming home?"

"What are you two doing here?"

"Mommie came to school at lunchtime and brought us here."

"Dad, I want you to know that I've got everything under control at home. So you just lay back and chill. Get well, and don't worry about a thing." James said.

"Trying to take your old man's place as the head of the house?"

"No, not really. I'm just trying to fill in until you get well. We miss you."

"I'll be home soon, son, don't you worry." I was so proud of the way my son felt responsible for his mother and sister. He reminded me of myself when I was a kid after my father had died. I'm happy that I could see him develop this trait.

"When are you coming home, Dad?"

"Soon, I'll be home pretty soon."

"Where's your mother?"

"Downstairs in the lobby, She said she wanted us to spend some time alone with you."

"I'm glad she did. I miss you two knuckleheads."

After the kids left, I took a nap. When I woke up, Angie and my nurse were hovering nervously over me.

"Sorry to wake you up, Mr. Stewart, but I've got good news fro you. I just talked to Dr. Bajari and based on the preliminary results of some of your tests, we're going to transfer you to a regular room."

"Why can't you just send me home?"

"Mrs. Stewart, how do you ever put up with him?"

"That's a good question. He's normally not this bad, when he's at home. So please indulge him if you can."

"I can, since he'll be out of my hair in just a few minutes," she laughed as she left the room.

"Thanks."

"For what?" Angie asked a bit perplexed.

"For bringing the kids. It was good to see them."

"I'm glad you're not mad at me."

"Sometimes I don't think before I act."

"Ang, don't start on your guilt trip again. It's not necessary."

After a nice visit, I sent her home to get some rest. I was sure she thought I was mad at her, or blamed her for my being here. But I didn't want her to see me like this.

Doug came by an hour or so after I was transferred to a regular room. 'What are you doing here? I told you wife to tell you I didn't want any visitors."

"Man, you need to get a grip on yourself. I just came over to see how you're doing because you're my friend. Is there a law against that?"

"No, but there oughta be. You know, you never answered my question. Why doesn't anything ever worry you?" I asked.

"You wouldn't understand." Doug replied.

"Try me."

"You know I haven't always been like this. When we met, I was more frantic than you normally are. I guess I reached a point in my life where I decided to find inner peace."

"Man, knock off that new age mumbo jumbo. I know there's something going on. And I want to know why you won't tell me."

"I've already told you the truth. One day, you'll understand."

"Don't hold your breath."

Bill and Georgette called, he was recuperating at home. He was discharged from the hospital yesterday, "So you couldn't stand for me to get all of the attention? You had to do this to yourself for some sympathy. Man, don't you know that there are better ways to do this? You're too young to have chest pains."

"Yeah, you're right."

"So when are you going to take it easy and relax?"

"Now you sound like Doug and my wife."

:Take it from me, it's the truth. I've been running and ripping my whole life, and if this experience had taught me anything, I learned life is too short and unpredictable not to enjoy it."

"So what are you going to do?"

"I'm retiring."

"You mean you're not rebuilding Chez Georgette's?"

"That's right. I'm going to take my insurance money and run. Maybe I'll buy a Winnebago and Georgette and I will do the traveling we've talked about for years."

"You can do that because you're ready to retire anyway."

"Age has nothing to do with this. It's a state of mind."

Even though I couldn't see him, I continued to feel my father's presence. I wish I knew what he wanted to say to me; I'm sure he was trying to communicate, but I just didn't get it.

The poking and prodding continued for the rest of the day. Angie came by after dinner time.

"What did your doctor say? How do you feel?"

"Baby, I'm fine—you need to quit worrying about me. I'll be outta here in a day or two."

"Okay, if you insist," she said meekly. "Miss Zoli said to tell you that she's still praying for you."

"How's Mrs. Henderson handling her?"

"Being in the hospital seems to have increased your concern about Miss Zoli."

"Ang, you know I'm not a totally heartless person. I do have feelings."

"I never thought that you didn't. I know that you don't want her in the house, and I'm going to find a place for her to stay. She's already caused us enough trouble."

"I told you, you don't have to do that, And I meant that. She can stay with us until we locate her family."

"Are you serious? What changed your mind? What's happened to you since you have been here?"

"Nothing's happened to me. It just wouldn't make any sense to get rid of her now. She's been with us for almost two weeks, and it would set a bad example for Ashley and James."

"Mr. Stewart, all of your tests have come back within normal limits. And you heart has been beating normally for the last twenty-four hours." Dr. Bajari's words were music to my ears.

"So what's wrong with me?"

"That is an excellent question. I suspect your arrhythmia was induced by severe situational anxiety attack."

"So when are you going to send me home?"

"I will fill out the discharge papers and you can go home today."

"You mean to tell me, I've wasted the last three days of my life in here to find out I'm stressed, when I could have been working? I could've told you that on day one."

"Mr. Stewart, you should be celebrating. The situation could've been far worse. You could've had a serious medical problem."

Angie picked me up around noon and drove me home.

"Honey, I'm so grateful you're coming home. I hope you'll find it in your heart to forgive me."

"Come on Angie, there's nothing to forgive."

"Mr. Stewart, you're a sight for sore eyes! It's so good to have you back home!"

"Thank you, Mrs. Henderson. I appreciate that. It's good to be home."

"I want you to know that I held you in my prayers."

"That's probably why the doctor let me come home so soon."

"Prayer does change things. I'm a witness to that," she said with a smile. "Can I so anything for you?"

"Mrs. Henderson, that's very kind of you, but I'm not an invalid. I just overreacted to stress, that's all."

Since I felt fine, I didn't feel like going to bed and resting anymore. So I sat in the library and started to read a book on African history I'd been trying to read for over a year.

Shortly after I came home, Miss Zoli stumbled into my office. "Suh, it sho nuff is good to have yah back at home. It's nice having a man around de house. I know yah doesn't likes havin me aroune heah, an I don't wont yah tah worries no moh bout mah bein heah, cause Momma Zoli is gonna be on huh way, jist as soon as I can gits mahsef straight. I is gonna had on mah way back to 'Sippi.

"Miss Zoli, you know you don't have to leave. You are more than welcome to stay here until we locate your family."

Her face burst into a bright smile. "Is yah sho 'bout dat?

"Yes, ma'am, I most certainly am.

"Yah know yah remines me ah ole Joe, back on de ole 'tation. He ain't nevah had no familee, ah he own, but he always be looking out foh ev'rybody. I see his strength in yoh eyes."

I just smiled as she backed out of the room.

"'Cuse me suh," she said as she stopped dead in her tracks. "I jist gots one moh thang tah axe of yah."

"What's that?

"Whot do dem chilrens ah yohs be disappearin to in de mawnin?"

"They go to school."

"De ain't workin in no fields is dey?"

"No ma'am they don't."

"Whot does dey be doin theah?"

"They're in school to learn."

"She was completely confused, almost disturbed by my words.

"Yah means tah tells me that colored chilrens be goin to school, an ain't nobody be stoppin dem?"

"Yes, ma'am they do."

"Lawd a mercy on me!" she exclaimed, shaking her head. "I ain't nevah seen nothin likes dat."

"I always wanted tah learn how tah read, an back in 'Sippi dey would kill us if we came close to a book. "She hesitated, then asked, "Suh, does you think dat yoh chilrens can hep me tah learns how tah read? I axed dem and dey said dey would, but you bein dey pappy an de man of de house, I ain't wanna be doin nothin dat was wrong."

"I'll ask them, if they'd be willing to teach you. I don't think it should be a problem."

"Oh thank yah. Thank yah so much. God bless you suh."

I agreed to Miss Zoli's request without thinking about it, I guess because I was truly happy to be back home. I hadn't felt this good in a long time. It was funny how little things, like a quick trip to the hospital, can make you appreciate, in a way you never did before, the little things in life that were really important.

Late in the afternoon, I received a huge floral arrangement form Charlie Kim and the Korean American Chamber of Commerce. The note said:

Mr. Stewart,

I was very sorry to hear that you have been hopitalized. I fear that the stress of our meeting contributed to your illness. You were absolutely correct, and it's courage and honesty like yours that has caused us to rethink African American's contribution to our history.

We hope that we can build a bridge between our communities, and I hope that you will be a part of that effort.

Thank you for showing us the light.

Peace and Unity,
Charlie Kim

Doug stopped by later that day, "Glad to see you back at home."

"Yeah, man, it's good to be back where I'm supposed to be."

"You know you need to take it easy."

"Come on, man, don't get started on me today."

"Alright, I'll give you a break."

"Tomorrow I'll get back into the swing of things."

"You mean to tell me that you can't take a couple of days off?"

"No, man, you know how critical time is."

"Yes, I do, but I also know how critical your health is."

"Man, the doctors, including your wife gave me a clean bill of health. It was just a little scare. I'm fine. That reminds me—I need to thank Kathy Lee for putting up with me.

"If you say so."

When the kids came home for school, they were happy to see me back home. When I asked them about teaching Miss Zoli how to read, they were excited by the opportunity. "Are you sure you can do this?"

"Yes, Dad. It'll be fun," replied my son.

"What about you, Ash?"

"I want to help Miss Zoli, too."

"Okay, just as long as you don't let it interfere with your school-work."

"Dad, we've done this before. Remember?"

"What are you talking about, son?"

"You know we used to tutor the kids down at mom's center."

"Oh yeah. You're right. I did forget. But, I think Miss Zoli might be a little different. She's a lot older than those kids you were tutoring, and it might be harder for her to learn."

"Don't worry Dad, we can handle it. We'll have her reading in no time flat," James replied.

twenty-eight

Words couldn't describe how happy I was to have my husband back at home, safe, sound and healthy. Thank God he didn't have a heart attack. Maybe this experience will slow him down—and help him to smell the roses. I desperately hoped so. This experience prompted me to realize how carelessly I had taken so many of my blessings for granted. That was something I would never do again.

I knew James and Ashley were very relieved that John was back home again. Their eyes were brighter and clear. The strain they had been carrying dissipated.

Since John came home last week, Momma Mae has called at least three times a day to make sure that her child was okay. She hasn't seen him in almost a year, and I knew she was very worried abut him. We needed to visit her because the children hadn't seen her in over a year. We also needed to see my dad. That was the only thing I didn't like about living out here on the West Coast—everyone was so far away.

Everything was still pretty much in disarray at the center. I hated to go to work, it was so depressing. To say that we were overwhelmed was an understatement. Sometimes the burdens we carried seemed to be too much to bare. The need in our service area had increased tenfold, while the resources seemed to have shrunken. The strain had taken its toll on everyone at the center. Even Doc Whitney was short tempered.

Miss Zoli seemed to be having fewer of her absent spells, and seemed to be adjusting to our home quite nicely. John had agreed to let James and Ashley teach Miss Zoli how to read. She had taken to reading like a fish to water. The kids were even planning to take her down to the city's main library. For some reason, she found it very hard to believe that Black people could read and learn of their own volition.

"Wheah I comes from, dey used tah poke niggas eyes out if dey try tah learn how tah read. An y'all can learn anythang yah wonts. I ain't nevah heard ah nothin like dis.

"Thank yah, Jesus, I is learnin how tah read!"

Some things still seemed to rattle her a lot—like the television. Seeing running water still got her goat from time to time and she said to me one day, "I ain't nevah seen a house wid so many outhouses on de inside." At least three or four times a week, she asked me to explain how things worked around the house.

"I guess you'll never understand."

"Chile, dere is a whole lotta thangs 'bout dis heah place dat I won't be knowin why dey is de way dey is."

That following Saturday before Father's Day, I hadn't been out shopping in months. So I decided to take Miss Zoli with me while looking for a gift for my husband.

We were walking down Wilshire Boulevard, when suddenly Miss Zoli stopped in her tracks. I thought she was having another one of her absent spells. But she pointed in the direction of a young couple, a Black man and a white woman walking in front of us holding hands and kissing.

"Look at dat!"

"Miss Zoli, what are you talking about?"

"Whot he doin wid dat gul? Don't he know dat he gonna git kilt?" she screamed, pointing at the couple.

"He ain't 'pose tah be wid huh. Somebody gonna string him up! Colored man ain't even 'pose tah look at a white woman, let alone be touchin huh."

"Miss Zoli, calm down. That's the way it used to be, but now, things are quite different. It happens all of the time."

"What yah mean?"

"Interracial couples are quite common out here."

She was utterly shocked. "Yah means colored mens an white womins?"

"Yes, ma'am, I do '

Shaking her head, she begged, "How can dat be?'

"That's just the way it is out here. There's nothing unusual at all about it."

"Lawd, I doesn't knows whot kine ah worle dis is, but it is sho nuff diff'rnt from mine. Back in, 'Sippi white mens can do anythang dey wonts tah do to a womin like me. But he bettah not catch a nigga lookin at his womin."

On Father's Day the family took John out to dinner, and then John and I went over to Bill and Georgette's to say good-bye to them. We left the kids and Miss Zoli down at Kathy Lee's. It was the first time we'd been alone in many months.

Bill and Georgette weren't wasting any time about getting out of town too begin their cross country tour. He was walking around pretty good, considering the fact that he'd almost lost his leg only a few weeks ago.

"I told those doctors not to count me out."

"Bill, quit bragging."

"We're so glad you two stopped by to see us before we left."

"Yeah, we're glad to have a chance to spend some time with you before you go. We're really going to miss you."

"Oh, John, that's so sweet of you to say," whispered Georgette with tears in her eyes.

"We're going to miss you all."

"Come on, sugar, don't cry. It's not like we're going forever. We'll be back."

It was hard, very hard saying good-bye to our dear friends. But I knew that we must. They had to move on with the rest of their lives and so did we.

When we picked up the kids and Miss Zoli on the way home, Kathy Lee pulled me aside and said, "I need to talk to you about Miss Zoli.

"I looked at her foot, and it's clearly not responding to the medication. I think she needs to see a friend of mine, Dr. Malika Collins. She's a holistic doctor. I've sent a few patients her way that nobody could help.

"Listen, I know it sounds funny—but one of my colleagues, another cardiologist himself, went to her as a last resort after he had a heart attack, and whatever the treatment was that she prescribed worked. Darwin is like a new man. I couldn't believe it and he refers a lot of his patients to her."

"Okay, if you say so. We'll give her a try," I said.

Amazingly, when I called the next day, the nurse informed me that they had an opening for that same day due to a cancellation.

"Wheah is yah takin me?"

"To see another doctor."

"Foh whot?"

"Because your foot isn't getting any better."

"Chile, I done tole you, mah foot is fine. It don't botha me, why is it botharin you?"

"That infection could get into your bloodstream and kill you."

"It ain't killed me so far. Why is it gonna do dat now? Ain't nothin gonna kills me till I fines mah chilrens."

Dr. Collins' office was one of the few remaining buildings on Vermont Avenue. Her presence radiated an immediate comfort and sense of understanding. She was tiny, no more than five feet tall and she looked even more like a little girl than Kathy Lee did. A forest of braids draped her warm brown face, and the only thing that was missing were the ribbons to tie them all together.

Miss Zoli didn't object as she was led into the examining room, while I waited in the reception area.

A half an hour later when Dr. Collins' nurse called me in, I wasn't prepared for what I was about to hear.

"Before we discuss Miss Steadwell's physical condition, I'd like to talk to you about her mental state. I know you might find this hard to believe, but Mrs. Stewart, it's my opinion that she could be telling the truth."

"What do you mean, Dr. Collins?" I was stunned. I couldn't believe my ears. "How can you tell me that it's possible that she's telling the truth?"

"I know it's hard for you to believe, but her story is quite cogent, and it is possible that she's telling the truth. Have you ever listened to her? Her only confusion rests with details on how she arrived her, on what happened to her on April 29th."

"You've got to be kidding. How can you tell me that you believe she's almost two hundred years old?"

"I lived on the continent, in West Africa, when I worked with the Peace Corps, and I saw things that were beyond my understanding. When I was there, I was told that during times of great upheaval and turmoil the ancestors will appear."

"Doctor, what are you saying? How could you say something like that?"

"Well, I know this sounds quite bizarre and farfetched to you, especially when you take into consideration how we've been taught to think—in the rational Western tradition. All I can say is that based on my experience in Africa, there is a good possibility that she is telling the truth. And furthermore, I don't think she's a threat to anyone."

"Let me make sure I got this straight. You're telling me that Miss Zoli could be telling the truth? What made you change your mind?"

"I really don't know. I guess you could say that I had a change of heart."

"I'm sorry, but I can't accept that. It's not possible."

"Give me a moment to explain. You see, there are things about life, mysteries of our existence, that we just don't know or understand. And it is possible that she was sent here through time. As a scientist and physician, I would say no it's not possible, that's my linear mind. But my being has told me as my experiences have shown me that God manifests in so many different ways, and that many of the mysteries of the universe are beyond our understanding. So in that vane, I would say yes. I believe that she is an ances-

tor that has come to visit us and to share with us something that
is very important.

"If she is telling the truth, and I think that she is, this is
something that I can share with my children and my grandchildren. Precisely let me say my grandnieces and nephews. Lord
knows if I'll ever give birth to a child, especially at my age!"

"So, what are we supposed to do?"

"Wait. If it's true, her purpose will be revealed. Why don't you
take her back to Mississippi?"

"I plan to, it's just that so many things have happened. My
husband was just released from the hospital, he lost his business
and since the riots my workload at my job has increased tenfold."

I left the office not knowing what to think. I never thought
about Miss Zoli telling the truth being a possibility, and I couldn't
consider that now. Strange things like this might happen in Africa, but I knew it didn't happen here.

"Whot did dat purdy little doctah say?"

"She said she believes you."

"Praise God! Somebody finally believes me! Thank yah Jesus.
Dat is music to mah ears,

"Why she believe me an yah ain't?"

"'Cause she has been to Africa, and has had experiences that
have led her to be more open-minded.

"She also gave me some vitamins and herbs to take to help
clear up your foot."

"We used tah boil roots an one ah de ole slave womin, Sistah
Fanny, was a root doctah."

I decided not to tell John, or anyone else for that matter. I
was sure if I did he would really want to have me and Miss Zoli
committed.

twenty-nine

Dere is ah whole lotta thangs 'bout dis heah worle dat I jist doesn't undahstands, dat don't make not one bit ah sense tah me, an I jist wonts tah gits on back tah mine as soon as I can.

I don't wanna keep on axin dem how I gots heah, cause I knows dey still be wonderin if I is crazy or not. 'Specially dat Mistah Stewart. Maybe I won't evah know foh sho how I gots heah, but dere is one thang dat I does knows is dat I ain't crazy.

Dey say dat dey name ah dis city, Los Angeles means de city ah angels. Well, de Lawd must 'cuse me, but I ain't seen no angel yet. Not ah one ah dem, an de Lawd knows dat dis place needs ah whole heap of dem.

Dey took me to dis heah colored gal doctah, an she de only one dat said dat I is tellin de truf. She gave me a whole bunch ah thangs tah be takin, and in a few days mah feets started gettin bettah an lookin bettah. De best dey has looked since I cain't remembas.

Lawd bless huh, cause she is de only dat believes me. Dey chilrens does too, but nobody evah listens ah long time to de truf de chilrens speaks.

Now I can walks in dese funny shoes, an wears de funny clothes, but I guess I jist gots tah makes de best ah dis heah siteeation til I gits back home.

I still ain't got use tah all dese 'traptions an funny machines dat seem like dey got a life ah dey own. De hot box dat cooks de food too fast, de box wid dem diff'rnt little peoples runnin aroune in it, de talkin box, what dey call de radio an dem music machines. I doesn't knows why dey needs all dem 'traptions, dey sho nuff be cloggin up mah mine. I doesn't likes bein roune dem too much, but I knows dere ain't much dat I can do 'bout dat right now. Dese people bin nice enough tah let me stay wid dem dis long, I cain't be tellin dem what tah do in dey own house. An dey seems tah like havin all dese thangs aroune. I keep havin dese dreams, I keep seein mah chilren in mah dreams, an I wakes up an dey ain't heah. It makes me awful sad.

But I is gonna get home one day soon. I jist knows dat I is, an I is gonna fine mah chilrens. Befoh I dies, I is gonna hold each an ev'ry one ah mah babies in mah arms, an all dem granchilrens dat I knows dat I gots. I is gonna do dat, cause I knows dat de Lawd didn't bring me dis far tah leaves me.

I done seen otha thangs in dis worle dat has knocked me off ah mah feet. Colored boys wi 'd white womens.

I is learnin how tah reads, an mah mine likes it. I nevah thought dat I would be learnin how tah do dat.

But I gots tah gits back tah 'Sippi soon as I can. I knows dat I ain't got much time left own dis heah worle an I jist wonts tah lay mah eyes on dey faces one moh time.

Each an ev'ry night even though I caln't see de stars likes I used tah do back in 'Sippi, -ray. I jist wonts tah goes home, befoh I closes mah eyes foh de last time.

Through many dangers,
toils and snares

I have already come

thirty

Time had slipped quickly through our fingers. It was already early August. It seemed like Miss Zoli arrived only a few weeks ago, and she has been here for months. We still hadn't found any trace of her family, yet she seemed to be adjusting nicely. She took to learning how to read like a fish to water. Yet, I still saw the sadness in her eyes whenever she talked about finding her family.

After John returned unscathed from the hospital, the man I married emerged. He was upbeat, happy and determined to rebuild Stewart Computers. He was even letting James help him out at his temporary office space. He brought back on board half of his staff, and planned to bring in the rest by the end of September.

The city was still quite tense in spite of the federal government indicting the police of counts of violating Rodney King's civil rights. No one believed that they would be convicted.

One Saturday morning after breakfast, John was lingering at the kitchen table. While I was putting away the dishes, he walked over to the counter and said, "Let's go to the beach. You know we haven't done that yet this summer. Let's pack up the kids and go."

"What about Miss Zoli?"

"We can take her, too. It's August already, and before we know it, the summer will be over and done with."

"John, what's wrong with you? We're in California! It's summertime all year."

"Baby, you know what I mean."

I paused and thought about it for a moment. "Oh, honey, I don't know, I've got so many things to do today."

"And if you wait until tomorrow or next week, or whenever to do them, the earth isn't going to shift on its axis because you didn't do them."

"You're right. It's been a long time since we did anything just for fun—let's do it."

We packed up the kids, and Miss Zoli.

"Wheah is we goin?"

"We're going to the beach Miss Zoli!" squealed Ashley.

"Whot's dat? I ain't nevah heard ah no 'beech'"

"We're going down to the ocean and the park."

When we arrived at the Santa Monica Beach shortly before eleven o'clock that morning, the sky was a bright clear blue, not a cloud present, and the gentle breezes, filled with salt air made me feel at least ten years younger.

"Whot's dat?" Miss Zoli asked pointing at the water.

"That's the Pacific Ocean, Miss Zoli," replied John.

"Dat watah is mighty purdy, an very peaceful. I could jist sit heah an look at it all day long"

"You're right Miss Zoli, it is very pretty," John said.

James and Ash had been walking by the water when they ran over to the bench where we were sitting and James asked, "Dad, can we go get some hot dogs?"

"Sure, son."

John and the kids were gone for no more than five minutes, when Miss Zoli looked at me and asked, "Can yah take me down by de watah? I wonts tah git closah to it."

As I led her down the stairs to the beach, she smiled and said, "Dis is beautiful. I ain't nevah seen nothin like dis back in 'Sippi. I seen de 'Sippi Rivah, but I ain't nevah seen no watah like dis."

"Yes, it is. I love it here myself. We don't come often enough."

When we reached the bottom of the stairs, there was a group of strange looking young white men. Maybe five or six skinheads, all wearing black leather.

As we got closer to the bottom, I heard one of them say, "Look at the nigga bitches comin."

"Excuse me," I said firmly, trying not to let them know how nervous I felt being near them.

No one moved out of our way.

"Bitch, we ain't movin."

Instead of confronting this idiot, I turned and held onto Miss Zoli's hand to go back upstairs, but they had already surrounded us.

"Whot's wrong wid dem?" she asked timidly. "We ain't hurtin nobody."

"Shut up, you old bitch!"

That was it. I could take him calling me a bitch with no problem, but not one of my elders. Not her.

"You can't talk to her like that."

Before I knew what had happened, something struck my head. It must've been a fist. I hit the ground, started seeing stars, and from what seemed like a great distance, I could hear Miss Zoli scream.

Through my cloudy daze, I saw the first one pull a knife and point it at Miss Zoli's throat. Before he could reach her, I picked up my foot, and with all of my strength, I kicked him in the groin.

John and James came rushing down the stairs. I didn't clearly remember what happened next, but I knew they beat the living daylights out of the ones who remained standing.

"Mom, are you alright?" I heard my son screaming.

I didn't tell them that one of them hit me. I didn't know what John might do if he knew that one of them hurt me.

Miss Zoli was crying and saying to John, "Yah kept dem off ah me. Ain't nobody evah done dat foh me befoh. Yah protected me from dem white men. My own husban and mah son couldn't do dat. Dey tried, but dey got beat worser dan me, so dey stopped tryin."

The Santa Monica police showed up a few minutes later to make a report. They said that before the riots began, a group of skinheads had been terrorizing Black people for months, but it had gotten worse since the riots.

We left shortly thereafter and headed home. On the way home, still shaken by the experience, we were all pretty quiet.

Suddenly, Miss Zoli started talking, "Would y'all, jist do one thang foh me?"

"What's that?" asked John.

"Call me Momma, Momma Zoli. Y'all is really de only familee dat I gots."

"Yes, ma'am," replied my husband softly. "We would be honored to call you Momma."

That evening, we were all in the family room watching television. For the first time, Miss Zoli came out of her room and sat down on the end of the couch. A few minutes later, a program came on about a reunion. It was heartwrenching watching three Vietnamese children who were now adults return to Vietnam to find their family.

The children, two girls and a boy, were very young, when during the fall of Saigon, their father brought them on his bicycle from a small hamlet where they lived with their five other older brothers and sisters. He left them in Saigon with a trusted friend, while he returned to get the rest of his family, hoping all of them could flee the country and come to America.

As Saigon collapsed, the children were separated from the friend, and placed on a plane headed for the U.S. They were taken off the first plane, and placed on another. The first crashed with all of their identification.

When they arrived in the U.S., they were adopted by a loving couple in Denver. They lived a good and prosperous life. They went to college, married, and raised families.

When they reached their late twenties, they decided they wanted to return to Vietnam and find their family.

They'd gone a few years earlier and distributed thousands of fliers asking anyone who knew the whereabouts of their family to contact them. They received many responses from people claiming they could help, but they wanted money first. Finally, they received a credible lead from a man who said he knew their parents and he asked for nothing in return

The two oldest children, one of the daughters and son, returned with their spouses and children to Vietnam. To actually see the reunion was the most moving experience I had ever had while watching television. First, they saw their oldest sister, then their father, a broken man who'd blamed himself for their loss, break down into sobs, upon their reunion.

We were all in tears.

"What's wrong, Momma Zoli?" John asked when he saw her crying.

"I jist want to go home, jist like dem slanted eyes chilrens did."

John looked at me, and with a firm determination said to me, "It's time."

"Time for what?" I asked.

"It's time to take her home."

thirty-one

I is so happy tah be leavin dis heah strange worle behine an gettin back tah 'Sippi so I can fine mah familee. Lawd ah mercy me, I is headed home, back tah 'Sippi. I ain't nevah thought dat I would see dis day dat I would be goin back home. An on dis heah airplane up in de sky.

I ain't nevah been dis close to de clouds. I feels like a bird, spreadin huh wings, ready tah fly. An dey tells me I is gonna be back home in jist a little bit. I still doesn't undastands how I got so far away from home.

Ev'rything is gonna be fine now. Jist as soon as I gets back home, I knows I is gonna fine dem, I can feel it in my bones. I cain't wait tah see dem red roads, and magnolia trees. I wonts tah see dem cotton fields, I nevah thought dat I would see dem again.

I is gonna fine me ah carriage, dat sweet chile Angela said dat we had some monee tah gits ah car tah gits aroune in. She don't know dat 'Sippi ain't a bit like Los Angeles bin like. She said she bin tah 'Sippi befoh, but de way she be talkin 'bout de part dat she bin to I ain't nevah heard ah no place like dat 'n 'Sippi.

I seen a lot in dey worle. Dey bin so good to me, and I jist thanks de Lawd dat dey foune me an took me in. Dey was good tah me, even hep me tah learn how tah read, somethang I nevah dream of doin. But dere is otha things dat is moh impotant dan readin, an all dey thangs dis worle gots. I wonts mah chilren back. Dey bin away from me too lon. Most of 'em ain't seen me since dey was youngins. Now dey is grown wid dey own familee.

I is finally on mah way home. An dis time, I is gonna fine mah familee.

thirty-two

The next morning, Momma Zoli was exuberant, almost walking on air. Her face was bright, filled with a clear radiance. She looked at least ten years younger.

"Thank yah Jesus! I is finally gonna gits back to my home an fine my chilrens agin. Oh praise de Lawd. Dat husban of yohs, he is somethin else. He gots a big heart. He just be hidin it. I gotta thanks him mahself."

At breakfast, I noticed that our children weren't too happy with the idea. James and John left the breakfast nook, while Ash sat around moping.

"Mommie, why are you taking her away? We want her to stay."

"Honey, we all knew this day would come. We can't keep her here. She wants to find her family."

"It's not fair."

"Ash, if you were away from home, wouldn't you want to get back here to us as fast as you could?"

"Yes, Mommie, I would."

"The same is true for Momma Zoli. Honey, you have to love with an open hand. Otherwise, holding on too tightly can destroy love.

"What's gonna happen when she finds her family? We'll probably never see her again,"

"Sugah, dat ain't true." Momma Zoli had slipped in the kitchen, without either one of us feeling her presence. "I ain't never gonna forgits yah, an if de Lawd is willin, I is comin back tah see yah, an I'll bring mah youngins wid me."

"You promise?" whined Ashley.

"Sugah, I promise." She turned to me and asked, "I jist got one question foh yah. How is we gonna git tah 'Sippi?"

"We're going to take an airplane."

"Take ah air whot?"

"You know, fly up in the sky."

"No. Dere ain't no way dat I is gonna gits up in de air an fly like a bird. I ain't got no wings."

"Momma Zoli, it's gonna be alright. Plus, if we took the train, it would take us three or four days to get there. And with the way things are on my job, I know I can't take off more than a week."

"I ain't doin dat."

"Momma Zoli, you can fly, it's fun," Ashley said.

"We fly all the time. We even flew across the ocean a couple of years ago to Hawaii."

"Wheah's dat?"

"In the Pacific Ocean."

"I done seen lots of dis heah worle an I is ready tah gits back tah mine. But I doesn't knows if I is ready tah fly. Goin up in de air like a bird jist don't seem rite."

"No, momma. It's really nothing to worry about. You're going to be alright.

"Yah thinks so?"

"Yes, ma'am. I know so. I can't tell you the number of times I've flown. Hundreds, if not thousands. It's okay. It's going to be fine."

"But Momma Zoli, I want you to be prepared for whatever we find in Misissippi. We might not find your children or your husband."

"Chile, I doesn't knows what yah is talkin 'bout. Of course we gonna fine dem dere. Yah outtah knows dat I doesn't wonts tah leaves yah, but I gots tah git back on mah way. I know dey is still lookin foh me, an dey is gonna be real happy tah see me again. I is so happy."

So much had happened in the few months she had been with us. She had adjusted quite nicely to our home and our world, even though it had been a challenge for her. I still chuckled at her unique descriptions of so many things we took for granted. I still couldn't figure out why the conveniences of the modern world had been such an adjustment for her. The radio, the television, running water and electricity, were as foreign to her as living on the moon would be to me. I just didn't understand. Maybe if we found her children, some of the missing pieces to her puzzle would be uncovered as well.

A few days later, we were at the airport and headed for Jackson. She said good-bye and thank you to John and the children in a most gracious way. It was touching to see her and John embrace finally, considering how much of a thorn she was in his side when she first arrived.

She turned to John and said, "Thank yah foh everything dat yah done done foh me. Even thoughs we didn't gits off tah a good start, we made up foh it in de end. I loves yah wid all of mah heart." She reached over and pulled him by the collar, and hugged him like a little brown bear.

Once we boarded the plane, she looked at me and asked, "How is dis big ole tub evah gonna git off de groune? I cain't see how dat is gonna happen."

"Just hold on, Momma Zoli, it will happen."

The stewardess came in and gave her instructions.

Momma Zoli gripped her hands into both arm rests, holding on for dear life, as the plane took off.

"Now dat is something! I cain't believe dis. Look, we is passin through de clouds. We is up highah dan de birds. I thinks dat heavin is own de othah side."

"Yah know dis here worle is somethin else. Colored folk doin some of anythang. Dey use tah tells us de only thang a nigga is good foh is pickin cotton. Dey tole us we cain't live in nobody's land of freedom cause our mammies and our pappies ovah dere in Africah lived in de trees wid de monkeys.

"Now bein heah among yah high fallutin colored folks an learnin 'bout all dat yah has done wif yah lives."

"Momma Zoli, why is it so hard for you to say 'black'?"

"Cause I ain't black! I might be a 'Sippi nigga, but I ain't black.. An ain't gonna nevah let nobody calls me dat."

"Momma Zoli, you and 1, we as Black people have nothing to be ashamed of. You are beautiful. Your color is beautiful. This is the way God made us. And all of us should be quite proud of who we are."

"Like I said. I ain't black, an I ain't nevah gonna be. So you might as well forget me even thinkin like dat. I is proud dat I can read a little bit now an when I gits back an finds mah chilrens, I is gonna teach dem how tah read. 'Foh I left I heard dat dere was places dat was teachin freed slaves how tah reads, jist like yoh chilrens showed me. Dats what I is gonna do.

"Look at dese clouds. I is up heah in de sky, Maybe I'll gits a chance tah see de face of de Lawd. It cain't be too far away, high up as we is."

"Momma Zoli, the way you are going, you're going to burst! You better calm down, just a little. We've got a long flight ahead."

"When is we gonna gits dere? How long is it gonna take?"

"Yah knows I bin waitin foh dis foh a lon, lon time. I wondas whot dey life been like wifout me dere. I wondas how many youngins do dey have. Wheah did dey gits sold off to. Wheah dey bin."

After at least an hour of constant talking, she finally settled down and fell into a deep sleep. When we landed in Dallas, she woke up suddenly and asked, "Is we dere yet?"

"No, ma'am. Not yet. It'll be a few hours."

"Wheah is we now?"

"We've just landed in Dallas, Texas."

"Texas? Dat's a long ways way from Sippi."

"Why don't you relax and take another nap?"

"I is too happy tah be gettin back home, I cain't go tah sleep! Mah heart is runnin an rippin like it gonna jump outta mah chest anytime now."

Finally, a few hours later, our plane landed. She shouted for joy. Looking out the window she yelled, "I sees dat red clay! We is heah!"

"Momma Zoli, calm down."

"I cain't. Don't yah knows what dis means tah me? I is finally back home."

"Now before we get off the plane, I want you to remember one thing. Regardless of what happens, you always have a home with us."

"Sugah, dats real nice ah yah, but I ain't gonna need no home, cause I is gonna fine mah family."

"I don't know if you're ready for this or not."

"Sugah, I is fine."

"I just don't want you to be disappointed."

"I ain't gonna be. Yah jist wait and see. I gots dis feelin in mah bone dat it's jist gonna takes a few moh days tah fine one ah mah youngins. I seen it in ah dream long time ago, and now its comin true."

My cousin, Mamie, whom I hadn't seen in years, was standing at the gate waiting for us. She had on a blue shirt dress covering her rotund body. She was loaded with bright costume jewelry on her arms, neck and fingers, and surrounded by the smell of heavy perfume.

Momma Zoli was so excited, and filled with anxious anticipation, I thought she was going to burst. At the baggage claim area, she grabbed and almost pulled my arm off. She pointed in the direction of a white porter, picking up the bags of an elderly black couple at the adjacent carousel. "Chile, I ain't nevah seen nothin like dat. White folks waitin on darkies. Are you sho we is in 'Sippi?"

"Yes, ma'am. I am."

"I doesn't knows what part we is in. But dis is a strange worle tah me."

When we walked outside heading for the parking lot, she stopped in the middle of the street and turned around, and with great distress asked, "Wheah is we?"

"We are right outside of Jackson."

"Jackson who?"

"Jackson, Mississippi."

"Oh no, dis cain't be. Dis looks like anothah worle, from de Jackson I knows. Wheah did all dese cars come from, an dese peoples wearing dem funny clothes?"

"They live here."

"Wheah is de horses, an mules an buggies?"

"Darlin, there are a few out in the country on the farms. But just about everybody these days has a car, or at least access to a truck."

"I jist don't undahstands."

Driving into the city. She was in and out of a confusing daze. "Where is de farms. Wheah is de animals, an dem ole dusty roles."

She began crying. "How can dis be? What's wrong wid mah head? How did dis place change so fast? Ah only bin away foh a few months."

"Please calm down, Momma Zoli."

"Look at dat. De Lawd jist done wiped away all de farms an houses. Wheah is all dem 'tations dat used tah be ev'rywheah? Wheah is de cotton fields?"

Cousin Mamie dropped us off at a small hotel located downtown.

"Are you sure you don't want to stay with us?" she asked.

"No, the hotel is better."

"We could help you with Miss Zoli, she seems to be a handful."

"She's not that bad and I can handle her."

Momma Zoli remained quiet for the rest of the evening. After I took a shower I discovered her on her knees praying.

"Please dear Lawd yah done brought me dis far by faith. Let me fine mah chilrens so dat I can come own home an be wid you. I jist wonts tah see dey faces befoh I leaves dis heah earf. Yah knows dats de only thang dat has kept me on dis heah side ah Jordan foh all dese yeahs."

"Momma Zoli, it's gonna be alright. In my heart I know we will find your children."

Jackson was a sleepy Southern town that stretched out it's arms to embrace the hot sweltering, unrelenting Mississippi sun. I hadn't seen it in almost thirty years, and its new face reminded me of a grand old lady having plastic surgery that only aggravated her obvious signs of aging. The changes seemed to only partially sweep the city into the modern industrial age as Azaleas, rich red clay, stately homes shared the spotlight with all the new buildings. The smell of sweet Magnolia trees, weeping willow trees, humming birds and mint juleps greeted me as a prodigal child returning home to the land of my mother's people. The sweltering heat and genteel southern hospitality only partially swept away the inherent brutality of the South.

Memories swirled fresh in my mind, of the times I'd spent here many lifetimes ago. I remembered the fear thick enough to spread on bread like stiff butter. I remembered my steely determination to come South with John during 'Freedom Summer' in sixty-four, in spite of my parent's reasonable objections. But I had to come. I had to take part in destiny's plan that would forever change the face of the South.

I remembered my mother's refusal to return to Mississippi when I was a child. "I got away, and I ain't never going back," she used to say. So my summers in the South were spent in my fathers homeland in South Carolina.

Momma used to say, "The only good thing I can say about Mississippi is that I'm gone."

I never wanted to know more about her great distaste for the land of her birth, until the summer of sixty-four. It wasn't until after her death that I discovered the root of her pain. Daddy told me that my grandmother told him that my mother, who'd never talked about this to anyone, had been raped by a white man at a very young age. And to add insult to injury, she got pregnant, but the baby was stillborn. Momma took that secret to her grave, never knowing that my father knew and didn't care.

With tears in his eyes, Daddy said the day we buried Momma, "I only wish I'd been there to protect her."

I picked up a rental car and we headed for the countryside. "Momma Zoli, we're going to drive around Jackson and see if you can find any landmarks. Do you remember where the Steadwell plantation is?"

"It's jist outsidah Jackson."

"Which direction?"

"I thanks it's south"

According to a map I picked up in the hotel lobby, there were many plantations still left, but the highways had taken the place of many others..

"I cain't believes mah eyes. Dis heah place looks a lot like Los Angeles. How can dat bes? I jist left a little while ago, an dis heah whole place done changed. Like I ain't been heah in years."

"What did it look like when you left?" I asked.

"It looked like de real 'Sippi. It had horses, an buggies, an farms, an womin dressed in long clothes, not like de ones dat yah wears."

After a few hours of driving around, she broke down and started crying. I tried to console her, but she wouldn't allow me.

"Lawd ah mercy on me, what is I tah do? Wheah is mah chilrens? Lawd, please let me fine dem. Please hep me, dat's all dat I axes ah yah befoh I come on home."

The next morning, we had breakfast in the room. When the white waiter brought the food in, Momma Zoli looked like she was about to choke.

"I cain't believes mah eyes," she said after the waiter left our room. "White folk servin colored folk! I knows I ain't in 'Sippi."

"I told you the movement changed a lot of things."

"Whot is yah talkin about?"

"Oh, nothing really."

I didn't want to talk about all that I'd seen and lived through. It was too painful. For some reason that morning, I didn't have the energy to share with her my experiences during the movement.

"Dere is somethin dat yah is hidin from me. An even from yohsef. Whot is dat?"

"We just went through a lot when we were down here during the sixties. It was a hard time seeing some of our friends killed. Not knowing if we were going to live or die."

"I knows it hard, but let me tells yah somethin. From what yoh talkin 'bout Momma Zoli done seen a whole lot worser and I is still heah tah witness it. An dat's what yah 'pose tah be doin, too.

"Don't evah shut yoh mouth tah what yah done lived through."

"Yes, ma'am."

"I wonts yah tah promise me, dat yah will always remembas whot I is sayin."

"Yes, ma'am. I promise."

thirty-three

We drove around Jackson and crisscrossed the entire state for several days. We traversed dusty roads and highways in Mount Bayou, Tupelo, Columbus, Albany, Oxford, Grenada, Ofahoma, Winona, Hebron, Hattiesburg, Meridian and Corinth, and found nothing. We even made a foray into Alabama, northern parts of Louisiana, up and down more dusty roads than I wound ever remember in hot pursuit of a familiar site, a trace of Momma Zoli's past, and found nothing.

With each passing day, she became more and more depressed.

"Dis ain't de 'Sippi dat I lef behine," she'd say shaking her head while pointing at businesses and modern buildings along the roads time and time again. "Dis wasn't heah when I left. "

She'd turn to me with great sadness and say, "Dis look like yoh worle, not mine."

Doubt began to slip into my mind. I found myself wondering whether or not John was right all along. Maybe she really is crazy, maybe she was not from Mississippi, maybe she was just hallucinating about a past that never truly existed. Yet, my heart insisted otherwise, refusing to let me yield into my escalating doubt. Somehow, I knew we're going to find her children, and I couldn't figure out why.

Toward the end of our first week there, I woke up in the middle of the night and found the balcony window open, the curtains flapping against her bed and Momma Zoli on the balcony, praying on her knees.

"Momma Zoli, what are you doing out here?"

"I tole you dat each an ev'ry nite I prays beneath de moon and de stars, axin de Lawd tah let me fine mah children." She grabbed my hand. Her gnarled, bony fingers dug into my flesh, as she pleaded, "Yah gots tah hep me. I ain't got much time left."

"Don't worry, Momma Zoli, we'll find them. I promise you."

"How does yah knows dat?" she asked with tears in her eyes.

"It's just a feeling that I have."

"Dis ain't my worle. I ain't seen nothin dat I knows 'cept dat ole state buildin. It's like I bin away a lon, lon time, an ev'rythang done changed.

"I gots tah fine mah chilrens."

"Momma Zoli, I promised you the day I found you that I'd help you find your children, and in my heart, I know that we will."

Since our arrival, I hadn't had a chance to visit with many of my relatives. I definitely wanted to see my great-great aunt, Mary, my mother's namesake before I left. At one-hundred-ten years, she's our oldest living relative. I had not seen her in almost thirty years. She was the first person in our family to attend and graduate from college. She spent all of her life teaching grade school around Jackson. Because she helped to start several schools for Black children, the Klan threatened her life on more than one occasion, yet for some strange reason, they never harmed her.

Cousin Mamie's granddaughter, Regine, agreed to take me to see her. Regine was home for the summer. She had a Ph.D. in literature and teaches at Lincoln University, a small college in Pennsylvania.

Aunt Mary still lived right outside of Jackson's southern city limits in the house her father built at the turn of the century. Aunt Ethel, her youngest daughter, has care for her for years. At eighty-five, she probably needed to be taken care of herself.

It wasn't very surprising to me that not much had changed in Aunt Mary's house since my last visit during my movement days. The living room was filled with doilies, fake pink roses and a suffocating, sweltering heat that laughed in the face of a sputtering fan that was almost as old as me. I sat uncomfortably on the same ivory French provincial couch that I did when I was a little girl visiting with my parents. And the same hot plastic covering the couch stuck uncomfortably to my flesh like a second layer of skin.

"Momma doesn't like air conditioning," Aunt Ethel said, wiping her brow with a white laced handkerchief. "She really doesn't care much for the electric fan, either." She moved like a butterfly, and fussed over us giving us her famous spicy iced tea and coconut cake. Momma Zoli sat quietly on the turn of the century rose colored sofa, seemingly lost again in her private world.

"It's no problem, Aunt Ethel," I said lying through my teeth. It was so hot in the room, I thought I was going to pass out.

"You know, Angela, Momma doesn't get out of the bed much. She fell a couple of years ago and broke her hip real bad. But that doesn't stop her from wanting or trying."

After we finished the tea and cake, she led us along the paneled hallway into Aunt Mary's bedroom. We found her frail little body in the middle of a big poster bed. The dark brown pillars seemed to be carefully guarding her as she rested comfortably on top of the neatly made bed covered with a white chenille spread with an occasional tattered fringe.

Aunt Ethel leaned over and said, "Momma, you have visitors here to see you."

"Who is it?" she asked, raising her head slightly, as her eyes tried to focus on Aunt Ethel. I leaned over and said, "Aunt Mary, do you remember me?"

She paused and studied my face for a moment and said, "You looks like Sarah's girl, Mary."

"No, ma'am. You're talking about my momma. It's me, Angela."

"My Lord, girl," she said with a strong whisper. "You done grown up a lot since I last seen yah. An you is a real pretty thing. You takes that after our side of the family, and not that rascal daddy of yohs!"

We all laughed, except for Momma Zoli. Aunt Ethel lead her to a chair next to the dresser. When she sat down, she commenced to investigate a couple of old pictures resting on top of yet another doily on Aunt Mary's dresser.

She pointed to the photo of a woman I knew was a relative, but had forgotten, and asked, "Who dat?"

"That's my grandmother," replied Aunt Mary.

"Whot's huh name?"

"Eula Tecora Washington."

"Eula Tecora? Is yah sho?"

"Yes. She was named after her aunt Eula and her mother Tecora."

"She look jist like mah daughta Tecora."

I was thunderstruck. Something was happening that didn't make sense. "Wait a minute, do you understand what's going on?"

"Sounds like another one of those coincidences, I'd say," replied Aunt Ethel. "You know how colored folks is, we all look alike."

"Aunt Ethel, do you still have the old family Bible?"

"We sure do."

"May I see it, please?"

"Of course you can."

When she left the room, something made me ask Momma Zoli, "What's the names of your children?"

"Nehemiah, Homer, Eula, Tecora, Roy, Raymond and Jeremiah."

Aunt Ethel entered the room, carrying in both hands a huge old black Bible. She dropped it on my lap as I sat on the bed next to Aunt Mary. A thick layer of dust covering its surface caused me to sneeze. As I turned its parched yellow pages, a heavy musty aroma filled my nostrils.

"That Bible been in our family ever since freedom broke," said Aunt Mary, pointing to it. "My grandmother told me that she got it right after she was free. Even though she didn't know how to read and write, granny said she wanted one to pass down to her children."

My heart pounded harder and harder with anticipation as I turned the pages. There it was in the book's center, a family tree. Just as I suspected, it was there in black and white.

Tecora Steadwell married Frank Washington and gave birth to eight children, the youngest was Eula Tecora. She had the names of all of her aunts and uncles, which matched the names of all of Momma Zoli's children.

"Oh my God! Momma Zoli this proves that what you say is true! Here are the names of all your children."

"But wheah is mah chilrens?"

Regine said, her face filled with disbelief, "Angela, how can you believe this?"

"I know it doesn't make any sense. But I know it's true."

"Ang, it's impossible," her voice of doubt echoing my husband's. "She should be dead, it's been over two hundred years! If she is Aunt Mary's great-grandmother, then she is related to us as well!"

Momma Zoli sat there in a cloud of disbelief. "Dat cain't be." She looked at Aunt Mary and asked, "If yah is mah granddaughta, den wheah is yoh mammy?"

"She's dead. My mother died a long, long time ago. And I know my grandmother died in 1893."

"Dat cain't be!" screamed Momma Zoli. "Mah chilrens is alive."

Aunt Ethel looked at me, and said, "Angela, what's wrong with you? This woman can't be momma's great-grandmother. She'd be dead by now."

"Aunt Ethel, I know this all sounds quite strange. But something is going on here that I can't explain. We have to find the proof. I know this isn't a coincidence."

My mind was reeling. In spite of what I knew should be an obvious impossibility, we had discovered, by some strange hand of fate the key to Momma Zoli's true identity.

I couldn't say another word to Aunt Mary or Aunt Ethel. I didn't want to confuse them by telling them the significance of our discovery.

Momma Zoli sat there dumbfounded. She couldn't speak either.

While driving back into town, Regine turned to me and said, "Angela, this is all very strange, I think I know someone who can help us figure this out. I think we need to talk to Professor Brown."

"Who's he?"

"He's my mentor, the reason I went into teaching. He's spent a lot of time in Africa and I have a feeling that he might be helpful."

Later that evening, back in our hotel room, Momma Zoli was in a very quiet, pensive mood.

"A penny for your thoughts. What are you thinking about?"

"Yah knows, mah husban Andrew is on mah heart somethin fierce, cause when I finds out dat I was comin back tah 'Sippi, I says tah mahsef, 'I wanna fine mah husban first.'

"I nevah talks 'bout him de way I be talkin 'bout mah chilren cause I been missin him de most.

"We bin through so much togetha when we was livin on de 'tation. He a good man, but he live in a worle dat ain't let him be all de man dat he coulda bin.

"Sometime, when we first got married, he wake me up early in de mawnin, 'foh de crack ah dawn, an we go down in de woods tah de creek. He say tah me when we be wadin in de creek an prayin tah de Lawd, 'Zoli dis is de way a man 'pose tah live. We is part ah nature, we 'posed tah be free like dem birds.'

"He was tall an good lookin, a real big buck of a man. He work out in de fields all ah his life. I ain't nevah heard him complain 'bout anythang, not until dey started sellin our chilrens away. Den he got real mad. Sometime he be mad at me, but I know dat he was mad at hisself, and ain't know whot tah do wid it, so he take it out on me.

"Yeah, I remembas real good how mad he got aftah de started sellin our youngins away. His eyes got blood red, an he said tah me, aftah de last one, mah baby boy Jeremiah was gone, 'I oughta go up tah dat ole varmint an kill him. I oughta ring his neck and suck de life outta him, dey way he be suckin it outta me.'

"I miss him so much," she said with tears in her eyes. "I miss him moh dan I can evah say. Yah jist doesn't knows how lucky yah is. Yah got a good husban dat's wid yah. Chile, yah is truly blessed."

The next morning, I left Momma Zoli in our hotel room with Mamie. Regine had set up an appointment with Professor Brown. I prayed he held the keys that would help us solve this mystery.

It was another hot, sweltering Mississippi day. The blossoms on the magnolia trees seemed to be melting beneath the unbearable heat, as the azaleas stood at limp attention. Professor Brown's office was located in a building that stood in the middle of the campus. An elegant old building, it looked like it must've been a stately home at one time. I stood on the steps and surveyed the campus. Not much had changed since I had last visited the campus nearly thirty years ago during the summer of 1964. Jackson State had been one of the major training sites for the voter registration drive.

Regine said that after she explained the situation to him when he returned her call last night, he wanted to meet last night. But she decided it would be best to wait until today.

My head was still spinning. How is this possible? Was this just a strange coincidence? My mind could not grasp all that had happened. How could this be true? How was it possible for an ancestor, my great-great-great-great grandmother, to appear in 1992?

"This is all too strange for me. But it feels right," Regine said.

For some strange reason, she was now more than ready to accept, and my mind was filled with anxious doubt.

"Let's suppose cousin Angela, just for a moment, that all of this is true. Of course, you have to suspend your rational way of thinking to do this. But if we accept that the proof we've found is true, think of the tremendous blessing that her presence is."

"I don't know, Regine. How could this be possible?"

"Stranger things have happened in this world. Sixty or seventy years ago, we'd never have believed that it was possible for man would go to the moon and return safely. Our great-grandparents would've never thought it possible to fly in an airplane or that people thousands of miles apart could communicate by phone. So, if you open your mind, yes, it may be possible."

"Regine, what made you change your mind?"

"I had a long discussion with Professor Brown and he convinced me that it was possible."

When we reached his office, Professor Brown stepped through the door as if he knew the precise moment of our arrival. He beamed a bright, wide full-tooth grin. "Regine! One of my favorite students. How good it is to see you! Do come in, my dear," he said with a clipped British accent. He stood at the door ushering us in as if we were two dignitaries.

"Professor, I'd like for you to meet my cousin, Angela Stewart."

"Mrs. Stewart, the pleasure is certainly mine," he said, shaking my hand and bowing ever so slightly. His hand was damp, thick with perspiration.

We sat down on brown wing-tipped leather chairs in front of his cavernous oak desk. Light streamed from a huge bay window facing the campus green, behind his desk, making his office like an oven.

As I surveyed his office, I discovered an eclectic array of art, walls of books and interspersed memorabilia. Some portions were in fine order, those most distant from his desk, while those in closer proximity to him were in a state of disarray. His desk contained loose papers, files, books on top of books and a few small wooden African carvings.

Behind him stood a huge glass cabinet filled with memorabilia, probably obtained during some of his journeys. I noticed a yellow, green and black flag of Jamaica, a huge photo of him shaking hands with Nelson and Winnie Mandela and several wood carvings. On top of one end of the cabinet stood a huge ebony wood carving of a mother sitting on an Ashanti stool suckling her child. He noticed me admiring it.

"I see something's caught your eye. You like?"

"I most certainly do. I have one in my family room at home. However, mine's a miniature compared to your magnificent work."

"Yes, it is truly a gem. It was presented to me by Nkrumah himself in 1959 during the independence celebration when Ghana became a free state."

"You knew Nkrumah?"

"Not only did he know him, he taught him when he was a student at Lincoln!" interjected Regine.

"Yes, he was quite a young man. So regal and sure of himself. I knew then he was destined for greatness. I was just a young graduate student when I taught him, but we struck up quite a friendship and maintained it over the years."

The professor was a short, stocky tank of a man. He was very proper, with a fastidious face, big wide features and rich, chocolate skin. He possessed a charming, big toothed grin. He wore a little black bowtie, a green and blue plaid vest and a heavy, dark blue suit. I wondered in the midst of this unbearable heat, why his forehead lacked one drop of sweat and why he wasn't suffering from a heat stroke.

"Ladies, you look so uncomfortable. Please pardon the lapse in my Southern hospitality. I'm am a Northerner by birth and even though my Southern roots run deep, I sometimes forget. Would you care for something to drink? A cool glass of water or lemonade? And for the daring soul, mint juleps are available," he said, with a wink and a playfully wicked grin.

"Professor, you're still such a card!"

"The water's fine, but quite honestly, a little bit of air conditioning would do me better. How do you manage to make it through the day without it?" I asked.

"It's a matter of conditioning the mind. It's just that simple. I see myself in a cool place and my body responds as if it was there."

He picked up the phone and rang his secretary. I could hear her phone ringing through the thick wooden door. "Mrs. Beasley, would you please bring in two cold glasses of lemonade and one glass of spring water for our guests."

Through the door, her muffled reply drifted slowly into the room, "Right away, professor."

I studied him carefully. Somehow, I knew that his youthful, bright smile had been a carry over from a slightly checkered adolescent past. His exuberant and vibrant charm overshadowed his stunted form. His eyes danced across the room in childlike wonderment, making brief, warm contact with each one of us. His teeth were stained a faint yellow. I was sure he smoked a pipe like my father did. I looked on his desk and saw an empty ashtray. It was black, oval shaped with gold trim.

My eye continued to survey the office. To his right, was a glassed-in shelf, containing hundreds of leather-covered books, probably rare. There was a fading color photograph of Nkrumah, bleached by the intense sunlight and a fading black and white photo of the professor and Patrice Lumumba, the fallen leader of the Congo, shaking hands They both wore bright smiles, with their eyes twinkling, but a hint of trouble seeped from the corner of Lumumba's eyes. There was also a larger one of the professor with Thurgood Marshall and Fannie Lou Hammer, a vanilla-skinned woman, with short-cropped curly hair. "Professor, I see you have quite an interesting life. And some famous friends."

"Patrice, I met at the United Nations during the early sixties, shortly before the Congo gained its independence. He, too, was a brilliant man. Nkrumah was more emotional, while Patrice was quite intellectual, and lead with his reason."

"You worked at the U.N.?"

"Yes, I was an interpreter. I am fluent in several languages— French, Spanish, Swahili, Twi, German and Chinese.

"Professor! You never told us any of that."

"Well, my dear, I'm not one to brag, although my behavior today may not indicate as much. Plus, I must keep a few secrets," he said with a sly smile.

"Who is the woman in the picture with you and Lumumba?"

"That's Marie, my late first wife."

"Now I did know about her, no thanks to you, I might add. Marie Shoemaker Brown was a scholar and a brilliant intellectual in her own right. She worked on archaeological digs in the forties and fifties all over East Africa. She was a protegé of Dr. Cheikh Anta Diop, the world-famous Senegalese scientist and historian."

"Ladies, I do apologize for not getting on to the subject at hand. Thank you for indulging me. Rarely do I have stimulating conversations such as this. Students are rarely interested in history these days. They're quite lackluster and more interested in rap than in reading. It's not that they aren't bright, but their developing minds have been diverted, off the highway of education and to the backstreets of commercial diversion and obsessive self-indulgence.

"They can be so unfocused, so unaware of the need to know who they are, so consumed by the notion of instant gratification. What they lack is discipline.

"Let me stop here. As Regine will tell you, Mrs. Stewart, I'm quite long-winded. What do the young folk say? I can really let it rip! My mouth that is," he said chuckling.

"As I understand from our conversation, you are looking for proof of the existence of a certain plantation that was located just outside of Jackson in the 1800s. The Steadwell plantation. Is that correct?"

We both nodded our heads in agreement.

"And furthermore, you want to document the owner's name and see if there are any records of the Africans he owned.

"You are interested because you, for some strange and wonderful reason, believe that a woman, a Miss Zoli Steadwell, could in fact be your great-great-great-great grandmother.

"This woman insists that she was a slave on this plantation, and does not understand nor can she explain how she got to Los Angeles on April 29, 1992?"

"Yes."

"Professor, I don't mean to be rude, but for such a strange story, you certainly seem to be taking this all in stride, quite matter-of-factly. I'm quite surprised," I said.

"I apologize. Please excuse me once again for not explaining to you my reasons for being so open-minded and accessible to this idea. First of all, I think it's possible that she is who she says she is."

"Why do you think it's possible? This experience, and I'm the one who's lived through it, is still very disturbing to me. Now, you and my cousin are sitting here acting like we're having a very civilized discussion about an academic issue. I don't get it. I found her. I've had her evaluated by psychiatrists, they say she's crazy, a severe case of delusional psychosis. She floats in and out of reality the way we change TV channels."

"That's it!" he yelled.

"What's it?"

"Mrs. Stewart, I have spent a lot of time in Africa—since the early fifties, long ago when most of us colored people didn't want to have anything to do with Africa. We Negroes back then considered Africa to be the 'dark continent.' I was drawn to go there by a force I cannot adequately describe or explain. Perhaps I should say I was called. And that calling lead me to my life's work—the restoration of the African mind.

"What I discovered immediately, across the continent, was that Africans, regardless of their location, have a very different concept of time, in comparison to us Westerners. There is no linear time. Time to them and for them, the past, present and future all exist concurrently, like streams of light, like the colors of a rainbow, reflecting different aspects, wavelengths of the entire spectrum. Like channels of different vibrations, varying frequencies traveling through space like waves. They believe we are in contact simultaneously with the past, the present and the future—the eternal now.

"Throughout all of Africa, but especially along the West Coast, the geographical location where most of our ancestors were stolen from, there is an oral tradition among the vast majority of the cultures, including the Ashanti, the Ibo, the Mandinka, the Yoruba, the Akan, the Kru and the Fulani, that hold this belief as one of the most important tenets of their existence.

"They—our African brothers and sisters—believe that in times of great turmoil and upheaval that the ancestors return to provide guidance and sustenance. They return to show the way."

"Professor, how is that possible?" asked Regine.

"I cannot explain that to you logically, because it's beyond traditional rational thought."

"Professor Brown, let me make sure I understand you. You're saying that it is possible that Momma Zoli is who she says she is?"

"No, I'm not saying that it's possible, Mrs. Stewart. What I'm saying is that it is highly probable. Yet, you know that. This is not the first time you have received this information is it?" He asked with a sly smile.

I gasped. He was right. My mind raced back to Dr. Collins. "Professor, how did you know?"

"I cannot reveal my sources," he replied with a wiry grin. "Suffice it to say that a little cosmic birdie has informed me that at least three months ago, a Dr. Collins provided you with the essence of what I have shared.

"Ladies, I have seen things that are beyond belief. My first trip to Africa, when I visited Ghana, was such a paradox. I saw the slave castles where our ancestors were shackled and packed in tighter than sardines. To this day, I do not know how they survived. I could feel their anguish rushing through me and I cried like a baby.

"I entered my motherland as a Negro, confused and ashamed, and after spending a night in the dungeon of Cape Coast Castle, I was reborn. I emerged from that night after hearing the screams and cries of a million Africans condemned to this new world and having my body wracked with their pain, an African, reunited with the essence of my soul.

"I also experienced the remarkable, unbelievable work of African spirit men-some ignorant souls have dared to call them 'witch doctors' and 'pagans,' while in fact they are highly evolved and spiritually developed beings.

"I saw men walk on water, disappear into thin air, step into a blazing fire and step out unharmed. Yes, I've seen miracles. But when you understand, there are really no 'miracles'—only higher, more refined expressions of universal law. Of course, my rational mind wanted to reject what I saw, but it was so provocative, I couldn't avoid the reality of my experiences. It tried to convince me that I had been drugged or tricked, but I tell you I am a witness, what seems impossible is possible."

"Professor Brown, please bear with me—it's going to take some time for me to digest the significance of what you're telling me."

"I think it is highly significant that you found her on a very crucial day in our history in this country. Those uprisings were far more devastating than most of us realized and have been led to believe. It's vital at this juncture that someone return to help us understand. I've seen so much hopelessness that I don't understand, considering all that we have experienced.

"Perhaps Miss Zoli comes as a standard bearer, returning from a far more difficult time to help us see something we've closed our eyes to?"

"What could that possibly be? She rambles on and on about finding her children, and her faith in God," I said.

"Pardon me, Mrs. Stewart, but listen to yourself," he said, as his deep baritone staccato voice filled the room. "Have you ever read slave narratives?"

"Yes, I read a few in the sixties."

"What, if anything, did you glean from them?"

"I learned that it was pretty rough back then, and that they suffered an awful lot, more than I could ever bear."

"And—"

"And, I'm glad I didn't have to live through that."

"Mrs. Stewart, bear with me, this is one of my major pet peeves that I have with my students in general and African Americans in particular. Suffice it to say, you don't know your history. You failed to read through the lies and the lines."

"Yes, I do," I responded.

"No, you don't. Because if you did you would not respond in such a manner. What you know my dear are facts. You know African American History 101. But history is more than facts. It is the living expression, the human and superhuman qualities of your lineage, those giants. It is but for their indomitable spirit, their strength, their simple refusal to succumb to death, the will to live, the resistance and faith that rests in your blood, in my blood, in all of our blood, pardon me, in your genes and mine, that has allowed us as a people to survive the most destructive and devastating circumstances ever known to be visited upon a people in the history of human civilization. A lesser people would have collapsed under such a suffocating oppression.

"How did they endure such unspeakable pain? That I do not know. How did they live in spaces tight enough for one hundred men, rammed with one thousand? That I do not know.

"How did they survive the middle passage? Can you imagine being packed—tighter than sardines—in a space where you couldn't sit up, shackled in chains at the bottom of ship? Forced to lie your own waste for three to six months? If there was ever a hell on the face of this earth, surely the bowels of those slave ships must've been the place.

"How many children died? How many souls were lost? How many generations yet to be born are to this day still resting at the bottom of the Atlantic?

"What kind of people survived this holocaust? Nothing but a strong, determined people of faith, and this frail little woman has come with a message. Her mere presence is a glorious testament to the strength of our people. You know I can't tell you the number of times I find myself frustrated by the moaning and groaning of my people. This is not the worst time of our existence on this side of the Atlantic. This would be a break, a quick relief, a piece of cake for our ancestors.

"And what really gets my goat, what sticks to my skin like hot grits, far more than anything else, rather than being proud—we have the nerve to be embarrassed by the fact that our foreparents survived slavery! Nobody wants to talk about it, just glide over it. A student said to me one day, 'We all came over on the same boat.' I informed her that saying implies the middle passage was a cruise or something like that. To say we came over on the same boat is like saying General Custer's last stand was a tour group.

"In 1933, the Federal Writer's Project—it was hard to get former slaves to talk in detail, to reveal the most important aspects of their lives. How did they feel? What did they do to survive? They had either been encouraged to be silent by their family, usually their children, or their stories were edited by the writers.

Every time I read them, I feel they are holding back, as if their tongues are being pulled out. I get the sense of choked words. Quite different from the detail of other slave narratives like Frederick Douglass' or Linda Brent's.

"Enough of my grandstanding," he said with a sigh. "Ladies, I do thank you for your indulgence, but I travel so much and speak across the country to numerous groups and this malaise, this growing sense of helplessness and hopelessness, I see among not only African Americans, but most Americans is the most frightening change upon the face of the American personality that I've personally witnessed during my entire life."

When he finished speaking, I was exhausted.

"Back to subject at hand. I have a plan. I would like your permission to check the archives at Ole Miss up in Oxford. They contain records and memorabilia from the old plantations. If there's any records of this Steadweell plantation still in existence. As a last resort, there are records at the Library of Congress in Washington, D.C."

"Professor, what is your fee?"

"My dear woman, the only fee I have is to request that you allow me the honor of meeting this ancestor."

He blew me away. We said our good-byes and walked outside into the sweltering heat of the noon day. I felt like a limp flower wilting before an unforgiving sun.

On the way back to Cousin Mamie's house to pick up Momma Zoli, Regine said, "Do you understand what this means if Miss Zoli is really from the past?"

"No, I don't think I understand anything right now."

"Well, I do. It means that we are witnessing a miracle."

When we returned to the hotel, Momma Zoli was in a very foul mood. Cousin Mamie said she stayed to herself and refused to talk, and when her husband, Cousin George, stopped by, she didn't have anything to say to him, either.

"Dis ain't de 'Sippi dat I knows," she said to me in an accusatory fashion. "All I wants tah do is fine my chilrens. How come dat be so hard? How come y'all cain't gits me back tah wheah I needs tah be?"

"Momma Zoli, we're doing the best that we can. We went to see somebody today that's going to help you."

"Oh yeah?" she said smiling.

"Is he gonna fine mah chilrens?"

"We'll have to wait and see what he finds. He did say that he thinks you were sent here for a reason."

"Whot reason is dat?"

"Well I don't quite understand myself. He said there are many stories in Africa, where our people came from that make reference to the ancestors returning."

"Return foh what? An side from dat I don't wanna hear nothin 'bout no Africa. I done told yah how I feels 'bout dat place."

Four days later, early in morning, the ringing telephone startled me out of my sleep.

"Mrs. Stewart?"

"Yes—"

"My dear, Mrs. Stewart, I do deeply apologize for disturbing you so early. This is Professor Jacque Pierre Brown. I have acquired some very interesting information that I think all of you would be excited to hear. Can you get over to my office immediately?"

"Yes, sir. We most certainly can."

"One more thing. Mrs. Stewart, would you please bring Miss Zoli with you?"

"Yes, sir. We'll be there with bells on our toes." In my heart, I knew he had found the proof. I could understand why he didn't want to discuss it over the phone.

When I called Regine, she screeched so loudly through the phone it hurt my ear.

"Cousin Angela, this is great news! I'll pick you up in fifteen minutes."

When we got to Professor Brown's office his secretary smiled at us and buzzed him. He rushed out of the room. "Ladies! How good it is to see you. Do come in."

"Professor Brown, this is Momma Zoli Steadwell." He reached out his thick, brown hands, and said, "It is such an honor to meet you." He leaned over and kissed her hand.

"Nice meetin yah, too. Can I axe yah somethin?"

"Yes ma'am. You can ask me anything."

"Is yah gonna hep me find mah chilrens an gits back tah de real 'Sippi dat I lef behine?

"My, my, my! I'm honored that you think so much of me. I'm not certain that I can do all that, but perhaps I can help shed some light on this situation."

Tears welled up in her eyes, "Suh, I jist wonts tah gits back tah wheah I is from. Dat's all dat I wonts tah do."

"Momma Zoli, it's going to be alright," I said, trying to soothe her fears, "Let's give the professor a chance to tell us what he's found out."

"I have some very exciting news to share with you!"

Regine and I sat on the edge of our seats.

"As it happens, we were able locate a considerable amount of records regarding the Steadwell plantation. My friend, Professor Wentworth, put two of his graduate students on the search, and they uncovered a lot."

"What did they find?"

"We discovered that in fact, there was a Steadwell plantation that existed south of Jackson from 1800 to 1870. It seems that the plantation was built by a family that moved to Mississippi from Georgia and North Carolina. Unfortunately, the records at Ole Miss were not complete. They did not have all of the records pertaining to the slaves the family purchased. However, we did find other pertinent data."

We sank into our seats and perked up immediately. It was like being on a rollercoaster ride.

"Because of the nature of this expedition, back into time as it were, I made a trip on Tuesday to Washington and to the Library of Congress. My contacts there were vital in assisting me. Prior to my arrival, they had already begun to review the records for the geographical area where we believe the plantation was. And we did find something!"

I left behind my logical mind and didn't bother to try to understand what was going on. My entire being was humming with pure excitement.

Momma Zoli wasn't paying a lot of attention. She sat there seemingly unimpressed.

"My friends at the university examined other parts of the archives. As it happens, there is a plantation memorabilia section. He opened a large manila envelope sitting on top of a pile of papers. "Miss Zoli, do you recognize this person?"

"De devil couldn't keep me from remembarin dat ole face. Dats dat ole evil man, Massa Steadwell, when he was young. If I recollects correctly, dey took this pitcha right aftah his pappy died, when he took ovah de 'tation."

"Correct, that's him, Wadsworth Armstrong Steadwell. What about this woman?" he asked pulling out another picture. "Do you know who she is?"

"If I knows who he is, yah bettah knows dat I knows who she is. Dats his ole evil wife."

He pulled out five or six more photographs of the Steadwell family, all of whom she recognized. Then he said, with beads of excited sweat pouring down from his brow, "Do you know who this is?"

Her eyes glistened as a stream of tears flowed down her cheeks. "Dat's mah daughtah. Mah beautiful chile, Eula." The picture captured a pretty, little brown-skinned girl, perhaps ten or eleven who possessed Momma Zoli's determined forehead and owl-shaped eyes.

He passed other faded brown pictures. One by one, Momma Zoli recognized all of them, other slaves on the plantation.

"And last but not least. Miss Zoli, I'm sure you know who this is?"

"Dat's me! Dat's me! Dat's me when I was young!" She leaped out of her seat, started hopping around, even her bad leg moved with new life. "I cain't believes mah eyes. Dat's me! Dat's me. I told y'all de truf, now yah can see. Dats me, dats me. I is who I says I is. "

In the midst of her dance, she dropped the picture on the floor. I bent over and picked up the photo. It was a picture of a young woman. Her face was graced with a steely determination, her owl-shaped eyes contained a fresh pain, tinted with deep sorrow.

"Now I remembas," she said looking at me and pointing at the daguerreotype. "De man wid de contraption. He went aroune takin pitchas ah all de slaves. Cause Massa Steadwell said he want tah have a pitcha of us an if we evah ran away, dat would make it easier tah track us down."

I couldn't believe my ears. My mind was stunned with the discovery that Momma Zoli was in fact who she said she was.

"Here's a copy of her bill of sale," he said while handing it to me. "Winzola Mary, Negro wench, age six. Purchased on March 15th, 1806 by Quinten Steadwell, Steadwell plantation, Jackson, Mississippi.

"Do you know what Winzola means?"

"No, I doesn't," replied Momma Zoli.

He turned to Regine and I, we shook our heads "No" in unison.

"It means daughter of the lost people."

Oh, my God. It was true. She is who she says she is. The reality of the discovery was sinking in. Finally, everything made sense.

Suddenly, the reality of the discovery struck her like an avalanche. She leaped out of her seat and screamed. "Dis cain't be! Dis cain't be! If dis is de futuah, I wonts yah tah tells me wheah is mah chilrens an mah husban?"

"Momma Zoli, I'm sorry, but they're not living," I said softly, trying to buffer the shock.

"Dat is a lie! Dey gots tah be alive. Dat's de only thang dat keeps me hangin on."

"Momma Zoli, we're your children, we're your family."

She roared fiercely like a wounded lioness, "Dat ain't de same. NO! I ain't give birth to yah! I doesn't knows yah like I knows mah own!"

I tried to put my arms around her and comfort her, but she pulled away. When she finally calmed down, she began to cry. "I doesn't wonts tah be heah. I wonts tah be back in mah worle, not in dis one."

"Momma Zoli, can't you see what a blessing this is that you were brought to the future? Can't you see how God's hand is in this? God led you to me. I don't understand it completely, but you did find your children's children, the generation that has followed who are still alive and well."

"Dis ain't no blessin. Dis is a curse," she cried angrily. "I doesn't wonts tah be heah in this worle." Her body shook as she screamed, incessantly shaking her head, "No! Dat cain't be. I jist wonts tah go home. I jist wonts tah fine mah chilrens."

I thought it would be better to take her back to the hotel to calm down. "How much do we owe you for such a tremendous job? How can we ever repay you?" I asked.

"My dear, Mrs. Stewart. There is no need. This is such a great, unbelievable opportunity. I am just grateful to have been a part of it. I thank you, Regine, for that." She bowed her head humbly and smiled. "But there is one thing that you can do for me," he continued.

"Before you return to California, I'd like to spend a day or two with Miss Zoli recording her voice."

"Foh what?" Momma Zoli asked.

"Momma he wants to put your voice on tape, the listening box, that's what you call it. To hold your memories of the past for future generations. Am I right, professor?"

"Yes, indeed you are, Mrs. Stewart. This is an incredible opportunity for the world to know, to discover the voice of our ancestors who have gone on. Doing this will be a remarkable contribution, not only to our academic understanding of slavery, but for our people to understand our true strengths.

"She's already said a lot. I don't remember much of what she said because I thought that she was hallucinating," I replied.

"There are literally thousands of slave narratives that provide great detail. However, it is my feeling that she can make a specific contribution, not only in terms of adding to the authenticity of the existing narratives, but I think it is far more important for us to record her observations of the twentieth century society, which is a world quite foreign to the one she left behind.

"That may give us insights as to what her specific purpose is. Also, you might want to keep a record, a diary of sorts, in terms of your experiences, dreams, visions, anything that is out of the ordinary."

"You know, when she first came, my husband and children had a dream that they were separated and sold away from one another," I mused.

"You know, this is a very critical time, not only for our people, but for the entire world. Many prophecies predict great changes, and perhaps her appearance at this time has something to do with that. This is a time of cosmic speedup, which is why we're seeing upheavals in so many expressions, from the breakdown of our institutions, families, relationships and the horrific wars we now see.

"She is the greatest living link we've ever had to the past. And Miss Zoli, I have a few people who would like to meet you. We'd like to have a little reception for you tomorrow evening at my home."

"Why yah wanna do dat foh me? I ain't goin nowheah else, 'cept back to de 'Sippi dat I knows. Suh, cain't yah heps me fine mah chilrens an mah husban? Can yah heps me gits back to dah real 'Sippi?"

"Miss Zoli, I'm very sorry. But I can't. This is all that remains of the world you once knew. It's one hundred and twenty-five years since 1867, and I'm afraid I can't do that. And it's not because I don't want to. The only one who can do that would be those spirits who sent you here."

"But suh, I don't undahstan dat. How could dat be true?"

"Miss Zoli, as I explained to your relatives, there are things that happen in the world that we just don't understand, that just don't make sense, but they happen nonetheless. During my visits to Africa, I discovered in the places where our people were stolen from that there is a belief among the secret traditions that is called 'Sese ne kwe ani,' or, 'the return of the blessed ones.' You are an 'Ani pisa dolun,' 'the blessed one who has come home.'

"Your presence for us—you are a waymaker, a precious gift from our past, and the ancestors have sent you here for a special reason, to remind us how strong we are. You have a mission. I don't know exactly what that mission is. That in time will be revealed."

"Mistah Professah, whot yah is sayin sho nuff sounds sweet an purdy, but why me? Why is I heah rite now?"

"You are here because, I am sorry to say, we have forgotten the way. Our children have failed to see how strong we really are. What strength, what spirit, what faith courses through our veins. Otherwise, how else could we be here today? Miss Zoli did you ever dream of freedom?"

"Yes suh, many, many times I did, moh dan I can remembas."

"This is the place of freedom that you have dreamed of."

"But I just wannah gits back tah de ole 'Sippi. Dats all I wonts tah do."

"Miss Zoli, I don't know how that would be possible. But what I will do—I have a friend in Togo, West Africa. He is a very powerful healer. I will contact him and find out if there is anything I can do to help you. This is a very delicate situation, as I'm sure you all understand, and I don't want to do anything that would have catastrophic consequences."

"Thank yah suh. Yah gots tah fine a way tah send me back home. I gots tah fine mah chilrens."

"Miss Zoli, I want you to understand something. That day in April when Angela found you by her car, you did find your family. Your children's, children's, children's, children's, children's children. This is the dream you have prayed for."

"How could dat be?"

"The ancestors, the spirits, sent you here. Your eyes have been blessed to see the future, to experience what we have made of ourselves."

"Suh, I sees whot yah is sayin, but I doesn't like dat. Why me? Why was I picked?"

"I can't say precisely why. But it is a great honor to have been selected."

"Suh. I thanks yah, but all I wonts tah do is go home."

"There may be a way of sending her back. Let me make a call to West Africa."

We hugged him, left his office and took Momma Zoli back to the hotel. She cried all of the way back. "I doesn't wonts tah be heah. I doesn't wonts tah be in dis worle. " She cried all evening long and finally fell asleep.

The next morning, around two a.m., the phone rang. "Mrs. Stewart, I'm sorry to call you in the middle of the night, but as you probably know, it is afternoon in Togo.

"I just spoke to Akuete, my friend from Togo. He is a powerful healer, with special powers and contact with the spirit world. People from all over the world seek him out for assistance. Air Afrique even makes special arrangements for stretchers to bring in patients from Europe.

"I explained to him in great detail what has occurred. He was far more excited than I anticipated. He called me back after consulting with his spiritual guides. They said yes to everything that Miss Zoli had described as the conditions of her arrival. She walked through the doorway of time. According to him, it's a one-sided thing. She cannot return until her work is complete. And that is something that the spirits would not reveal to anyone but her. Akuete says he cannot interfere."

"There's nothing he can do to help her?"

"I'm afraid there isn't. Not in the sense that he can help her to return. He said time travel is beyond his abilities. Plus, he said even if he could, he would not interfere. According to him, this is a delicate situation, and much is hanging in the balance."

"Professor, thank you. I just don't know how I'm going to break this news to her."

"I can imagine, you have my deepest sympathies on this matter. And if there is anything I can do, don't hesitate to give me a call. I am at your service. This is a paradox—a joyous return also harbors the seeds of a tragic departure. She lost her biological children and found her descendants in the land of freedom."

"Well, maybe I'll have you talk to her after I do. You can better explain the situation to her than I can."

My rational mind wouldn't let go. Quickly, I'd grown to ignore that part of me, it really was acting like an overgrown child. It whispered, "Explain to her? How you gonna explain, Miss Lady, that you can't get Momma Zoli back to her world? What's there to explain? How you can't get her back to the past? Don't feel bad, I'm sure Einstein would have difficulties with this one, too. So don't feel bad. You've already done your best."

It demanded, "What's John going to have to say about this? And what about all of your friends? How are they going to react to your adventures in time? You better be glad your mother isn't here. She'd have you committed."

"Shut up, shut up!" I cried.

Momma Zoli rolled over and said, "Somethin wrong?"

"No, ma'am. Everything is gonna be alright."

After breakfast, Momma Zoli asked, "What's wrong? You ain't eatin yah food, like yah should be eatin."

"Momma, Professor Brown called me early this morning."

"He did? Yah knows, I likes him. He really de first person dat don't looks at me like I is crazy woman or somethin wrong wid me.

He listen real good, an I likes hearin mah voice in dat little talkin' box of his. Whot did he say?"

"I'm afraid I have some bad news for you." Her face dropped into sadness.

"He talked to his friend, the spirit man in Africa. Akuete says the ancestors sent you here, and he cannot help you return to your time. There is something special about you and they want you to stay here until your mission is done."

"I wonts tah go home," she said with a steely, forceful determination.

"Momma, there is nothing we can do, but to help make your stay here as pleasant as possible."

She broke down and cried again, "All I wonts is tah fine mah familee. Dats all I wonts.

"Why cain't yah hep me?"

"Momma, you've been through a lot. Why don't you go on and lie down? I'll call the professor and let him know that you're not up to going in today."

"No, no. I'll go. I knows I is gonna feels much bettah latah. So I will jist lies down foh a little while. I doesn't wanna lets him down. He was de only one heah in dis worle dat believes me in his heart. He ain't wonderin nothin but me. He knows I is tellin de truf.

I sat there on the edge of the bed taking deep breaths. When I closed my eyes, I saw my mother's, my grandmother's, my great grandmother's and finally all of their faces blending into Momma Zoli's. Then I saw her hand reaching out to all of us, stretching across the portals of time.

thirty-four

Dis cain't be, dis ain't possible. Dey is tryin tah tells me dat I is in de futuah? Why is I heah? I doesn't undastands. An if I is in de futuah, dat means dat mah chilrens an mah husban is dead. I doesn't knows why de Lawd done put dis on me. It jist ain't right. All I evah wonted in dis life was tah be wid mah familee. An now dey is tellin me dat I cain't be wid dem, dat dey is dead an gone on home tah be wid de Lawd.

Den why is I still heah, an who sent me to dis heah strange worle, an foh whot? Whot is I supposed tah be doin heah? I doesn't likes it, an I jist wonts tah goes back tah where I came from. My head just be spinnnin aroune like a top, cause I jist doesn't undastands.

Why me? Why is I heah? I ain't nothin but a broken vessel. I is ah tired ole woman an all I evah wonted was tah be free an tah be wid mah familee. Ain't nothin special 'bout Zoli tah end up like dis.

Dat little man keep on talkin bout he got proof dat I is who I says I is, and dat I was sent by de spirits. I ain't neah heard ah nothin like dis.

Whot he mean? De spirits sent me? Angela said he says dat dere is no time? He sho nuff be talkin outta his head. I think he plum crazy.

I jist wonts tah fine somebody dat can hep me be on mah way, back tah mah worle, cause I ain't got a lotta time left on de earf. I jist wonts tah fine at least one ah mah youngins befoh I closes mah eyes foh one last time.

Talkin bout Angela bein some kin to me. So what if she is? I ain't give birth tah her. I wonts mah own. Or else I is ready tah die.

I jist wonted tah be free an live in a worle wheah I doesn't have tah worry 'bout nobody evah takin mah chilrens from me. Now dat I is in dis worle ah freedom I doesn't knows if dis is wheah I wonts tah be.

I jist wont tah live mah life de way I was 'pose to.

I doesn't like bein in dat place. It ain't no land ah milk an honey, an it ain't no place foh me tah be. I doesn't cares what dey be sayin. An why didn't dey believes me in de first place?

I went back tah 'Sippi lookin foh mah own flesh an blood. Now dey tellin me dat dey is dead, bin long gone. I st'll doesn't knows how I gots heah. It be very confusin tah me.

I 'ist wonts tah git back home so I can fine mah husban an mah chilrens. I is trapped in dis heah place, an I doesn't wonts dis worle. I is ah ole woman an des heah bones ain't gettin no youngah.

Dis is a poison, dyin worle. It be drainin de life outta me. I sees it jist seepin away from me. I doesn't wonts tah be heah. I wonts tah go home.

thirty-five

"Woman, have you lost your mind? What do you mean she's telling the truth?" I couldn't believe my ears. My wife was on the phone telling me that Momma Zoli had been telling the truth. If I didn't know better, I would've sworn that she had been putting something up her nose. I didn't know what her problem was.

"Honey, I know it sounds strange, but we have proof!"

"Proof! What kind of proof are you talking about? Angie, have you lost your mind?"

"Professor Brown found proof that a Winzola Mary Steadwell lived on the Steadwell Plantation outside of Jackson, and even found a photograph of her."

"Angela, get a grip! There can't be any proof that confirms Momma Zoli is who she says she is. Just because someone with the same name existed over a hundred years ago, how does that mean that she's who she says she is?"

"Because everything matches."

"But Ang, common sense tells you that if she lived that long ago, she should be dead."

"Not if she was transported through time."

"Now I know you've lost it. You're telling me you believe in time travel? Do I have to come down there myself and bring you home?"

"No, honey. We should be home in a day or two. I didn't believe in time travel, before this. But now it seems possible. Professor Brown explained everything, based on his experiences in Africa, and I know in my heart it's true."

"Ang, I don't like the way you sound."

"And there's more than that!"

"Do I need to sit down for this one?"

"Honey, trust me, I'm fine."

"How can I trust you? You sound like a crazy woman."

"But, I'm not. She is really who she says she is, and she's my great-great-great-great grandmother."

"Now I'm sure you've lost contact with reality now. I think you need to see a psychiatrist."

"Honey, I've got to run. Give my love to the kids."

I decided not to tell the children anything because I didn't believe Angela. What am I supposed to tell my kids, "Guess what? Momma Zoli was telling the truth. She was sent here from the past. Even though this has never happened before, you're supposed to believe this."

Doug came over. I didn't even know if I should tell him. He was so out there, he had probably believed her story all along. Before I could stop myself, I blurted out, "Man, I think my wife has lost touch with reality."

"What's wrong, man?"

"She says Momma Zoli is who she says she is."

"I believe her."

"You what?"

"I believe her. I always have."

"Why didn't you tell me?"

"Because you wouldn't believe me."

"Now, I know the world has gone stark raving mad."

During dinner, Ash gave me one of those, I'm-looking-into-your-soul looks and asked, "Daddy, when are Mommie and Momma Zoli coming home?"

"I don't know for sure, honey, but I suppose some time soon."

"I wish they'd hurry and come home. I miss them."

"Baby, why do you think Momma Zoli's coming back? They might've found her family by now."

"No, she didn't. At least not who she expected to find."

"What are you talking about?"

"I had a dream last night, and in the dream this man told Mommie that Momma Zoli was related to us, and I know it's true. And he said that she was telling the truth."

"Ash, have you talked to your mother today?"

"Daddy, I haven't talked to Mommie since last week when she called."

If I didn't know better, I'd swear my whole family was losing it. I didn't know what to make of it. Maybe Ash's dream is a coincidence. But I still didn't believe Miss Zoli was telling the truth. Anybody with a drop of common sense would know that it's impossible. I just wondered why my wife was so gullible to this hocus pocus stuff.

thirty-six

Before we left Jackson, I tried several unsuccessful times to get Momma Zoli to see Aunt Mary.

"I doesn't knows huh. She ain't no kin tah me. I wonts tah see mah own."

"But Momma Zoli she is your own great-granddaugheer."

"No, she ain't!" she replied shaking her head. "I ain't got nothin tah say to her."

And that was the end of the conversation. I'd never seen her like this. She'd have tremendous mood swings from angry adamant defiance to severe, almost suicidal depression.

For several days after we returned to Los Angeles, Momma Zoll remained sequestered in her room, and refused to eat or sleep. Every time I checked on her, I found her sitting quietly on the edge of her bed staring into another space, seemingly trying to will herself into death. In spite of his disbelief, even John tried to pull her out of her shell, as well as the children and Mrs. Henderson, but no one could reach her. She refused to let us touch her.

"Momma Zoli, please, you've got to eat."

"I don't wanna be heah, I wonts tah go home."

"This is your home. The place you knew doesn't exist anymore. I am so sorry that you're upset, but like Professor Brown said, there is a reason that all of this happened."

"Whot is de reason? Can yah make dat clear tah me?"

"I don't know for sure, but we'll understand it better by and by. I know how you feel."

"How could yah evah knows what I is feelin? Yah ain't me!" she snapped, pulling away from my touch.

She remained in a deep depression for weeks. Everyone seemed to be affected by her unhappiness, as if we were in a death watch, witnessing her desperate attempt to will herself into death. I'd often find her on her knees praying, "Lawd, please take me, I jist wont's tah be wid mah chilrens."

Work at the center had only slowed down a little bit since the riots, and it was beginning to take its toll on everyone. Even Doc Whitney was carrying a short fuse. Geneva spoke often of retiring, and I didn't know how much more of this constant pressure I could take.

Shortly after our return, As I was entering the center one day, I ran into Jacqueline, the strange Jamaican woman.

"How's that woeman doing?" she asked, confronting me with her insistent presence.

"All things considered, she's doing alright," I sighed.

"I tole you to leave her be, and now you knows de truth. Dat woeman is special, an yah bettah take good care of her."

Startled, I replied, "How did you know that?"

"Chile, when you gonna learn? De spirits done tole me a long time ago. An yah know what? It's gonna git bettah, bettah with her here now. You just wait and see," she said smiling.

I didn't have time to try to figure out how she knew. I decided after the discovery, aside from John and our children, not to tell anyone, even K.L., because I didn't want my friends reacting to me the way my husband did.

Gloom settled throughout our home like a layer of thick dust, covering everything with an agonizing, palpable despair. There were few smiles, little if any laughter, and somehow I began to feel the subtle presence of impending doom, the same way I felt on the morning I found Momma Zoli. No matter what I did I couldn't shake that feeling.

Finally, one evening, Momma Zoli emerged from her room and sat down to eat dinner with us, for the first time since our return from Mississippi.

"Momma Zoli!" John exclaimed jumping to his feet. "It's so good to see you again. Angela, fix her a plate, I know she's hungry."

"I ain't hungry," she said, almost snarling at my husband. "I doesn't wonts tah be heah."

"Come on, Momma Zoli, being with us can't be all that bad, is it?"

"It's terrible in dis place. I doesn't undastands dis worle, an yoh ways, it's like bein in de valley ah dry bones. Yah ain't like de folks in mah worle de way yah be raisin yoh chilrens. I ain't nevah seen nothin like dis."

"What are you talking about?"

"How can you let dat boy ah yohs listen tah all dat crap?"

John looked at James, who said instantly, "She heard me playing my rap downstairs."

"Is dat whot dey calls it? It ain't nothin but vermin an vile. I bin called a lot ah thangs in mah life, a whole lotta names, but I ain't nevah heard nobody talk 'bout colored womins dat way. How can yah let him listen tah dat?" she asked pointing her finger at John and me. "If he ain't knowin no bettah, den at least da two of yah should. Yah is his mammy an his pappy, an Lawd knows at lease one of yah oughtta have de sense tah knows dat he ought not be listenin tah all dat cursin an carryin on."

"Momma Zoli, we talk to him about it and we let him listen to it here, because all of his friends are doing it. And it's better for him to do it in our home than to sneak behind our back and do it in the streets."

"Is dat what yah be thinkin? Lawd, I doesn't knows whot be wrong wid yah niggas in dis heah land ah freedom. Cause he gonna do it anyway, yah gonna let him do somethang dat yah know ain't right.

"Is yah gonna let him call any woman dem names when he be aroune yah?"

"Of course not," replied John.

"Well, listenin to dat kinda music is lettin him do jist dat wid out openin his mouth.

"I doesn't wonts tah be heah in dis worle. I jist wonts tah go home an be wid mah Lord." She got up and walked away.

The next morning, as I got dressed for work, she appeared at the entrance to our room, scrutinizing me.

"What kind ah work does yah do?"

"I work at a social service agency. We help families in need."

"Ain't nobody else aroune tah help dem? Whot's wrong wid people?"

"This world is very different from the one you left behind."

"De moh an moh I sees dat, de less an less I likes dis place."

"Why ain't people helpin each othah like we did? Why dey gotta come to yah foh help, when ev'rybody oughtta be heppin each othah?"

"I wish I knew, Momma Zoli. I wish I knew."

She refused to relinquish her anger. She held onto it with a predatory tenacity, and for some reason later that day she continued to direct it at me.

"Missus Henderson done tole me all ah dem thangs dey be doin down wheah you be workin an I doesn't understands, why people be givin up dey babies? Why ain't de pappies raisin dey chilrens wid de mommas? I ain't nevah heard ah no colored folk given dey chilrens away. What's wrong wid dem?" she asked with tears in her eyes.

"You don't understand. Today, people have a lot of problems, and places like our agency help them to cope."

"Why ain't familees takin each othah in an heppin each othah out like we did? We ain't has nowheahs tah go but to each othah."

I didn't know what to say.

"We loved our babies so much. Dats all we had. An we did ev'rythang we could tah keep dem. I know one momma even chopped off her baby's foot tah keep Massa Steadwell from sellin him, aftah he done sole de rest ah huh chilrens.

"An now y'all gots folk throwin away dey chilrens like it ain't nothin. An dis is 'pose tah be de land ah freedom? Whot happen tah all de lovin dat we gave each othah when we was slaves?

"Aftah freedom come, I saw folk dat done foune dey chilrens, an a whole lot moh like me who was lookin each an ev'ry way dey could turn tah fine de ones dat de love an slavery done took away from dem.

"Now yah gonna tells me in dis heah worte yah gots pappies dat jist turn dey back an walk away from dey own? An mommas dat ain't half raisin dey youngins? Why it be like dis?"

I escaped into a numbing silence, because I didn't have one answer to the words that pierced my heart. I tossed and turned all night long and couldn't sleep because her words haunted me like an ancient spirit.

thirty-seven

I still didn't believe this supposed proof that had been con-
jured up. It wasn't not logical, and it didn't make any sense at all.
Even though I didn't believe this crap about Momma Zoli being
who she said she was, I decided to keep it to myself. The only
thing about this situation that me and my wife agree on was that
we shouldn't tell anybody. I hated that I told Doug, but I was sure
he would keep his mouth shut.

I felt very sorry for her. She looked so pitiful, and it seemed
like there was nothing we could do to pull her out of her funk. She
only had dinner with us once, and she was so angry she could
barely contain herself.

Late one evening, when James and I were watching the news
in the family room, she slipped up on us while we were having a
discussion about the latest news report on the truce between the
Crips and the Bloods.

When we noticed her, she was standing behind the couch like
a tiger about to leap on its prey.

"Whot y'all talkin 'bout?"

"Momma Zoli, we were just talking about the gang truce."

"Whot's a gang?"

While I was trying to find the words so she would understand, James blurted out, "It's a group of people who get together
and do bad things."

"Do dey be hurtin niggas?"

"Yes, ma'am, they are. But it's hard for me to explain to you.
I guess you'd have to live in this world a long time to understand
the conditions that caused this situation to arise."

"Dat ain't no 'scuse for nobody tah be killin dey own! You cain't 'splain it cause yah knows deep down insidah yah dat it ain't rite."

"I agree with you, Momma Zoli, that it isn't right what they're doing, but it's not their fault. For years they've been killing a lot of people, selling drugs and committing all sorts of crimes. But since the truce happened last spring it seems like the killing has slackened off considerably."

"Why dey stop killin?"

"I think they realized that it doesn't make any sense for us to kill each other."

"Hold on. I doesn't undastands. Whot yah sayin is dat dese gangs is niggas killin each othah."

"Yes, ma'am. But we don't call ourselves 'niggas.' We're Black people."

"Befoh I finishes wid talkin 'bout dese heah gangs, I is gonna tells yah whot I thinks 'bout yah callin yohself black, but befoh I do dat, I wonts tah knows why is dey killin demselves?"

"There are a lot of reasons, Momma Zoli."

"Like what?" she replied with disbelieving eyes.

"Like racism," James said.

"What's dat?"

"It's the way white people systematically treat us by discriminating against us and limiting our rights. It's the way they hate and hurt us because of the color of our skin."

I was quite proud of my son's articulate response. But before I could bask in the rays of my fatherly pride, Momma Zoli shot back, "Whot dat got tah do with anythang?"

I said, "Momma Zoli, that's the root of our problem. If we had all of the opportunities and rights that white people have in this country, then our people wouldn't be in this condition: poverty, poor education and lack of a fair chance to succeed. We wouldn't have all of this killing. Plus, they are the ones who bring in the guns and the drugs into our community."

"I doesn't undastands somethin, an I wonts yah tah make it plain. Is it de white folk dat is killin niggas?"

"No ma'am, but they might as well be."

"How yah figuah dat?"

"They've created the conditions in which these young Black men are killing each other."

"Ain't nobody puttin a gun to dey head an makin dem do it is dey?"

"No ma'am, not really. But because of these conditions, you might as well say that someone is. "

"But dey really ain't doin dat is dey?"

"No ma'am, they're not."

"Just about each an ev'ry day dat I bin heah, I bin seein on dat box wid de little peoples somebody talkin 'bout niggas gettin kilt. An if I ain't seein dat, den dere is somebody on dere gettin killed, but y'all be tellin me dat ain't real. It's just make believin, but it be lookin mighty real tah me.

"Let me tells yah somethin bout colored folks in dis heah worle. I still doesn't knows why I is heah, an moh dan dat, I doesn't wonts tah be in dis place wheah yah is killin one anothah like flies, an den yah go blamin de white folks, who mite have somethang tah do wid it, but dey ain't makin yah do nothin dat ain't already in yoh mind. Yah gots whot de Lawd done give yah when yah was born and dat is de sense tah knows dat killin nobody ain't rite, an killin yoh own kine is even worser."

"Momma Zoli, it's quite complicated, and I know you can't see that with your way of thinking, but it's just not that simple."

"And why ain't it? If yah got de sense dat yah is born wid, an I supposed dat ev'rybody do, den it is dat simple."

With her voice trembling with anger and her eyes seemingly on fire she said, "But, befoh I leaves dis room, I done tole y'all befoh—I ain't Black. An foh dat mattah, yah ain't eithah! All ah us got brown skin. Ain't no Black tah be found nowheah on yah or on me. I ain't nevah bin Black, an I ain't nevah gonna be Black, an don't yah evah calls me Black agin! I might be a nigga but I sho nuff ain't Black."

"Momma Zoli, I know you weren't happy to come back to Los Angeles. Like I told you when you returned, this is your home, and it will be your home for just as long as you want it to be. But ma'am, this is my house, and I must ask you not to talk about our people and disrespect who we are while you are here."

"Disrespect? Yah sayin I is disrespectin yoh house cause I say I ain't Black?"

"Yes, ma'am. You are."

"If I is disrespectin yoh house, like I axed yah an yoh wife de othah day why is yah lettin yoh son have all ah dat cursin up in heah? Callin womins names I ain't nevah evah heard dat ole varmint Massa Steadwell use, but I knows dey is vile from de way dey be hittin mah ear. How does yah figuah on dat?"

"Y'all got so much in dis worle, but yah be actin like yah ain't got nothin. Yah gots so many yah cain't even count all ah de blessins dat yah got. Look at yah livin in dis big ole house, wid all ah dese high fallutin 'traptions. Yah got moh outhouses insidah yoh house dan I evah seen outside ah de big house. Yah got food ev'rywheah, yah got hot boxes dat cook food so fast til I is 'fraid tah eat it. Yah gots dem machine carriages dat go fastah dan any train I evah seen, but yah sit aroune heah complainin all ah de time 'bout somethin or othah. I hears yah, yah might think I ain't listenin, but I is.

"Yah can come an go as yah please, do what evah yah wonts tah do, an yah ain't nevah gots tah worry 'bout no overseah breathin down yoh back or beatin de life outta yah foh no good reason at all. Yah ain't nevah gots tah worry 'bout nobody sellin yoh chilrens aways like mine.

"When dey was babies, mah husban, Andrew, used tah gits mad at me, cause I would stay up all night long holdin dem. I wonted tah remembas ev'rythang 'bout dem dat I could, and I wonted dem to knows me. Cause I knows in mah heart, sure as de sun be risin dat one day dey was gonna be stole away from me, an I wonted tah have as much ah dem as I could befoh I had tah let dem go.

"How can yah sit here an talk about killin like it ain't nothin an forgitin tah count all ah yoh blessins is moh dan I will evah knows how tah undastands."

I didn't know what to say.

She looked at both of us, turned and went back to her room.

"Dad, what do you think about what she said about the gangs?"

"Son, I think she's very confused."

"Well, it made some sense to me."

"Son, maybe one day you'll understand."

"Dad, I hope so."

The next morning, I talked to Angela about getting her out of the house and taking her down to the center. Maybe being around other old folk in the senior citizens program might help her to bring her mind back to this reality, instead of the one she believes she's a part of.

A few days later, Doug asked me to come over and help him get that old van of his started. Kathy Lee was waddling around the house like she was about to deliver that baby any moment.

"How's Miss Zoli doing?"

"Not too good. She's very depressed and angry about not finding her family."

"Yeah, Doug told me how she's been behaving. I'm sorry to hear that," she said knowingly. "John, things sometimes happen in mysterious ways, so just be patient with her."

"Wait a minute—I thought you were my staunchest ally!"

"John, I told her the whole story about what happened in Mississippi."

"Man, why did you go and do that?"

"John, it's okay. I haven't told anyone else."

"Listen, you two are the only ones that know about this cockamamie discovery. We didn't even tell the kids what happened. At least Angie and I agree on that."

"John, I know how you feel about Miss Zoli, but considering everything that's happened, it could be the truth."

"Not you, too? Kathy Lee, I thought I could depend on you not to get caught up in this craziness unlike your husband and my wife."

"At first I did think she was crazy, but you know John, I had something happen to one of my patients that's caused me to rethink the way I look at the world."

"What happened?"

"One of my oldest patients, Miss Mary, came in a few weeks ago, actually while Angela and Miss Zoli were in Mississippi, and told me a story that is unbelievable, but I know it happened. She's in her late eighties and suffered a stroke and a heart attack back in June. It was touch and go, but she's such a spunky little lady that she pulled through, which was quite miraculous to all of us.

"When she came back to see me on her follow-up visit, she told me a story that sent chills down my spine. Miss Mary lives alone in South Central. She's a retired school teacher, never got married and her children have been the kids in her neighborhood. Over the last couple of years she became very close to Danny, her paper boy. I've even heard her mention him during some of her visits. She said that he was 'the grandson I never had, and I was the grandmother he never knew.'

"Danny never came to visit her while she was in the hospital, which she thought was quite strange. And she didn't hear from him after she returned home. One morning while trying to light one of the burners on her stove, she slipped and fell with the unlit burner on. Danny walked into the kitchen, turned off the stove, picked her up, put her in the bed, and left. She said she was so grateful she didn't even want to scold him about not coming to visit her.

"A little while later, one of her neighbors came in to check on her and was surprised to find her in the bed. When Miss Mary told her what had happened and how Danny had saved her, the neighbor said that couldn't be, because Danny was killed in a drive-by shooting on the same day that she got sick.

"Miss Mary insists that he is her guardian angel, and that Danny was there and saved her life. She even described the clothes he had on, which, according to his parents, was what he was wearing on the day he was killed."

"That's a very interesting story, Kathy Lee, but what does it have to do with me and my situation?"

"I think Miss Zoli is telling the truth, and the proof is valid."

"Okay, okay. You're entitled to your own opinion. But please, for our family's sake, and my own sanity, don't tell anyone else."

"John, your secret is our secret. One day soon you'll understand."

"If you say so, but don't hold your breath."

thirty-eight

I don't know why de Lawd done me like dis. I doesn't wonts tah be heah in dis valley ah dry bones. Dey be sittin aroune heah talkin bout thangs like ain't nothin wrong wid dis worle, de way dey be killin each othah, like dat's alright. It don't make no kine ah sense.

I remembas de way dem nightriders was killin niggas aftah we got set free. Dey come along an string up niggas, jist foh de fun ah it, foh no good reason at all. Now in dis heah land ah freedom we is killin each othah.

Den dey tells me dat in dis land ah freedom peoples don't hep raise dey chilrens, dey jist walk away from 'em like dey ain't got nothin tah do wid dem gettin heah? Why is dey doing dat? I cain't figuah it out.

An den dey axe me, "Momma Zoli, whot's wrong wid yah? Why is yah so sad?" Why is dey so blind tah what de Lawd done foh dem?

Den dey wanna knows why I ain't wantin tah be heah. All I has evah wonted bin takin away from me. An dey keep on tryin tah tells me dat dere is a reason why de Lawd done sent me tah dis heah place. Whot is I 'pose tah do heah? I doesn't fits in tah nothin. Even though I bin heah a few months, ain't nothin rite 'bout dis heah worle foh me. Dis is a worle foh new fangled niggas an new fangled white folks, dat don't hold nothin foh me but mah teahs. I jist wont's tah die, so I can go on home an be wid mah Lawd an mah chilrens. An I jist wishes dat somebody would hep me tah do dat, instead ah tryin tah keep me in dis place.

T was grace that brought me

safe thus far

thirty-nine

It was getting to the point that I hated going home. Momma Zoli's presence had enveloped our home with a dark film of sadness.

I often found her wandering throughout the house praying, "Oh Lawd, please sen me back tah my home, return my chilrens tah me on de wings of yoh great spirit. Dats all I wonts rite now."

The aura of her presence was the exact opposite of what it had been before we left for Mississippi. She had been so vibrant and happy, bubbling over with anticipation and a steely determination to find her family. She was so certain she was going to find them, and when she didn't, her light faded. I felt responsible for the way she was now. I didn't warn her enough and I knew she was so hopeful. Now she walked around the house like she was in the land of the living dead. Now that we knew the truth, I think she felt slighted because we didn't believe her before.

My heart went out to her, but nothing seemed to reach her. Her disappointment and anger created a wall around her.

One morning at breakfast John asked me, "Baby, why don't you take her down to the center? Maybe that will help to pull her out of this slump. Didn't you tell me the senior day care program is at the main office now?" It was a good idea, especially since Mrs. Henderson was going on vacation. One of our satellite facilities had sustained a lot of water damage during the riots and we were forced to move our senior citizens program to headquarters. I thought being around people her age would help. And maybe it did a bit.

But it only seemed to make her feel lonelier and remind her of her plight. "I don't like going down there wid dem ole folks," she said to me one morning.

"Why not, Momma Zoli?"

"Cause I ain't got nothin tah say tah them. We ain't got no memories tah share. All dey be talkin' bout is ah growin' up in de depression an how bad it was den. Whot does I knows about any depression. When I tries tah tell dem about my worle dey runs away from me, like its somethin' dey is shamed of. Well I guess I cain't blames dem too much. Dey jist doin what dey was taught tah do."

But a day never passed where she didn't mention her desire to find her family, "I still wonts tah see dem. I hang on—y'all been real nice tah me, an I undastands dat yah is my own flesh an blood. But dis heah is a lonely place. I feel worser heah dan I did when I was back on de 'tation after de sole away my last chile. But dis heah loneliness is jist a wedge in mah heart, like a big wooden stake drivin through it.

"But Momma Zoli, you've got to make peace with the fact that you are here. And that this is your home."

"Why does I have tah do dat. I ain't axe for dis? Sometime I wondahs why yah took me in. Yah doesn't believes me. But now jist cause somebody else tells yah, and gots de papahs tah show foh it dat I is who I says I is, yah believes dem. Now yah be lookin at me all wide-eye an funny, holdin on tah ev'ry word I says, wheah befoh yah jist thought dat I was dis heah crazy ole woman talkin out ah her head.

"And dat ole bald headed colored man, he says dat de spirits sent me heah. Well I tells yah one thang, I wonts tah talk tah dem spirits. Cause I ain't told nobody de could send me no wheah. How come dey could jist pick me up an plop me down heah? Whot is I 'pose tah do heah foh yah dat yah cain't do foh yahself?"

I went to check on her one afternoon during the lunch break, and I found her sitting at a table by herself. "Who dat gul?" she asked pointing at Jacqueline, the Jamaican. "I know huh, or somebody dat looks jist like huh. She look like Hagaar."

"Who's Hagaar, Momma?

"Hagaar was one of dem fresh off de boat Africans. She came to de 'tation maybe two or three yeahs befoh de wah started. She was at anothah 'tation up in South Carolina. But dey said she was a haint, an put spells on people. I doesn't knows why ole Massa Steadwell wonted tah buy huh, but he did. She was a mean ole woman. Had dese sharp evil eyes. She was black, de blackest women I has evah laid eyes on. She was so black till she was almose blue. She ain't have much tah say tah nobody. She be mumblin some ole African stuff an walkin aroune lookin at peoples.

"Den one day, I was at de well drawin up some watah, an she come up from behine an almose scared de living daylights outta me. She said, 'Gul, I knows yah knows dat I be a watchin yah but dey is othah eyes dat is watchin yah, too.' I say, 'Who else is watchin me? I see yah is, but I doesn't see nobody else.' She said, 'Gul yah jist doesn't knows how many spirits be a watchin yah, too. Dey always gonna be watchin ev'rythang dat yah gonna do.' Her voice sounded deep like an ole man's ridin on de wind.

"An den she say, 'Don't yah be worryin. Cause dese eyes be watchin out foh yah. An if dey is anybody dat be makin yoh life hardah dan it 'pose tah be, jist let me knows. Den I can works mah roots on dem. I is a root womins. Dats whot y'all calls it heah.'"

"What did they call it in Africa? Did she ever tell you?"

"I done toles yah dat I doesn't wants tah know nothin 'bout no Africa. I jist doesn't wonts tah knows a thang."

"Did she talk to anyone else?"

"I doesn't knows. Den she started telling me all sorts of thangs, bout Africa, dat I didn't wont tah heah. She tole me bout how she was a queen, how dey cast huh familee an huh tribe to de win an dat dey is all over de worle now.

"Den one mornin, I woke up an she was in mah room, standin by mah bed, jist ah watchin me. I axed huh whot she was doin, an she said, 'De spirits tole me, tah watch ovah yah. An dat is whot I is doin.'"

"I didn't wants tah believes how bad it was. Sometime I have dreams about dat place. I feels trapped. Like somebody put some chains on mah hands, and won't let me goes wheah I wonts tah go. I can't believes we lived through all dat.

"Whot evah happen tah dat li'l colored gul? Mah furst doctah? I wants tah see huh?"

"Why is something wrong?"

"No, I jist wants tah see huh. She been real nice tah me, an I wonts tah talk tah huh."

After a few days of going to the center, she came into my room one morning while I was getting dressed for work and said, "I doesn't wonts tah go dere no moh."

"Why not?"

"I doesn't likes it dere."

"Momma Zoli, getting out of the house is doing you a lot of good."

"No it ain't. I doesn't wonts tah go tahday. I jist wonts tah die."

"Momma Zoli, please don't talk like that. It makes me so sad."

"I ain't intendin tah do dat tah yah but I can't lie tah yah eithah. I ain't got no reason tah live foh."

"I thought going to the senior citizens program might be doing you some good. At least you're getting out of the house."

We ain't got nothin alike. Dey sit aroune complainin 'bout ev'rythang undah de sun. Dey chilrens, dey drugs, dey security check, dey dis, dey dat, dey aches, dey pain. I doesn't means no harm, but I doesn't wonts tah be dere.""Momma Zoli, I'm sorry, I wish there was something I could do. But there isn't. I hate to hear you talking like that, I know it's hard for you to be here, but there is a reason."

"I doesn't wonts tah leave dis house. De next time I go, I wont to be going home tah be wid mah Lawd."

"I can't leave you here alone. The kids are going to camp and John won't be here either. So if you won't go. I guess I'll have to take the day off."

"I doesn't wont yah to miss workin, so I 'pose I has tah go."

The day was a whirlwind of work. I was so busy, I only checked on Momma Zoli a couple of times during the day, but I knew Jacqueline would be looking out for her. When I did see her, she was sitting at a table by herself staring into space. I knew what she was doing, she was trying to find her way—at least in her mind—back to Mississippi, and a world that was more familiar to her than ours.

After a long, trying day, as I was walking out of the center, I ran into an old colleague of mine, Lucinda Gray.

"Girl, look at you! You're a sight for sore eyes," she screamed. I hadn't seen Lucinda in at least nine or ten years, since she and her husband moved back to the East Coast the year their youngest son left for college.

I was lost in conversation, when suddenly I heard gunfire—two shots rang only a few feet away.. My heart dropped. Oh, my God, I thought, where's Momma Zoli? I almost knocked Lucinda down, trying to get outside. I found her on the sidewalk covered in a pool of her own blood.

"Momma Zoli, what happened?" I screamed as people rushed around us yelling and screaming. I couldn't hear a word they said. I was drowning at the thought of losing her. Her glassy eyes peered up at me helplessly as I cupped her head in my hand. Blood was gushing from her abdomen. She made gurgling sounds as blood trickled out of the corners of her mouth.

I was shocked into a numbness that turned the swirling confusion around me into one painful, gray blur. I vaguely remembered Doc Whitney ordering someone to call the police, and when they arrived, one of the officers saying, "We can't wait for an ambulance. If we do, this lady's gonna die."

In the back seat of the police car while holding her head in my lap, I pleaded with God not to let her die, and begged Momma Zoli to keep fighting. I knew she wanted to die, but this was not the way for her to leave us.

I couldn't stop crying. I pleaded, "Momma Zoli, please don't die! It's not your time to leave us, we have so much more to do together."

I could see the life force draining from her as blood drenched my clothes. I had seen trauma before. I've seen children shot, and people die, but I'd never ever seen anyone I loved injured.

Geneva and Doc Whitney followed us to the hospital and arrived only moments after we did. She called John, and he and the kids were there maybe a half hour later.

The police tried to interview me to find out what happened. I was too upset to talk and didn't know any more than they did. I knew that my momma had been shot and was probably dying because I wasn't paying attention. Who did this to her? Who could've injured a poor, helpless woman like this? Who could be so cruel?

It seemed like forever, but John said it was less than a half hour after he and the kids arrived when the emergency room doctor came out to talk to us.

"How is she, doctor?" asked John.

"I'm sorry, but it doesn't look good."

"Oh no!" I screamed. "Don't let her die, you can't."

"Ma'am, we're doing the best that we can. She's lost a tremendous amount of blood, and for a while she was in cardiac arrest. Fortunately, we stabilized her enough to get her to the operating room. But I must be very honest with you. It doesn't look good. She suffered two gunshot wounds to the abdomen, and probably has sustained extensive damage to several organs."

"Thank you, doctor. When will we know something?" asked John.

"If she pulls through, she'll probably be in surgery for hours"

"Don't worry, baby, she's going to be alright."

"How do you know that?"

"Trust me. I know she's going to pull through," he said sadly.

"I hope you're right," I replied with tears streaming down my cheeks.

We waited for hours in the surgical waiting room. I'd never felt so guilty in all of my life. This was all my fault. I should've paid attention, I should've let her stay home. I knew she didn't really want to die, she was just afraid and disappointed. I prayed, I begged, I pleaded with God to let her live. I wasn't ready to let her go.

The kids were in more shock than I was. I knew they didn't want me to see them crying, but they did many times throughout the night. Geneva and Doc Whitney left around midnight, after John insisted that they go home and we promised to call them as soon as we heard something.

Finally, around two a.m., a bleary eyed doctor emerged from the operating room. John and I jumped to our feet, while the kids slept on the couch across from us.

"How is she, doctor? Is she still alive?" I begged, while holding onto my husband's hand.

"It's amazing, but she is."

"Thank God," I screamed.

"I must caution you not to be overly optimistic. She lost a lot of blood, and to be quite honest with you, I am amazed that she pulled through the surgery. We had to remove a portion of her stomach, liver, all of her spleen, and several feet of intestine, as well as one of her kidneys."

"Doctor, is she going make it?" I asked.

"It's hard to say. She's one tough cookie. I've seen teenagers succumb to lesser injuries, and several times during surgery, I thought we were going to lose her. The next forty-eight hours will be critical. If she pulls through that, she stands a good chance of survival."

"Doctor, can we see her?" asked John.

"No, I'm sorry, but you can't see her tonight. She's in the recovery room, and she can't have any visitors there.

"You folks need to go home and get a good night's sleep and come back in the morning. She'll be in the surgical I.C.U. by then."

"Doctor, thank you so much," I said shaking his hand.

"Yes, thank you for saving our mother's life," said John, with tears in his eyes.

I couldn't go to sleep. My heart ached with guilt. I tried to cry myself to sleep, but couldn't. I wouldn't let my husband hold me because I didn't feel that I deserved his comfort. I knew my tossing and turning was keeping him awake.

"Ang, I know you're feeling guilty, but it's not your fault."

"You don't understand, I wasn't paying attention."

"No, Angela, you don't understand. This is in God's hands."

Finally, I drifted into sleep, and saw my mother's face, then Momma Zoli's in a pool of her blood. I woke up shaking, and then startled because John wasn't in the bed. Our room was drenched in moonlight. I found him on his knees praying next to our bed. In the darkness of the early morning, draped in the silence of a new day, we prayed together on our knees, lifting our voices to the God, our hearts linked as one encircled by the presence of the holy spirit in a way that I had never felt before.

The next morning, we returned to the hospital. James and Ashley insisted on going with us. They had to wait outside because the I.C.U. only allowed two visitors a fifteen-minute visit per hour.

Momma Zoli looked so weak and fragile. Her presence flickered like the light of a small candle in the face of a strong wind. As she hovered between life and death a sallow, yellow cast covered her face. Her eyes were glassy. I leaned over and said, "Momma, it's me Angela. John and I are here for you."

Her eyes registered a brief moment of recognition. As I touched her hand, I noticed her arms were strapped to the bed's railing. Seeing her restrained unleashed something inside of me I did not know existed. Suddenly I was encircled by chains. In my mind, the room was filled with all kinds of painful instruments of capture that my ancestors were forced to wear—leg irons, neck irons and wrist chains. "Why is she tied down?" I demanded, remembering her words about the chains that had weighed her down before.

The nurse responded carefully, "It's just a precautionary measure that we take, Mrs. Stewart, so she won't harm herself."

"Take them off, now!" I insisted. "She must not, unless it is absolutely necessary, be restrained."

"Baby, calm down. They're just trying to help her out," begged my husband.

"You don't understand what this would do to her if she wakes up and is restrained like this. John, you just don't understand.

"No!" I screamed again. "Take them off, now!"

The nurse relented and did what I demanded.

Momma Zoli was attached to the respirator through a big tube in her mouth. There were IVs in her arm, monitors everywhere and alarms going off continuously.

John was noticeably solemn during the visit. He just stood there over Momma Zoli, holding her hand. When our fifteen minutes were up, he leaned over, kissed her on the forehead and whispered something into her ear. As he straightened up and tried to release her hand, her tiny fingers clamped down into his hand and refused to let him go. For several moments, she held on to him for dear life. He stood there stroking her hand gently, and whispered in her ears. After a few minutes, she finally released his hand.

On the way out of the unit, he put his arms around me. I looked at his face and saw a river of tears streaming down his cheeks.

"Honey, what did you say to her to make her react like that?"

Once we were outside he looked away from me down the long, corridor and said, "I told her I'm sorry."

"Sorry?"

"What are you sorry about?"

He sighed and paused again, wiping the tears from his face. "I told her I'm sorry I wasn't there to take the bullet for her. Because that's what a son is supposed to do.

"I've always wanted to shield and protect you and the kids, protect my family from the madness of this world. But I didn't do that for her. Momma Zoli is a part of our family, and I'm supposed to protect her, too. I should've been there to spare her this pain. It's something I know I'm supposed to do as a black man in this world. Most of us feel like that, we never say it."

I collapsed in his arms. Whatever had anchored my fragile heart released and opened in me the gates of an ancient, restless pain. Overwhelmed by festering old wounds, that perhaps were not even mine, the tears wouldn't stop flowing as I held onto my husband for dear life. As a rush of searing anguish and pain relinquished itself on me, for the first time in my life, I understood not only my husband's pain, but the unspoken pain and unsung grief I had seen in my father's eyes, my brothers eyes, all of the black men I've known, and those I've never seen. The crushing, suffocating anguish of constricted expression, of unrealized strength of not being allowed to be a full man in this world, hit me. I now understood why many felt incomplete and only a shadow of themselves as they were prevented from taking care of and protecting their own. In his arms, I cried the tears of a million women, of the mothers who had lost their men and children, who stood in this world alone and unprotected.

forty

I hated to see others suffer. It just made me sick to my stomach to see someone hurt and knowing I could have done something to prevent it from happening. It was my fault that Momma Zoli got shot; I should have known something like this was going to happen. I should have been there. I should have taken that bullet for her.

My wife took it so hard; she felt so guilty. There was nothing I could do to pull her out of her pain. I didn't know why she did this to herself. I was supposed to be the protector in this family, that was my responsibility, not hers.

For the first time in our marriage, she hadn't let me comfort her. She wouldn't let me hold her. She said over and over again, "It's all my fault that this happened. I should have paid attention," as her grief-riddled tears flooded our room. Aggravating my guilt, it made me feel even worse.

Last night when I fell asleep for just a few minutes, I saw my father in a dream, and he just stared at me like he did at the hospital. I woke up knowing that he was disappointed in me, because knowing the kind of man daddy was, he would have prevented Momma Zoli from getting hurt. But I was not that man the he was. I would never live up to his stature and I was ashamed of myself for not being able to do what my daddy would have done.

It was not my wife's job to protect her, it was mine.

Seeing Momma Zoli that way was so hard for me. I didn't know what to do. I had to tell her I was sorry, and when I did, she held on to me. More than that, I felt her holding me in my heart. I knew she had understood. At that moment, nothing seemed to matter anymore. I just wanted her to live.

I didn't want to go work. I just wanted to stay at the hospital and gather my strength for her. That was the least I could do, since I couldn't save her from that bullet.

The day after Momma Zoli was shot, the police came by and told us that they had a suspect based on the interviews with the witnesses and a young man the perpetrator was trying to shoot. The witnesses were standing in the parking lot and across the street when they saw Momma Zoli step in front of a kid pointing a gun at another child running through the parking lot. They put out an all-points bulletin for this eleven-year-old kid. But before they could arrest him, the suspect was found dead, shot in the head and stuffed in the trunk of an abandoned car on 103rd Street.

I didn't know how to feel when I heard the news. I was just so numb inside. Nothing seemed to make any sense when our children were killing each other and innocent victims like this. We agreed not to tell Momma Zoli should she pull through.

For several days, Momma Zoli teetered precariously between life and death. She developed numerous complications. Both of her lungs collapsed and she had to have chest tubes inserted. She became jaundiced, due to her liver malfunctioning. Her intestinal system showed signs of obstruction, but fortunately, she was never completely obstructed. Her blood pressure would shoot up and drop like a rollercoaster, and as Dr. Richard predicted, she developed a severe infection in her blood stream. Each time we went to visit her, we were surprised to find her tenaciously clinging to life.

Dr. Richard was boggled by her refusal to die. "I've never seen anything like it. I don't know why she's still here. Considering all of the complications she's having."

Angle and I practically lived at the hospital. Fortunately, I had completed most of the work need to rebuild my company and at this point, it really didn't need my complete attention. Most of my staff was back at work, and I'd found such a good deal on an office downtown that I was thinking about not rebuilding the building.

I couldn't believe how much attention the media were giving to Momma Zoli getting shot. According to our friends, every day at least one of the stations had a story about her progress. The hospital was flooded with flowers, cards, messages and well-wishers stopping by to visit her. Several ministers called and said their churches were praying for her. Maybe that was what was keeping her here with us.

In the midst of all of this uncertainty, Kathy Lee gave birth to another little girl. Doug called me late one evening shortly after we came home from the hospital.

"Hey, man, I'm a proud poppa of another beautiful little girl."

"That's great," I said halfheartedly. "Is Kathy Lee okay?"

"They're both doing great. John, I know this is a hard time for you with Momma Zoli in the hospital. But I wanted to share this moment with you."

"I'm glad that you did. Man, I appreciate you telling me."

"There's one more thing I thought you might like to know."

"What's that?"

"We've decided to name her Joy Winzola Garrett after Momma Zoli and all of our ancestors."

I was speechless, I didn't know what to say.

Angie cried when I told her. "I just hope she pulls through so she can see her little namesake."

"Ang, she's gonna be fine."

"How do you know?"

"Trust me, I just know," I'd say, trying to convince my unrelenting guilt as well as my wife.

The kids wee handling the situation better than us. They had absolutely no doubt that she would recover, and were already talking about her return.

"Dad, are you going to let Momma Zoli sleep in the guest room upstairs when she comes home?" asked Ashley.

"I don't know. We'll have to take it one day at a time."

"Don't worry, Dad. She's going to be alright," said James with the authority of an old man.

My children's faith helped me to hold on to hope that she would recover. At the end of her second week in the hospital, we ran into Dr. Richard in the hall. "Mr. Stewart, I've never seen anything like this. She's one tough cookie."

"Do you think she's going to pull through?"

"I can't say for sure, but I'm feeling better about the possibility that she might."

We decided to go to church that following Sunday to thank the Lord for sparing her life. I was in the shower when Angie came rushing in, her voice filled with panic, "John, get out of the shower! The hospital just called. They said to get over there immediately."

My agitated stomach churned all the way there like an unbalanced washing machine. I thought she was gone. I could visualize her funeral. And the guilt surrounded me again. Angie cried all the way to the hospital. She kept saying, "I know she's gone, I know she's dead. Oh God, it's not her time."

When we arrived at the Intensive Care Unit, we rushed in and found Momma Zoli sitting up in bed smiling. The respirator was turned off and the tube in her nostrils was gone.

"Dat's him," she said, smiling with a hoarse, raspy voice, pointing at me. "Dat's mah son an yah ain't touchin not one part ah me til he tells yah dat it's alrite."

Still in shock, I asked the nurse, "What happened?"

"We're not quite sure, Mr. Stewart. About a half hour, forty-five minutes ago, Mrs. Steadwell woke up out of her coma, sat up in her bed and yanked the ET tube from her nose. She refused to let us touch her or do anything like change her dressings until you got here."

Angela was crying. "Momma Zoli, you're back. Thank God you're back."

"Yes, sugah, I is glad tah be back. I done bin on de othah side of dah Rivah Jordan an seen de bright an mawnin star."

"What are you talking about?"

"Yah knows I ain't wonted tah be in dis worle. An I wonted tah die. At lease I thought I did. But it ain't mah time."

"What do you mean?" I asked.

"When dey gots me tah de hospital, I was in bad shape. Blood was ev'rywheah, I ain't nevah felt no hurtin like de one I did dat day. I was weak, hurtin real bad, I knew I was dyin. All ah dem people runnin aroune me, tryin tah save mah life. Dey was yellin an screamin, doin all sorts ah things tah me. Den all of a sudden I was lookin down at mah body. I said, 'Lawd ah mercy on me, how can dis be?'

"All of a sudden, I was in dis heah tunnel, movin real fast. At de end ah de tunnel, a seen dis tiny light, but de faster I moved, de biggah it got. When I reached de light, it wrapped itself aroune me, like it was alive, den I was in de most beautiful place dat I has evah seen. Ev'rythang was brite an glowin with its own light. It was a garden, full ah de prettiest flowers dat yah evah seen, an bright green grass. I ain't got de right words tah tells yah how wondaful it was tah be in dat worle.

"I was on de othah side. An yah knows what? Ev'rybody was dere! I seen mah family, aftah all ah dese years, I seen mah husban an all ah mah youngins. An yoh pappy was dere, an yoh mammy, all ah dem chilrens y'all was gonna have dat ain't make it heah was dere, too. Even mah own granchilrens, an some ah mah kin folk. Dey was happy tah see me. Real happy, an I was, too.

"I ain't nevah felt so much love. I was happy, very happy dere. An I wonted tah stay, but dey tole me dat I had tah come back tah dis heah worle, dat it ain't mah time yet. Dey say de Lawd done chose me for a special reason tah be heah, an dat I had tah come back heah, cause I gots plenty ah work tah do, 'foh it's time foh me tah return tah de othah side."

She looked at me, and grabbed my hand. "I knows how yah is feelin. I knows yah thank it's all yoh fault, but it ain't. Dis heah an all dat happened is God's will. I could feel yah spirit givin me strength tah stay heah, when I was so weak.

"I seen yoh daddy on de othah side. He tole me tah tells yah dat he is very proud ah yah, an dat yah is a good man an a fine son. He had on dis heah uniform, a good looking man. He say he be watchin ovah yah an yah mammy foh a lon, lon time, evah since he bin killed in de wah. He said tah tells yah dat yah ain't crazy, dat yah is seein him when yah do. Jist like yah did when yah was in dis heah hospital a little while back."

Angie looked to me with utter disbelief. I was stunned, couldn't believe my ears and didn't know what to say. But in that moment, I finally knew in a way that I couldn't explain that Momma Zoli had been telling the truth all along, and I believed her.

"John, what is she talking about?" Angela asked

"I've been seeing my father since I was a boy. Momma thought it was just my imagination. I saw him for the first time since I was a kid, when I was in the hospital."

"I ain't through yet. Angela, I seen yoh Momma. She said dat she real proud ah yah too, an dem fine granchilrens ah yohs. An she be lookin out foh yah, watchin ovah yah."

"Why did you come back?"

"I had tah come back. I didn't wonts tah, but de spirit sent me back. Dey said dat de spirit sent me heah foh a reason dat wadn't no mistake. Said y'all needs tah see an knows close up bout wheah yah came from an all dat yoh peoples bin through.

"Y'all gots ev'rythang dat yah needs. De Lawd done already given dat to yah. It jist dat y'all needs tah come to ah undastandin 'bout who yah really is."

She turned to me, her glowing eyes radiating warmth. "Yah is moh dan dis flesh," she said, grabbing my hand again. "Yah is a beloved chile of de most high God. All dese chilrens on de earf a lot of 'dem, specially colored chilrens ain't nevah knowed dat. Dat's why dere is so much confusion runnin all ovah de land.

"If yah only knew who yah really is. Yah would live a betta life. Yah gots so much hep comin from de othah side it ain't funny. On de othah side de angels an de heavenly hosts be sendin yah so much. Dey be ovah dere echoin dey mercy an whisperin dey love.

"So dat's why dey sent me back. Tah sho yah de strength dat be runnin in yah blood."

"An now dat I is heah, de Lawd done showed me de truf when I was on de othah side. We is his angels wid clipped wings. I ain't got nothin tah be shamed of foh who I is an how I was born into dis worle. All ah mah life dey tole me dat I was 'pose tah be a slave, cause dat was de Lawd's will, dat mah people ain't nevah done nothin, but be slaves. Now I knows de truf. I is a chile of a great God, an mah peoples done great things. What's insidah me is somethang beautiful. It ain't nothin but love.

"We is blessed in so many ways, yah jist doesn't knows. I had tah die befoh, I could live.

"I even seen dat chile dat shot me. Y'all knows dat somebody done killed him, cause ah whot he done tah me? I seen dat in a dream, rite befoh I woke up, an he said tah me dat he is sorry foh whot he done. He was only eleben yeahs ole. I wonts tah see his momma an tell huh dat he is alrite. He in a much bettah place.

"An yah knows whot? I could heah all of dem peoples prayin foh me when I was in dat deep sleep. I wish I could thanks all of dem foh prayin foh me, cause I knows dat dey hepped me tah stay in dis worle. I know dem prayahs hepped bring me back, an heal me up real fast.

"Cause yah knows what?" she said laughing. "I ain't no spring chicken noh moh. I is old. Real ole, an it 'pose tah take me a lon time tah heal up like dis.

"I wonts tah learn moh 'bout dis worle. I was sent back tah learn as much as I can, an dat's what I is gonna do."

She turned to me and asked, "Sonny, can yah bring me some books? I wonts tah read agin."

"Yes, ma'am. I most certainly can."

I couldn't understand her. She'd returned from the throes of death happy. Not only happy, but she didn't have any anger or bitterness about almost losing her life. I'd never seen anything like it in my entire life. When I thought about all that she had lived through and all that I had lived through, my self-indulgent pity now deeply embarrasses me.

Doug stopped by that evening and I decided to tell him about Momma Zoli's description of dying.

"Can you believe that?" I asked.

"Yes, I can."

"Why? Come on brother, let me in on your secret. What do you know that I don't know?"

"The same thing happened to me."

"Come on, man, you're pulling my leg."

"No, I'm not. It happened when I had my heart attack. Remember, my heart stopped beating?" He took a deep breath, and sighed. "I don't talk about it because I didn't want to come back and I knew nobody would believe me."

"That's exactly what Momma Zoli said."

"I had never experienced such intense, excruciating pain before. Then all of a sudden, I was out of my body. I didn't feel any pain anymore, actually it felt pretty good to be free of all that pain. I looked down from the ceiling, and man, I could see everything that the doctors were doing. I tried to tell them that I was alright, but they didn't hear me.

"Then all of a sudden, I'm in a dark tunnel, and I see this little fleck of light, and I'm moving toward the light. It gets bigger and bigger. It was the most beautiful light I ever saw. I can't describe it completely. It felt like living love. I know that sounds kinda strange, but that's the best way I can put it.

"And I saw Lizzie. Man, she was there. I'd never seen her so happy. She was beaming. She told me not to worry, that everything I did and did not do was forgiven. My parents and grandparents were there, too. I even saw a couple of my partners I grew up with who'd passed on.

"I wanted to stay there in the light, but I was told I had to come back, that my work wasn't completed here on earth, so I returned.

"When I came back, I told my doctors about it, told them things I could not have possibly known, about my resuscitation, and they looked at me like I was crazy. I stopped talking about it because I thought they were about to send me to the psychiatric ward."

"Wow, that's deep. What did Kathy Lee have to say?"

"She was a little better, but not much than the rest of her colleagues. Of course, she didn't know me that well, I was just another one of her patients. She did her best to comfort me, but I never sensed that she really believed me.

"Why didn't you tell me? I'm your best friend, your main man!"

"Don't take this personally, but would you have believed me? I didn't think you or anyone else would believe me after my doctors reacted so strongly. I thought you might think that I was crazy too, if I told you I saw Lizzie."

"No, I believe you now."

"Why is that?"

"Because Momma Zoli told me she saw my father when she died. It had to be him from her description. It couldn't have been anybody else."

"And you finally believed her?"

"Yes, I do."

"Do you believe that she is who she says she is?"

"I hate to admit it, but I was wrong. She is who she says she is." I conceded. "What are you smiling about?"

"I knew one day you'd come around. I just didn't know it would be so soon," he said still beaming.

"Man, tell me something. How has all of this changed you?"

"You've seen I have a different way of looking at life. I am much happier now. And the experience allowed me to relinquish my fear of death. I discovered when I was dead that we truly have nothing to fear. That's why losing my businesses really doesn't bother me. I've wanted to get rid of them for a long time. It's time for me to move on to other things now. I want to make a contribution—help these kids that don't have any hope for tomorrow."

"What took you so long to tell me?"

"I guess I didn't know how. But now I do. Sometimes it takes a while for things to be manifested from the spirit. It's about cultivating patience. I need to relinquish these material possessions, not because they're bad, but because my heart tells me it's the thing to do now. I've already set up a substantial trust fund for my girls and I have a good life. I've been blessed with a second chance. I'm going to live the rest of my life to the fullest.

"I ended up not needing a bypass. Dying turned out to be a very healing experience for me."

"What does K.L. have to say about all of this?"

"I didn't tell her for a long time. When I finally did, I think she believed me, although she didn't have a lot to say. I don't think her medical training was conducive to the spiritual side of life. Modern medicine is about machines, gadgets, technology and let me examine the specimen that is your body. A medical version of 'wham, bam, thank you ma'am,'" he said with peaceful, gleaming eyes.

"But a few years ago, she had several patients almost back to back that died and came back, with accounts very similar to mine. She's come along way, and is now very much open to the notion that science can't explain everything."

Mrs. Henderson returned a few days after Momma Zoli came home. One day, her car broke down, and I drove down to Watts to pick up her husband so he could come and fix it.

As we drove past an old, abandoned, dilapidated building, he looked at me and said with a smile, "You know John some folk look at this raggedy, empty factory and feel nothing but shame. They see it as empty and think it needs to be tore down. But that's not what I see when I look at it. You know what I see?"

"No, sir, Mr. Henderson, I'm afraid I don't."

"I see all of the blessings of my family. My Uncle J.H. and Uncle Rob came out here from Texas in nineteen-twenty when that factory first opened up and they both got jobs in that place. I don't know if he was exaggerating or not, but Uncle J.H. said that they walked half the way out here, and the other half was spent on the back of an open truck with thirty other people trying to escape Texas and find the promised land here. When the truck broke down, instead of going back home, they all took to walking, and made it here safely.

"It's because my uncles found work that I'm here. I came out here once in the late thirties looking for a job and nobody would hire me. I ended up going back home. But I came back after serving my country in the war and found a good paying job. Right here in this factory. Then my brothers came out here and other relatives, too. They all got jobs that helped them to live better than their wildest dreams back in Texas. We bought homes and sent our children to college—a few of 'em are lawyers and doctors. We even have a promising actor in the bunch," he said laughing.

"So when I look at that abandoned old building, I don't see anything but the hopes and dreams of my family fulfilled."

forty-one

I doesn't remembas ev'rythang dat happened tah me, but I do remembas most ah it. I was comin out ah de buildin when dis youngin ran pass me an almose knock me down. Den 'foh I could git mah balance good, heah come anothah one of dem runnin real fast, too. He stopped rite in front ah me an pointed dis heah gun at de first youngin who be runnin through de parkin lot.

I got in front ah dat youngin an tole him, "No, yah cain't do dat. Yah cain't shoot dat chile."

He look at me wid nothin but evil in his eyes an say, "Bitch, if yah ain't get outta mah way I is gonna shoot yah."

I tole him, "I ain't movin. Yah is gonna has tah shoot me tah gits tah him."

An he did. Rite in mah belly. I ain't nevah felt no hurtin like dat in all ah mah life. Even when I was gittin de life beat outta me wid a big ole bull whip it ain't felt nothin like dat.

Den I doesn't remembas too much aftah dat. I can heah Angela screamin an cryin, an holdin mah head, beggin me not tah die. An I was ready tah go den. I knows I was dyin. I could feel de life justa runnin outta me.

De next thang dat I knows I is lookin down at mah own body in dis heah room. All ah dese folks is runnin aroune me, doin all kine ah things. I heard dis man jist ah yellin "Code blue! Code blue! We is losin huh. Get me some blood!"

Den all ah ah sudden, I was movin, f'lyin through dis long, dark tunnel with dis little bitty lite at de end. An as I got closah de lite got biggah, an biggah. When I got tah de lite, it was all aroune me. An I felt nothin but love. It was like de lite was de love. De lite was shinin on me was nothin but pure love.

Den all of a sudden, I was in de most beautiful place dat I has evah seen. I was in dis field wid flowahs dat was brite like dey had dey own lite.

An den I seen mah familee. Mah husban an chilrens was dere, an dey chilrens an dey chilrens chilrens was all dere. Even Angela's momma, John's pappy, an de chilrens dat dey loss was dere.

I was so happy, I ain't nevah felt so good. I had a new body, I was as lite as a feathah.

But dey tole me dat I couldn't stay, dat it wadn't mah time yet. Dat I had tah come back ta de earf an hep yah chilrens down heah.

I didn't wont tah come back. I wonted tah stay wid dem. But mah chilrens tole me dat I had tah come back. Dat I had work tah do. I had tah come back an hep dese confused chilrens undastand who dey really is, an why dey is on de earf. Foh I knew it, de spirit done sent me back, an de next thing I knows I is in dis place, wid all a dese funny noises an I ain't feelin nothin but a whole lotta hurtin.

I was heah in dis worle an sometime I was dere on de othah side wid dem. De doctahs said dat I was in a coma. I guess dat was like bein tween dese heah two worles.

I could still see mah chilrens watchin ovah me when I was in dat deep sleep. I could heah dem whisperin dey love tah me, an ev'ry now an den I can feel dese wonderful stirrins in mah heart. I could feels all ah dem peoples down heah prayin foh me axin de Lawd tah hep me git bettah, an I knows dat dey prayahs hepped me tah git bettah.

Den one day I jist woke up, feelin fine. I snatched dat ole tube dey had in mah mouth out. I ain't need it no moh. I ain't have no hurtin, mah insides just feels a little sore. I is on de mend real good, I knows cause so many was prayin foh me.

I knows dat John an Angela cain't believes dey eyes when dey seen me sittin up an smilin. I knows dat dey thought dat I was dyin. Guess I fooled dem!

I is ready tah go home. I knows whot I has tah do. An I is gonna do it. I is ready tah be on dis earf an do whot I gots tah do. I is ready tah do de Lawd's work foh my chilrens dat is still heah.

forty-two

When we got the call to return to the hospital immediately, I just knew that Momma Zoli had died. My heart trembled all of the way there. I couldn't believe my eyes when we arrived and there she was sitting up in her bed, like nothing had ever happened. I was so grateful that she survived. Still feeling the sting of my guilt, I wouldn't be able to live with myself if she had died.

The nurse said she had yanked out the tube that had connected her to the respirator, and she simply refused to let anybody touch her until John showed up and gave them permission. He was so touched by her faith and confidence in him, 'til I thought he was going to burst with pride

Momma Zoli told us about what happened when she died. "I seen yoh Mammy. She is happy an very proud ah yah. She tole me tah tell yah dat she be watchin ovah yah all ah de time." She even described her to a tee. I guess there were so many things about the mysteries of life, we'll never be able to understand.

"Bring me some books. I wonts tah finish learnin how tah read. An when I gits outta dis hospital I wonts yah tah take me to dem museums so I can learn about mah peoples an all dat dey done since we be in dis heah place."

Her progress over the next few days was miraculous. Everyone in the unit was talking about her—even the relatives of other patients. One evening while he was on rounds, Dr. Richard scratched his head, and said, "I can't explain her progress. She's a miracle."

Even the remnants of the rash on her foot healed. We were startled to see her walking with the assistance of her nurse, only a day after she came out of the coma.

A couple of days later, Dr. Richard transferred her to a room. She started eating, walking and her wounds healed quickly. She asked us to bring her books, "I wonts tah learn ev'rythang 'bout dis heah worle. I was sent back foh a reason, an I is gonna do ev'rythang dat I is supposed tah 'foh I leaves dis place."

She recuperated so quickly it almost gave me whiplash.

The only ones who weren't surprised by her astonishing recovery were my children. "Mommie, see we told you Momma Zoli was gonna be alright." And she was.

Less than three weeks after she had been shot, Momma Zoli came home. The day we brought her home, she refused to leave before personally thanking everyone who'd help to take care of her. She even refused to ride in the wheelchair and slowly walked out of the hospital on her own strength.

John had the spare room upstairs turned into a hospital room with a bed. He even hired a part-time nurse. The room was filled with flowers and bright pictures.

She came home happy, healthy and with a zest for life that I'd never seen before.

The day she came home Kathy Lee and Doug brought the baby by for Momma Zoli. "She is such a pretty baby. I ain't nevah had nobody named after me."

"Yes, you have Momma Zoli," replied Ashley. "Aunt Mary, Grandmomma and Mommie. They all are named Mary."

"Yah is right. I ain't nevah thought about dat."

To tell the truth, I hadn't either.

Her new-found zest for life blessed us with an energy of excitement and anticipation. Her bright eyes glowed with peace.

She began to speak of her world. Each evening after she recuperated we'd gathered around her and listen.

Her stories were spellbinding and her observations were intriguing. No longer were we listening to a confused, old homeless woman, but to an ancestor who'd returned from the past.

Doc Whitney came by to see her a few days after she came home. It was amazing what happened to him. When he came out of her room his eyes were glowing.

"What happened, Doc?"

"She told me she saw my mother standing next to me. She described her perfectly, everything, even told me about some things that's been going on in my life that no one could ever know about, much less her.

"I don't know who she really is, or where she's really from. I've heard all sorts of things, mostly from the seniors back at the center, about what she said, but one thing I do know is that she's blessed my life in a way that is beyond my ability to express. Thank you for letting me see her. I'll never be the same."

Then next day, Geneva came by to see her. She emerged from the room weeping like a baby. "It's alright Gen. She's going to be fine."

"It's not her I'm crying about, it's me," she said, blowing her nose into her monogrammed white lace handkerchief.

"What do you mean?"

"She told me to stop pretending, to stop wasting all of my time trying to be something that I'm not. She said I didn't need to pretend to be this grand ole Southern belle, that I needed to just be me and people would love me even more.

"And she's right."

"I've never been secure enough to be the woman I'm supposed to be. She hit the nail on the head.

"When I asked her, 'Where do I find myself?' You know what she said? She said, 'Sugah all dat yah gots tah do is look inside ah yoh heart.'"

Momma Zoli spoke with a new grace and wisdom. Her anger was replaced by a tenderness I'd never seen before. She and John grew closer, as if he was her direct descendant instead of me.

"I sees de worle wid new eyes. I knows ev'rythang is gonna be alright."

Not a day passed by without her talking about the child that almost took her life. She always spoke lovingly of him. "I doesn't blame him. I jist wonts tah know when is all ah dis killin gonna stop?

We took her to see the child's mother. As we sat in the small, hot living room, Momma Zoli's faced beamed with a golden light. She said, "I seen him. He is in a bettah place, an he is alright. I can feel him all ovah yah. You ain't got no reason tah feel no guilt, like yah done somethin wrong. It is alrite."

"But I should've seen this coming," the boy's mother said weeping inconsolably.

"No, Sugah, don't say dat. Some thangs can't be stopped. If he hadn't ah done to me what he did, I coulda nevah done whot de Lawd meant foh me tah do. I is jist sorry dat somebody hurt him.

"All ah dis killin has tah stop, an peoples got tah start actin like dey knows who dey is.

"I learned on de othah side dat we ain't got nothin tah be shamed ah, dat God loves us an made us who we is. I is Black, I can say dat. I thought it was somethin terrible, but we is made from nothin but God's love."

"I wonts tah git outtah dis house. I wonts tah learn bout dis heah worle an all dat yah done."

The children began to take her on regular excursions to the library. She had a vociferous appetite for learning. Not only reading, but she watched literally hundreds of videos on African American history. We also took her to the African American museum and other cultural places.

She became an inspiration to all of us. She filled us with laughter and wisdom in a way that I couldn't have imagined. Her common sense and simple grace awed me and filled me with a new zest for life. Finally, after so many months of trials and tribulations of darkness and despair, our home had become a place filled with light and love.

One night, when John and I went to check on Momma Zoli, we found her looking out of the window.

I asked, "What are you doing, Momma Zoli? Looking for stars again?"

"No sugah, I is talking to de Lawd."

"About what?" John asked.

She turned, her eyes were shining, almost glowing in the dark. "I is thankin him foh makin me who I is. I ain't shame no moh ah bein African. Cause dat's who I really is. Cause I is a chile ah de most high God. I knows de truf, an I wanna thanks yah foh lettin me see de lite."

forty-three

After months of turmoil and upheaval, uncertainty and confusion, our lives finally slipped without us noticing, into a rhythm of normalcy. Finally recuperated from her injuries, Momma Zoli had made peace with being here. The kids were in the midst of enjoying their summer vacation. In his spare time, John began working with Doug and several other businessmen to create a network of community, economic redevelopment and enrichment programs. And my work had finally settled back into its normal hectic pace.

"Baby, let's have a Labor Day cookout. There's gonna be a lot of people in town that weekend, and we need to do some entertaining since we haven't had one in at least two or three years," John said.

Since it sounded like a good idea to me, we invited Kathy Lee and Doug, Geneva and her husband and the new couple who owned the restaurant. Several friends from Howard were in town to attend one of the numerous Black conventions being held that weekend.

It was a casual afternoon filled with barbecued ribs, potato salad, baked beans, cole slaw, junk food for the kids, swimming, sunning by the pool, bid whist inside, billiards, video games for the kids, recalling old memories, exchanging new stories and plenty of laughter.

Late in the evening, we were in the family room, sitting around, talking crap, playing cards and the kids were watching a video. It was like old times, sitting around laughing, talking, cracking jokes, and having a good time.

For some reason, Momma Zoli kept to herself throughout the day. She never left her room. I checked on her several of times, but her cranky mood seemed to make her want to be left alone. The last time I popped my head in, I found her reading a book.

"Momma Zoli, don't you want to come out and meet some of our friends?"

"No, I doesn't."

"Are you feeling okay?"

"I is fine," she replied, almost barking at me.

"Well then, why are you cooped up in this room?"

"I jist wonts tah be by mahsef tahday."

I couldn't understand why she wanted to stay away. It didn't make any sense to me. But I decided to leave well enough alone.

I was sitting on the couch when Kathy Lee and Courtney, the wife of one of John's classmates, were playing bid whist against Spider Leach and Randy Brown, two other classmates of John's, on a card table next to the couch.

When I was at Howard, I had never taken a liking to Spider. He looked more to me like a little dirty rat instead of a spider. He was such a nasty character. He wore his sleazy charm like a snake that impressed only the most naive women on campus. I never wanted to have much to do with him. The straw that broke my camel's back was when he got one of my friend's, Carol Lee Stinson, pregnant and denied even knowing the girl.

Now, nearly thirty years later, he looked much older than everyone else in the room. His drawn, weary face wore the signs of too much alcohol and too little sleep. Even though I didn't like him, I couldn't help but feel sorry for him.

He turned to me and said, "Baby, umm-umm-umm. You sure do look good. John is a lucky man to have you all these years."

Because I couldn't muster up even a phony smile, I just ignored his sleazy compliment.

After Courtney dealt the cards, Spider said, with a tooth pick bobbing at the corner of his mouth, "Four low."

Kathy Lee, sitting next to him, smiled slyly with a Cheshire cat grin and said, "Five no."

"What did you say?" he asked with a tinge of anger.

"You heard me. I said, 'five no.'"

"Damn," he sighed, slumping back into his seat. "That's just like a Black woman to take a brother out."

"Excuse me?" shot back Kathy Lee. "What did you say?"

"You heard me, what you did is exactly what I expect a Black woman to do these days."

"Look, I don't know what your problem is, but we're playing cards here and that's all. So if you've got a problem with my bid, you should've bid higher. It's just that simple, my brother."

He turned his head, not responding to her, and started talking to Milton, who was sitting on the couch next to me. The toothpick picked up speed in his mouth and bobbed around like a ship that was about to capsize in an angry, unpredictable sea.

"Yeah, man, you know one thing, and I'm sure you can relate to this, my brother, it's rough being a black man in this world. And with women like the ones we got here in this room, it's even harder. We got to fight two battles in this world. One with 'the man' and the other with our women. That's something women just don't understand. The white man makes it harder on us, they get the jobs we are supposed to get."

Kathy Lee countered, saying, "You know, Spider, I don't know you from Adam, but I do know men like you, and I heard this argument all the way through medical school. There were brothers, Black men I went to school with, who suggested that I should not be there, because I was taking a brother's slot, preventing him from being able to support his family."

"And those brothers were absolutely correct."

"Excuse me!" she shouted back. "You have no idea as to what you are talking about."

"Yes, I do, my sister. Black women have been used as pawns in the white man's game, used against their own men, and you should be ashamed of yourself for doing that."

"Ashamed? All I know is that you can't see past your own sexism. Not only do Black women have to deal with white men, we have to deal with brothers like you who are retroactive, and wouldn't know what progressive meant in terms of women's issues, and what we have to deal with—racism and sexism. The problem is you've got a chip on your shoulder and you want to take it out on me, and probably all of the other women in your life."

"The problem with you sistahs of the nineties, you just won't listen!"

"Listen? How can we listen, when all we hear is garbage like the crap that's coming out of your mouth? 'Nobody understands me, 'cause I'm a poor Black man. Woe is me. Come help me lick my wounds.'"

"Kathy Lee, come on, give the brother a break. It is rough out here for brothers," added John from across the room.

"Rough? Men are so sensitive to pain, if you had to give birth and take care of the children, we'd have a population shortage, in less than one generation!" howled Geneva.

"See, there, that's exactly the attitude that Spider is talking about. You women are out of your proper place. You are not supportive or respectful of us and our ordeal."

"And you brothers don't listen to our pain either."

"I don't recall seeing no videotape of no sistahs getting beat by the police. Tell me this my beautiful Black queen, have you seen one? We get our head busted each and every day of the week, three hundred sixty-five days a year. Why hell, the L.A.P.D. don't even take a holiday off on Christmas. I got a friend that was almost beat to death in the police station last Christmas. His only problem was that he didn't have no white boy around to do a videotape.

"What point is that? The police don't have to beat us. Brothers do it for them. We are the ones who are beaten and abused. How many sisters slap their husbands around and used them as punching bags whenever a white man does them wrong?

"And as long as it's not your mother, or your sister, or your daughter, so some other significant woman in your life, like a good friend, you turn your head and pretend that it's not happening."

Spider's dropped his gaze to the cards he held in the palm of his hands. "Yes, my sister, You know you is right about that."

"Sisters have a hard road to trod. Not only are we expected to take care of the children, keep the house clean, cook and be a man's second mother, we are supposed to work a full-time job, too! It's amazing to me that sisters are not dropping dead like flies with all that we have to put up with," she said sarcastically.

Nervous chatter erupted throughout the room. Everyone was agreeing and disagreeing, mumbling and starting up their own two- or three-person conversations about the controversy. The bantering between K.L. and Spider continued for several minutes. Some teasing, but the tone of the discord was growing in intensity.

Then Spider turned angrily away from the table and looked across the room and said, "Okay, I'm gonna put an end to this right now. Let's take a vote. How many brothers think that women have it worse?"

Suddenly, the room was filled with tense silence. No one moved or said a word.

"Come, cain't none of you niggers in here speak? What's wrong? Cat got your tongue?"

Randy leaned over and said, "Come on, man, why don't you lay this thing to rest? Get off it and go on back to playing cards. That's what we are here for, isn't it?"

Spider didn't say a word. He just sat there in a smoldering, almost palpable anger and glared at him.

Suddenly, before anyone uttered another word, Momma Zoli bolted out of her room, yelling and screaming, as if the house was on fire, "Stop dat! Stop dat! Put dat down now!"

John jumped up and ran over to her. He touched her arm, but she yanked it away with tremendous force. "Momma, what's wrong? What are you talking about?" he begged, his voice almost two octaves higher than normal.

"Stop dat!" she screamed again, paying John no attention, glaring at everyone in the room. Her voice filled the room with an acidic, caustic rage. "Why is you talkin like dat?" she asked pointing her finger at Kathy Lee and Spider. "What's wrong with yah? Y'all in heah actin like yah ain't got the sense yah was bon wid!"

"An why ain't nobody in dis room got de sense tah stop dem?"

The room trembled with silence.

"Yah is in heah all of yah jist a breakin mah heart into li'l bitty pieces wid yoh crazy talkin. Yah oughta be 'shamed ah yohsef. Cause I knows if yoh mammies an pappies was heah, dey sho nuff would be shamed ah de way yah is actin."

"Momma, calm down." I pleaded.

"How can yah sit aroune dis room, arguin, axin dis heah kinda questions, talkin 'bout pain de way yah is, arguin bout who hurtin de mose? Yah should be runnin into de woodshed to hide yah faces. Ain't nobody can ansah dat! Yah oughta be shamed, very shamed of yohsef."

"How can yah tell me, how can yah measure mah pain or yoh pain or anybody else's pain? Whot rite does yah have tah axe dese questions?

The trembling stopped. Her words trapped all of us against the wall of our shame. I felt like I was suffocating.

"Dat is a question dat only de good Lawd can ansah. Everybody's pain is diff'ent. Don't yah know dat? We all is in pain. Dis heah worle done heaped a whole lotta pain on all of us. Yah should have de sense yah was born wid to know dat!"

"Talkin bout who be hurtin de most is like tryin tah count de stars in de sky. Now tells me who can do dat? Who knows how many fish dere is in de sea? It would be easiah tah count dem dan to say who is hurtin de most.

"De way I sees it, y'all gots it pretty good compared tah whot's gone on befoh yah. Do yah thank foh one minute dat all dose who gone on befoh yah went through all dat suffah'n so y'all could sit aroune dis heah arguin like dis?

"If yah thinks dat, den yah betta thank agin.

"We git down on our knees each an ev'ry nite prayin to a Lawd we didn't even know was listenin, axin for 'liverance from de lion's den, in spite of all de hurtin, waitin foh de day dat we would be free. An if our eyes wasn't gonna see freedom, we sho nuff was prayin foh our chilrens.

"Does anybody in heah knows how many ah yoh ancestas prayed foh a day dey cain't nevah see. An now dat de day done come, heah yah is actin like a heap ah fools wid yoh disrespectin mouths."

With fire in her eyes, she turned toward John and I and screamed, "I thought dat de two of yah shoulda known betta dan dis! Dis is crazy, 'specially doing dis kinda talkin in front of yah chilrens. Whot is dey supposed tah think bout somethin like dis? Why is yah lettin somebody do dis in yoh house?"

I shuddered with guilt.

"I praise de Lawd for His grace an His wondrous love, I doesn't knows what tah thinks about yah.

"Let me tell yah about de pain I done seen wid dese eyes an carried in dis ole heart. An den I wonts yah tah tell me, who hurts de most, who is livin in worser grief. Does yah knows how it feels tah have yah chile, yah baby stolen away from yah an yah cain't do nothin about it? Does yah know how much pain a mothas feels in her heart? An each time it happens yah thanks it cain't git no worser, but it do! Ev'ry time dey took one of mah chilrens away I thought my heart was gonna crush from de weight of mah grief. An I thought if dey did it agin, it won't hurt so much. But I was wrong, dead wrong.

"Each day dat I lived an breathed aftah dey was all gone, de only thang I could think about, de only thang dat kept me ah goin was de prayah, de knowin dat one day I would see dem agin.

"But did I suffer moh dan anybody else? Hell I ain't do dat. An yah know whot? All de pain an suffah'n I seen, 'mongst de people I knew, ain't bin one time dat anybody say, 'I is hurtin moh dan yah' cause dey knew bettah dan de sorry chilrens y'all turnin out tah be.

"Tell me dis—was my pain worser dan dat purdy li'l Beatrice, who was youngah dan Ashley when ole Massa Steadwell bought huh to use cause he growed tired of his wife? He raped that poh chile day in an day out. Doin all sorts of ungodly thangs tah her, tearin up huh body like a plow rippin up fresh land. I could heah huh screamin upstairs in de attic when his wife had left de house, goin tah town. An den when he wasn't rapin huh, he would lock huh up so she couldn't run away, an nobody could hep tah soothe huh wounes. Den when dat ole evil dried up Missus Steadwell got ah hold of de poh chile when she was pregnant, bout tah bear dat ole evil man's chile, she strung Beatrice up an nearly beat huh tah death. Den dat ole woman pour hot oil, den lye up in huh body, tryin to scar huh body shut so massa won't want huh no moh. Caused dat baby tah be born dead.

"De poh little gul went crazy an hung huhself dead, licky split.

"An what about Jeb? He been on de 'tation longer dan me. He al'ays was fightin back, an dey was al'ays tryin tah break his spirit. 'Dis nigga will not rule me!' dey say. Dey ain't let him keep no wife. Dey sold dem off an his li'l chilrens. But dat wasn't good enough. Yah know whot dey did when he come down sick? Dey wouldn't give him no moh food. Said he was a dyin nigga an didn't need none. Den when he got real weak, dey took him out in de barn and dey put him in a bin where dey be keepin corn an food. Dey knew rats was up in dere, an de rats came in an gotta hole of him, ate de flesh offa his face, an his fingers.

"An if dat ain't enuf evil foh one man, when dey finally took his body out, aftah a couple of weeks, it was all rotted. But do yah think dat was 'nuff to stop dere? No it wasn't. Den dey put his body up on a tree, so dem vultures could eat whatevah was left. Dey kept it dere for a few days, made othah slaves stand aroune an' guard it so nobody would sneak off an give it a proper burial, like the decent thang to do, sayin, 'Dis heah is whot happins tah rebellious niggas.' An dey burned his body on dat tree, made all of us watch it. Tarrin an feathahin woulda bin a blessin seein whot dey did to him.

"An what about all dem little chilrens, who lost dey mammas an pappys? Nevah tah see dey smilin faces agin in dis worle. De only comfort dey knew was at de hands of dose who suffered too, who had lost dey own. Did yah suffah more dan dem? An who suffahed de mose? Was it de motha, de fatha or de chile?

"Did I suffah moh dan dem Africans like Hagaar? Do yah knows whot happined tah dem? Maybe yah thinks dat yah does, but I knows yah cain't. I still remembas what Hagaar tole me, 'bout what happened tah huh. She was de only fresh African dat I evah seen. She said dese white men an Africans from other tribes came tah huh village in de middle ah de nite. Dey killed de old peoples like huh mammy an huh pappy. Den dey took huh an huh husban an huh chilrens, an chained dem up wid de rest ah de young folks an made 'em walk across de land foh weeks, til dey got tah de watah. Den dey separated dem, put de mens in one dungeon, puts de womins in anothah, den puts dey chilrens in dey own. Can yah undastands how she feel when she heah her chilrens cryin, an she cain't git to 'em tah stop dey tears? Dey ain't nevah seen dey chilrens or dey husbans agin. Dey ain't knowin wheah dey is on de face ah de earf, if dey is dead or alive! Dey is scared, dey ain't knowin what gonna happen next, an den, aftah months a bein in de dark places dey is put on dese ships, tah live packed so close togetha some of dem gits crushed tah death? Lyin dere in dey own waste, not knowin wheah dat ship was takin dem, oh if dey was gonna live oh die? Does yah have any idea how dat be feelin?

"An heah yah is sitting aroune talkin 'bout pain, like yah is braggin on somethin. So since y'all knows so much, tell me—who suffered de mose. Whose pain was burstin' outta dere heart moh dan mine? Tells me dat!" she roared like an angry lioness.

"We ain't axe dem kinda questions. All we did was tah try, de best way we could, tah ease each anothah's burdens. Dats whot yah 'pose tah be doin' now, not dis heah arguin' ovah somethin that cain't fine de ansah.

"It was mercy an grace dat seen us through tah de light of dis new day. Doesn't yah know dat?

"My pain is yoh pain, an yoh pain is my pain. How did yah hearts git so narrow an small, tah be only worried bout yahself an yah own?

"I is speakin for dem dat ain't got no tongues tah speak. I is speakin foh de pase, de blood ah mah blood, an de bone ah mah bones.

"I wish I could tells yah dat I suffered moh dan yah, an maybe in a way dats true. But when I sees yah, wid all dat yah got painin each an ev'ry day in dis heah worle, I ain't so sure.

"Who is this crazy woman?" asked Spider, looking at me. "Where you get her from?"

From across the room, John yelled, "Shut up, Spider. Shut your trap right now and listen."

"I wonts yah tah thinks 'bout dat long an hard. How do yah thinks yah would feel, use tah bein free like de burds, losin ev'rythang dat evah made any sense, treated worser dan animals. Don't yah think dat would drive yah crazy?

"I done seen suffah'n dat I still to dis day cain't even speak 'bout. It's too terrible to remembas. But when I looks in yah eyes an see de weight of pain dat yah is carryin aroune I cain't say who is worsah dan who, an' if I could I wouldn't wont to.

"Cause in spite of all mah pain, all dat I seen, an all dat I went through, I nevah gave up hope. If I could jist lift up mah eyes to de hills from whence cometh mah hep, I would fine de place of faith dat made me go on.

"How could yah, all of yah, gits tah dis heah place of confusion wheah our own chilrens feels so unloved dat dey can shoot each othah down an anybody else dat gets in dere way. When one of mah own chilrens, an who knows if he is or ain't one of mah own flesh an blood, shot me down like a dog? Dey hearts is like dat cement pond right outside filled with nothin but rivahs of pain.

"Whot y'all heah is fohgittin is dat somebody pained yah into dis life. Somebody knew dey eyes was gonna see freedom through yohs. Dey knew dey was gonna breathe de sweet fragrance of hope realized through yoh body. But y'all seem to fohgit. All of yah heah, an all of yah livin in dis worle tahday got heah cause yah is standin on de shouldahs an de chains of all dose who came befoh yah. Think bout dat sometime in yah suffah'n an in yah arguin!

"An yah know what? It was men an womin, boys an guls who suffahed foh yah. Dey ain't nevah seen de light of a free day, an dey has bin all but forgotten cause of yoh shame an yoh pain. But dey won't lets yah fohgits cause I is speakin foh dem.

"An if de suffah'n is gonna tah stop, an Lawd knows dat it need tah, den ev'rybody's suffah'n needs tah go 'way at de same time. Nobody should be suffah'n in dis heah worle. Dat's not why de Lawd put us heah. But man in his wicked ways has brought about de suffah'n of too many nations of people. An dats what needs tah end.

"So don't do dat no moh. Don't let me evah catch yah talkin like dat tah one anothah. I is sho dat yoh ancestas is hollerin in dey graves, crying out tah yah tah stop dis heah madness.

She turned and walked out of the room—closing the door, sealing us in with her words, as they reverberated and vibrated in and around us.

For a long time, we sat there in the silence of our guilt. Most of those in the room hung their heads in obvious silent embarrassment. Kathy Lee started weeping.

Then she got up slowly, "Kathy Lee where are you going?" asked John.

"I need to go apologize to her. This is all my fault. I should've never started arguing. It never touched me, as deeply as it does now, all that our foreparents have gone through. She's right, you know. We have no right to do this to one another. We are dishonoring the memories of those who have gone on before us when we get lost in these petty, divisive arguments."

"Man, I've never heard nobody talk like that. Where is she from?" asked Spider.

"It's a long story, one that I'll have to share with you another time," John said, exhausted.

It seemed like we all sat there for ages, wanting to reach out to one another, to say something, not knowing what to say or how to say it. Then, Ray who'd been sitting silently on the couch, looked at the bar where his wife Sarah was sitting. He said, "Maybe we'd better pack up the kids and go home."

Courtney, his little six year old daughter, rushed over to him and said, "Wait, daddy, before we go, can we say a prayer?"

"A prayer for what, baby?

"A prayer for all those people who are hurting."

forty-four

For the first time in my life I was thrust into another reality that was the pain of my elders. The pain of others that I had only thought about superficially. Maybe it was too much for me to bear. Trapped by the inescapable reality of her words, I sat there frozen. I had tried to get things to cool down, but Momma Zoli took care of it better than I ever dreamed of doing. She shamed us, all of us, and our arrogant victimhood. She set us straight the way my momma used to when I was out of order.

She stripped me of everything, and the last walls of my defenses came tumbling down. Even if I wanted, I couldn't ignore her. Ever since she first showed up here, a part of me kept her at distance. She made me uncomfortable and stirred up something that was hidden in me that I didn't want to face. She forced me to wrestle with the ancient demons of my lost father, my father's father, my lineage. She made me face those old wounds I did not want to face. The oozing wounds of self-hatred, the mutilating thoughts that I had accepted and the way of being which stripped me of my strength.

I didn't know what do. I didn't known what to say to myself, to my children, to my guests. I sat there in a daze of remembrance. We were the vessels of the days gone by, the triumphant children of a forgotten people.

Since she left the hospital, we had grown closer, but I still kept her at a distance. I treated her way I did everyone I loved because of the fear I have buried deep in the crevices of my soul. Maybe it was my ancestor's rage that I had felt on days I had lost control. Maybe it was my grandmother's pain that had made me

such a protective father—especially over my daughter. What would
I have done in a world where I could not protect them? That I did
not know, nor did I wish to consider. It was far too painful for me
to ever know. What would I have done if someone tried to take
Ashley away from me, sell my son into a place that I could not see
or rape my wife at will? Would I have gone mad? Would I have
rebelled? Would I have killed them instead of allowing continuous
suffering, or would I, like Momma Zoli, have just held on?

I was grateful that I didn't know the answers to those questions. I could only sit in awe of those magnificent spirits who had
gone on before me. But I did feel deep guilt and great shame in
terms of dishonoring all that they survived.

The children watched us. They did not know what to make of
the situation. They had always seen their parents in control.

What was I supposed to say to my guests who did not know
the story, the truth about Momma Zoli's presence in our world? I
had just told them that she was Angela's grandmother and left it
at that. But then again, it really didn't matter. Even if they didn't
know or wouldn't believe, they still had to face the truth, the unavoidable reality of her words.

The brutal truth of her words moved though my soul like a
distant voice crying in the night.

"We didn't go through all dis heah hurtin just tah let y'all gits
heah to argue 'bout who hurts de mose. And if yah could decide, do
it really mattah? Whot difference do it make?"

I had never, not in my entire life, heard anyone say such
things. She made me feel little, selfish and stupid. How did I get to
this point of being so self-centered? How could I get locked up and
lost in such a meaningless endeavor? I did not know. So I sat there
stunned, wondering and trying to figure out what to do next. Now
I knew why I hadn't wanted her in my home. The truth of discovery
crushed me again. She reminded me of a past I did not want to face.

I wanted to rush into her room like Kathy Lee to tell her I
was sorry—like I was taught to do. But I knew, for the time being,
it was best to leave her alone. Angie sat there stunned. I could see

everyone else was trying to make a comeback, to regain their lost composure, return to their normal thinking. But we couldn't. In just a few short moments, she totally disrupted our way of thinking and being. How had we become so lost in this world that we could not acknowledge each other's pain?

Spider said nervously, "I guess she shut my mouth. Yes siree. That little lady put a clamp on my style."

"Man, be quiet. You still don't get it, do you?" I said, my voice overflowing with disgust.

"No, like what is there to get?"

"You just heard the voice of the ancestors. Speaking through someone who was sent here to help us."

"You gotta be kidding me. So now I am supposed to believe that this is some kind of mystical event that I was privileged enough to participate in? Give me a break."

"Whether or not you believe in where she came from, what she said is still true."

Angie said, "John, leave him alone, let him go. He can't handle it. He's in too much pain."

Angela looked into my eyes and said, "I feel like a thick old heavy veil has been lifted from my eyes. I can see clearly now."

I couldn't go to sleep that night. I tossed and turned for hours. It felt like my body was chained and I couldn't set myself free. Every time I began to doze off, the sounds of terrified voices surrounded me. Moaning, screaming, agonizing voices haunted me. I couldn't escape them.

I didn't know where I was. I was crushed in a small space filled with stench. I could barely breathe. I couldn't move because ev'rywheah I turned there were people packed almost on top of one another. Screaming in different tongues, coughing, choking, gasping for air.

Trapped in the belly of a living hell, I wanted to die.

Finally, when I yanked myself out of that place, I woke up drenched in sweat. I was completely drained, yet somehow set free, liberated from ancient wounds that had lived far too long in the deep dark corridors of my mind. I laid there for a moment. Then I decided to get up and pray. I fell down on my knees and began to give thanks for all I had never been thankful for. I was lost in a world of thanksgiving. Suddenly, I felt my wife's soft hand touch me as she joined me on her knees.

"I had never been so grateful to be alive in this world. Momma Zoli shined a new light into my dark confusion."

Angie replied, "I know how you feel. I had all sorts of dreams last night like I've never had before. It was so painful and hard. I don't know how our ancestors survived.

"Do you ever wonder why she came to us? Why I found her?"

"We'll probably never know. For whatever reasons, it was simply meant to be." I used to say, very matter of factly, "We all came over on the same boat." That is dishonoring the middle passage.

She shamed us, shamed each and every one of us as she uncovered the arrogance of our limited suffering. When she placed the content of our lives in their proper perspective, she made all of our worries seem quite small. How much time had we wasted? How many deeds had gone undone?

How did I get so lost in my own pain, so limited in my view? How did my foreparents contend with so much and survive? I was sure it was God's amazing grace.

When Momma Zoli came to the breakfast table, she peered into my eyes and said, "I is sorry."

"Sorry for what?"

"Whot I done was wrong. I ain't got no rite to disrespect yoh house like dat. Do yah wonts me to leave?"

"Momma, you shouldn't even talk like that. This is your home and you have every right to say whatever you want to say. What you said was very true, and something all of us needed to hear a long time ago."

"I doesn't knows whot came ovah me. All of ah sudden mah room was filled wid all ah dem ole slaves dat I knowed back on de 'tation. An dey was jist a lookin at me, an dey eyes was axin me 'Whot is yah gonna do Zoli? Is yah gonna let dem keep on talkin like dat? Ain't yah gonna git out dere an tell dem de truf?'

"I jist had tah stop dem from kickin dirt in de face ah dere blessin.

"Aftah I came back in mah room, I started thinkin 'bout mah Andrew. I miss him so much, even though I knows he is waitin on me on de othah side. But I see his strength in yoh eyes," she said looking at me. "Yah know I knows how much hurt he carried around aftah dey took our chilrens from us. But he nevah said one word cause I know he feel de guilt dat only a man can feel. I know he felt might awful bout not bein able tah take care ah his familee de way he 'pose to. Cause dat's whot he tole me when I was on de othah side.

"John, I wonts yah tah do something for me."

"Anything, Momma Zoli, just name it."

"I wonts yah tah take me tah see dem chilrens dat is in trouble."

"Who are you talking about?"

"Yah know de ones dat be killin folk like de nightridahs."

"Oh, you mean the gangs?"

"Yeah, dem. Dat's who I wonts tah see."

"Okay, Momma Zoli, I'll see what I can do."

I asked Angela to arrange through her contacts at the center a meeting with some of the members of the Crips and the Bloods, some of the younger ones. If Momma Zoli was going to get through to anybody it would probably be them, yet I had no idea as to what she was going to say. Doug volunteered to join us.

We went down to a community center in South Central on 110th Street. As we entered, the gang members were sitting around the edge of the room, almost frozen in a ritualistic harshness. I didn't explain that much to the director as to who Momma Zoli really is. They had been told that one of the elders in the community wanted to spend some time and share some of her insight with them.

She seemed to grow stronger in the presence of so much anger.

"I was shot by a chile dat somebody in heah probably knows. An I died. But de Lawd seen fit tah send me back tah dis heah worle. What makes me so sad 'bout de siteeation is dat de chile was killed by somebody else 'foh I or anybody else had a chance tah hep him change his ways, an it ain't 'pose tah be like dat.

"Now I undastands dat y'all got some kine ah agreement dat yah is gonna stop killin each othah. All I wonts tah know is does dat mean yah gonna stop ev'rythang dat be hurtin othahs like sellin dope?"

"Who is you to be axin us anything?" said one.

"I is somebody who cares. Dat's who I is."

"And why do you care?"

"Because dat's why I is heah, an dat's why I came back from de dead. Y'all is actin like a whole bunch ah fools de way y'all bin killin one anothah an innocent people dat ain't evah done nothin to yah. An dats gotta stop. If white folk was doin now whot y'all bin doin tah one anothah, a whole lotta colored folk would be upset and rarin tah fite."

"Colored folk? Man, where you from?" said another young man disrespectfully.

"Junior, watch your mouth," Doug cautioned.

He ignored Doug, and said, "Yeah, what you care ole woman? What you hear for anyway?"

"Show some respect for your elders. She's old enough to be your mother," I said.

"She probably older than that," shot back another young man.

"Yah is rite," she said rising up from her seat. "I is a lot oldah dan yah knows. An de worle dat I comes from ain't like nothin yah evah gonna know an yah should be thankful foh dat."

"What chu talkin 'bout lady? Break it down."

"I is talkin bout a place dat yah cain't nevah undastand. Wheah we worked from sun up tah sun down, an ain't nevah got paid foh nothin dat we did. Wheah white folks did some ah anything tah us, jist cause dey felt like bein mean an evil, wheah dey took our chilrens away an sole dem, nevah tah see dem agin, wheah dey beat us, an took womin's bodies anytime dey wanted, wheah dey killed colored men, strung dem up on a tree, jist cause dey felt like huntin down a nigga. An heah yah is doin jist about de same thin to yah own.

"All ah dem black folk dat come befoh yah ain't die so yah could be doin all ah dis killin an craziness in to yoh own people.

"Tell me dis—how is yah sellin somethin to people dat yah knows ain't no good foh dem. How come all mah dese chilrens is takin drugs?

"We ain't got no othah choice."

"I doesn't sees any white folks down heah makin y'all sell it!

"When I was a slave dey used to give us a whole lotta licka aroune Christmas time an all ah dem niggas on de 'tation would git real drunk. Den ole massa he come down tah de cabins, sayin, ' Looka heah, I done tole y'all yah doesn't needs tah be free. Cause if yah was, all yah would do is tah drink up licka. Yah ain't good foh nothin but bein a slave. Y'all bettah thank de Lawd foh us comin ovah an savin yah from yahsef in Africa.'"

"Let me get this straight," said another gang member. "You tellin us that you was a slave? Right?"

"It might be hards foh yah tah believes dat, but we got proof." She pulled out the picture and the sale."

"And you was sent here to the future to talk to us?"

"Dat's right, an I ain't axed tah come."

"What did you do?"

"I was a cook on de Steadwell 'tation right outside ah Jackson, 'Sippi."

"Did you fight?"

"Fight who?"

"The white folk who was making you a slave?"

"No, I cain't say dat I did."

"Well if you tellin the truth. Did you ever think that maybe if you had fought back a little bit we wouldn't be in the shape that we're in?"

"I'm sorry," I interjected.

"Whot yah sorry 'bout?"

"I'm sorry about the way they talked to you."

"Sugah, yah ain't got nothin tah be sorry foh. Dey axed me somethin dat I shoulda though 'bout lon, lon time ago.

"An dey is right. I shoulda fought back. But dey heped me tah see somethin dat I ain't seen befoh. Yah heah in dis worle, is carryin our pain, all ah dem beatins, an separations, de middle passage, an ev'rythang else dat we bin through. Dat's why thangs seems tah be fallin apart. Cause y'all is carryin de burden of many generations."

"Y'all is carryin aroune memories from a lon, lon time ago. Lawd ah mercy on me, no wonda dis heah worle is full a colored folk dat on de edge ah losin dey mines.

Momma Zoli quietly spoke her truth and answered questions for another hour. Everyone left the center slowly. One of the gang members said to us, "Yo, yo brother, I got some othah homeboys you need to check out for your own education. It might be a good learning experience for you. Here's the number of a sistah whose doin good things. You might want to take the mother over there to see her. She's doing some good things."

On the way home, as drove down Pico Boulevard, suddenly Momma Zoli screamed. "Stop! Stop dis cah!" I thought she was sick. However, as I turned to look at her, she was pointing to the drug rehab center. "Takes me in dere! I gots tah go in dere now! Somebody needs me."

Before I or Doug could say a word, she was out of the car and running into the center. As soon as we parked the car we followed her inside.

We found her hovering over a man who was stretched out on the floor, appearing to be having a seizure. The Jamaican woman that worked at Angie's office was there.

"What happened?" I asked.

"I was callin Momma Zoli, cause I needed her hep. I brought one of my neighbors over heah, and he went into a convulsion. All weekend long he hasn't had any heroin," she replied.

"I knows somebody needed me. An dat's why I was yellin like dat. But he gonna be fine, he coulda died," Momma Zoli said. "Dem drugs is worser dan licka."

"Momma Zoli, you can say dat again."

"Why does peoples takes it? I doesn't undastands."

"They have nothing to hope for."

"Seems like y'all jist be tryin tah run away from somethin dat be hurtin. I feels kinda sorry for y'all.

"It seems like a whole lotta folk in dis worle be walkin aroune in a daze, cause dey got so much comin at dem. Dere ain't much time foh bein quiet. Back in 'Sippi we used tah go out an look at de beauty ah de stars, sometime I git up jist tah watch de sun rise ovah de land, or tah watch it settin an it be beautiful. Listenin tah de crickets an de whippawills. But y'all gots so much workin in yah mines."

Finally, the man calmed down. As we left the center Momma Zoli said, "Son, I undastands why yah used tah git so riled up. Dis heah worle can make yah crazy in a way dat yah almost cain't sees."

"Yes, momma, you're right."

By that time I was ready to take Momma Zoli and go home.

forty-five

I doesn't knows whot I woulda done if I bin born in dis worle, maybe I be thinkin like dem. But it seem like dat's jist de way dis heah worle is rite now. Full ah folks complainin 'bout somethin. Not jist colored folk. I seen dem white folk in dat box wid de li'l people talkin bout some ah ev'rythang dat be goin on in dey life. An I ev'n seen somebody on dere talkin bout dey killed dey mammy an dey pappy cause dey beat 'em when dey was youngins.

Lawd a mercy on me. I ain't nevah thought dat de futah would be like dis! Dey gotta wake up an see how blessed dey is befoh it's too late. Cause dey blessins ain't gonna last forevah if dey keep on actin like dis.

Maybe it's too much for dem tah bear. I doesn't knows foh sure why dey is actin like dey doesn't know whot went on befoh. Dey knows de truth, cause it's runnin in dey own blood.

forty-six

The days had slipped quickly through our fingers, and before I knew it, it was almost Thanksgiving. I loved the holidays. I was absolutely my most favorite time of the year, tracing back to my earliest childhood memories. I remembered getting out of the bed on chilly Thanksgiving mornings to find Momma already in the kitchen cooking, with the delicious smell of candied yams, macaroni and cheese, homemade rolls and cornbread dressing gently caressing my senses.

Thanksgiving dinner on those crisp November Thursdays in Milwaukee was always absolutely delicious. Each morsel of food seemed to voluntarily melt in my mouth, and by the end of the evening, my stomach felt like it was about to burst. Thanksgiving was still the most joyous time of the year for me. I loved to cook a huge meal, the way my mother did when I was growing up.

I knew this year was going to be a very special Thanksgiving, considering all that had happened and the blessing of Momma Zoli's presence. Early in November, Professor Brown called and asked to come visit. John suggested that we invite him to spend the holiday with us.

The night before Thanksgiving, I was in the kitchen lost in my own world, as I made the cornbread dressing, when I noticed Momma Zoli had eased up on me and was standing no more than two or three feet away carefully studying me.

"What's wrong Momma Zoli? Why are you looking so sad?"

"Ain't nothin wrong wid me. I jist bin thinkin."

"Thinking about what?"

"Dat it's 'bout time for me tah be goin home."

"Momma, I thought you'd gotten over wanting to go back to Mississippi a long time ago."

"I ain't talkin 'bout goin back tah 'Sippi. I is talkin 'bout goin home tah be wid de Lawd."

"Momma! Why are you talking about dying? You're in good shape, healthy as a horse."

"Cause, sugah, I knows dat it's time foh me to go. I can feels dat in mah bones. I can see dat Rivah Jordan straight ahead ah me, just waitin foh me tah cross on ovah."

"Please don't talk about leaving us. I can't think about that now."

"Angela," she said firmly, "dis heah is somethin dat yah cain't run away from. I is jist tryin tah git yah ready foh whot is goin tah be. I done all dat I is 'pose tah do heah, an I is tired."

"Listen to me. You're not going anywhere. It's not time for you to leave us yet."

"No, sugah, yah de one dat needs tah listen. It is mah time."

"Momma, please don't talk like that. I can't imagine what our lives would be like without you."

"Oh y'all gonna be fine," she said slowly, beaming a bright smile. "I was jist sent tah be heah wid yah foh jist a li'l while. Yah knows dat. It's time foh me tah put dese weary bones ah mine tah rest."

Burning tears suddenly streamed from my eyes.

"Baby, don't cry. Dere ain't nothing foh yah tah be cryin 'bout. Yah should be happy. I is gonna finally gits mah rest.

"I wish I could tells yah how beautiful dat heavin is. I ain't nevah felt dat good in all de days dat I done bin on de face ah dis heah earf. De Lawd had just wrapped all ah his lovin sef aroune me.

"Listen tah me, an listen good. De angels is callin me home. I doesn't wonts yah tah cry, cause I loves yah so much. I bin so blest tah see mah futah tah knows dat mah chilrens chilrens is livin in a worle dat I ain't nevah dreamed ah. Dat yah is free tah be a familee, an tah stay togetha an love one anothah, an short ah death, cain't nobody pull yah apart. And now dat I done done whot I 'pose tah do, I can walks in de lite ah a new day ah freedom. Lawd ah mercy on me."

"I don't want you to go. It's hard for me to remember what my life was like before you found us. You've been the mother I lost a long time ago, and the grandmother I never knew. I'm sorry I didn't believe you when you told me the truth."

"How could yah knows? How could anybody?"

"Yes, I suppose you're right," I sighed.

"But listen," she said grasping my hand with her long, cold, crooked fingers. "I wonts yah tah do somethin foh me."

"Anything, Momma Zoli, you know you don't have to ask."

"I doesn't wonts yah tah tell John or de chilrens whot I done tole yah."

"But Momma—"

"No, don't tell dem," she said, "Dey can't take it. Dey ain't ready tah knows. Let me tells dem in mah own way."

"Alright, but it's not going to be easy."

"Baby, it ain't gonna be easy foh me tah go. Y'all bin so good tah me, I cain't fine de rite way tah thank yah, 'specially yahsef. Yah took me in when I was nothin but a strangah to yah. Gave me food an shelter, an heped me fine mah own way home. Even when I almost died befoh it was mah time, yah saved me agin, got me tah de hospital so de doctahs could fix me up. I knows in mah heart dat de Lawd is gonna bless yah in a mighty fine way."

"Momma, having you in my life is a greater blessing than I deserve."

"One thang dat I does knows. If yah hadn't takin me in dat dey when I was lost, I might nottah lived through all dat fightin an killin. Yah saved mah life.

I tried to keep myself busy and not think about what she'd said. Yet somehow my heart knew she was telling the truth.

Thanksgiving morning I got up early to fix breakfast and then we all headed for church. It was a very special service, "Umoja Karamu," a joyous celebration of the Black family and the most wonderful service of the year. Everyone dressed in traditional African clothing. The bright colors were mesmerizing, a cacophony of the beauty our people possessed. The service was spiritual, uplifting and put us in contact with our ancestors.

The service recreated Africa at the dawn of civilization and proceeded through our experiences in the new world.

The service was riveting and intoxicating with its colorful pagentry. A-ten-foot tall stilt dancer, African drummers and fluid, moving dancers, expressed the joy and pain of our people. The aura of an ancient mystical spirit filled the sanctuary. For a moment, we were suspended in time. The past, present and future were weaved together in the bountiful circle of life.

A few years ago, I took a friend of mine from Milwaukee, who was in town for the holiday. Andrea was several years younger than me, like a little sister, when we were growing up. As the choir marched in, I looked over at her and found her crying like a baby.

"What's wrong?"

"I feel them."

"You feel who?"

"I feel the presence of the ancestors."

We took Momma Zoli. She wore a beautiful African gown of a bright yellow print from Kenya and a matching head wrap called a 'gelee.'

On the way to the garage, while holding her hand, John said, "Momma Zoli, you look like an African queen."

She blushed like a teenager. "Chile, you oughta shut your mouth. Angela, what we gonnna do wid him?"

I laughed and remembered how far they had come. I never could have predicted they would reach to this point of tender affection

She loved it. After service, her eyes were filled with the wonderment normally reserved for precious childhood discoveries. She grabbed and kissed me and John and said, "Thank yah so much for bringin me heah tahday. All ah dem pretty peoples—dey look so good. Guess I use tah see5n us covered in rags."

I took a deep breath, momentarily hoping she'd forgotten her desire to leave us.

"I learnt so much 'bout wheah I is from," she said with a burst of excitement. "I bin tah dem colored peoples museums, but dis was bettah. It was like livin de past. An de Lawd showed me how much I gots tah be proud of."

That afternoon, our home was filled with joyous laughter, and a warmth we hadn't felt in years. Professor Brown came, joined by my father and John's mother. Geneva and her husband, Doug, Kathy Lee, Imani, and Joy Winzola came; Bill and Georgette parked their Winnebago in the driveway after spending several months in Mexico and Central America. And Doc and Mrs. Whitney, a few of my staff, and John's employees stopped by.

The table was covered with the biggest turkey I'd ever cooked, cornbread dressing, green beans, collard greens, potato salad, cole slaw, macaroni and cheese, scalloped potatoes, Waldorf salad, candied yams, sweet potatos, banana pudding, bread pudding with rum sauce, coconut and German chocolate cakes, pumpkin and pecan pie.

Because so many of our loved ones wouldn't be here during the Christmas holidays, we decided to celebrate the last day of the Kwanzaa ceremony, Imani. After the last piece of pumpkin pie was eaten, we all gathered in the livingroom. We had set up a table in front of the pond. As the water softly trickled down the rock wall, even the goldfish in the pond stood still.

Just as we were about to begin, the doorbell rang. Everyone we'd invited was already there, so I answered the door thinking it might be someone lost looking for directions.

A smiling man stood at the door with his arm wrapped around a woman that must have been twenty years younger than him.

"Can I help you?"

"Yeah, baby you sure can," he said, still smiling.

"I beg your pardon?"

"Angela, it's me, Spider."

I didn't recognize him. He looked ten years younger and had a peaceful countenance.

"Spider, what are you doing here?"

"Angie, I'm not here to intrude. This is my daugher, Rita. I had never seen her before last week. But after that little lady read the riot act to me, I couldn't sleep for days. I finally faced the fact that I had to find my child and make up for what I did not do. It took me a long time to track her down, but here we are, and I just wanted to thank Miss Zoli her for what she's done for me."

I was stunned. There were no words to respond to the visible healing I could see in Spider's eyes. He was beaming. The snake had finally shed his burdensome old skin.

I invited them into the livingroom to share the service with us.

After lighting six of the seven candles on the Kinara, a hand-carved wooden candle holder, Professor Brown poured a libation and offered a prayer to God and our ancestors.

"In the name of the ancestors who have gone on before us, we here gather today to celebrate Kwanzaa. It is a celebration of the seven principles of the Nguzo Saba—Umoja, unity; Kujichagulia, self-determination; Ujima, collective work and responsibility; Ujaama, cooperative economics; Kuumba, creativity; Nia, purpose, and Imani, faith.

"This is indeed a special occasion as we gather to celebrate our rich heritage and our glorious African past, as well as to acknowledge our future. In the unending circle of life, where the past, present and future flow together like waves in the ocean, we are truly honored to have Momma Zoli present today. We gather here today to honor the circle of life, the sphere of love which contains all things and all possibilities. We come from many people, Ibo, Yoruba, Akan, Fulani, Mandinka. We who are now one tribe.

"I've stood at the door of no return, on Goree Island, and wept for all those who were lost, and for those who have survived. We are a miracle people. The children of those who refused to die.

"We give honor and praise for their lives, and we are most grateful for their faith, not in man, but in the God of our weary years, the God of our silent tears, the God who has brought us thus far on our way. The God who has by His might led us into the light, to keep us forever in His path. We pray.

"The God of Issac and Jacob, the God of Solomon and Sarah, the God of Cleopatra and Ramses, the God of Nzinga and Nelson Mandela, the God of Martin and Malcolm, the God of millions of lost ancestors whose bones now lie at the bottom of the Atlantic.

"We remember the distant, silenced voices that have stretched across the gate of eternity, and now come with the voice of Momma Zoli.

"Her presence not only represents our past, it signifies our future. Her faith and indominatable spirit brought her thus far along the way.

"According to the New Testament, faith is the substance of things hoped for in the evidence of things not seen. Today, we know in a new way, thanks to the gift of Momma Zoli's presence, the true meaning of faith, and of holding on to hope in even our darkest hour."

Then Ashley and James stood up. James said, "We wrote a poem for today that we want to dedicate to Momma Zoli and all of our ancestors. It's called "Our Family's Tree is not Made of Pine."

Our family's tree is not made of pine
It grows beneath an African sun
Its seeds were kidnapped, taken away
When God and the universe were one,

Our family's tree is strong and tall
Its branches sway to and fro
We continue to love our roots from afar
Regardless of where we grow.

Our family's tree cannot be pierced
By arrows of deceit and spite
It's hard to withstand the venomous tips
Of evil men who roam at night.

Our family's tree plays with the wind
We've learned to change with time

The weeping willow taught us how to bend
Whenever we're in a bind.

Our family's tree is but a shelter
To the animals of the land
Coming whenever danger lurks
Alone they could not stand.

Our family's love has sustained
Its children through the years
We've held each other inside our hearts
And cast out afl the fears.

Our family's tree is a landmark
For those who must hold on
To the glorious past of African people
And days that now have gone.

Our family's hope is deep and strong
God sent the rain from above
We've learned to rise above our plight right now
While He nutures us with His Love.

Our family's tree is happy
In spite of weary days
Life's nothing without a smile
To chase the pain away.

Our family's heart isn't made of wood
It's too easy for us to feel
The joys and sorrows life has to offer
A varnished heart's not real.

Our family's tree is like Gibraltar's rock
It stands through rain and snow

We've learned to draw from its inner strength
And let our worries go.

Our family's tree is waiting
For a better world to stay
So its children can flourish in springtimes of love
And for evil to go away.

Our ancestors taught us long ago, we've learned our lesson now
To ask and it shafl be given, to seek and we shall find
We've seached through the forests of our motherland
And found indeed, our family's tree's not pine!

I had never been so proud of my children. I stood there basking in the light of a mother's humble pride. When they finished, Momma Zoli stood up and walked to the ceremonial table.

"I didn't wont tah say nothin, but de Lawd done put somethin on mah heart dat I gots tah do it now.

"I nevah knew whot de futah would hold, but I always prayed dat de Lawd would deliver to mah chilrens to a betta day dan de ones dat I done seen. An he did. I is so happy dat I was sent tah dis heah worle. It took Momma Zoll a lon time tah git use tah bein heah, an I ain't sho dat all ah me is used tah dis place yet. But I is glad dat I knows dat de generations dat followed me is alright.

"I knows dat dis heah worle ain't very easy, but I wonts y'all tah remembas one thang, if yah is gonna remembas anythang dat I done said. It don't mattah how bad things might seem tah be or how dark de night is. As lon as yah know dat yah is a chile ah God, an dat God is gonna make a way outta no way like he done foh me, an all of dem Black folk dat came befoh yah, yah is gonna be alright. Y'all is chilrens of a great God. Y'all is strong people. An cain't nothin in dis worle or de next evah change de truf. You is strong, an you is gonna do wonderful thangs.

"I done seen thangs dat I couldah nevah dreamed of, an done things I would nevah think 'bout doin. I learnt how tah read an write, I learnt how tah be proud ah who I is. I learnt how much mah people has done, an dat we wadn't born tah be slaves, we was born tah be free. An no mattah what lies feelingdat has tole de truf will always rise tah shine like de sun.

"I has seen beyon de dream ah mah dreams. I doesn't knows why, but I has bin blessed tah see tomorrow's tomorrow an I is grateful tah know dat ev'rything gonna be airight. I is in a worle dats way past mah biggest dream.

"So y'all go on in dis worle. Knowin dat wheah evah yah go, no mattah whot yah do, dat de ancestors be watchin ovah yah. Dat dey be lookin out, echoin dey mercy an whisperin dey love. Even when yah cain't heah it. Dey is dere, doin de Lawd's biddin foh yah.

"I bin in dis worle jist a little while, and now it's time for me to be on mah way.

"Y'all done done so much foh me, took me in when yah didn't even know mah name, and as de Lawd would have it, yah is de chilresn dat I bin searchin foh. De Lawd brought me tah dis land ah freedom, which ain't nothin like de worle I came from. But it is because he sent me heah dat I foune mah soul. I undastands an knows thangs dat I nevah could've known befoh.

"An I wanna thanks yah foh bein so good tah me. I wanna thanks yah foh bringin me in de way day yah did. It was so kine. I is jist an ole slave who ain't nevah done nuttin, nevah bin nuttin, nevah knowed nuttin moh dan workin foh nuttin an prayin an workin some an takin on somebody else's pain dat ain't got nothin in dey heart but hatred foh who dey is. I was always tryin tah hold on tah what I loved, cause dats all dat I evah had. De Lawd blessed me wid a good man an ah heap ah youngins dats waiting foh me on de othah side. I knows dat I is gonna see dem real soon.

"Because ah all dat you done done, de Lawd is gonna bless yah in a mighty fine way.

"I done seen things wid dese heah eyes dat ain't nobody evah needed tah see. But I seen beautiful things too, 'specially in dis heah worle, dat I could nevah even dream of in mah worle. I has seen de bright light ah dis new day. I learned in dis place not tah be shamed ah who I is an de color of mah skin, cause I is a chile ah God an I is made ah nothin but love. We is all made ah love because we is made in his image.

"De joy dat I has foune in dis heah worle is from de love dat yah has given me. Yah is all gonna be alright, jist as long as yah lean on de Lawd, an walk by faith an not by yoh sight. Yah jist keep on keepin on."

She walked over to John and touched his cheek. "Yah is a good man, John Stewart. Yah gots a big ole heart dat yah be tryin tah hide. Yah ain't got nothin tah be shamed of. I wonts yah tah knows dat I loves yah wid all ah mah heart like yah is mah own. I is gonna miss yah. But don't worry I is gonna be alright, an so is yah.

"It is time foh me tah be gone. I done done mah work. But don't worry, I ain't goin too far, I is gonna be watchin ovah yah too, makin sho dat yah is airihet in dis heah strange worle.

"Momma Zoli, don't die, you can't leave us yet. What are we going to do without you?" cried Ashley.

"Come heah sugah." Ashley walked over and Momma pulled her down into her lap. Wiping away Ashley's tears, she said, "I doesn't wonts tah leave yah But its time foh me tah go.

"Yah gots a lot moh livin tah do an more tah give. It's folks like y'all dat makes holds up de sky, yah make dis worle a bettah place. Don't evah let nothin break yoh spirit.

"But why do you have to leave us now?" pleaded Ashley.

"Because de Lawd is callin me. I has tah go."

This time I knew she was telling the truth. And even though I didn't want to let go, I knew for her sake I had to.

That night, after everyone had left, John and I went down to Momma Zoli's room. It was filled with rays of luminous moonlight.

We found her sitting on the edge of her bed looking out of the room.

"It's not dat I wonts tah die, dat I doesn't wonts tah be heah, it's dat de spirit is tellin me it's time. I is tired, an dese weary bones need a rest.

"De whole worle is changin. De kingdom ah God is at hand. And yah is gonna see a lotta stange thangs happin in de days tah come. Strife, an fightin, things fallin apart, but I assure you dat deLawd is gonna make a way foh dem dat trusts him.

"Live yoh live in accordance wid his will, an you is gonna be alright. You jist doesn't knows how much hep we got on de othah side. How is it dat aftah all we bin throuh we is still heah? 'Cause we is so strong. Cause our strength comes from de Lawd.

"See me in de sunshine, see me in de trees, see me in de sparrow, see me in de clouds, in de raindrops.

"I doesn't wonts tah leaves yah. Yah bin so good tah me, took me in an treated me like I was one ah yoh own, when you didn't even know mah name. How can I evah thank yah?"

With tears resting in the corners of his eyes, he said, "You don't have to."

She looked at him and smiled, as her radiant eyes gleamed. "Yah is a good man, John Stewart. Yah bin like a son, a real good son. Yah protected me an done thangs foh me dat mah own sons couldn't evah dream ah doin. An you did em even when you thought I was a crazy woman dat yah didn't wont in yoh house. Yah is a strong man. I see de strength of a thousand generations ah men flowin throw yah like a mighty stream. Yah is gonna be alright, too. Cause I knows in mah heart dat dere is nothin in dis heah ole worle dat can evah break yoh spirit.

"Son, I wonts yah tah takes good care of mah chilrens foh me."

"I will. You know I will do that."

"An deres one moh thang I wonts yah tah do?"

"I'll do anything for you, Momma."

"I wonts yah tah takes good care of yohsef. I wonts yah tah enjoy yohsef. You is always so busy workin, an doin foh ev'rybody else. Take time tah see de beauty dats all aroune yah, an tah enjoy what yah got."

"Yes, ma'am. I will."

"I is gonna miss yah, an bein in dis heah high fallutin worle ah yohs. But I done finished up mah work. An ain't I old enough?"

she asked laughing. "When I looks aroune dis heah house tahday an saw what I did on y'all sweet faces I knows in mah heart dat mah work is done done, an it's time foh me tah rest dese weary bones. It bin a long, long life an it's time tah give dis heah ole body a rest."

She looked at me, an said, "I knows what you is thinkin. But like I tole yah dis mornin you is gonna be fine, an you gots all de strength you need tah carry on."

"I jist wonts yah tah remembas dat no mattah wheah ya goes or whot yah do, de Lawd's lovin protection is always wid yah. Lawd knows I is a witness tah dat.

"Who wouldah evah thought dat me, li'l ole Winzola Mary Steadwell, wouldah bin sent tah de futah? Not me. But dat's how de Lawd works. Dis is mah father's worle.

"I ain't nevah really knowed dat God loved me, not til I died, an seen his mighty hand.

"Don't evah let nobody turn yah aroune, an forgits how strong we is when we is wrapped in de Lawd's lovin arms."

When she made a deep sigh and yawned, John said, "Come on, Momma, let me help you get in the bed."

He hugged her for a long time. Then she turned to me. My eyes were filled with tears.

"Don't cry. Dere ain't nothin tah cry about. Cause I ain't really leavin you. I jist won't have dis heah ole body anymoh, but I is always gonna be watchin ovah yah. An when it's yoh time, I is gonna be dere tah meets yah. One thang I knows foh sho, dere is no death, we is jist bein born inta anotha worle."

I hugged her, didn't want to let go. Finally, she pulled away and said, "It's time foh me tah git some sleep. I'll see yah on de otha side."

The next morning, John and I woke up before the sun rose. The room was filled with spirits—old men and women, clothed in raggedy tattered clothes. At first, I thought I was seeing things, but John said he saw them, too. I wondered if they were the slaves from her plantation coming to take her home. I could see them watching us. Suddenly, Momma Zoli appeared, amidst all the spirits at the foot of our bed, and smiled lovingly at us. In unison, all of them raised their hands, waved good-bye and vanished.

In that moment, we both knew that she was gone. No words needed to be spoken. We went to her room and found it filled with the same golden light I'd seen radiating from her eyes last night.

She was gone. She lay in her bed, smiling the most serene smile, while her body glowed in the light. My heart whispered, "She's resting in God's hands."

I rejoiced, knowing that finally after nearly two hundred years after her birth Momma Zoli was finally resting in peace, and reunited with her beloved family.

The miracle of her life and the mystery of her presence in our world remained an experience I could not fully understand.

We took her home, back to her beloved "Sippi" and beneath the fragrant shade of a beautiful, blooming magnolia tree we laid her to rest in my family's cemetery next to Shoal Creek Baptist Church.

And grace will lead me home

epilogue

John

God does work in mysterious ways.

Our lives, my life, would never be the same. How could I ever begin to measure what this little lost woman had done to my life? This miracle, this mysterious happening, came from someone I thought was a crazy, dangerous, homeless woman. She has had the most profound effect. She frightened me as she touched hidden parts of my life I wanted to forget. She made me proud of who I was. She made me stronger than the strength I thought I knew.

Her presence shattered my beliefs and opened me to a brand-new way of thinking and seeing my life and our world. In just a few months she taught me what it really meant to be a man. She showed me through her simple, broken words the folly of my own self-pity and how I had overlooked the river of blessings that have flooded my life.

What shall I do with the love and wisdom she poured over me? Only time will tell. I didn't feel the need to do everything and be everything for everyone. She showed me how important love is in ways that I could never fully explain. How this love for our family and God should be at the center of our lives. She taught me not to falter and fall into the den of my own inequities.

Nothing in our lives had prepared us for this. Perhaps nothing should have. The greatest blessings come with unexpected invitations that only the beating of our hearts could extend, opening the door to miracles and blessings.

When I looked at my family, I saw how much we had changed by the mere presence of her spirit. We were more loving, much kinder, and didn't take each other for granted.

With the sweetness of her gentle spirit and the majesty of her truth, she healed us, changed our lives and set me free. She showed me the truth that God was inside of me and at the center of our lives. For these blessings and others, I owed her more than I could ever repay. I was just grateful, so very grateful that she came to our world.

We had lost our way, we had forgotten the songs of our ancestors and lost sight of the triumphant path of those who walked on this bitter earth before us.

I appreciated what I have been given. Now when I look back over my life, I no longer felt the weight of the shame I once carried.

Our work had only begun to reach out to those in our community and wrap our arms around them to create a circle of love.

History will one day have its say. And the voices of those once silenced shall be heard.

Angela

I couldn't find adequate words to describe what overflowed from my heart. That little old woman, initially an enigma, our ancestor. From the moment I laid eyes on her, my heart leaped out to capture her. I held on to her for dear life, and never wanted for one moment to let her go.

What were we ever going to do without her? Before she died, I refused to imagine how I could go on without her guiding light nearby. Now I felt her presence enlightening me the way beams of shimmering moonlight illuminate the surface of a peaceful lake.

I knew the strength I needed rested quietly inside of me as did the wisdom in her that took so long for me to see. She waited and watched at the edge of my heart. I knew could always call upon her strength when my own was far away.

The miracle of her life would never be forgotten. She touched me and showed me how many of my blessings I'd taken for granted; she showed me how I had turned my back on the legacy of the strength that flowed through my veins. She made me stronger yet softer. She showed me who I really was.

She showed me a side of myself I never knew existed. She was a light, an example—quite simply and profoundly—she taught me what it meant to be a Black woman. She taught me the importance of living one's truth, of overcoming brutality with face, of withstanding hopelessness with grace, of seeing beyond today and peering into a tomorrow that I may never see.

Her dignity, grace, faith and endurance were a living testament to the strength of our ancestors, and a powerful reminder to all of us of the truth. And I now knew that the strength of this long stretch of humanity that endured the most unbelievable atrocities flowed through me like a mighty stream.

Nothing but God has seen my people through, and nothing but God using us as his vessels will heal the pains of the life storm battering our people today.

As we moved on to meet the challenges of this unraveling world, I knew the only lasting solution to the bullets not deflected by innocence, to the raging seas of despair, to the crumbling institutions, the dissemination of families, the absence of hope, and the belief that tomorrow will only bring more of the same, was that to go inside to the core of our being and rescue our fate with love.

The only thing that we had was love, the substance of all form, the only thing that would exist after all else had ended.

We must embody the same unrelenting expressions of love, faith and hope that my noble ancestors possessed in the face of the most brutal expression of human cruelty the world has ever known. In my heart I know for the rest of my life, I would find my family surrounded by the shelter of their love.

Momma Zoli

They thought I was a crazy ole woman. But now dey knows bettah, dey knows de truf. I still doesn't knows how I gots tah dat new worle. I still wondas why de Lawd sent me.

I done seen pass de dream of mah dreams. I done thangs I nevah couldah dreamed ah doin. Mah eyes has bin opened to de truf. Mah soul sang de song ah freedom. I still doesn't knows why I has bin blessed tah see de futah ah mah own, but I is grateful tah know dat dey is gonna be alrite.

Lawd knows whot happined tah me was strange. Somethin dat was v'ry diff'rnt. I didn't knows whot did Lawd had in store foh dis life, but it was moh dan I could evah thank of. I has bin truly blessed by His power and His grace. I has lived a full life. I is blessed tah see de land ah freedom. Tah be in a place wheah I knows dat mah chilrens is free an livin wid plenty, moh dan I evah thought any Black person could have. I done seen de face ah freedom, I seen de sunshine, I bin tah ah worle wheah dere was plenty ah food.

I knows who I is. An I is proud of de color of mah skin. I cain't say dat was feelin dat way 'foh I got to dat new worle. But it taught me tah be proud ah who I is. An comin to de othah side de firse time showed me dat I is made of nothin but love. Cause I is made in de image of God an God is love.

Heah I is on de othah side, an I is happy tah be wid mah chilrens. I is happy tah be at home wid mah Lawd. I wish ah couldah brought dem all wid me but it ain't dere time yet. So I is gonna be heah watchin ovah dem in de days to come an waitin foh dem tah cross ovah to de othah side.

Dere ain't really no need tah say good-bye. Cause one day soon we will all be togetah agin on de othah side.

legacies

In 1619, millions of African people embarked upon a forced journey into a new world. Their lives to that point had been lived fully and joyously, filled with love and incredible thanksgiving. As a people, they accomplished many things valued by the world. They created the first civilizations that gave science, art, literature, medicine, astronomy and mathematics to the world.

The Africans had many teachers along the way. But the teacher that taught them the most was the teacher called slavery. It was one of those gifts in life that come wrapped in ugliness, deprivation and shame, in a box of unspeakable despair, but when it is opened, one finds unexpected blessings. It taught the sons and daughters of Africa and the generations that followed in a new way the things in life that are valuable: love, hope, faith, joy and peace.

It taught them that life is not an endless round of suffering and struggle, of brokenness and pain. Instead, each and every day all around them wonderful things were happening, and they became the recipients of God's grace, receiving miracles and blessings more than words could ever express. Slavery taught our ancestors the meaning of the word "survivor."

To their descendants and others still looking for the path to survival, they left this direction: Go deep within yourself and find the presence of the God of our weary years, the God of our silent tears, the God who has brought us thus far on our way. God's presence within is the essence of love.

Bring it to the forefront of your life and greet each person, each challenge, each roadblock experience of racism and discrimination as an opportunity to be surrounded by the presence of love without conditions.

Once you have done that, your life will become a marvelous adventure and you will discover the courage and freedom that allowed our foreparents to survive against unbelievable odds.

about the author

Elaine R. Ferguson, M.D. is native of Highland Park, Michigan, a suburb of Detroit. She is proud product of the Highland Park Public School System, a graduate of Brown University and the Duke University Medical School, and completed her postgraduate training at the University of Chicago's Hospitals and Clinics in pediatrics.

Her internationally acclaimed first book Healing, Health and Transformation: New Frontiers in Medicine is now considered a classic in the burgeoning field of holistic and complementary medicine. Dr. Ferguson is currently the medical director of the Chicago Public School System.

She is a member of various professional and civic groups, and an active member of the Trinity United Church of Christ in Chicago, where she helped to found the church's Healing Ministry.

In her spare time she spends many hours with children and young adults in various settings, including volunteer work with babies born to women addicted to cocaine, which she has described as, "The most meaningful thing I do in my life."

About herself, she says, "I was very blessed to be born into a family and a community that instilled in me at a very early age the understanding that we are all linked together in the fabric of life and we are responsible for helping others.

"By word and example, my parents have been my greatest teachers of unconditional love. At this critical juncture in our society and world I believe it is imperative that we open our hearts and share the blessings we have been given with those in need— our elders, our children, and the poor."